# SPELL OF THE SINISTER

Books by Danielle Paige

*Stealing Snow*
*Before the Snow*
*Queen Rising*

—

*Wish of the Wicked*
*Spell of the Sinister*

# SPELL OF THE SINISTER

DANIELLE PAIGE

BLOOMSBURY
LONDON OXFORD NEW YORK NEW DELHI SYDNEY

BLOOMSBURY YA
Bloomsbury Publishing Plc
50 Bedford Square, London WC1B 3DP, UK
29 Earlsfort Terrace, Dublin 2, Ireland



First published in the United States of America in 2024 by Bloomsbury YA
First published in Great Britain in 2024 by Bloomsbury Publishing Plc



A catalogue record for this book is available from the British Library

ISBN: PB: 978-1-5266-4161-8; eBook: 978-1-5266-4163-2; ePDF: 978-1-5266-4162-5

2 4 6 8 10 9 7 5 3 1

Typeset by Westchester Publishing Services

Printed and bound in CPI Group (UK) Ltd, Croydon CR0 4YY

FSC www.fsc.org
MIX
Paper | Supporting responsible forestry
FSC® C171272

*To Mommy, Chris, Andrea, Daddy, Josh, Sienna, Fiona . . .*

*For Mather McPherson, a prince in the making . . .*

*And to anyone who has ever made a wish . . .*

*I'll let you in on a little secret: You don't have to say your wishes out loud for them to be heard. A wish is a thing that seeks to be answered. Seeks to be acknowledged. The act of wishing—of admitting who you are and what you want—is revolutionary, is a step toward what you wish for. I am here. I can hear you. I am listening.*

—Farrow

*The Entente were a secret, then a rumor, and now we were finally stepping into the light. They called us monsters, they made us monsters, and for that and only that do we owe them our gratitude.*

—Bari

# PART I

# CHAPTER 1

## — FARROW —

Hecate was here. And she was alive.

I touched her face and her hair and her hands. Her skin was surprisingly soft and smelled sweet and new like an infant's. Hecate didn't say a word; she just allowed my touch, something she never would have done in her very first incarnation and something she could not do when she was made of ash.

A wide smile played on her lips. It was unfamiliar. Maybe it had been too many years since Hecate had been able to smile. But I had studied her then. I had not known that she was my mother, but perhaps in my heart or in my magic I had sensed that our connection ran deeper than those I had with my other sisters and the rest of Les Soeurs.

There was another wrinkle, one that I couldn't fully wrap my head around. One that seemed impossible. But what was more impossible than her coming back from the ashes, back to her flesh?

Still, Hecate was younger somehow—years younger—and now she looked only a few years older than me. We had the same magic, my wish magic, which had given Hecate back her flesh and blood and bone. Had it also turned back the clock?

"Farrow," she said, breaking the silence.

Suddenly, she shivered.

I slipped off my coat and wrapped it around her nakedness.

"Oh dear, you must be cold," I whispered.

"Cold . . . ," she repeated, as if testing out the word.

How would it feel to be released from a prison of ash? I wondered as I searched her eyes for the Hecate I remembered.

"How are you here? How is this possible?"

"Magic. Your magic specifically. You granted my wish to come back to you. When the Queen died, I was revived," she said simply.

"And how are you so young? Hecate, you look like you are barely older than me."

Hecate looked at me with an expression of absolute puzzlement, as if her resurrection were commonplace but her newfound youth was unthinkable.

"What do you mean?" Hecate asked.

I paused for a moment, wanting to find a way for her to understand.

"Wish for a mirror," I demanded.

Hecate hesitated. It had been so many years since she had seen her own face. But then Hecate closed her eyes. And I could hear her wish even though it did not cross her lips.

*I wish for a mirror to see myself as I am . . .*

I pulled out my wand and drew the shape of a mirror in the air in front of us. A physical mirror appeared, suspended in air.

"You can open your eyes," I said.

Hecate blinked and marveled at herself for a moment in the floating mirror. She snatched the glass and held it at an angle up to her face.

Finally, she spoke again. "You are right, I haven't aged a day. In fact, just the opposite."

I could come to no other conclusion than that it was the spell—somehow it hadn't just frozen her in place; it had given her back the years she had lost.

She tossed the mirror away, over the cliff. It made a distant din as it landed below.

"Oh, Mother, I did not mean to upset you."

"Mother . . . ," she repeated, her face sill inscrutable.

I realized then that this was the first time she was acknowledging that I was her child since she'd returned to the flesh.

"You are my mother, that is the truth. I hope it does not offend you for me to call you such."

Hecate reached for me and crushed me into a hug that took my breath away. I did not care. I could have stayed like that forever. I was filled with a warmth like no other I had experienced in all my eighteen years.

When she let go, she proclaimed, "Say it again."

"Mother," I said.

"It is how it should have been from the start."

The wind picked up, and Hecate's face shifted again. Her eyes went wide, and her body tensed as if she sensed some kind of threat that I could not see or feel.

"My wand. I need my wand," she said fiercely.

"I'm sorry. I gave it away. Don't worry, we'll make you a new—" I began, but before I could finish, Hecate said, "Then I want yours."

She thrust out her hand. I felt my wand rustle in my pocket, and it flew into Hecate's outstretched hand.

"This will do for now," she said, seemingly satisfied. Her smile returned and her face softened.

I studied her for a beat. Hecate before the ashes never would have taken my wand from me unless it was a punishment. I tried to dismiss the thought—after all, what would it feel like to be trapped in ashes for years and years? Wouldn't anyone, even Hecate, be affected by that?

"Very well, you hold on to it for now," I said, but as I looked at Hecate's hand grasping the wand, I could see that there was blood dripping from her fingers.

As I reached over to gently pry the wand from her grasp, Hecate's words from just after she had transformed echoed in my head again.

*Be careful what you wish for.*

# CHAPTER 2

## — BARI —

For me, magic began with a beetle. It was the first creature I used my magic on. Others do not see their beauty. The way they catch the light. Sometimes appearing black, sometimes iridescent blue, sometimes both at once. The way they wear their skeletons on the outside. Nature's most perfect design providing protection and beauty at once.

Galatea used to say that I could fly before I could walk. It was a kindness perhaps, or something else. Perhaps it was inspiration. Les Soeurs were not supposed to lie, but Galatea had done many things that the Entente was never supposed to do. Even then. You just had to look closely enough.

We left the Queen's body in the square for a single day. Galatea wanted to send a message, but she also wanted to show the people that it was time to move on, with her as their leader.

As we watched the Queen burn, Galatea had seemed completely at peace and completely satisfied. I, on the other hand, felt uncharacteristically unsettled. I looked down. My fingers were covered in black feathers. I concentrated. They went back to their normal fleshy color. As the flames lapped, some part of me wanted to fly away. Not because I was squeamish—not because I didn't believe she had been given her due. But because no matter where I was, I would rather be flying.

It was happening more and more lately. I attributed it to the stress of the last few weeks.

South looked over at me. Had he seen my feathers? Did he know that their appearance wasn't voluntary? Now he had magic. More than "had magic," he had his mother's power, a power equal to Galatea's and to Hecate's before the Burning. To me, he would always be the same nosy kid who was forever watching and forever interfering. He was also the man who had just betrayed us and ruined our original plot.

I was supposed to have married the Queen's son and then killed the Queen and taken her crown for myself. Instead, Farrow and South had stopped me from using my love spell on the prince. Galatea discovered the plan too late, but she made the bold choice to face off with Magrit, and after showing surprising mercy on the battlefield, she'd turned Magrit's guard against her. Magrit had been forced to surrender, and Galatea had made haste to burn her as the Queen had burned Hecate once upon a time.

South should have been in chains for his role in thwarting our plans, but instead he stood beside us.

Killing the Queen hadn't felt like it was supposed to, but the next one would be better. At least that was what I told myself.

"I have seen this day in my head so many times. But the reality is so much sweeter," Galatea whispered, apparently having the opposite experience.

Suddenly, Galatea's smile got even wider.

"What is it, Galatea?"

"She's alive."

"Magrit? She's crispier than our dinner."

"Hecate. She's not on our side, but she will be."

# CHAPTER 3

## — FARROW —

I pried the wand out of Hecate's hand. An angry, bloody welt had formed where she had gripped too tightly. "Your hand!" I gasped as I reached for my handkerchief and prepared to staunch the blood and wipe away the rivulets.

Still undaunted, Hecate reached for the wand again.

"Hecate, no, I have to clean this out." But as I wiped away the blood, I noticed that her wound was already knitting itself whole.

She followed my gaze and turned over her hand to examine its condition.

"That's new," she exclaimed, more curious than horrified.

"Does it not hurt?" I asked, concerned even more by her placid expression than by the wound itself.

"It did for a moment and then it did not," she assessed. The wound was completely gone now. It was as if it were never there.

"Maybe the protection spell is still working," I suggested.

"Give me your blade," she said with the same intensity as when she had demanded my wand.

"Hecate," I warned.

She waved her hand, and I could feel my blade rustle in my pocket before I saw her holding it. Without hesitation she sliced the blade through the center of her palm, and the skin began healing immediately.

Entente have all kinds of different powers—rapid healing was not one I had seen without the aid of a spell or a wand. I glanced instinctively at the cliff behind us. Before Hecate got any ideas about throwing herself off it to test her new skill, I gently moved her away from the edge.

A breeze danced around us, bringing a whiff of the fire from the burning of the Queen. Even though Hecate had returned with new gifts, even if she was possibly impervious to pain, she was not impervious to Galatea.

"We have to get someplace safe. We have to make a distraction spell so that Galatea doesn't discover us."

"She already knows," Hecate said, her words like an anchor of dread.

"Then why hasn't she followed us? Why isn't she here right now?" I asked, trying to fight the sinking feeling. Hoping against hope, or rather a Fate herself, that she was wrong.

"Galatea is busy with the burning of Queen Magrit. And she thinks what she's always thought—that she can sway me to her way of thinking."

I paused, considering Hecate's words.

"Can you humor me, then? Let's get inside. Let's do the spell—I'd like to put as much distance as I can between us and our sisters for the time being. At least until we can figure out our next move."

"I can still see the Futures, and in none of them does she find use in trusting me. I want to go home."

It was Hecate's turn to look at me. To my surprise, her eyes were not pleading; they were knowing. She seemed so very certain. "Home" meant the Reverie. I had been back countless times, almost always with the ashes of Hecate in my pouch. To go back with her in the flesh . . . with her hand in mine . . .

I sighed a deep sigh. Hecate's flesh was now only moments old. How could we really know if her power to see the Future was truly intact? What if she saw what she wanted to see? Or worse, what if she saw what Galatea wanted her to see?

Hecate spoke again: "You have every reason to doubt me, Farrow. But we have come this far, why not a little further?"

"Hecate, Mother. I want nothing more, but—"

Before I could express my doubts, she closed her eyes and made the wish.

"I wish we were home," she said resolutely.

I took out my wand and granted it.

In a blink we were back at the Reverie. It was in disrepair. Cracked stone walls and cobblestones. Overgrown greenery. Some of the destruction was nature-made, and the rest was by the hands of humans.

I had been back many times with Hecate, and she had flown and walked through the rooms in her ash form. Now she could tell me what she really thought, and even without her saying a single word, I could tell how much it hurt her to see our home like this.

Galatea and my sisters had been here too, but none of us had transformed the space to its former glory. Doing so might have signaled our presence to the guard, which Magrit had ordered to sweep the grounds regularly. The irony, of course, was if either the rest of the Entente or my mother and I had left any trace of coming here, then we would have been reunited years before. What then? Would I have killed the Queen myself? What of Mather? Would I have killed him too? Or would the path of Fate taken us somewhere more peaceful? I knew not.

Hecate motioned for my wand again. "This will not do."

I shook my head and held the wand tightly in my pocket.

"The Queen is gone now. We live in fear no longer," she said.

But the specter of Galatea loomed larger than my childish wants.

"What of Galatea? I know what you said back on the cliff, but need we actually invite her to find us?"

"We will deal with Galatea another day. Now we must begin to heal. Let us start with our home. I promise I will hold it more gently this time," she added as I gingerly handed the wand back to her.

Without Hecate even whispering a spell, the columns of the courtyard righted themselves and stood at attention for her like good soldiers. I could almost see the sixteen of us practicing our arts, with Hecate or Galatea leading us. Tere making it rain, Bari making spiderwebs, Amantha disappearing at will . . .

Hecate's eyes were watering too. I knew she must also have been remembering.

"Mother, you're using too much magic. You just got your strength back," I warned. *I just got you back*, I wanted to say. But Hecate was adamant. The disrepair of the Reverie was making her increasingly agitated.

"This isn't right. I have to make it right."

"It can wait. Until you are stronger," I said gently but firmly, still not completely certain that Galatea would not look at the Pasts and see us here.

"It cannot wait," she said, her voice full of impatience.

"Then wish for it. Let me help you," I offered.

Hecate paused and looked at me with an expression of surprise, as if the idea of me helping her with something of this scale was new to her. She smiled and said, "I wish that it was as it was."

She handed me my wand. Then she closed her eyes, and I closed mine. I could feel the rest of the home begin to transform. Warmth flowed through me as the cracks in the marble floors closed and the walls rebuilt themselves. The greenery, which had become an uninvited visitor, began to recede back into the woods. Only Galatea's room, whose walls were papered with live flowers, remained filled with flora, and even those plants shrank back into the subtle pattern they had made long ago.

Hecate clapped her hands together with glee; it was a gesture I had never seen before from her in either flesh or ash.

She swayed a little. I thought she was literally moved by the excitement of re-creating our home.

But then, she stumbled into me, holding on to my arm to support herself. I caught her around her waist and noticed that her face had lost its color.

"Mother, I told you it was too much. You've had such a monumental day. No more magic. It is time for you to rest."

I led her back to her room and helped her into bed. The room was now exactly the same as she had left it the day of the Burning, complete with the brushes she kept to pull her away from the Futures that haunted her.

When I got her onto the bed, she looked up at me pleadingly. "Can you stay with me?" she whispered.

"Of course," I replied. I hadn't ever actually thought of leaving her alone for even an instant. But she didn't know that. We curled up in bed facing each other. Hecate was tired, but after years of not being able to talk, she had much to say.

"I am so sorry that you were all alone without your sisters, Farrow. Without me . . ."

"I still had you." I tried to quiet her, reminding her of her exhaustion. She required rest.

"Not in the way that you needed."

"What you taught me stayed with me. I know it may not have always seemed that way," I said, recalling how even in ash form Hecate had made known her objections to my plan to avenge her and my sisters by killing Magrit and Mather. Ultimately, I could not go through with it, but I felt a wave of shame. "Can I ask you something? How much did you know? How much did you feel? How much did you understand?" I asked.

Hecate looked at me without saying a word for the longest of pauses. "Oh, Farrow, I understood everything."

I slid closer to her, warmth flooding through me. My biggest doubt answered. I had believed she knew what was happening. I had believed she knew me. Now I knew for sure.

I felt a rush of contentment, coupled with the embarrassment that she had witnessed my worst moments. I pressed on though. My head was full of so many questions that could finally be answered. "You came back because you were bound?" I said, looking for confirmation.

"And because of my love for you."

"What about Iolanta—is there any way back for her?" I ventured to ask.

Hecate put her head down and began to cry.

"We should have bound her. As vulnerable as she was. We should have bound her to us so we would never lose her."

I had never seen Hecate cry. In the few hours she had been in the flesh, she had shown more emotion than in all the years I had spent with her in ash form.

I put a hand on her shoulder, comforting her, and she curled up beside me.

Another thought occurred to me. "What about Galatea? Did you bind her?"

Hecate looked at me sharply.

"You're asking because you want to know if you can kill her."

"That's not . . . ," I began. "I just want to know what we're up against. If she doesn't think she's vulnerable to death, there's no limit to what she can do."

"You don't understand Galatea. She's been living with death all her life. The Ever After holds no fear for her."

"Then what does?" I asked, my voice impatient.

Suddenly, there was an impossibly loud buzzing sound echoing through the Reverie. "Bari," I whispered instinctively. Could she possibly be here? Had she found us? "Wait here—" I ordered. Hecate thankfully was standing still, not following me, but her wishes wafted down the hall after me.

*I wish Farrow's wand would light her way as clear as it was day.*

My wand lit up in my hand, and I sighed in relief, as the hallway was completely insect free. The buzzing sound grew louder—it was coming from the room that I had shared with Bari. Before I opened the door, I could almost still see her lying there on her bed, tossing back her dress to reveal that she had replaced her legs with beetles.

*If you crush them, you crush me*, she'd boasted loudly.

I put my hand on the knob and gave the door a gentle push. It creaked open.

It was exactly as I remembered it—except there was no Bari. Both beds appeared to be mercifully empty.

The buzzing began again, and the quilt that covered Bari's bed began to move—within seconds whatever was buzzing beneath the covers had taken on the exact silhouette of Bari at age seven and a half.

“Bari doesn’t own every flying thing in the world—at least not yet,” Hecate said, appearing beside me.

“I told you to stay in the room,” I scolded.

“That isn’t her. That is a swarm she left behind,” Mother said with certainty.

“But what if she left them to keep watch . . . ?”

Hecate shook her head. “Like Galatea, her energies are elsewhere today.”

“Why am I still not comforted?”

“Bari is completely in Galatea’s thrall,” Hecate reassured.

“But you said, ‘yet’—is there something that changes that?”

“Not something . . . some*one*.”

Before I could ask who, the beetles became aware of us, and they flew toward us, lifted up the blanket, and rushed to the open door.

Hecate grabbed my hand and put up her palm. She’d stopped the beetles in midair just before they reached us. She’d slowed time itself without the aid of her wand. I shut the door and handed Hecate my wand to seal it.

“When we leave the Reverie, I promise I will set you free,” she whispered through the door to the beetles.

As we walked back to our room, I wondered, would the beetles tell Bari? Or were they just left over from her childhood magical experiments? And then something else occurred to me.

“You didn’t have your wand.”

“I didn’t, did I? Wands help channel magic—they are not magical. We have always strived to bring order to chaos . . . order to magic. Perhaps it is another self-inflicted restraint.”

"What you said before about Bari, I can't imagine anyone changing her path."

"There is a version of Bari who lives beyond all rules, the Entente's and nature's. That Bari could see through the eyes of every flying thing at once, could transform and terrorize at will . . . and if your other sisters give in to their baser instincts as well . . ."

Hecate touched my temples without the aid of the wand. She showed me a vision of the Queendoms. There was a dragon breathing fire in front of a Queendom's palace. She showed me realms in turmoil and other places under siege, each more terrifying than the last.

As I shuddered, she removed her fingers. "If we do everything right, we can help her and the Queendoms to avoid that Fate."

"Let's do that then," I whispered.

# CHAPTER 4

## — BARI —

The next morning, the fire in the square, where Galatea had burned Magrit, was still smoldering. I could smell it from our perch in the palace.

Amantha wondered aloud again if it was time to remove what was left of Magrit from the square.

"Leave her, as a reminder to the people of what happens to those who cross the Entente. Let her become ash as Hecate had. A proper end for the human Queen," Galatea insisted.

"Couldn't it also inspire vengeance? The humans, they have pledged their allegiance to us, but how can we be sure that they do not harbor revenge in their hearts?" Amantha countered gently, remembering what Hecate's Burning had inspired in us. A decade of plotting and revenge, which had culminated in Magrit's death.

We had changed course from our original plot. Galatea's and Farrow's actions necessitated this detour, wherein Galatea killed Magrit and revealed the Entente to the Queendoms. Our original plan had been to wait, with every sister taking over a Queendom before we took on Magrit. I was supposed to marry Prince Mather, kill him and Magrit, and take over the First Queendom. I would have done it in the dark, and the humans would never have known they were being ruled by the Entente. But now we were improvising. I could see Galatea thinking, recalculating.

I found myself recalculating too. I felt a rush of anticipation. We were no longer a secret. We were in the light. We were finally equal to the humans. No, we were their betters. They would all see now; they would all bow down to us.

When Galatea finally spoke, her words were surprising. "Preparations for our coronation must begin in earnest."

"Our coronation?" Amantha said.

"We must all be crowned, my loves," Galatea said simply, as if it were the plan all along. "If I am to be Queen, you are both to be princesses."

As we digested this, Galatea insisted there was something else we must do.

With sweep after sweep of our wands, we removed the Black Glass that had covered the palace and the surrounding buildings. The glass had been everywhere: on the exterior and interior walls of the palace, on the sides of the buildings throughout the village. It had been the desperate act of a Queen trying to hold on to power.

In her madness, Queen Magrit had even begun paving the streets with the glass. It was meant to ward off the Entente, but it turned out that its only power in this form was to reveal our true faces when we disguised them. When set afire the Black Glass could wound us, even kill us, as it had Iolanta—but as a solid, it was relatively harmless.

Now I wore my true face, or at least half of it. The rest had been taken from me on the day of the Burning. I filled in the space where the flesh had been with my beetles. And a wave of my wand created the illusion of skin and bone.

Amantha's Fate has been worse than mine—her entire body was destroyed by the fire. And somehow she survived. She was like a ghost, appearing to us through pure magic. If you touched her, you could feel her flesh, but she flickered in and out of existence at will or sometimes with the pressure of emotion.

"Perhaps we should stop," I suggested as Galatea suddenly leaned into me, weak from her expenditure of power.

"No, there is too much to do."

"We can finish deglassing the city after the coronation."

"But you won't be here then."

"Where will I be?" I asked, surprised.

"After we are crowned, you must ready yourselves to leave. Time is of the essence now."

"I don't understand. You need us to keep the guard at bay," Amantha said. "You do need us, don't you, Galatea?" she added plaintively.

"Of course I do, but right now I need you to do something else."

"What could be more important than maintaining the ground we have gained?" I asked.

"Taking new ground."

"What does that mean?"

"You and Amantha are of little use to me here. The prince is gone. "

"We could track down Prince Mather," I offered.

"Or you could find another prince," Galatea said with a smile, clearly enjoying delivering this new information.

"There's no such thing," I said. Prince Mather was an anomaly. His very existence as the first male heir to any of the Queendoms was in some ways the catalyst for Magrit's desperate plan to retain absolute power.

Galatea explained, "There is another. Queen Delphine of the Eleventh Queendom had a daughter, Helene, and a boy out of wedlock—a year after Mather. Queen Delphine hid the son for all the obvious reasons."

Of course Galatea had known. Had all the other Les Soeurs known as well?

"Who is he? Where is he?"

"He is an actor, of all things. And a rather successful one at that. He is completely ignorant of his parentage. I imagine having already had success on one stage, he'd happily trade it for another. You and Amantha will find him, and you will bring him to light only after he has fallen madly in love with you."

Amantha flickered again, her eyes suddenly unfocussed. I could see that her interest was piqued by the idea of the stage. We had never met an actor before, but plays held a particular fascination for her. She was probably already spinning some story in her head about him.

I shot her a cautionary look, and she straightened up.

I didn't want to leave Galatea, and despite her momentary lapse, neither did Amantha. But the look on Galatea's face—stern and fixed—said there was no changing her mind. My sisters were spread out across the Queendoms—each with a mission to take over their respective Queendom. Every day we were a step closer to having our revenge. For a few moments, I'd had the pleasure of thinking the Entente could skip ahead in the plot and take down the other Queendoms right now by the force of our wands. But instead, Galatea urged restraint, and I found myself in a new marriage plot. How could I again be stuck marrying a prince?

"When do we leave?" I asked.

"After the coronation of course. I wouldn't want you to miss it. It wouldn't be happening if not for you and your sisters."

"With all due respect, Galatea, shouldn't I—shouldn't *we*—be going after Ella and Farrow and Mather?"

"I cannot see the Future, but I know that this is the right course."

"But, Galatea—"

"I know the Rooks. They have magic, but they are completely without honor. They are tricksters through and through. Farrow and Mather think that they have gone to enlist the Rooks' help to defeat us. They are in for a surprise. It is very likely that Mather and Cinderella will never return from the Thirteenth Queendom."

"Do you mean that they'll be killed?" I demanded.

Our sister Farrow had betrayed us. But she had been my favorite sister when we were small, before we were separated on the day of the Burning. I still blamed the humans and the years she'd spent with them for her betrayal.

"I meant that the Rooks are known to spin a web of magic that is almost impossible to extricate oneself from—in a way, Iolanta was still stuck in that web until the day she died."

"Do you think South's father used a spell on her?"

"Even the Rooks do not have a love spell. Their leader, King Waid, then a prince, was ever so charming."

I felt myself freeze in place at the sound of the word "king." There was no such thing in the Queendoms until Magrit wanted to make her son king. But the Rooks had lived for centuries apart from the Entente and apart from the humans. They had their own hierarchy, including kings and princes.

"And Iolanta said that when they were together it was if they were the only two people in all the Queendoms. For Iolanta, who felt everyone's Presents all at once, that was no small feat. She called it love."

Upon hearing this, I felt even more of an urge to go to the Thirteenth Queendom—and see what the Rooks were all about. The prospect of going to find a prince who did not know he was a prince and seduce him paled in comparison to a true adventure with a real challenge filled with magic.

Galatea brushed her hands against her gown, a gesture I knew meant she was done with this topic. There was no more arguing, but I found myself unable to obey her in this moment.

I tried another tack. "But what if Farrow and Hecate have followed Cinderella and Mather? Shouldn't we be stopping Farrow, not chasing another throne? It took us years to get this one. To me, it seems the problem of Farrow is more immediate."

"Are you worried about Farrow? Or the plot at hand?" Galatea challenged.

If we were to put an Entente on the throne of every Queendom, we were going to have to use magic and wit in equal parts. Amantha and I were to go to Queen Helene's Queendom and pose as her nannies while Helene attended the Queen's Council. But what did it matter if we dismantled Queen Helene's Queendom now or weeks from now? Farrow was out there doing Fate knew what.

"We have to switch princes—Prince Mather is lost to Farrow—he is no use to us now."

"I can get him back—spell him back," I said, sounding defensive even to myself.

"This is not a failure but a change in course," Galatea replied and paused before continuing. "Think of sailing. You hit rough waters and you try and find a new destination. This is all we are doing now."

Both Amantha and I looked at her for the longest of moments, confused beyond measure. Galatea had never been on the water. But beyond the metaphor, the sentiment made no sense. We had spent years on this course.

"So we abandon the plots altogether. They know about us now. Every Entente can rise up in their respective Queendom and take over by magical force," I said, finally voicing what was in my heart. "Think about it, Galatea, no more marriage plots. No more stupid crowns. Just us in the light as ourselves—not bowing down to anyone."

Galatea shook her head. "That is a lovely picture, but not a realistic one. Not yet. We have never wanted a bloodbath—there are still a millionfold more humans than us—the guard laid down their arms in this Queendom because they did not believe in their Queen. In other Queendoms that is decidedly not the case. We must sway them slowly. A union between you and Mather would now seem to the public as orchestrated by us. We must start anew—with another Queendom, another prince." Her voice was firm, signaling that she would brook no challenge.

"It seems that you have thought of everything, but perhaps there is one thing you have missed," Amantha began tentatively.

Amantha wasn't done trying to find an escape from the plan yet either. "You have told us repeatedly how our presence here at court is imperative, to maintain the illusion that we are more like the humans than previously thought. Won't we be missed?"

Galatea considered this, then pulled a velvet rope that was attached to a bell, which alerted the staff when Galatea needed something from them.

Sadie, head of household in the palace, was knocking on the door within moments. A middle-aged human, she was unfailingly polite and kept her eyes mainly on the floor unless spoken to. I could not tell if her behavior was left over from her fear of the previous occupant of the palace or if it was reserved for us. I'd disagreed with her presence here, thinking of how our household staff from the Grays' home had played a part in our change in plans. They'd helped disrupt the prince's ball, where I was supposed to make Mather fall in love with me, by bringing in animals from all over the Queendom—it had been an embarrassing melee. One that I did not want to repeat. But Galatea believed that keeping Sadie on was a sign to the people of continuity. We had punished Magrit, and the punishment began and ended with her.

Behind Sadie there were two maids of slender build.

"Sadie, please leave us—" began Galatea.

Sadie looked concerned for her girls. "Whatever you need I can certainly handle and delegate. There is no need for you to have to waste your time by instructing them personally."

"That is where you are wrong, Sadie. I think that was one of the mistakes Queen Magrit made—she did not get to know her people. I intend to."

Galatea turned toward Sadie. "I have decided to send the girls on an errand. It won't take more than a few days, and you'll get to ride in my personal carriage. Now, how does that sound?"

One of the girls lit up like it was a holiday; the other's face creased with fear.

Sadie bowed. "Girls, please report to me in the kitchen when you are done." But before taking her leave, Sadie straightened and faced Galatea. "If the girls are not back in the palace at the end of the week, they will be sorely missed. They have parents—they are very connected to the town and to its people."

“Oh, they will be back in plenty of time.”

Galatea had grown tired of Sadie’s subtle attempts to secure her charges’ safety and walked Sadie to the door of the room herself, then closed it firmly.

Amantha looked at me and whispered, “I don’t get it—what is the meaning of this?”

I got the meaning, and I shared a look with Galatea.

“We won’t be missed at the court because the maids will be at the court.”

Galatea clapped at my cleverness. And frowned at Amantha for not catching the plot immediately.

The two maids shifted uncomfortably. The one who was smiling got the plot and was anxious to get on with it. The one who looked scared hadn’t put it together yet, but she did gather that what was about to happen was probably not good. She got to her feet and began to walk toward the door.

“Your Majesty, um, Majesties . . . We’re honored by the invitation, but I think I am better suited for kitchen work.”

“Speak for yourself—I want to see the inside of the carriage. We are always outside. Never in.”

“I don’t think there is an inside of the carriage for us.”

Galatea waved a wand and froze both maids in place.

“Why must humans be so tedious? I would much rather do this at the Reverie, but there is not much time, girls. After tonight’s ball, may these maids wear your faces and mirror your every gesture and manner for seven days.”

We repeated the chant.

The girls’ faces shifted into ours for a moment—mine showed up on the face of the smiling one, and Amantha’s on the one smart enough to be scared.

"Take a look, dear maids, it's not so bad. You won't remember a thing—but oh so much fun you will have."

A mirror appeared before them, and they gazed at it blankly. Amantha stepped to the mirror as well. Seeing her beside herself was too much to resist. I followed suit.

There was a knock on the door.

Galatea waved her wand and undid the magic for a moment.

"Girls, we will see you promptly back here after the ball."

"Yes, Your Highness," they said in a trance.

As she escorted the girls to the door, it opened to reveal South, who bowed before her. He'd made no secret of the fact that he did not agree with the sisterhood's plans to take over the Queendoms. But he'd also sworn his loyalty to Galatea. I was surprised when Galatea accepted him back into the fold. But he was a Fate, which afforded him special privileges.

The three Fates, Les Soeurs, had once been Iolanta, Galatea, and Hecate. But Iolanta had been killed by Black Glass arrows set aflame, and Hecate had been turned into ash the day of the Burning. Galatea had told us that Hecate was returned from the ashes, but she had not said if Hecate was at all changed by her time as ashes. Hecate had somehow remained a Fate even when she had been reduced to ash on the day of the Burning. The fact that she had remained here, still animated and still able to communicate through rudimentary gestures even in ash, was a testament to her power. But how would she return? Did she still have the same power? Was she still a Fate? Was she set against our plan like Farrow or would she join us in our rightful revenge?

I received a sudden flash from childhood, the day South got his wings. Amantha and I had teased him. Farrow, wanting my favor, had spelled him, giving him wings. Hecate had punished us all.

She'd taken Farrow to see Iolanta, who showed the truth of her Present, how much she had hurt South.

Hecate had shown me a glimpse of my Future, but I did not believe it had the effect that she'd wanted. She showed me transforming into a dragon. It was a magnificent feathered thing that breathed fire and had so much magic and power. She thought it monstrous. I thought it wonderous. And from that moment on, I had redoubled my efforts to make that transformation possible. I had never told anyone what I had seen that day. Not even Amantha or Galatea or Farrow, who had been my closest sister once upon a time.

Galatea nodded again, and the girls swept out of the room with purpose.

"We will be back after the ball, your Highnesses."

South turned and watched them go. No doubt he'd use his power to learn what we were up to, and he dared interrupt us.

South's very presence made me angry. I had never liked him when we were children. I had never understood how he, then believed to be a male, human child, had been allowed to be raised alongside us. It turned out he was one of us, the only male Entente and Iolanta's child, but we hadn't known it then. Now, with Iolanta gone, he had inherited her role and her powers as the Fate of the Present.

When I was young, I hated him for not belonging. Now I hated him for taking the power that should have been mine. I knew in my bones that I was meant to be a Fate . . . and there would not be another chance until another Fate died. Galatea was in her prime, South was the same age as I, and Hecate had defied nature again with her magic by coming back from the ash.

Looking at South was just another reminder that I wouldn't be a Fate for a very long time. The power was wasted on him. Like Farrow, he'd spent too much time with humans, and also like Farrow, his loyalty was in question.

South said, "With your permission, Galatea, I'd like to accompany Bari and Amantha."

Amantha looked at South accusingly.

"You were listening to us?" she said.

"He doesn't have to be outside the door to listen. He's a Fate. He can see every Present everywhere all at once . . . ," Galatea countered.

"You have the Queendom in hand. And you are right, as much as I want to go to the Rookery and find the truth about my father, at the moment I present too much of a risk to our mission. I know you do not trust me completely, but I can prove my worth to you and to the rest of the Entente if I accompany Bari and Amantha. Please give me this chance," he said carefully. I had no doubt that he had chosen every word in advance.

Galatea stared at him intently, then she said, "Very well."

Amantha spoke up again. "Don't you think that we should have a say in whether or not he goes with us?"

Her body flickered in and out of corporeal form, but she remained solid. I was impressed. Usually when she was stressed or angry, she was gone.

I backed her up. "You cannot be serious—he is a threat."

*How could this actually be getting worse?* I thought, looking from Amantha to Galatea and then to South, who had a smug smile on his face, as if he had already won. The triumphant expression he wore was a further insult.

"Since when could you not handle a threat, my dear?"

I held in a sigh.

"I can handle anything and everything," I vowed.

“That’s my girl. Now, we have to get ready, Princess.”

She smiled as she said it. “Princess” was meant as a joke . . . but technically that was what she had made me and Amantha. When Galatea had first proposed her plan all those years ago, I had known there would be crowns. But there was a difference between the idea of a crown and actually wearing one—even if it was just for a day. We were the Entente, first and always. We had served the Crown, we had fought the Crown, and now we wore the crown. It did not rest easily on my head. But Amantha seemed to be fine with it, and Galatea seemed to be positively gleeful.

“Come on, Princess . . . ,” South echoed, and it took everything in me not to turn into a swarm of bees and sting him.

# CHAPTER 5

## — FARROW —

In the middle of the night I woke with a start to find that Hecate was gone. "Hecate," I whispered. I was about to crawl out of bed when I heard breathing just above me. Grabbing my wand, I looked up and could make out Hecate's silhouette in the moonlight. Had the magic worn out at moonrise? Had she returned to ash? Mercifully the moonlight intensified and the beams fell on her still-flesh-covered form. She was plastered to the ceiling like she had done to hide when anyone had come into a room while I was at the Couterie.

"Hecate," I whispered again.

I coaxed her down. She hesitated for a moment before letting go. Instead of floating down, she descended rapidly, landing with a thud on the wooden floor.

"Hecate . . . It's all right, Hecate," I said as I reached her and helped her up and back into bed.

"I thought I heard someone. Someone's coming . . ."

Hecate's fear seemed so real that I peeked outside through the window of the cottage. With my gift, I should have been able to hear the wishes of any humans that were coming near. But there was only the sound of wishes miles away.

"Can you sense Galatea? Are she and the other sisters coming?" I asked.

Hecate's eyes focused on me. She shook her head.

"Then who? Who's coming?"

Hecate's eyes glassed over as if she was having a vision.

"Farrow?"

"I'm here, Mother. I'm here. Just me and no one else."

"I heard footsteps . . . I thought someone was chasing me . . . It must have been a dream. But it felt so real," she explained, her breath still shallow.

"It was just a dream. It is just going to take some time. I promise."

But as I said the words, I wasn't really sure. What if it was another Future?

We spent the morning readying Hecate to face Galatea again. We took a bath in the Reverie's healing spring, and after, I braided my mother's hair. We then went to the spot on the edge of the Reverie where I had made wands for my lost sisters before I knew that they had survived the Burning. Despite her show of magic without a wand yesterday, Hecate had decided she still wanted one.

Hecate took in my mixed emotions. "Such painful memories . . . We cannot replace them, but we can give you happy memories to sit beside the sad ones."

"It wasn't all sad. I still had you," I blurted. I knew that Hecate hated sentimentality, but I did not apologize. It felt important to tell her what it meant to have her with me. To know that she had not gone into the Ever After so that she could stay with me.

To my surprise, Hecate did not scold me for my show of emotion;

instead she matched it, her eyes glistening. She took her hand in mine.

"Ah, to hold your hand instead of having my ashes sift right through your fingers. This is a happy memory to sit beside the sad. Indeed."

"Let's make you a new wand," I said. But she did not let go of my hand as we walked through the little wood looking for the perfect tree.

"None of these will do," she said petulantly.

Hecate raised her hand, and the ground began to shake until it cracked open and the giant trunk of a tree sprouted out of it.

The tree was alabaster white and bigger than any other in the forest, and it continued to grow as we spoke—branches extended in every direction. One branch grew literally right up to where Hecate and I stood, as if offering itself to her.

I reached in my pocket for my knife. But Hecate stepped closer and broke the branch off in her hand.

She sat down on the stump I'd sat on to make wands for all the Entente when I thought they were dead. The day I had met Mr. Gray, Cinderella's father, and given him one of my wands.

I handed Hecate my knife, and she began to whittle. I sat at her feet and watched her work.

It was the happiest I had been in years.

# CHAPTER 6

## — BARI —

I awoke in the middle of the night to see Amantha's shadow leaving our sleeping quarters.

"Amantha," I called, expecting her to flicker away again.

But instead, she opened the door and seemingly drifted into the hallway.

I slipped out of my nightgown and transformed into a flock of moths—and I followed her in the dark. Unsurprisingly, she was already halfway down the hall. I followed her deep into the palace, wondering for a second if I would be able to find my way back. Finally, she stopped in the throne room. She was carrying something in her arms. A stack of books. Had she actually snuck down here just to read?

"Amantha, why did you come down here?" I demanded when she finally faced me.

"You will think it is silly. Let's just go back to bed."

"There are no secrets between us and no embarrassment either," I proclaimed, meaning it.

"I wanted to practice," she said simply.

"Who cares if we curtsy wrong or get the words mixed up? We are Entente—we are not meant to wear crowns; we are meant to wield wands."

"I know that." She pouted.

"Then what are we doing here when we could be sleeping blissfully through our last hours as non-princesses?"

"I do not like them, but I do not want to be embarrassed before them."

"How could you be embarrassed? They are humans and you are Entente. You are made of magic, which means you are perfect. And they are not." I had asked the question wanting sincerely to understand her meaning.

"What if the crown falls right through me?" she said, her voice cracking slightly. "I was going to practice with the books on my head," she explained.

"Oh, Amantha . . . They do not deserve an iota of your concern," I whispered.

Amantha had felt a sting of embarrassment when her foot could not fit in the slipper, and she had made her toes invisible. Then, there had been the prince, Cinderella, Farrow, Hark, the household staff, and the guard in attendance. Now a grand hall of hundreds of humans she did not know would apparently have a greater effect on her.

I smiled at her encouragingly.

"There is no need to fret. If you want to practice, why use that pile of books? Let us use the real thing." I closed my eyes and summoned our crowns.

*Give us our crown for our use when no one else is around . . .*

They appeared, one in each hand.

"Galatea would give you poor marks on that rhyme," Amantha said, but the tears that had been threatening had receded.

"If I don't get to sleep, then why should anyone else?" I mused. I waved my wand again.

Sadie, who acted as our lady-in-waiting in addition to her other palace duties, appeared, still in her nightdress. It had been a surprise that Galatea had kept on the household staff. Amantha and I thought it would have been better to do the reverse of what we had done at the Gray mansion and find some animals to turn into servants. We had turned the servants into animals there—and it had worked out well, until it hadn't. The night of the ball that Magrit had held for Mather to choose his bride, the animals had gathered others and ruined the festivities by arriving with hundreds of other real animals.

Galatea clearly remembered. She'd said, "I think the palace should be an animal-free zone, save the horses. One cannot do without horses."

Now Sadie stood in front of us, looking a bit like a scared and sleepy mouse.

"Tonight you will not remember, but teach us now your silly rituals." I paused to formulate the rhyme.

*Teach us how to be royal.*
*Show us you can be loyal.*
*But for you tonight is not as it seems.*
*To you it will be but a dream.*

A slightly dazed Sadie nodded and then got straight to work. "You have been trained to be ladies, to project grace and beauty. But now you must also project power."

"That won't be a problem for us," I said, hoping my confidence would be infectious for Amantha.

"A princess projects power without raising a wand or her voice. She commands, but she also is aspirational. Her example is the one we all follow after the Queen. Do you understand?"

Amantha gave me another panicked look. In the years we'd spent at the Grays', Amantha had retreated into her books when she wasn't with me or Galatea or our other sisters. Now Galatea was asking her to be the center of attention—the center of society, not just for one night, like the ball, but for as long as it took for us to complete our plot to take over the Queendoms. Amantha flickered again, her nervousness not at all quelled.

I grabbed her hand. "Hey," I whispered. "Tomorrow there is only you and Galatea—the rest of them are just wallpaper. You are going to pretend that you are in one of your novels or plays. You are the brilliant wayward witch who has discovered that she is not just a witch but a princess."

Amantha smiled dreamily, as if imagining it. But her nervousness lingered as she bit her lip.

"Now we are going to practice getting our crowns on, and that will be that . . . ," I said firmly.

Amantha nodded.

We spent the next hour with Amantha going through the drill of where to stand and sit and speak, as we were instructed by the ever-patient Sadie. The crown fell through Amantha only once.

As the sun broached the stained glass windows, I deemed us ready.

"I think we should get a few hours of sleep."

"Thank you, Bari," Amantha whispered as we made our way back to bed.

# CHAPTER 7

## — FARROW —

Mother stood up with the wand in her hand, and the sky split open with light and sound as a bolt of lightning met the tip of it.

I stood up. Something was different. I had seen Hecate do this trick a million times when I was young. But this time the lightning was not captured by her wand. It flowed through her. Her veins lit up with electricity.

"Hecate!" I screamed. I had just gotten her back. I did not want to lose her again.

"Step back," she said with trembling lips. But her eyes were focused and steely—she was seemingly in control.

But I was not comforted.

The lightning continued to flow, and the ground began to shake. Two cracks formed where her feet were planted and merged as they cracked open the earth through the center of the Reverie.

Hecate rapped her wand at the sky again, and I watched as the lightning reversed itself, moving up and out of her veins, out of her and back through her wand, and up into the sky.

She turned her attention to the singed dirt beneath our feet. She touched her wand against it, and the earth began knitting itself together. Within moments, it was as if it had not opened at all. Hecate twirled her wand around her fingers.

"Hecate, Mother, I think we need to get out of here. There is no way that Galatea could not have heard that."

"I wanted her to hear it. I wanted her to know that I did not lose anything to the ashes but time," she said stoically.

"If that was your aim, you have exceeded it," I said, wondering if Hecate's boldness would be something we would live to regret.

# CHAPTER 8

## — BARI —

Even after living among humans for years, I found the idea of being crowned by them strange.

This had been part of the plot, and my sisters all were prepared to wear crowns as part of our ruse to take control of the Queendoms. But Galatea, Amantha, and I would be the first Entente crowned by humans who knew exactly who we were.

The morning of the coronation, Amantha asked, "Don't they remember Prince Mather? What if they start to miss him?"

Galatea reassured her: "Prince Mather is far from here and far from the humans' thoughts. If he comes near, we will make quick work of him."

I felt Amantha's trepidation, but Galatea was so incredibly certain that I found her confidence infectious.

I stood up taller in the uncomfortable gown that Galatea had picked for me. It was a pale lavender, and I wasn't quite sure which was more painful—the corset beneath it or the color of the silk itself. I touched the hem of my gown with my wand, deepening it to a shade of dark blue. Galatea touched it with her wand immediately after, returning it to the palest purple it was before.

"They already know who we are. Why not just be completely ourselves?" I protested, turning it back to blue.

Galatea sighed. But I defiantly tapped my wand to my face, revealing the space where the beetles filled in for my skin. Galatea did not flinch; instead she put a loving hand on my other cheek.

"It doesn't matter if they see. It only matters if I and your sisters see you. Beetles and all."

I felt the beetles in my cheek speed their movement.

"Then why must we do this? We won—to the victors go the spoils. Where are our spoils?"

"They have their rituals, we have ours," Galatea said impatiently.

"But ours result in magic. Theirs are ceremony for ceremony's sake," Amantha objected.

"Everything is wrong. I should be chasing down Mather and Cinderella or chasing down Farrow and Hecate, not standing here debating dress colors. My talents are being underused," I protested.

"At this moment, the humans believe that Magrit was more of a danger to them than we ever could be. We don't want to dissuade them of that—that is our advantage. I love your face, Bari, your real face. But I fear the Queendom may not be ready for it." This time Galatea's voice was not laced with softness. She had made up her mind, and it would not be moved.

She turned to Amantha. "And, Amantha, don't you dare flicker away at will or they will wonder if you can flicker into their private moments and spy on them. We must maintain this fragile trust for a bit longer."

Amantha, in her pale lime dress, nodded dutifully.

I tapped my wand to my cheek, and the beetles melted back into a facsimile of skin.

Just then, Sadie gingerly opened the door and curtseyed.

"It's almost time . . . Your Highnesses," Sadie said, pausing to stifle a yawn and immediately looking at the floor instead of meeting any of us in the eye. I could not imagine that her loyalty lay with Magrit, who was notoriously awful to, well, everyone she met except her son. But I couldn't imagine Sadie would be loyal to us, seeing as how we had just burned Magrit alive. And it seemed she had no remembrance of her late-night coronation etiquette lesson with us. The spell had worked.

"Your pardon, Your Highnesses, I swear I went to bed early to be ready for today."

Amantha laughed a belly laugh, then, remembering herself, quieted immediately and adjusted her posture.

"Don't be late," Galatea said as she followed Sadie to check on last-minute preparations for the reception. Whatever Galatea was planning, she had said it was a surprise.

The ceremony was to be hours long, and Galatea had invited all the townspeople—the palace was open to the public again. It hadn't been when Magrit was Queen. Magrit had lived in constant fear of the prophecy, in constant fear of the Entente, even though she thought she had eradicated us. What if one of us had lived? What if someone out there was out to get her? She hadn't been wrong.

As for Amantha, when the moment came to walk down the aisle for the ceremony, I would not have guessed that she'd spent last night in the throne room, practicing with a book because she was so worried about looking foolish, if I hadn't been there myself. The second she walked into the throne room, now in daylight and filled to the brim with humans, she smiled brightly and waved as if she were in our drawing room at the manse or back at our real home, the Reverie. I was struck with a very different range of emotions.

I had never been in a space with so many humans. Not even at the Royal Ball we'd attended for the prince. We were to follow Galatea down the aisle to the altar where three thrones awaited us today. Galatea's throne was larger and more ornate. She was to be crowned by the head of the church, and then she would crown each of us. But as I looked down the aisle, I found my feet had stopped moving. I could not follow.

There were so many of them—too many of them. I had a flash of the day that they'd come for us in the square the day of the Burning.

The feathers on my right hand threatened to turn my whole arm into a flock of birds. I was never nervous. But I was now.

On my other hand, under the voluminous sleeve of my gown, as surreptitiously as I could manage, I changed one of my fingertips into a beetle. I squashed the beetle between two other fingers and felt a tiny prick of pain that I hoped would distract me. I had been crushing my beetles for years, to make myself stronger—to make myself regenerate faster in anticipation for battles to come, but the act itself, the pain itself could be centering, even comforting. Right now it had no effect. What was wrong with me?

South surprised me by pushing me into the shadows behind a column and touching my hand with his wand. He transported us to a cliff high, high in the sky.

It was overlooking a Queendom. But it wasn't our Queendom; it was one I'd somehow never been to before. Snowflakes fell all around us, and there was a glittering silvery green palace, nestled above us on a neighboring mountain.

"Where are we? What are you doing? Why did you do that?"

"We're in the Twelfth Queendom. Amantha seems to be bearing up well, but you . . . you look like you could use a moment. And I find snow quite calming."

"I don't need a moment. And I find you quite infuriating," I barked back, but I didn't move. "Do you think I have never been to high places before?" I asked.

"Not this place."

I looked again at the massive castle above us.

"That's not a Queendom. That's the Rookery," South pointed out.

"That's forbidden," I said.

"Technically, we are still in the neighboring Queendom. Iolanta used to bring me here when I was a child. I just never knew why," South explained.

I shifted uncomfortably. I was sorry that Iolanta was gone. And in this moment, his mention of her now made it harder for me to properly insult him.

"You're ruining the coronation," I protested.

"How much would you mind that, really," he said lightly. "As a Fate of the Present I can slow time. We will be back before anyone notices that we are gone."

"Galatea will notice."

"Galatea's mind is on the moment. She will not notice . . . ," he replied.

I felt a twinge of offense at realizing he was right. Galatea had been particularly preoccupied with the ceremony.

"There are just so many of them . . . ," I admitted finally.

I had spent years among humans, even attended a ball in the very palace where Galatea was now being crowned—but this was different. There were hundreds of humans and they had all been looking at me.

"I want to turn them all into crows. No, beetles—or spiders—or both—"

He laughed, which I wasn't expecting. "So not nervous? More murderous . . . ?"

"You disapprove?" I asked, assuming that I already knew the answer.

"I felt the same. Imagine being in the middle of the guard, surrounded by them," he said intently.

I had not expected this response, given his untiring defense of humans.

"So what did you do?" I asked, surprising myself by how genuinely invested I was in hearing his response. He paused then, leaving me in suspense.

"I didn't have any powers. I just had to keep my knife sheathed in my pocket. If I'd had powers like yours—I would think the temptation would be even more extreme."

"So how did you stop yourself?" I blurted, wanting to know.

"I imagined the day I would put that knife in Magrit. But of course, that has already happened, though by fire instead of my blade. You will have to come up with another incentive to stall your rage. Perhaps you can imagine transforming them all into flying things . . . like the Fallen," he suggested, still seemingly sincere.

"I truly do not understand. Why are you helping me?"

"Who says I'm helping you? I just stopped you from devouring half the Queendom."

"I thought it would be different. I thought we would burn down their palaces, not move into them," I exclaimed. "I thought we would melt their stupid crowns, not wear them. I thought we would show them that their stupid rituals were just that, pomp and circumstance. Instead we're participating in them— What did you think was going to happen?"

He sighed a big sigh. "I never imagined any of this. The scope of Galatea's plan is breathtaking. I didn't even think I was going to be in the throne room. At best, I would have been lucky to get close enough to make a single strike and take down the Queen."

"And then what?"

"I was alone. I didn't have the rest of the Entente—there was just me. I was realistic about my prospects. If I got my knife in the Queen, it was enough."

He would have given his life to avenge us. Even though we were gone, even though we never accepted him, even though we had afflicted him with wings that did not work. And most importantly, even though he thought he was human then.

"Taking down all the Queendoms wasn't even in my mind—because I do not think they are all to blame."

There was judgment in his tone, and I felt myself snap back to my senses.

Before I could come up with a proper retort, he took my hand and said, "We should get back."

He tapped his wand. We were back in the throne room, next to the same column we had leaned against before. When we stepped out of the shadows, no one had indeed noticed. With a wave of his wand, everything sped back up to real time again.

I took my place beside Amantha, who was still waving enthusiastically.

And I could feel South take his place behind us.

I glanced at Amantha again, glad I hadn't missed her crowning. To my surprise, Amantha had borne up better than last night's nervousness would have indicated. It was as if she became more present and more radiant the more eyes that were on her. She was almost glowing.

South's words did ease my need for immediate vengeance, though I would never tell him so. While the music swelled and the people cheered and the ceremony dragged on—with us at the center of it—I did as he had suggested. I imagined the guard as scorpions and the people as other flying creatures. In my mind's eye, there were moths and beetles and bees dressed in human finery filling every pew. And instead of the expected rage as I glided down the aisle, a laugh tickled and climbed up my throat and threatened to escape from my lips. South had been right for once, even if his motives were misplaced. His proclivity for preserving human life was troubling at best, dangerous at worst. But in this moment, it was useful. His advice had stopped me from ruining all of Galatea's plans.

By the time Galatea rested the crown on my head and Amantha and I took our vow to take care of the people of the Queendom, I had made it through without flying out of the throne room or actually transforming any of the humans.

"That's my girl," Galatea whispered as she put the crown on my head and I stood before the congregation. There were cheers—but when I looked up, all I saw were winged things, just like South had suggested. And Fate help me, I had to suppress a laugh that threatened to escape from my lips.

Luckily, Galatea didn't notice; she was already turning back to the crowd. But South's eyes were on me, and from his position near the altar, I could see him flash a triumphant smile in my direction. I met it with a sneer. I owed him nothing. He smiled broader still.

Now Galatea began. "You have seen our might—and the Black

Glass is gone because you no longer need its protection. You have ours . . ."

The crowd looked around, not yet sure how to react. The removal of the Black Glass was welcome. But the burning of Magrit, no matter how hated she was, could not have given the humans certainty that they might one day face the same fate if they displeased us.

Galatea cleared her throat and tried another approach. "I know all your Pasts: every secret, every lie—the good, the bad—the losses, the loves, the secrets, the joy . . . I know you, but I do not know the Future. I know that may not give you comfort, that you are fearful of us, and we in turn have cause to be fearful of you."

There was another murmur in the crowd—I for one thought that it was good for the people to fear us. But I knew from what Galatea had expressed last night that she was seeking the humans' trust and obedience, as well as their fear.

"But I and my daughters seek a peace. One that we can forge together. Take comfort in knowing that I never intended to sit upon this throne and to wear this crown. I had always been told it was meant for another," she continued.

She was not lying, but she was not telling the truth—she had intended for the throne to be mine, not hers. Still, her moment of honesty seemed to sway some of the onlookers—their faces softened. Their eyes widened; they were enraptured. She had not won them all, but she was having an effect on them that was not based on fear.

"So I stand here with one crown—but there are two of us beneath it. The Entente and I will always be your Queen until the Ever After claims us both."

Amantha and I shared a look of appreciation for Galatea's artful choice of words. Entente and Queen . . . it did have a ring to it.

The crowd took a moment to react. But now there was enthusiastic clapping and some seemingly genuine cheers.

Galatea feigned an expression of modesty and rewarded them all with a show of magic. Flowers hung suspended in air overhead, blooming and cascading down, and then up in the sky again, arching over the palace.

There was a reception after the coronation, but Galatea, eager for us to get on with the plot, insisted that we begin to ready ourselves to leave the second the last carriage pulled away and the square emptied out, after more waving from the balcony.

We returned to our rooms and finished packing. Later, Galatea entered with our doppelgängers. We were to leave our crowns in the hands of our magical twins. Amantha wondered if she might keep the crown and give the doppelgängers some other object that she could transform into one.

Galatea shook her head—it would be enough work casting and recasting the spell to change their faces every night until our return.

"We have to meet Madame Linea. We're late," Amantha insisted.

I rolled my eyes. I wasn't sure who I was annoyed more by—South or Amantha.

"Aren't you forgetting something?" South said archly.

I looked around. I did not know what he meant.

"You're still dressed like a princess. Not a nanny."

I touched my wand to the hem of my dress, changing it back to the subtle gray of the Entente. And then I touched my face, choosing a rounder, sweeter countenance. Amantha did the same.

South shook his head.

"What?" Amantha demanded.

"Nannies tend to be more cheerful, less dark and stormy," South explained.

"We're late," I exclaimed.

Without saying anything more to South, I grabbed Amantha's hand and we were gone in a blink.

# CHAPTER 9

## — FARROW —

The world had stopped when my mother had come back into the flesh on the cliff, and it seemed to begin again once she had finished carving her new wand and then tested her power.

She stood up and focused on me. "The world has paused for us. I wish we could stay here forever, my child—but every moment Galatea grows stronger. And the others who have trusted their lives to you—they could soon be in danger . . ."

It was my second sunrise with Hecate in the flesh, and guilt flooded me as I realized I'd let a full day go by without allowing myself to think about what had become of Mather and Cinderella while my own personal dream had come true. My mother was back, and I had sent Mather and Cinderella to the Thirteenth Queendom, where the Rookery was hidden.

I had hoped they would find help there to overthrow Galatea. The only way to fight magic was with magic, and mine was still new and was no match for that of all my sisters combined. But with Hecate back in the flesh and South now a Fate, perhaps we did not need the Rookery after all. Perhaps it was time to bring Cinderella and Mather home.

Hecate could still read my Future. I wondered for the briefest of moments if this new version of her might actually answer me if I asked her to read it for me now. I told her of what I had done, unsure if when she was in ash form she had witnessed the moment I had granted Cinderella's wish to take her and Mather to the Rooks.

"I need to know what has become of them. And what will become of them. I need to be where they are so I can see for myself that they are all right."

Before she could even open her mouth to respond, I continued to press. "Wish me to where they are," I said pleadingly. I could imagine Cinderella's open face and Mather's arm around me. I could also imagine them in peril.

Hecate twirled the wand in her hands. She had barely let it go since she had made it. Her grip had loosened a little though, and her hand had remained healed.

Finally, she answered firmly. "I can't do that."

"Why not?" I asked, not understanding.

"Because in every Future I see, if we go to them, your sisters Bari and Amantha will follow."

"They're going to follow anyway." I pouted.

"Bari will find them, and you don't want to know what happens next."

I shuddered. I had seen what Bari could do. She could become a swarm of bees or beetles or a murder of crows. Or any number of flying things.

I sighed. *What now?* Another idea crept into my head, and I smiled at my mother.

I knew, looking at Hecate's face, that she had already gathered what I was thinking.

"We can't travel without Galatea knowing. But we can still see them," Hecate reasoned.

Hecate closed her eyes suddenly and whispered some words I could not hear. The mirror I'd seen in her room when I was small was now in her hand. She could use it to see the Future.

Hecate opened her eyes. And I nodded as I realized Hecate wanted to show me Cinderella and Mather in her mirror. It felt like spying. But I needed to know if they were safe.

*Cinderella and Mather presented themselves in front of the largest gold door I had ever seen. The palace itself was also gold and impossibly large.*

*"I am Prince Mather of the First Queendom, and this is my friend . . . Ella Gray. We bring tidings from the Entente," Mather said.*

*They were led by a small man down a series of corridors and then brought to a giant throne room. They approached the throne, but no one was there. There was the sound of a lock turning.*

*Mather asserted, "It's a trap."*

*Cinderella was calmer. "Or it's a tactic. They want us to know they control the situation."*

*"Well, message received."*

*He began looking around the room for a way out.*

As I watched, I clutched Hecate's arm.

"We need to help them leave."

"Our magic is no good there. Just as the Rooks' is no good here."

I thought for a moment and studied Hecate. Her face was set in certainty of defeat.

"Is that a rule that you agreed to, or a fact?" I pressed.

Hecate considered.

"Just as we protected the Entente with the Veil so have they protected their home. The ground beneath Ella and Mather's feet is magicked by the Rooks. It weakens our magic. We have done the same with the lands of the Entente, particularly the Reverie."

"Why did you never tell us the Rooks were truly real? I thought they were just a story you made up to keep us from misbehaving."

"Only the Fates needed to know. You're right, we do have a covenant with them. The Rooks and Les Soeurs have always come together to produce the next generation of Rooks and Entente. If a girl was born she became an Entente, and the boys became Rooks."

"So what happened with South? Why did Iolanta keep him?"

"Iolanta broke the rules. She fell in love—" Hecate put her new wand to my temple, and I got a flash of Iolanta and her Rook kissing. "And children born of magic and love are rare indeed. Iolanta and the Rook created South through physical intercourse instead of by magic alone. There is a superstition that says such progeny are an abomination that will undo the covenant. So when South at birth appeared to be completely human, the Rookery wanted no part of him. They wanted him tossed to an orphanage to be raised with other humans. Iolanta, even in her most frenetic state, could see the truth of their intentions and she brought him to live with us."

"And you and Galatea agreed?"

"Reluctantly, I am now ashamed to say—but yes. Just having him near seemed to calm her."

From what I had seen of Iolanta, she had been so very far away from calm. If South's presence tempered her, I hated to imagine how much worse she might have been without him.

"But you could see the Future—you could see what he was to become. Why didn't you ever share that with all of us? Or at least with him. You let him be an outsider among us."

"In my mind, in all that I had seen, I believed that it was important for him to identify as human first—to develop a love of humanity. Perhaps that was the path to peace for all of us."

"But what of the prophesy? The end of the covenant?"

"The more I knew of South, the more I saw of his Future, the more I believed that he belonged with us."

I absorbed this and ventured, "What of my father?"

As Entente we were never to know our parentage. But the day of the Burning, all of that changed. Hecate as she burned informed me that she was my mother. I had never had the opportunity to ask about my father until now.

"We created you the old-fashioned way, by magic—and I never knew his name, but I can show you his face."

My heart leapt. The concept of fatherhood had never been part of our existence—we had in some ways thought of all three Les Soeurs as our mothers, and there were no males at all in the Entente except South.

"What was he like?" I asked, my voice dropping to a whisper.

"From what he allowed to me to glimpse, he was funny, kind—but he was a Rook, so all of it could have been theater."

She put her wand to my temple again, and this time I got a flash of my father. He had his hands on Hecate's belly. It was lit from wishing. Glowing as I was made.

Hecate had not lied after all. At least not about this.

"What was his name?" I asked.

"Laurel," she said.

"Laurel." I tested out the name. Now I had a name and a face and an image. I wondered how much of me came from him and how much from Hecate.

I certainly had her eyes and, before the doctor altered it, her nose. What had I gotten from him?

Hecate interrupted my musing. "I am so sorry to change the subject. But there is something you must see in the mirror."

*Mather was tearing at the tapestries that lined the hall. Cinderella was calmer. Perhaps after having lived with Galatea, Amantha, and Bari, she was more accustomed to having to stay calm in dangerous circumstances.*

*A Rook entered.*

*He surprised Mather and Cinderella by bowing to Mather.*

*"King Mather. We meet at last . . ."*

*"I may not become the king. There is a new Queen. Queen Galatea. My mother is dead . . . And this is Cinderella. A dear friend of the Queendom," Mather said.*

*The Rook bowed again and kissed Cinderella's hand.*

*When he rose, he again trained his eyes on Mather.*

*But Cinderella cleared her throat and asked, "And you are?"*

*"Forgive me, I am Waid, king of the Rooks. But we recognize only one ultimate monarch. And that is you, the true king. Long live the king," the Rook King said.*

*Perhaps the enormity of his mother's death now truly hit Mather.*

*"I have not come here on my own behalf. I have not come here to seek the crown. The truth is I never want to be king. I just wanted to stop her . . . My grandmother taught me to care about the people; my mother showed me what it was like to just protect oneself. After years of watching the latter, I decided that my grandmother was right. The people are my purpose. I want to make up for all my mother's ills."*

*"So now you want to stop the one who has taken her crown."*

*Mather paused and looked at Cinderella. Hearing it aloud must have driven the point home.*

*"Yes, that is what I want."*

*The Rook King smiled as if he had won a battle that Mather clearly did not know he was taking part in.*

*"I sense your hesitance for claiming the throne. You realize that*

*the only way to do that is to pick up the crown after it is removed. Are you prepared to take your rightful place as king when we relieve her of that crown?"*

*"Is that the condition for your help?"*

*"It is a condition. King Mather, we have just begun our negotiation. In the meantime, we shall have tea."*

*Cinderella squeezed his arm in assurance, and then Mather spoke. "We would love some tea. I take mine without sugar."*

I could sense Mather's desire to be anywhere but there, although that emotion wasn't at all present in his voice. I could also feel his disdain for the Rook. I wondered if the Rook could feel it too. How did their magic work, really? In the wake of learning what Hecate and Galatea had kept from me all these years, I did not take Hecate's account of how the Rooks' magic worked as the truth. I wanted to hear Mather's thoughts on what he had seen in the Rooks' presence.

Beside me, my mother cleared her throat—

"There is something else I must show you," she said suddenly.

We watched the coronation in the mirror. Amantha was preening—she loved the crown. Bari wore an expression of fury as if she might devour their guests. Galatea was oddly calm, as if this weren't her first coronation.

The ceremony was objectively beautiful, and the castle was restored to some semblance of what it had been before the Black Glass—and Galatea had begun to make the palace her own. There were flowers everywhere: in the tapestries on the walls, in giant urns throughout the place. The carefully cultivated royal gardens had grown exponentially. The animal topiaries were now almost as tall as the palace itself. I stopped and stared at a lion topiary, which had captured the fierce feline in midpounce. Knowing my sister's penchant for transformation, I had to stop and ask if the lion was real.

Hecate shook her head.

"All the Black Glass, it's gone," I whispered as I looked at the newly, most likely magically resurfaced buildings in the square, including the palace itself.

"Oh, Galatea, even with all of our sisters . . . that must have taken too much power . . ."

I absorbed Hecate's words. I knew that it was going to take some time for Hecate to fully grasp that Galatea and our sisters were who we were fighting against, even though she had witnessed their crimes when she was ash. But aside from reacting to her concern for Galatea's well-being, I latched on to the idea that at this moment Galatea was the most vulnerable we'd seen her.

"You hinted at it before, but I cannot allow it."

"What?"

Hecate was resolute. "I can't give you the tools to injure my sister. That's against the rules of the Fates."

I felt offended and seen at once, as only Hecate could make me feel. I would do everything I could not to hurt Galatea. That did not mean I was past using force; I just didn't want to have to.

"I don't want to injure her, I want to stop her—or at least slow her down until we can change her mind. Please, Mother," I begged. Hecate still required honesty in a way that no one else I had ever encountered had.

From what I had seen from Hecate since she regained her flesh, she was not the same as she had been before. She was torn between the old rules and what had become of us.

Hecate remained silent and gestured back to the action in the mirror. We continued to watch in silence.

After the ceremony, after the party, which seemed to be an enormous success, Hecate informed me that Bari and Amantha disappeared, with South seconds behind. Another Bari and Amantha appeared moments later on the dance floor. But Hecate said they were spelled doppelgängers.

"Where did they go? And why go to such lengths? And what could be so urgent they would skip out on the ball?" I asked.

"South will tell us. He is with them—"

I called out to South in my mind, but for once he did not answer.

I realized too late that I should have set up some new way to communicate with South. He was firmly in my corner—I knew that. I trusted him completely. But I should have planned better; Galatea had planned every moment of her coup. With the notable exception of executing Magrit. And even then, within hours Galatea seemingly had the Queendom in the palm of her hand. She'd brought the guard and the people to heel. Relative to her deft, albeit fallacious actions, I felt like I was just scrambling to catch up. And Hecate was still acclimating to being back in the flesh.

"Galatea's just so far ahead of us, Mother. She's been planning this for years."

Hecate looked at me sharply, having seen what I was going to think before I had even thought it. "You're wrong about that, you know. Galatea's improvising. She never expected to take the crown. She was going to give it to Bari while she continued to orchestrate everything from behind the scenes. The crown was never meant to be hers. She was going to be a Queen Mother a dozen times over, with a dozen different faces, as each of your sisters took over one of the Queendoms while none of the people were the wiser. Instead, now she's in the center of the court in the center of the most powerful of all the Queendoms, and all eyes will be on her. She will make a mistake, and we will be there to stop her."

Hecate's words were encouraging, but she could see I wasn't entirely convinced. She added, "You forget. I am the Fate of the Future. She will never be truly ahead."

"So what do we do, Mother? How do we stop her?" I countered.

"If we get close enough to Galatea, perhaps I can see her Future and we can thwart it."

# CHAPTER 10

## — Bari —

I didn't change my dress. I grabbed Amantha's hand and blinked. We traveled to where Madame Linea was waiting, just outside Queen Helene's palace grounds.

Madame Linea looked startled as we appeared next to her in her carriage.

South appeared, wearing his annoying grin, across from us.

We had never met Madame Linea the night of Queen Magrit's ball for Mather, but Linea had a longstanding special relationship with the Crown of every Queendom and, shamefully, with the Entente. She trained companions for every royal and every member of the nobility, for a price. The companion was raised to know the royal's or noble's history and likes and dislikes and to defend them from harm. Oftentimes, they fulfilled their charge's romantic needs as well. Les Soeurs had sanctioned the practice, even helping pick the companions based on what the Fates knew of their Futures. I found the practice archaic and distasteful, even for humans. And when I saw Madame Linea's opulence, as evidenced by the finery of her dress and jewelry, I couldn't help but bristle at how she achieved it. Farrow had spent years as a Shadow to the Couterie before becoming one herself. Her face had been surgically altered to match the Couterie she Shadowed. If something happened to the Couterie, Farrow was meant to serve as backup. Farrow had made the most of her position and challenged her Couterie, to take her place, in an effort to kill Queen Magrit. She hadn't succeeded, but in that action at least, Farrow had my respect.

Madame Linea had finally found her voice, and she used it to scold us.

"There you are. Being early is on time for Queen Helene. Oh, and you must change your dresses. Pastels are nonthreatening. And a fuller skirt . . . and you must smile. You'll look more . . . trustworthy. As you are, I would think you wanted a baby for a sacrifice."

"Before we begin, I just want to be clear. This arrangement was not our idea. I don't like you and I don't like working with you," I said, needing to establish our higher ground before Madame Linea uttered another word.

South coughed loudly, covering a laugh.

Amantha was more direct. "You work for us, not with us."

"Of course, you must have your reasons for your tardiness. It must be a significant undertaking suddenly acquiring a Queendom," Linea demurred.

South smirked.

I didn't like Linea. I didn't know how Farrow had spent all those years under her thumb. I was half tempted to turn her into a flying frog or squirrel. But I remembered the mission and what we were supposed to do. I could not disappoint Galatea. Not now.

"You and the rest of the Entente have loftier schemes to think of than fabric colors. That's what you are thinking."

"Exactly," said Amantha.

"My reason for changing your dresses has nothing to do with the latest fashions. It has to do with our mission. You want Queen

Helene to trust you with her child. She is only going to do so because she believes you have nothing to do with the Entente. Because she believes you are Couterie. Because she believes in me," Linea explained. "But your dresses undermine all of that. A Couterie wouldn't be caught dead in dresses the color of gravel and peat. The Queen knows that, and when she sees them, she will know something is amiss and our plan is ruined before it has begun." Linea concluded, "Now, you have two choices: you can use your wands or you can use me. From what Galatea intimated, you wanted to do this as quietly as possible. But it is your choice. I can take my leave—"

"There's a third option." Amantha's arm went to her pocket, where her wand was. "I could turn you into a—" she began.

I cleared my throat. "We will proceed with the plot." I slipped out my own wand and touched the hems of both of our dresses. "Pastel it is," I said resolutely.

"You look . . . like someone a Queen could trust," Linea said, rapping on the carriage for her driver to take us across the moat and to the palace.

She took a final appraising look at us before the footmen opened the carriage doors. Madame Linea then led us to the entrance of the palace and pulled the velvet rope that hung there. I could hear the loud, hollow echo of a bell.

A valet greeted us, and we entered.

"Queen Helene is expecting you," the valet reported, and we followed her to the nursery. There was a crib and there were toys and a chair that rocked but no sign of the infant.

The Queen herself was young, our age, and pretty. And welcoming.

This palace was unlike Magrit's in every way. It was cheerful. It was more rustic, which reminded me of the Reverie, and I felt a pang for the place where I had grown up. We had improved upon the palace, but it still lacked the warmth of the Reverie. And more important, it lacked all my sisters under the same roof.

"Thank the Fates that you are here," Helene said. "The carriages are packed. And I must leave before the hour is through. And you must too."

Amantha sighed loudly. She clearly had not reconciled with the idea that we would not be staying in any palace.

Linea apologized for our tardiness and made introductions. "Your Majesty, I present the sisters Esmerelda and Gertrude, and their guard. I vow on my life that they will be perfect protectors for Her Highness. And the cottage we have found is secluded and literally the last place the Entente would search for. Princess Dora will be safer than she has ever been."

I wished too late that we had chosen our own names like we had chosen our own faces.

I found curtsying to the Queen to be almost as difficult as bowing my head to have a crown placed upon it.

Amantha felt the same, as evidenced by her wobbly curtsy. South steadied her before taking a bow. His military training was annoyingly apparent in his posture, even when he bent before Queen Helene.

"It is an honor to meet you, Your Highness," I said, ungritting my teeth.

"I have been summoned to meet the Entente Queen—" she began.

Then she corrected herself. "The new Queen of the First Queendom, Queen Galatea, for her Queen's Council. We all have, but given the circumstances . . . I want to leave my baby behind. In your safekeeping. I have trusted the Couterie with my life and my secrets.

Linea vouches for you and her word is golden. But I would like to have yours."

"Pardon?" Amantha blurted. She frowned, considering, I assumed, exactly what I was considering. Was swearing some kind of human oath a betrayal of the Entente?

"I would like you to vow on all that you hold dear to treat this babe as if she were your own, and to protect her with your life."

I cast a warning look at Amantha, and then looked Queen Helene squarely in the eyes. "I promise on all that I hold dear to protect this baby with my life."

Amantha and South repeated the vow.

I could see her shoulders visibly relax, and she clapped her hands. The valet rushed out of the room, and two maids rushed in—one was carrying an infant wrapped in a seemingly excessive number of blankets.

Queen Helene lifted the baby from the maid's arms and held her to her own chest.

She murmured to the child. "Dora, Mommy loves you so much. Mommy will miss you, but these two kind ladies and their guard will take the finest care of you. They will keep you safe. It will be but a blink. Don't grow up too fast without me. And don't you dare say your first word without me being there."

The Queen remembered we were in the room and ended her embarrassing display.

Then she handed me the squealing baby. It was heavier than I imagined, and when I looked down at its round pink face it cooed and then had the audacity to smile.

"Cook will provide you with enough food for a week. And Linea will contact you if there is any delay in my return. Dora likes to be told a bedtime story before bed. And if she gives you any trouble at all, sing for her."

The baby didn't cry, and I didn't cry. I hadn't since the day of the Burning. But I certainly felt like it. We had been victorious over Magrit, so why in this moment did I feel like Amantha and I were the ones being punished?

# CHAPTER 11

## — FARROW —

I think we need more magic," Hecate said suddenly. She was holding the wand again, twirling it between her fingers. We were sitting in the drawing room of the Reverie. It felt empty and full all at once. Our sisters were not here, but Hecate was. The question was, which Hecate was she today? Her moods seemed to be shifting moment to moment, hour by hour.

Despite what she had said, I was still worried about her use of magic calling attention to us. I could hear the wishes of the people. Some of them were happy about Magrit's execution. Others feared that they would be next. So I did not want to be found by anyone, magical or human. If we were to approach Galatea as Hecate wanted, it should be on our own terms and in our own time.

Hecate had already proved that she was in possession of her power again. Maybe more so than ever before. So what were we waiting for? That was, unless Hecate had reversed course and thought the better of her idea. Maybe, with a little urging, I could get her to come with me to help Mather and Cinderella or tell me exactly what she saw of Bari's and Amantha's Futures. They were clearly up to something that we would regret later.

"I don't understand, you just showed me your magic—I think it is more than ample. If anything you are more powerful than ever before," I began.

"I didn't mean me—I meant you," Hecate said matter-of-factly.

I was caught up short. Not having power at all and now only having the power of the wish had caused me so much insecurity and so much pain. And now the person whose opinion I valued the most was saying what I'd suspected all along out loud: I was not enough.

"Can you unbind me?" I ventured.

Hecate had bound my magic the day of the Burning, and when the sisters finally tried to unbind it years later, my magic had been changed. I was the only Entente with wish magic. I could only grant wishes. I could hear desires. Other spells, all other magic, even the smallest magic, like lighting a wand or changing the weather, escaped me unless it was directly in service of a wish.

"Oh, Farrow, I believe that you were forever changed that day. Like South, like Amantha . . . and me."

"Mother, it wasn't forever for you. You are back, and you are just as powerful as you were before. Maybe more. You are the same in all the ways that matter."

"Look at me. I am not the same. Not in looks or deed—or in magic."

"How does your magic feel?"

"Wilder somehow—unpredictable."

"I'm sorry, Hecate."

"Don't be. I have lived the alternative in the ashes. This is better."

I nodded, pretending to accept it, but the wall of guilt was still there.

"So what do you mean? What are you proposing?"

"Unlike Galatea, I do not believe the Past is worth revisiting for too long. Otherwise there is a risk of getting lost in it. I believe we should move forward from where we are with what we have. We accept our new gifts . . . ," she mused as she took in her reflection again, as if she was talking about her new gift of youth as well. "And we learn to use them. Perhaps they are the key to defeating someone who is by her very nature mired in the Pasts," she finished, looking back up at me.

The speech was stirring. Still, I did not know how she supposed we were to acquire more magic for me, but I could not wait to find out.

"I have something for you," Hecate announced, thrusting her wand in the air.

A cloak appeared, floating. It was the palest of blues. And when the light caught it, it shimmered as if hundreds of stars were twinkling all at once.

I raised my arms and welcomed the cloak around me. The cloak felt like a living thing, coursing with the tingle and warmth of magic.

"Mother, it is beautiful."

"No one says that armor can't be beautiful."

"What do you mean?"

"I cast a protective spell on the fabric. When you wear it, you will be unnoticed by the Entente—and no harm will come to you. It is impenetrable by arrows or blades or weather. It will keep you warm and safe even when I am not with you.

"There's one more thing," Hecate enthused, twirling her wand. The cloak itself changed colors and then became an exact camouflage matching the tapestry behind us.

I remembered once upon a time when I was small and Hecate had surprised me by indulging my desire for a yellow dress on the morning of the Burning. Back then, she had usually favored and encouraged us to wear the gray dresses of the Entente. And allowing me the yellow dress was a huge departure for her from her usual adherence to the ways of the Entente. Now, this Hecate had made me a cloak that could be any color.

I hugged her.

Hecate's plan, it turned out, was for me to grant wishes. But not just any wishes.

"Our power is tied to emotion—even yours. When you grant a wish for someone with whom you have a difficult history, you will garner more power from that wish."

"I can't grant the wishes of the Entente. They will go counter to our mission—"

"There are others with whom you have had difficult Pasts."

"You mean the Couterie. Mother, you just told me how we did not want to get stuck in the Pasts, and now you want me to revisit mine."

"We are making an exception because it can be of use to us."

"Please say you don't want me to help Madame Linea."

"Never."

"You mean Lavendra and Tork?"

My mother nodded.

"But you showed me a glimpse of them. They are happy."

"I have glimpsed them again. Perhaps they can be happier."

*I wish with all my might that Farrow, Lavendra, and Tork—* She began, smiling sheepishly as if she was still getting accustomed to making wishes and having me grant them. She stopped mid-wish, taking in my hesitation.

I sighed. Other Entente could make magic happen with a wave of the wand. My magic was completely dormant unless it was in fulfillment of another's desire. Now I had to help someone who I could have gone a lifetime without seeing again.

Lavendra's and Tork's were the first lives that I had affected both before and after I had reacquired my magic. I adored Tork like a brother, but Lavendra was another story. Still, I had felt regret about changing their course. Taking Lavendra's spot in the Couterie had been essential in my quest to kill the Queen. Lavendra had run away after I bested her in that challenge. And I thought we had made our peace the night that she had left. Tork loved her so much he had left the Couterie for her. And she had left the Couterie for her freedom, which I respected. When I had run across Tork again in the village pub, I had shown him where Lavendra was. I thought reuniting them had closed the door on my regret and on the pain Lavendra had caused me.

And yet, at the mere suggestion of helping her, I felt my insides rise in protest. Neither time nor action had erased the years in which Lavendra had been cruel to me.

"How is it I understand what I must do . . . while at the exact same moment in time, I do not want you to finish that wish?"

"Forgiveness is much harder than forgetting. The former may well be more rewarding in the long term, though."

I was heartened by Hecate's words. Still, as I raised my wand, I did so with trepidation.

"Don't fret. The monsters of our youth are rarely as big as we remember them."

I thought about Bari. She had gotten only more powerful—but then again, so had I.

*I wish with all my might that Farrow, Lavendra, and Tork reunite.*

*When the hour is up she will return, with the magic she has earned.* Hecate smiled again. I wrapped my cloak snugly for comfort, and I granted the wish.

In a blink I was standing in front of a small cottage in the Thirteenth Queendom. It was winter here. I pulled my cloak around me even closer.

I looked into the window of the cottage and saw that Lavendra was baking. I had never once seen her enter the kitchen in all my years as her Shadow at the Couterie. At this moment in time, she was humming beneath her breath as if she was completely at home and completely content.

My nose perked up in recognition at the sweet scent emanating from the oven. One thing hadn't changed: Lavendra still loved honeybread. Only now she was making her own.

She took a tray out of the oven and placed it on the table. I watched her for a moment, remembering the countless times she had demanded I go to the baker to retrieve more of her favorite treat, regardless of weather or time of day. Her wants always superseded my own.

Now, in the Present, Lavendra turned around and took me in. She screamed in surprise.

"Well, Shadow, still lurking around behind me, even after you took my place. Tork was right, you are Entente." Her words almost sounded like an insult, but she smiled as she said them. Her eyes met mine, and then she cast them downward.

After she offered to take my cloak and I refused, she pointed me to a chair in their kitchen and began making me some tea.

"How did I not know when you were under my nose the whole time? The Couterie pride ourselves on our powers of observation. I obviously failed," she said matter-of-factly.

"Imagine how Madame Linea feels," I said, trying to keep the mood light.

"I would trade all my honeybread to see her face when she realized you were Entente."

"I think I'd trade some of my magic for it—"

"Farrow, I owe you an apology. A proper one."

"No, you don't. You already apologized," I said firmly, trying to remember Hecate's words about forgiveness.

"I was terrible to you."

"You were."

"I wish I had some excuse for it. I was so unhappy and I took it out on you. Not because you deserved it. But because as my Shadow you were simply always there. I realize that now. And I know I can't turn the clock back on all those years. If I could, it would all be different. I would have been different. Maybe we could have even been, dare I say it . . . friends."

"I was unhappy too. Profoundly. I would have liked having a friend. Yet there's the rub . . . Linea didn't set us up to be friends, she made us rivals. She made everyone rivals." As I said the words, I did feel a little of the hurt and anger toward Lavendra flow out of me. It wasn't all gone. It would never be gone. But it had lessened. Her acknowledging what she had done was a part of it. But I was the other part of it. Standing in her kitchen in my cloak made of stars—with my power back, with my mother back—I realized I was no longer the Shadow she had insulted; I was the Entente who could no longer be sent out for honeybread.

"That's the rub," Lavendra repeated. Then she rose with alacrity, announcing she wanted to show me the source of the honey in the honeybread. I sensed what she really wanted was to shift the mood.

It was a particularly surreal experience seeing Lavendra—my Lavendra—slip into a bee suit and take me out to her beehive.

"Come, I want to show you what we've built—what Tork and I built."

I stifled an instinctive laugh at the idea of Tork using his hands to build anything.

She put gloves on me and a baggy suit like the one she wore that covered every inch of me, except for a web of fabric that protected my face. After years of helping Lavendra dress, now she was helping me.

When we were both properly attired, we walked outside, and she showed me her garden, which was filled with fragrant flowers that I recognized as hibiscus and lavender blooms. At the end of a winding walkway there was a wooden structure: a hive where Lavendra raised her own bees.

"I never would have imagined you keeping bees."

"Would you imagine me being a nanny?"

I shook my head reflexively. I had seen through Lavendra's wishes that she had found herself here and in the employ of a family in town. But I had not actually witnessed her caring for the children.

"Lavendra, I am sure you are a wonderful nanny," I lied.

"How could I possibly be? You took care of my every whim. I had no idea how to take care of myself let alone two incredibly needy, incredibly curious children."

"I'm sorry, Lavendra," I said, feeling for her predicament, but also feeling a pang of recognition that she was right—she would have been a horrible nanny.

"Don't be, it was a relief to get away from those little tyrants. And I like to think it was a bit of Fate that led me here to the bees.

When I first came here, I bought a honeybread every day. It was all I could really afford if I intended to make my purse last. The baker sussed out my situation and took pity on me. She offered me an apprenticeship, and it turned out I have a bit of a knack for it. The same baker hired Tork, and now we are starting a little shop of our own across town with the baker's blessing. You should see Tork behind the counter—he is a natural salesman."

From her beatific expression, I could tell it meant a lot to her and that she was proud. And from her wishes, I knew she was hoping that I did not find her enterprise beneath her.

*I pray that, after everything, she does not look down on me and Tork and our simple life*, she wished. I wanted to reassure her without letting on that I could read her wishes.

"I have a sister who would love this," I volunteered, thinking of Bari.

"You have a sister?" she asked.

"Lots of them—not by blood but by magic."

"Wish you'd told me back at the Couterie."

"You would have used it against me."

She thought for a minute, then added, "Yes, I would have. Or I would have blackmailed you into granting my wishes . . ."

"I didn't have the power when I was there," I explained.

"That makes sense. Otherwise you never would have been there to begin with."

She showed me how she took the honey from the trays with a kind of spoon and jarred it, all while we wore these enormous suits covering us head to toe. The bees didn't want to sting us.

In fact, they seemed to be humming happily.

We retuned with our fresh honey, and Lavendra insisted on making me a cup of tea with it.

Just then, Tork was at the door with a bale of logs, freshly cut, presumably by his own hands.

"I am victorious!" he boasted as he entered.

My urge to giggle returned.

Lavendra smiled and said, "Yes, you are, and we have a guest."

He dropped his logs in the metal bin by the fireplace.

He ran his hand through his hair reflexively and smoothed down his shirt.

He rushed up to me and picked me up and swung me around and deposited me on the ground.

"It's good to see you too, Tork."

"I didn't know if we'd ever get to see you again. Or if I would get to thank you. Thank you, Farrow, for telling me how to find Lavendra."

"It's the least I could do after what I did to both of you—my plan kept you apart."

"When I was here on my own, I used to hope that we would find our way back to each other, Fate willing . . . and now I know that that's you, right?" Lavendra said.

Tork took her hand.

"Oh, I am not a Fate—just a member of the Entente," I corrected.

"I think you don't have to be modest after you appeared out of thin air outside our cottage," Lavendra countered in jest.

All of a sudden, the clock behind us seemed to tick louder.

*Tick, tick, tick . . .*

Lavendra cocked her head a little. She could hear it too.

"Are you doing that?"

"Hecate, my mother is. She's reminding me that I haven't much time."

"Your mother?"

"Time for what?" Tork said as if it wasn't the most surreal thing in the world to have a clock's volume increase by magical means. Even I, as Entente, marveled at how far Hecate's magic now reached.

"My mother was returned from the ashes. It's a terribly long story, and we haven't time, I'm afraid. You see, I am not just here for a social call. I am here because I want to do something for you. I want to grant your wishes to restore some of what you lost."

Without missing a single beat, they looked at each other and spoke at once.

"We want for nothing," Lavendra said.

"We have each other," he seconded. But I could hear their wishes.

It took me a moment to focus as their wishes overlapped.

*I am perfectly content, but I know Tork must miss his library.*

*I am perfectly content, but Lavendra toils for so long. I wish she had a bigger oven and a bigger hive. And a new dress for every single day.*

With the right wish and a wave of the wand, I could put them in their new Queen's Court. But given the state of the Queendoms and, more important, their own wishes, why would I put them in the eye of danger when they were currently safely ensconced away from it?

I spent a few moments talking with Tork. He peppered me with questions about the First Queendom.

He also asked about Jacoby.

"Do you know how he is? Is he well?"

"I promise I will check on him."

"If there are any wishes to grant, maybe you can grant his in our stead. It was, I am afraid, rather chilly in my shadow for my twin."

I had hoped that there were private moments between them

that were warmer—that when Madame Linea could not see them they behaved as true brothers. Tork disabused me of that notion. I still hoped that maybe Tork was being hard on himself because of guilt.

"My brother knows me, but I don't know my brother. I was a selfish brute to Jacoby."

Lavendra touched Tork's arm to comfort him.

"He doesn't know the real you. We're both figuring out who we are now. We are going to be better people."

"I believe you already are," I said, before kissing them both and answering my mother's wish to wish me home.

Despite what they'd said, I could still hear their real wishes. She was making wishes for him and he for her.

*I wish for a library with every book that Tork wants to read. And clothes, poor Tork left the Couterie with only the fancy clothes on his back. And, Fate help him, I am the worst seamstress in the world.*

*I wish for an oven big enough so that Lavendra does not have to spend so many hours over the stove. And dresses. I know she misses having them.*

It had been only a few short weeks, but they both had indeed transformed so much. If there was hope for the two most selfish humans I had met besides Magrit, was there not hope for the Entente, as twisted as they had become?

I could hear Hecate wishing for me to return.

"I have to get back. But I am a wish away if you need me," I offered as I raised my wand.

I granted Tork's and Lavendra's wishes first, before I got to Hecate's.

When I arrived back, my face was wet with tears.

"It was different than I thought—they are different."

"For the better I hope?" Hecate said, even though I knew she'd seen everything in her mirror.

"Yes, for the better."

We watched in her mirror as they realized that their wishes had come true.

Lavendra was pointing at the oven, her eyes wide. "Do you see that? It's growing . . ."

"I see it." Tork stood in front of her protectively, but he was smiling.

The oven was indeed growing—its iron frame was stretching in every direction. This was accompanied by a screeching sound, and the metal warped itself into an identical oven of exactly twice its original size. The flame inside reignited.

Lavendra said, "I don't understand. How did she know? I never wished for a bigger oven . . ."

There was a sound in their living room as the front door swung open and slats of wood floated in.

The wood assembled itself into a bookshelf along the wall, and books began to appear until they lined every shelf.

"And I never wished for a library," said Tork.

"I wished it for you," Lavendra admitted.

"And I wished the new oven for you," Tork whispered in response.

They were about to embrace, when their clothes began to transform.

"Your dress . . . My shirt . . . pants . . ."

Lavendra rushed to the closet in their bedroom and flung open the doors. It was filled with dresses for her and new shirts and pants for him.

Lavendra looked down at her feet, which were still encased in her scuffed dress shoes from the Couterie.

She began to laugh.

"We should have wished for shoes."

Still watching in the mirror, I nodded at Hecate and granted their wish.

"Thank you, Farrow," Tork whispered.

Hecate's mirror clouded over as they came together in a kiss.

I thought about the letter that Tork had written to Lavendra well over a year ago. *I would forgo today to have you forever.* They had written those words to each other. They finally had their forever.

"That felt good," I admitted, "and I feel stronger."

Hecate nodded in agreement but then added, "That was lovely, but we need bigger wishes. We're going to need a lot more power for what's to come. It is important for you to know the weight of every wish, as well as the joy of granting them."

I found myself tapping my fingers against my wand—a habit I had developed when I was nervous.

"You have done well," Hecate assessed. But I felt myself sink a little from the high sense of satisfaction I had felt only a moment before.

"What is it, my child?"

"It feels as if it is not enough. The Couterie forced us all to study the history of all the Queendoms. All that study, and now they will never put it to use."

"There is value and beauty in the life that they have chosen."

"I know that. I see it. I felt it. There was so much love in those rooms . . . I just meant they are both masters of people and books. Have I sent them into a life where they are missing out on their potential to affect more than each other? They were supposed to move Queens and nobility."

"Perhaps . . ."

I felt my face fall. Hecate was much more kind than she once had been, but she was still honest, and brutally so.

"Or perhaps the smallest change could still change everything."

She showed me the mirror. A book fell from the shelf and opened on the floor. Tork picked it up and examined it.

It was a history of the Thirteen Queendoms.

"Why did you do that?"

"Tork's skills could be of use to the Queendoms someday. Lavendra's too. Because of the wish you granted, he will be prepared when the Queendoms shift again. And perhaps he can be of use to us as well."

Before I could ask which shifts, a new vision appeared in the mirror.

# CHAPTER 12

## — BARI —

Linea insisted on holding the baby when we got back into the carriage. Her driver drove us out of the palace grounds and the city and into the woods. We stopped at the woods' edge.

"This is as far as you go, Linea. Amantha, take the baby," I commanded, thinking it was a terrible idea for Linea to know our exact location. She was betraying Queen Helene by making her believe she was entrusting her baby to Couterie instead of the very thing she was hiding her baby from—the Entente. What would stop Linea from crossing us as well? Galatea was sure she was on our side, but from what I'd heard of her from Farrow and what I'd seen for myself, I was pretty certain that Linea had only one side: her own.

"No, you take the baby," Amantha protested, rolling her eyes.

"I already held the baby in the palace," I countered.

My eyes flicked to Linea, who was watching us intently while pretending to be interested in the stitching on her dress. Knowing the Couterie's penchant for observation, I did not want this tiny disagreement with Amantha to undermine my authority before Linea.

"It's no trouble. I can drive you to wherever you are taking the child. Or I can keep it at the Couterie. We both know what Helene doesn't. The baby has nothing to fear from the Entente," Linea said the last as if she was convincing herself. Or at least justifying the betrayal. Then again, perhaps Linea felt not even an iota of concern for the child. Her practice of mutilating children to match one another so that one might replace the other in service of the nobility of the Queendoms was barbaric. My thoughts drifted to Farrow and her nose and ears, which had been surgically changed to match her Couterie before she replaced her.

South looked at Linea squarely. I assumed he was reading her Presents, but the barely veiled look of fear in her eyes was enough for anyone to know she was scared of us and scared for the baby.

"You don't think that we are capable of keeping a human baby alive and healthy?" Amantha demanded.

"I never said that. I never thought that. I just . . . I am sure that you have other magical business to attend to. I can take care of the babe," she said nervously.

"Considering what you do to children, I think the baby is much safer with us. Now hand the infant to Amantha. I will not ask again," I said, steely.

She sighed and complied.

"And how do you propose I get home?" she asked as she made a dignified show of getting out of the carriage.

South raised an eyebrow of agreement with her. He was right. We couldn't leave her here on the edge of the forest. What if she never made it home? Galatea had been quite clear that Linea would be of further use to us.

"She can have the carriage," I announced.

Amantha and I joined hands over the baby and blinked away to the cottage.

"This place is worse than the Gray manor," Amantha said when we arrived at our new temporary home. I could not disagree, taking in the abandoned woodman's cottage, completely devoid of magic and charm.

She took out her wand and waved it, making it look like the interior of the Reverie. I took out my own wand and gave it a wave and changed the cabin back to its original rustic awfulness.

"Why can't we make it a little more livable?" she whined.

"We are supposed to use only essential magic so that no one can detect us," I countered.

"It's essential that I don't have to look at those ugly wooden walls."

South looked around and assessed, "It's not so bad. It's rather cozy."

"You can only say that because you spent most of your life in Magrit's dungeon for the Fallen and then in the barn behind the manor," I countered.

He smiled a wry smile that did not contest my point.

"If I didn't know better, I'd think all those years at Cinderella's spoiled you," South added finally.

I couldn't let him have the last word on this or any subject.

"The Reverie is much nicer than the manor." Amantha attempted to back me up, but I was focused on South.

"But that's the thing, South. You don't know me anymore. We are very different than we were as children."

"Then you don't know me either. Not really . . . Hopefully, that will change now that we're stuck together," he said defiantly.

He sat down in a wooden rocking chair. I squeezed my wand in my pocket, and one of the chair's rockers broke in two, landing him on the ground. The chair made a sound. But South didn't give me the satisfaction.

Amantha cleared her throat as if she was bored with our conversation.

"We have to put the baby away and start working on the love potion for seducing the prince."

"You do realize that Linea was right about one thing. Babies don't just take care of themselves. There isn't a single spell for that."

Amantha, frustrated, bit back, "Well, there should be."

South raised an eyebrow. I assumed he was going to ask questions about the spell—but instead he simply offered, "What do you need me to do?"

Amantha and I debated whether to use South's immense power in the love spell. We weighed his power against his intention. With enough will and enough magic, you could do anything, Hecate had taught us. Well, South's will wasn't necessarily on our side. Neither was Hecate's.

"We've actually given it some thought, and your help is not needed for this spell," Amantha said.

South sounded unsurprised. "You have a pretty powerful Fate at your disposal, and you choose to pass on adding my power to the spell?"

"We don't want to dilute our wicked magic with all that pure, righteous magic you carry around with you."

Dora seemed to giggle as if she found my sarcasm funny. I stared down at the little human, and she began to wail. And South began to laugh.

"What are you laughing at?" I commanded.

"Your face," he said simply.

"What about it?" I shot back.

"You are perfectly comfortable transforming into scorpions but put a little human baby in front of you and you look positively terrified."

In response, an idea occurred to me.

"You do remember saying that you wanted to be helpful?" I said, before I cradled the baby in one hand and reached with the other for my wand in my pocket.

*"Baby take flight, find yourself in South's arms,"* I whispered beneath my breath.

South shook his head as the baby floated across the room in his direction. For her part, the tiny person seemed to enjoy being weightless, and she began making a not unpleasant cooing sound. He took it in his arms, at once awkward and protective.

"Galatea did not ask me to do this," he said, looking helpless for the first time since he had asked to accompany us on this mission.

It was my moment, finally, to smirk. And relief flooded me. I felt the tension in my body relax, as if I had been unintentionally holding every muscle at attention. It was because I was unaccustomed to taking care of children, I told myself. It was also because I was unaccustomed to spending this much time with someone as exasperating as South.

"You said you wanted to be helpful," I mocked.

South cradled the baby closer and headed for the kitchen. His surprise and alarm had shifted into something softer. He looked into the baby's eyes, and his own widened as if he recognized something in her.

"Don't mind them . . . Your caretakers are just working on a spell to dethrone your mother. Come on, little one who wants to eat. You do, yes you do . . ." As the baby quieted and cooed, I realized he was reading her Present. He knew exactly what to do for the baby because he could read what she was thinking and feeling.

"He is just so infuriating," I said, stomping my feet.

"He is. But he made that awful din stop so now we can get back to the spell, right? Maybe we can just keep South on baby duty and we'll never have to hold the little thing again," Amantha said, finding the bright side.

A few minutes later, we had gathered our supplies and found a clearing in the woods with some distance between us and the cottage in which to concoct the potion.

It seemed almost surreal that it had been only days since the last potion we'd made, since the prince's ball, since the execution of Magrit, since the coronation . . . and now Amantha and I were standing in the middle of the woods making another potion. The love potion we had created for Mather was specially tailored, using Farrow's hair—because he was already in love with Farrow, and we just wanted him to fall under my spell while I posed as her at the ball. This one would use my hair. This new prince would fall in love with me.

But when I pulled a strand from my head to put it in the potion, Amantha surprised me by batting my hand away from the caldron we had set up in the clearing.

"Why do you think you should be the one the prince falls for and not me?" Amantha said.

I was caught up short. It had never even occurred to me that Amantha would want to be the one leading the plot.

"Because the last time we used a love spell, I took the potion." I defended my position.

"And it was a complete disaster," Amantha replied unblinkingly.

"Through no fault of my own," I countered.

I bit back, feeling uncharacteristically attacked by my greatest champion.

"You know why it can't be you, Amantha. You couldn't even be crowned without practicing with a book because you were afraid it would fall through you. We have to be practical, Amantha. What happens if you disappear in front of the prince?" I said, in a less-caustic tone, but the effect was no less impactful on Amantha. Her face crumpled as the words hung between us. Amantha's cheeks went red, and her eyes flashed. And then, she disappeared.

When South ventured out to the clearing to check on us, the baby was sleeping in his arms.

"Where's Amantha?" he asked in a whisper as he looked around.

"Did anyone ever tell you that you are the embodiment of salt in a wound?" I hissed.

# CHAPTER 13

## — FARROW —

When I first met Hodder, he was a horse in Cinderella's barn, and then I began to hear his wishes and the wishes of all the other animals nearby. In a twist of dark Fate, my sisters had turned the household staff into animals to cover the Entente's crimes. I had undone the magic at the time. Hodder and the other animals had been set free. They had returned and helped us sabotage Magrit's ball, after which we sent them on their way as humans.

I wanted to grant his wish to be permanently human without him seeing, without him knowing it was me. One, because he didn't like me very much, which was fair given what the Entente had done to him and the others. But it also felt like a more magnanimous way to grant a wish.

Hecate gave pause, though.

"What if you grant a whim and not a true wish? Show yourself and be certain."

Hodder was surprised to see me.

"What are you doing here—?" he asked me.

"I could ask you the same question. Cinderella told you that you could stay at the house as long as you want. What are you doing in the Twelfth Queendom? Let me help you, Hodder."

"What is in it for you?" Hodder asked.

Hecate stepped in defensively. "She's trying to help you."

"Who are you?"

"Her mother. You don't recognize me. I was a pile of ashes when you last saw me. We shared a barn," she explained.

"And I was a horse. What strange new world is this?"

He suddenly looked as if he was going to cry.

"Hodder, what is it? Are you lost?"

"No, *they* are . . ."

"Who are they? Who are you missing, Hodder?" I asked, my concern growing. Was there some new threat to the Queendoms?

"My family," he cried.

Hodder had a family? I had not known, because I had not asked.

"I didn't know. What happened to them?" I asked gently.

"I sent them away when the Grays passed. I knew something was wrong. I promised I would follow. But then I got stuck. And now I can't find them. They're not where they told me they would be. They're not anywhere. Do you think that Lady Galatea and her daughters turned them into horses too, before they got away?"

I sighed at the idea that there were more victims of the Entente's magic. I wished I could defend my sisters and say they would never do that—but I had already seen so much evidence that they could.

"All you have to do is wish for them, and I can take you to them."

He searched my face as if looking for meaning. "What's in it for you?" he asked finally. I realized he was looking for an ulterior motive.

"Do you really care, if you get what you want?" Hecate added unhelpfully.

"I want to see them more than anything—I just do not want the cost to be something that I cannot live with," he said stoically.

For the longest time I hadn't understood human capacity for love and humans' strength. Perhaps Mother was right. My years without magic had made me understand better. And still, it was not enough.

"You have no need to fear. When I grant a wish, I get stronger. I want to be strong enough to contain Galatea."

"And no humans will be hurt?"

"No one will be hurt period if I can help it," I said resolutely.

Hodder looked at me a long beat before finally acquiescing. "I believe you."

*I wish I was with my family.*

I closed my eyes and granted the wish, hoping against hope that his family was alive and well, not anywhere dangerous.

Luckily for them they had made it to the Tenth Queendom—they were working for another family. They were safe and happy and so excited to see him. Hodder's wife had a gentle face and smile. And his twin sons were mirror images of their father.

I looked at the happy reunion. I felt my magic coursing through me.

"Hodder, if you ever decide you all want to return to the Grays' mansion when it's safe, there's a place for you there—all you have to do is wish for it."

"Thank you," Hodder mouthed.

I took my leave of them, and Hecate and I returned to the Reverie.

"That felt . . . amazing. I want to do it again."

Hecate said, "I think you have enough magic to face Galatea."

Before I could say anything more, a new vision appeared in the glass.

It was Amantha.

"Where is she? What is she doing?" I asked as we tried to make sense of the scene before us.

*Amantha was helping a young woman about my age across the street to a theater.*

*"I've got you," Amantha whispered.*

*With her other hand, she rapped on the door to the theater. A handsome boy filled the doorway and reacted immediately.*

*"Madame Corinne?"*

*Madame Corinne began to laugh hysterically, and as she did her skin began to turn a pale shade of blue.*

*"I believe she has the pox," Amantha whispered.*

*"The pox? Have you seen this malady before?"*

*"I'm afraid I have. She is not well."*

*Behind the young man in the door, a peal of laughter rang out and there was the sound of a crash.*

*Amantha and the man settled Madame Corinne on a couch onstage. And the man yelled out for a doctor.*

*A woman stepped out from behind a curtain and said, "Gamine too . . ."*

*Amantha asked, "Who's Gamine?"*

*"The understudy," the man said, sounding even more somber.*

*"Mother, we have no choice. We have to cancel the show."*

*His mother added, "Jon has run for the doctor."*

*The doctor appeared in minutes as the actor and Amantha and his mother tended to the patients onstage.*

*Amantha curtseyed and began to back away.*

*The man stopped her. "You say that you are familiar with the sickness. How long will this pox last?"*

*"We had an outbreak last winter where I'm from. Usually several days, and then a full recovery after more rest."*

*"That's a relief—for Madame and Gamine but not for the play. I'm afraid we're done for. No Dahlia and Casio."*

*"Oh, my favorite play. 'That the guardian of my heart comes from the heart of the enemy, that the soul of my soul is at war with mine . . . That I would be nameless and with you than have all the glories and the crown . . .' "*

*"You know it?" he said, surprised.*

*"It never left me, it seems. It's only my favorite. I'm no Madame Corinne, but I must have acted out her part in our drawing room a hundred times. I had my heart set on seeing her tonight."*

*His face lit up. "How would you feel about being her?"*

*Amantha looked taken aback.*

*"Pardon?" she said.*

*"I know that this will seem in equal parts callous and forward of me, but would you consider sharing the stage with me this week?"*

*"Me? I'm no Dame Corinne," she said innocently.*

*"No one is. But you are here—and you'd be saving the theater. You see, everyone's fortunes ride on every performance."*

*"In that case I have no choice but to say yes."*

*"Just know, I see you. I have been where you are."*

*"At the door to a theater—?"*

*"On the cusp of trying to become someone new. I did it once upon a time—it was worth it."*

*"I thought I was taking a role for a few days, not getting a new soul."*

*"The acting life is not for the faint of heart. If you choose it and it chooses you, it's transformative."*

*Amantha blushed, and as she did so she flickered into and out of sight. The boy was blinking hard as if he was unsure of what he had seen or not seen.*

*"Are you okay? You look like you've seen a ghost," he asked.*

*"Perhaps we have been out here in the sun too long or maybe you have the pox too," she excused.*

*Amantha leaned forward impulsively and kissed his forehead.*

*"You don't feel warm," she assessed.*

*He caught her by the wrist gently.*

*"You shouldn't get so close. If I have it, you would have it now too," he said, releasing her.*

*"I wouldn't mind . . . I mean . . . I don't know if it works like that."*

*"You're a brave one, aren't you? Have you decided yet if you are ready for your transformation?"*

*"Who says I will be any good at it? I have no training."*

*"We all pretend in big ways and small. Haven't you ever told a lie? Haven't you ever pretended to be something or someone you're not?"*

*Amantha nodded.*

*"I can teach you a few tricks—but I believe we are thespians all."*

*Remembering himself, he looked down at his hands on her waist, and her eyes followed his gaze. He pulled his hands gently away and stepped back from her.*

*"Pardon, that was forward of me."*

*"I didn't mind . . . My answer is yes. I would like to try."*

With that, Amantha followed him inside, but Hecate's vision stopped.

"Hey, we weren't done," I said impatiently.

"She takes the position. I believe it's fairly obvious," Hecate concluded.

I pursed my lips. I somehow had become invested in this small moment in Amantha's life. Was I rooting for her to hook the man's affections because she was so often in Bari's shadow? I felt a tiny bit of guilt wash over me. Whatever Amantha was doing was in service of Galatea, and that couldn't be good.

# CHAPTER 14

## — BARI —

I have to go find her," I said, not caring that South could see my panic.

"I'll help," he said immediately.

"I don't need your help. And someone needs to watch the baby."

Still, South put the baby in the crib and grabbed my hand. He tapped his wand, and the baby was frozen in place with her little hands punching up into the air. But South and I were still very much animated.

"There, problem solved."

"You stopped time . . . ," I marveled, despite the circumstances.

"Now I can help you find Amantha, and the baby will be just fine."

I turned into a murder of crows and flew out the nearest window; South was behind me. I didn't stop until we got to the Reverie. I went from room to room. No Amantha . . . Finally I stopped on the cliff at the edge of the Reverie. I could feel him touch down beside me. And I could feel the shadow of his wings.

For all my dislike for him, his wings were a marvel. Their span was twice his height, and their feathers were gloriously golden.

"Use your power. Tell me where she is," I ordered.

To my surprise, he closed his eyes and concentrated obediently.

"I can't find her. I already reached out. I am sorry, Bari."

"Then what use are you—to me, to this plot? I think we should get back. Maybe she'll be waiting for us."

He stood his ground, and I felt a strong desire to push him off the cliff. Remembering his gift, I shoved him hard and he began to fall.

South grabbed me around my waist, and I fell with him. Usually I loved the falling. It was one of the best parts of flying. But this time I had not jumped off the cliff of my own volition. I had been forced.

Before I could transform, he pulled us back up, still holding me lightly around the waist. As his wings fanned the air, he righted us, and we began to ascend. I had flown before, but I had never been carried. It was a different sensation.

I relaxed into him. I could feel my heart and his. My own body had betrayed me. I had never flown in my own skin before. I had always transformed into something else. There was exhilaration and pleasure in being held, being touched while soaring.

"Put me down," I insisted.

"Only if you're sure," he said, ascending higher and higher with every moment.

"Put me down," I repeated.

"Very well," he said.

I immediately realized my mistake. I felt his arms slide away from my waist. I screamed as I began to free-fall. I was falling even faster than I had ascended. My skirts were floating up around me.

It took me a few seconds to recover. It seemed as though the cliffs below were going to meet me and not the other way around.

*Remember, you can fly, Princess…* I could hear South's voice in my head.

I separated into an unkindness of ravens just in time and began to ascend and chase after him. He was faster than me; he was faster than my birds.

"You dropped me," I croaked.

"You pushed me," he screamed back at me.

"I knew you could fly," I countered.

"And I knew exactly the same thing about you."

"You are impossible."

"As are you."

When we landed, I regained my human form. I took out my wand again, and then I decided against it. I could not let him get to me. Not more than he already had.

South eyed my wand and smiled as I put it away. He thought he had scored a victory. He had no idea.

I made the decision in an instant. I was impetuous—not a bad thing, but not always a good one. Entente were supposed to be patient and thoughtful. I was the latter, but never the former. South looked down at me and inhaled sharply. Then he looked away.

It took me a second to realize what he was reacting to.

"Your dress . . . it's gone . . . ," South said, now purposefully keeping his eyes on mine. But his own were wide, and embarrassment washed across his features.

My dress was indeed gone. When I'd transformed, it had torn to pieces. It was in the wind. And my wand was in the wind too.

"I want nothing from you," I said to South. A part of me took pleasure in his reaction. South had spent his life with us and then in the dungeon. He had been a member of the Queen's guard for years before Farrow found him again. In that time had he had much experience with the fairer sex? Had he even ever kissed a girl?

"Would you make an exception for a shirt? You um . . . must be cold," he said in almost a whisper, as if my naked form deserved some kind of reverence.

His hands moved to the top button of his shirt in a chivalrous attempt to give it to me.

"I want nothing from you," I repeated. This time, when my voice came out, I closed my eyes and shouted into the wind.

*Return my wand,*
*Do as you are told, make me whole.*

The wand appeared in my hand, and feathers blew in from every direction, forming a dress around me.

"We should get back. Maybe Amantha's home by now," I asserted.

He reached for me, expecting to fly me home. I transformed again, leaving my dress behind on the cliffs.

"I want nothing from you," I repeated for the third time. This refrain somehow sounded less sincere every time I uttered it.

# CHAPTER 15

## — FARROW —

I remember you," Sadie said as she greeted me and Hecate. Hecate, of course, was wearing her true face, and it was younger now, so I knew that Sadie could not recognize her. She was addressing me. The last time I had been to the palace, I had visited Magrit before her execution, but I had not seen Sadie then. The last time I had actually seen her was right before I attempted to murder Queen Magrit.

I assumed she was not happy to see me.

"Lady Sadie, I—" I began. "Sorry" wasn't the right word. Because I would do it all over again.

Living in the palace that had once been Magrit and Mather's would have been strained and uncomfortable. Galatea had used her magic to make it her own and to wipe the Past from it.

There were live flowers growing through the tapestries and wallpaper. Even stranger, there was a portrait of Galatea and Amantha and Bari. They did not wear crowns, but in every other way it was distinctly a royal portrait. Hecate stopped and stared at it. We stood silently for a long moment.

"Wait here," Sadie ordered, before nodding at a couple of guards and then heading down the hall, no doubt to check and see if Galatea would see us. Hecate stifled a giggle and lifted her finger to point.

I pushed her hand down and held it.

"Hecate," I whispered, a warning.

"I've just never seen a painting of Entente before."

She was right. Our likenesses were not anywhere—not on any wall, in any time. We did not memorialize our lives in any way except in our own memories. This painting was a purely human act.

Sadie returned, clearing her throat and indicating that we should follow her. We continued down the hall toward Queen Magrit's old suite of rooms. I was surprised to see that Galatea had not changed any of the staff. I assumed she had spelled them into submission, but I could not be sure.

As we walked, Sadie explained, "I don't know how much time you will have. The Queen is readying herself for the ball."

"What is it in honor of?" I asked.

Sadie laughed and then said, "Need there be an occasion? The sun coming up or the moon rising. The taste of the strawberries. Our new Queen does love to celebrate . . ."

It had only been two short days, and Galatea had already made quite the impression on Sadie.

She collected herself. "Tonight's extravaganza is for the Queen's Council, who arrives this evening. There is a ball planned for every single night in perpetuity."

Galatea had instated nightly balls to unify the Queendom. Commoners and the court were invited alike. Another surprise. And all the Queens from all the Queendoms were en route for the Queen's Council, where Galatea and Amantha and Bari would make their grand debut as Queen and princesses respectively.

Sadie led us to the door to Magrit's old suite of rooms. I felt a pang of sickening déjà vu. If Hecate felt it too, I could not tell. I could not hear her wishes. She straightened her posture and glided forward.

Sadie knocked and pushed the door open.

"Mistress Hecate and Mistress Farrow of the Reverie to see Her Majesty," Sadie announced with an exaggerated curtsy before backing out of the room.

Galatea did not turn to face us. She was gazing at a mirror, a voluminous white gown billowing around her. Not turning toward us, it seemed, was a show of her new power, as if she was too occupied to even bother to properly receive us, to even look at us. I was bothered by her attempt to show her dominance. I glanced at Hecate, who despite her recent displays of emotion since her return to the flesh, showed absolutely no emotion now.

"Is that really you, Hecate? Back from the ashes . . ."

"It is I," Hecate said evenly.

We watched Galatea as two seamstresses approached where she was standing before the ornate floor-length mirror and began making adjustments to the gown. Everything about the scene we took in felt wrong. To begin with, Galatea looked pretty. Not that she wasn't already pretty. But it looked like she was making an effort to be pretty. The Entente as a rule tried to fit in, not stand out. Galatea's hair was carefully coiffed. I was not sure if it was by her wand or by the other, human members of her court. And the gown was as intricate and elaborate as one fit for a human wedding. The only thing that distinguished the gown from a human one was the delicate live flower stems that wove their way through the material.

And still she did not turn. She held herself in place as if the seamstresses' final touches were just as important as being reunited with her sister who was recently revived from the ashes.

"This is what they expect. The other Queens, the people . . . ," Galatea said simply.

"I thought you were trying to change their expectations," I interjected.

"Ritual makes them docile so they will never expect the real plan."

"And what is that exactly?" Hecate asked.

We already knew Galatea's plan was to take over the Queendoms. As she examined herself in the glass, seemingly pleased with her reflection, I wondered about the purpose of this moment. What did my mother seek to learn from Galatea?

It almost seemed as if she was enjoying the accouterments of being a Queen. The way she looked at herself in the glass—I had seen the look before in Lavendra back when I was following her for all those years as a Shadow.

Hecate saw it too, and I feared that she would not keep her tongue. One of her most fixed qualities before the Burning had been her ability to keep her thoughts inside, walled off from me and even the other Fates. But now, that point had shifted like a quake of the earth, and what she would do or say next was more a mystery to me than ever.

Another servant, another seamstress, emerged from beneath the bustle of the skirt.

"There, perfection," she assessed.

"Oh, company," she said nervously, realizing we were there.

"Your Highness, may we take our leave?" the seamstresses asked in unison.

"Yes, but the gown must be finished for tonight or I'll have one of my daughters turn you into a knot of toads."

I was not sure if Galatea was serious; neither were the seamstresses.

But she smiled an enigmatic smile, and they nervously smiled back before ducking out of the room.

A long silence followed the seamstresses' exit. Hecate was the first to fill it.

"Once when we visited Magrit, she was sitting for her portrait. I remember getting a glimpse of it. I remember thinking it didn't capture what I saw in her. It hid all that she was capable of... all that I could see with my wand. And now a portrait of the Entente hangs where it once did."

"And what do you think my portrait does, sister? Does it conceal or reveal?" Galatea asked pointedly, but I was not quite sure of her meaning.

"There was a time when we would never show our true faces to the world. There is a part of me that feels joy that we are no longer secret, while another still feels fear. As for your visage, the artist did capture your likeness quite well."

"I am so glad you like it," Galatea said, seemingly puffed up with pride.

"I didn't say that I liked it," Hecate deadpanned.

"I am open to critique—if it isn't the existence of the work itself that you object to," Galatea mused.

"The eyes aren't quite right. When I look at you now I can see that you are haunted by an infinite number of Pasts—including your own. What you have done to get the crown haunts you even though you say it does not."

"That is not true. I am quite content. This is what we have been fighting for no matter the cost."

Hecate shook her head.

"The fact that you still feel the consequences of your own Past—that gives me hope for your Future. For all of us."

Galatea went rigid for a moment and then composed herself.

"I thought we could cast aside the trappings of the crown. But the people demand them. Their ceremonies, their rituals . . . give them comfort, and allow them to more readily accept the Entente in the place where their human Queens used to be," Galatea defended.

"And do you think they have forgotten their prince?" I blurted.

"You clearly have not forgotten him," Galatea bit back.

I felt my cheeks warm. She was not wrong.

"As for the rest of the people, Sister Hecate, you can speak further as to the soundness of my actions. You have the gift of the Future after all. What do you see?"

Hecate frowned, and Galatea finally turned to face us.

"My word. You have aged in reverse," Galatea said, looking at her sister in the flesh for the first time after all those years.

She touched her face and embraced her. The giant gown was crushed almost comically between them. There were tears in both their eyes as they came apart and stepped back from each other.

"What is the meaning of this visit? What do you seek from me?" Galatea demanded, her eyes searching her sister's for the truth.

Hecate's gaze softened.

"Let us not quarrel, sister. We have the same gift. We can both see everyone and everything if we so choose. But you forget, I will always be a step ahead of you."

Galatea frowned, considering. Had Hecate bested her in their battle of wits?

"It isn't just the power you are given; it is what you are willing to do with it. We have both changed, but you are still tied to the old ways. Your loyalty to humans will always limit you. I have no such loyalty. And I am the better for it."

"We shall see... but I want us to be sisters and friends as we have always been."

"Friends who disagree."

"Sisters who disagree but share a roof," my mother corrected.

"I let Farrow live—that does not mean leaving myself open to another betrayal," Galatea said chillingly.

"We will be watching each other wherever we are. Isn't this more civilized? I for one don't want to let a little war get in the way of me spending time with my sister," Hecate said, not missing a beat.

"Very well," Galatea said with a smile, and she hugged Hecate again. "I insist that you stay as my guests. As Entente, my home is your home."

"I am glad," Hecate replied, her voice sweet, and she pulled Galatea into a second embrace.

Over Galatea's shoulder, Hecate's face changed. "Did you keep the cook? He made the most delicious confections. I have a hankering for that lavender cake," Hecate said suddenly.

"I kept on all the staff," Galatea said, clearly puzzled by her sister's shift in attention.

Hecate turned to me. "Would you mind if I just get something sweet to eat? I find myself suddenly famished."

"Hecate," I whispered.

I thought for the briefest of seconds that this was just another part of the plan. That she wanted to sneak off and search the throne room or something while I distracted Galatea with the most awkward attempts at a conversation ever.

Then I heard it. Her wish.

*I wish for the cake that we did not eat when we visited the Queen.*

Cake? I wondered, then remembered distinctly a time when Hecate and I had walked through the kitchen on the way to visiting

Magrit. There was a giant cake in the kitchen. It was taller than me and frosted with chocolate and berries. I remembered thinking it belonged to such a different life than ours—even though we could make any delicious thing that we could imagine with the wave of our wands. Those humans in the kitchen had made this beautiful, delicious-smelling confection, this delicious-looking feat, without an ounce of magic. They were capable of such beauty and such destruction. Sometimes all at once.

But it never occurred to me that austere, disciplined Hecate had been impressed by human cake. And yet here she was standing in front of me, desiring it.

Her eyes had glassed over with unadulterated want. She did not bother to shield me. *I wish for cake. The Queen's cake.* The wish grew louder as she grew more impatient.

How was our plot to compete with a craving for a treat that my mother had been denied for the better part of a decade?

Despite myself, I cast a look at Galatea, who met my gaze. And we shared an accidental moment of congruence. Despite everything, despite our conflicts, she saw what I saw, which was Hecate, starved for cake—and so much more. And even though she could have all she wanted now, it didn't make up for the time without—the time without cake had twisted us all.

"Go, Hecate. The baker will make anything you like."

"Go, Mother. I'll find you there."

I nodded. Hecate kissed her sister on the cheek and ran out of the room, momentarily forgetting about me, it seemed.

And leaving me alone with Galatea.

"I trust you are less thrilled with the idea of staying here than your mother is," Galatea assessed.

"We have been apart too long. I wish all my sisters were under one roof. Tell me again why that isn't possible now."

"There is more work to be done."

"Is there? Because we can just stop now—halt our revenge and begin living our lives again."

"You know I cannot. Now tell me. Have there been any other changes in your mother since she came back?"

"She seems otherwise unchanged . . . ," I lied, omitting the fact that my mother seemed to have more power than ever. "Will she remain like this?" I asked, needing to know, even though I wasn't sure if I could truly trust her response.

"Do you seek to remedy our miracle? We have her back—we cannot quarrel with her imperfections," Galatea reasoned.

"You remember everything. When she was young, was this how she was?"

Galatea considered my words for a moment.

Galatea waved her wand and showed me the Past in the mirror.

A young Hecate, Galatea, and Iolanta were walking through the woods. They were smiling and laughing. Their arms were interlocked. Hecate's face looked the exact same age as she looked now.

"That was a good day. Iolanta was having a good day. So we were happy. Your mother was the best of us. She was our moral center. She led us and we followed. We were so very content . . ."

"You could still follow her now," I offered.

The mirror suddenly went blank, and our own reflections returned.

"I no longer follow . . . and the Hecate who was just here, she is not that Hecate in the mirror. She is a new Hecate. She was burned alive and then torn from the Ever After. She is both the old Hecate and brand-new—she is reborn," Galatea said.

"Do you think she can be restored . . . to what she once was?" I asked.

Galatea's eyes widened in surprise.

"Why would we want that? Look at you, my child. Your magic works differently now, but that's what makes it extraordinary."

I didn't understand. A few days ago, she'd tried to force me to stay home while she and my sisters went to the royal ball for Mather, because my magic was too unpredictable and could lead to our discovery.

"Just days ago you did not want me to take part in the plot because you could not trust my magic."

"It appears that it was not the magic I couldn't trust—it was you," she said matter-of-factly.

She had me there.

"You don't understand, do you? We are not on the other side now. We have not yet won. But the fear of discovery in this Queendom—that we have most certainly conquered. Here that fear is gone," she continued.

Another idea occurred to me—one that I knew was not entirely fair to the people of this land. They did not deserve to be ruled by our vengeance.

"What if we brought all our sisters here? Why couldn't we make this our home? We could live in the light without any fear," I mused.

"You paint a lovely picture," she began, but then she frowned and shook her head. "If we did that the other Queendoms would raise their forces and surround us. We must conquer every Queendom—and not just conquer, hold the Queendoms and build upon that hold," she countered.

"Build what?" I asked.

"Our security . . . our Future," she said, sounding certain.

I couldn't make out what she meant. I knew, of course, that Galatea had a bigger plan in mind. I just could not fathom what it was. And my mother would not or could not share the worst possible Future with me.

"Oh, there are so many details I must work out before the ball. You and your mother should come. I'll have the seamstress make you something new to wear."

"You do remember what I did at the last ball I attended here?" I reminded her, incredulous.

"And if you were not thwarting all my plans then I would have been quite impressed. I trust you have not had the time to thwart this one. You've only just learned of it."

"I have no plan to thwart your ball. I promise by the Fates."

# CHAPTER 16

## — BARI —

When we got back to the cottage, there was still no sign of Amantha. And something had shifted between me and South. There had always been tension between us. As children it was the tension of pure dislike. Since we had been reunited it was the tension of distrust. And in the past hour, it was something I could not place.

Nothing was the way it was supposed to be, I thought as we stood in the exact same place we'd stood before we left to look for Amantha. South was about to reanimate the moment and the baby, and to start time again. But I stopped him.

"South, wait!" I said forcefully.

Before he could turn around, I put my finger in the rest of the love potion on the table, and I smeared some on my lips.

Once he faced me, he stood absolutely still as if waiting for me. I stepped closer to him and then closer still, and he leaned down as if he knew exactly what I intended. My lips met his with all the frustration and anger swarming in me, and he responded in kind, meeting me with the same intensity. Our lips parted as the kiss deepened, and his arms wrapped themselves around my waist just as they had when we were flying. Only now he was pulling me closer and closer as if he wanted nothing between us.

When we broke apart, I whispered the spell. "You are completely loyal to the plan. You will help me as if your life depended on it. You will not remember this conversation. You will love me more than you love Farrow. I will make her a shadow in your mind. And you will never tire of kissing me."

He looked at me quizzically. In my haste and fury, I remembered that I should have made my spell rhyme.

*From this kiss forward, you will do nothing untoward,*
*Whatever I say is right, you love me with all your might,*
*You follow me, like the sun follows the moon,*
*You love me, and to me only you stay true.*

A strange look crossed his face, and then he smiled a dreamy smile.

"I am true," he repeated breathlessly.

It was done. I had cast a spell on South. It wasn't part of the plot.

Behind me there was a gasp. Amantha had returned. How much had she seen? From her wide eyes, I could tell she had taken it all in.

"Where were you?" I asked as if nothing out of the ordinary had happened between me and South.

"South, would you mind going to check on the baby again," I suggested.

"I'd love to," he said brightly as if it was his favorite idea in all the world.

Amantha watched the exchange in disbelief as South dutifully went to the other room to attend to the baby.

"Where were you, Amantha?" I demanded again.

"I was setting our plot in motion. I poisoned the actress like we planned. I met Thiago, and he begged me to take her place."

I reacted. She had done the exact opposite of what we had discussed.

"More importantly, what were you up to while I was gone? What did you just do to South? You used it, didn't you?"

"You have to understand. I could not stand another moment of his smugness. I just used a little of the potion on South."

"He already agreed to help us." She persisted.

"He clearly had reservations," I argued. "I removed them."

"We already knew that. What changed? Did he try to stall our plot? Did he tell Farrow?" she said, blinking up at me.

"Not exactly, but he wouldn't stop talking."

"Bari, your shell is as tough as your beetles. Since when did a few barbs from South not roll off you? We have to tell Galatea." She frowned.

"No, we don't. We have everything under control—there's no need to bother her," I countered forcefully. I took a step closer to her, meaning to touch her arm, remind her of our bond, and bring her back to her senses.

"Are you going to use a spell on me next to make me do your bidding?" she said, stepping back from me, her voice's pitch rising in disbelief and anger.

"No, I'm going to appeal to your intellect and our bond. Please let me see this through, Amantha. We do not want to disrupt Galatea. She has enough on her plate," I said as gently as I could muster.

"From what I can see all she's doing is having big parties, which we are not invited to," Amantha hit back.

"We have to trust in Galatea and her timing."

"Which is why you went rogue and spelled South?"

"Surely you don't really have a problem with what I've done. You are just as mad at South and at Farrow as I am."

"For all his faults, *he* is one of us—he is part of our sect. We do not do this to one of our own. More than that, he is a Fate now. You spelled a Fate. We are supposed to honor the Fates."

Amantha's moral line was chaotic: on the one hand, she thought South had betrayed us; on the other hand, I had betrayed our sect by spelling him. Her unexpected moral stance was a surprise. We were usually in sync.

The more I tried, the more she resisted.

"Like Galatea said, the old rules don't apply," I replied finally.

"I thought that meant about how we treat humans, not how we treat each other," Amantha countered.

She took another step back from me, as if I was capable of hurting her. And maybe by telling her that I had to be the one who the prince fell in love with, I already had. Because in that moment, she thought I had underestimated her.

"You can't be serious, Amantha. I would never hurt you. I would never spell you."

Amantha began to fade.

"As Galatea says, the old rules don't apply." Amantha flickered away like she almost always did when we fought. This felt different somehow.

"Amantha . . . don't be this way. Amantha!"

South was staring at me with the most puzzling look. I recognized it: it was the way he looked at Farrow. Like he was in love with her. Now he had that look for me.

"What are you looking at?" I demanded.

"Did anyone ever tell you that your eyes are the same color as a raven? They used to scare me when I was small, but I see now that they are absolutely beautiful. She has eyes like the night; they make everything delight."

"A poet you are not," I said reflexively. But a part of me could not help but relish seeing South humbled by my spell into paying me an actual compliment, one that was tailored only to me. I couldn't imagine anyone ever comparing Farrow to a raven.

He looked hurt.

"If that's of importance for you, I will work on it, Princess."

But even the force of the spell had not stopped him from calling me princess.

"Princess? Never call me that again."

He looked hurt again. "But it is who you are—"

"Okay, enough, can we focus on the prince now?"

# CHAPTER 17

## — FARROW —

An hour after our meeting with Galatea, Sadie led me to Hecate, who was in the kitchen. Hecate was standing next to a colossal chocolate tower of cake sculpted to look like the palace. She was holding a fork, and a considerable chunk of the east wing was missing.

"Mother, was it as good as you thought it would be?" I asked, genuinely wanting to know.

"Better. You know when you want something for so long and you finally get it, there is the chance it might not be as good as you'd hoped—but this was so much better. It's a little like you, Farrow. I dreamed of you through the ashes, and now you are here and you are . . . you are like the cake."

Mother looked like she was going to burst into tears.

"Well, I guess I better taste the cake. Sadie, do you want some?"

Sadie seemed moved. But protocol stopped her from partaking. She shook her head.

"Sadie is going to show us to our rooms when you are ready," I said.

Behind her, the baker was reacting to the damage Hecate had done to the chocolate palace.

Hecate complimented him. "You have outdone yourself. That ganache is perfection."

I could hear the baker's wish. *Please, dear Fates, may Queen Galatea not punish me for the cake.*

Hecate did not appear to want to leave the kitchen anytime soon. I took a step closer to her.

My mother spoke between bites. "I must have walked by that kitchen dozens of times in my life. I smelled the most delicious things, saw them too, but I never once partook. Not once."

"I know. You wouldn't let me partake either," I said, my lips forming a wan smile.

"Perhaps it was the time I spent in the ash, but there is a difference between cakes made by magic and those made without even a hint of it. See . . . ?"

She suddenly scooped up a handful and pushed it gently past my lips. The taste was a revelation. The sweetness of the chocolate softened by an unexpected savory spice that brightened the flavor. Was it cardamom? Our Entente baker would never have thought of that spice. It was a wholly human choice. Or perhaps a happy accident. Whatever it was, the cake was indeed worth the wait.

"Galatea would not approve of us," I said, my mouth full of laughter and cake.

"I believe that she was this close to proposing etiquette lessons for me. Not for you though. Your manners are quite impeccable."

"My manners come from the Couterie."

She put down her fork and picked up her napkin to wipe away a bit of cake on my nose.

Her smile faded. She was thinking of what the doctor had done to me.

"Hecate, it's okay."

"It will never be okay. I should have been able to protect you—"

"You came back from the Ever After for me. How much more could any mother have done?"

"So much more. If it would not change the course of Fate, I would wish to turn back the clock and make it so the Couterie never existed," she said fiercely.

I noticed that she had picked up her fork and was now holding it with the same intensity that she had held my wand when she first came back from the ashes. Her knuckles were strained, and I feared that she might bleed again.

"Hecate, it's okay. I'm okay. We don't have to undo anything. All that matters is that we are here together . . . Hectate," I soothed. I put my hand on hers, and she loosened her grip on the fork.

She straightened her back and used the fork to take another bite of cake. "This is delicious, isn't it? Why am I so hungry?"

When she had finally had her fill, I wiped her mouth with another napkin and nodded to the baker, who was near tears. With a wave of my wand, I repaired the cake.

"Would you like us to have your things sent for?" Sadie began, when we finally reached our rooms.

Hecate waved her wand, and neatly packed satchels from the Reverie appeared around the room.

She looked at me. "I'm afraid that all you had at the Couterie is gone. But I can re-create each one."

I shook my head. I didn't want any reminders from the Couterie.

Hecate took in my expression, reading me.

"Of course you will have new things."

Sadie's eyes were wide with wonder. "It seems you have it all in hand. Please ring the bell if you need anything."

'This must be so terrifying for you . . . Let us assure you we mean you no ill," I said, reassuringly.

"My previous mistress was way more terrifying. I pray that that continues to be the case."

When Sadie was gone, Hecate and I settled into our rooms, which were adjoining and faced the palace's gardens. But even without asking, I knew that Hecate would sleep with me tonight.

"Galatea is planning more than balls," I said, finally giving voice to what we were both thinking about.

"Undoubtedly. I may have found something of value en route to the cake."

She grabbed her wand and my hand, and we were instantly back in the alcove where the portrait of Magrit and Bari and Amantha hung.

Hecate waved her wand over the three figures.

*May the paint run like water, let use what is under . . .*

The paint bubbled, and the figures melted away as the painting reconfigured itself into a map of the Queendoms.

"What is this?" I asked.

"Look closer, dear. Think about your training not just as an Entente but as a Couterie too."

I studied the map. Queen Helene's Queendom had a tiny beetle. "That beetle is for Bari . . . Queen Helene is first . . . Bari and Amantha are in the Eleventh Queendom? But how on earth are they going to dethrone her? Will they raise a resistance while Helene is away? You must know, Hecate. Why won't you tell me?"

"Because what is happening might reverse Bari and Amantha's course," my mother said with a knowing look that infuriated me. "We should focus our attention elsewhere—on your sisters and the Rooks. I promise I'll keep an eye on Bari and Amantha."

"So we just wait..." I pouted, wanting desperately to take action.

"Look closer."

Now there was a symbol next to each Queendom on the map. Each mark represented one of my sisters. And next to Helene's, two symbols had appeared: that beetle and, now, a translucent silhouette. "Bari and Amantha. That truly confirms it as Queen Helene's Queendom... Nimolet... that *must* be where they are."

"There is something else you need to see." Hecate took my wand and put it to my temple.

I saw. Galatea. She was still wearing her crown, but instead of one of the fancy dresses we'd grown accustomed to seeing her in, she was wearing a nightgown. Her feet were bare. She was walking through the Reverie at night. I could sense no other of the Entente. After several minutes, she entered the same room that Hecate had lain in her glass casket the night of the Burning.

A coffin stood near the entrance. I felt myself inhale sharply, thinking the worst. Was Hecate trying to tell me she was heading back to the casket or to the Ever After sometime soon?

"Keep looking," my mother whispered.

Galatea walked farther into the room. There was not only one glass coffin; there were several. I began to count: one, two, three, and all the way to twelve. One for each Queen except for Galatea herself.

Hecate had shown me other horrors before, and I should not have been surprised now. But I had no clue about how to parse these new visions. "Mother, what does this mean? You have shown me the Queendoms in various states of destruction before. What is different now?"

Measuring her response, Hecate finally spoke. "Galatea is different somehow, and Bari is becoming even more terrifying than I imagined." She put the wand to my temple again.

On the floor of the chamber there was a shadow cast from something outside. It had the shape of a dragon.

"Bari . . . ," I whispered.

"Do your worst," Galatea shouted to Bari.

# PART II

# CHAPTER 18

## — BARI —

South still wore my kiss; it was clear in his gaze and in his every movement. His eyes tracked me as I paced across the room. He inhaled sharply when I tucked hair behind my ear.

He was worried precisely because I was worried. In the past, whatever emotion I was feeling, he seemed to take the exact opposite position—now he mirrored me like a dance in which I was the lead.

"Why is this disappearance any different than any other time she surrenders herself to thin air?"

I sighed, exasperated. I could not tell him it was different because my sister and I had had a fight about the love spell that I had cast on him.

His lips made a stubborn line. "I don't like it when you are upset. And I don't need to know why. If it matters to you, then it matters to me, and I am compelled to help."

My mouth twisted at the irony. In any other circumstance, I would be making fun of South's almost comedic attempt to be my hero.

He tapped his wand on my temple, and I received a vision of Amantha.

She was at the Reverie, her face a ball of anger.

Satisfied, I said, "Enough."

"This pleases you?" he asked eagerly.

I hated seeing Amantha upset, but at least she had not gone to Galatea at the palace.

I returned my attention to the task at hand.

"We have to get ready for the theater. Now, hair up or down?"

"I like it down."

"It doesn't matter what you like. It matters what the actor likes. You can see what he likes, right? I can change my attributes. Blond hair? Red hair? A larger bosom? A smaller waist? Taller? Shorter? Whatever his dream girl looks like I can be with a twist of my wand..."

I leaned into the crib to make sure the baby was still breathing in and out. It reached out and wrapped tiny fingers around my pinkie and held on tight. I tried to extract my finger, but the baby just squeezed tighter, and as it did so the act elicited a surprising flutter inside my chest that I could not name.

"It's okay to like her," South insisted quietly.

I used my other hand and unclasped the little fingers one by one, and the baby began to wail. With a sigh, I extended a finger, and the baby grasped it eagerly.

When I pulled away my finger, there was more wailing, and South reached in and picked up the crying thing. "It has to learn that it won't always get what it wants," I admonished.

But even in South's arms, the baby was not content. It continued to cry.

"She doesn't have to learn that lesson today. Besides, if holding your hand is the price for enough quiet to lay out the plot, what is the harm?"

"I am not sure which of you I like the least," I said, and I reached into my pocket and put the wand in the baby's hand. She quieted immediately. I never let anyone else touch my wand, but it was better than surrendering my finger. I did not want to experience that horrible flutter again.

"Now, where were we?" I asked.

South grinned, clearly amused.

The plan was this: I would make such an impression on Thiago at the theater that he would ask me to step into the role that Amantha had created by putting his leading lady and her understudy out of commission. With a little lighting and magic and a bouquet of flowers I'd bring, he would find me irresistible.

"You were telling me if my eyes should be blue or green . . . ?" I pressed.

"Your eyes are the perfect shade of twilight. Lavender and gray at once with a touch of the approaching night."

"South . . . ," I warned, struck by his poetry and unaccustomed to any compliments on my appearance.

"I don't have Farrow's gift. I don't see wants and desires," he countered. "I see Presents. I only see what people are feeling, and at a precise moment."

"Then tell me what have you gathered from the prince this moment then," I said, irritation rising.

South began a description of the man Thiago was.

"He loves the theater. He loves slipping in and out of characters—maybe because he isn't completely comfortable as himself. He has many romances. They seem to last only as long as he is in a town—"

"That is helpful. That I can use. Or rather, we can use. We'll create the perfect moment. And when he kisses me, I'll seal it with a love spell. He will spot me on the balcony in the perfect dress. We'll part the clouds, maybe have a bird sing a night song, and he will not be able to resist me."

"It won't work," South said with annoying certainty.

"Why?"

"Because he doesn't care how you look—even though you look . . ." He drifted off, his eyes meeting mine and then flitting downward.

"Explain," I demanded.

South was still impossible. He still talked too much. Only now, he filled every silence with compliments instead of insults.

"He's a man with a huge ego and a huge appreciation of the arts—you have to do something more than be the most striking girl in the theater to grab his attention."

"And what do you suggest?"

"Not flowers and the prettiest dress."

"We'll see about that. You haven't seen the dress yet. Besides, I just need to get close enough to kiss him. I think this will do the trick."

I tapped the hem of my dress, transforming it from pastel to scarlet red. I dropped the bodice and raised the hem. South's eyes widened. He was clearly affected by the sight of my flesh.

The baby responded too, with a giggle, and pointed at me with her free hand.

"Maybe you should stay here and mind the baby," I said, not looking at him. Even with the spell, it pained me to see him be right. But somehow the thought of leaving the baby again, even if he slowed time, just seemed like an opportunity for a mishap.

Amantha reappeared just as suddenly as she had left. "I'll mind her. Since that's all that you think that I am good for."

"That's not . . . Amantha, you cannot still be cross with me?"

She shot a look at South, then looked back at me. "I think you lost your right to tell me that."

"South, can you give Amantha and me a moment?" I murmured an order for South to take the baby and hum a lullaby. "And you won't hear a word of our conversation."

He dutifully took the baby and began to hum. Amantha looked at him in wonder and at me with disgust.

I studied her a beat. Amantha had volunteered to mind the baby, which was strange after the tantrum she'd thrown before. Perhaps she had finally come to her senses. South and I were to go to the theater—where I would finally meet Thiago. We had lost a night with Amantha's theatrics, but I wasn't about to confront her on it again, given my own infraction. As for South, the spell did not seem to have worn off. I would have to kiss him again before moonrise—if I wanted it to continue. Which of course I did not.

"You've domesticated him. I swear it's worse than the time Em turned Selina into a tiger. I can still see her drinking tea—with her paws," Amantha mused.

The analogy didn't entirely work, but I got her meaning. I had tamed and defanged South, the moral beast we were sharing a home with. Amantha, for her part, was against it. I was quite pleased. I found there was joy in having my adversary at my mercy—before it seemed he was watching my every move because he was trying to thwart the plot; now it seemed he watched me for the sheer pleasure of it. He stole glances at me even now as he cradled the baby.

"Let the spell wear off and it will be almost as if it never happened at all. We will never speak of it again," Amantha said finally, clearly enjoying her momentary position of power.

I nodded. I wanted to explain why I had done it. I wanted a moment of peace, of control in a world that had suddenly seemed out of hand.

But I didn't utter those words.

Instead, I just said, "Very well . . . South, hand Amantha the baby."

He handed her the baby, and South and I stepped out of the cottage.

Without asking, South wrapped his arms around me and began to ascend.

"What are you doing? We might be seen. It's faster to travel without wands than to fly."

"But think of the view," he whispered, but he was looking at me, not where he was flying.

I did not like the divide between me and Amantha. I told myself it would dissipate at moonrise, as soon as I let the spell die. And I would—I really would let it die. I just had to get through tonight.

# CHAPTER 19

## — FARROW —

After the vision faded, my heart still raced and my thoughts flew even faster.

"Hecate, I have tried to be patient, but my mind is spinning—all those dead Queens . . . and Bari's shadow . . . I cannot shake the image," I began, and with every word more aware that Hecate was constantly confronted with such visions. I had only wishes to contend with, and I had learned to quiet them.

"Not all of them were dead. Not all of them were Queens, some were just sleeping—and it was just one possible Future," Hecate observed, attempting to sound light, but there was worry in her eyes.

"I am not comforted, Mother. The ones who weren't Queens were princesses, and they were sleeping eternally."

"True," she said simply.

"And Galatea ordered Bari to make them into ash."

"Also, true."

"Mother, I know you explained that we should see if what happens in the Eleventh Queendom changes Bari. But what if we just show her now? What she will become. Surely that could hold more sway than waiting to see if she changes during her plot."

"If we show Bari her future again, she will simply rise to meet it."

"What do you mean, 'again'?"

"Remember the day South got his wings? You went to Iolanta, and I showed Bari a glimpse of her future transformation. I think she took it as an inspiration, not a warning. And now I fear it would be even more so. Remember what happened when I showed Magrit the Future . . ." She drifted off as we both thought of the Burning.

"But Bari is not Magrit."

"No, she is not. Bari believes in this cause, and more significantly she believes in Galatea. I think Galatea is the key to stopping Bari's transformation. Really, to stopping all the bad things that are to come. Galatea is the heart and the mind of the plot. Bari and the others will stop if she stops."

I sighed, feeling defeated. "Have you seen any more of Galatea's plot? Are you purposefully withholding what you have seen? Or have your visions shifted?"

Hecate was silent. She had begun to busy herself with more unpacking.

"Are you not telling me, but you know?" I asked.

Hecate shook her head. "Galatea is blocking me."

"But you can still see the Futures of the people of the Queendoms. She must figure in them," I pressed.

"I can. And she does," my mother said somberly.

"And what do you see now?" I ventured to ask.

"There is chaos and burning. Everything is lost."

"We knew that was a possibility," I said.

"You don't understand. There is no Future that is happy. Every vision I have is horrendous."

"Maybe . . . maybe that's because you are still recovering. You're barely back in the flesh. Maybe your gift isn't fully back—it took me years and a spell to unbind myself," I said, not wanting to diminish Hecate's magic, but still searching for some other less-doomed Fate.

"I am not bound—and I don't think I need to heal. We have to do something different to make the outcomes different."

"Like what?"

"I don't know. But we will figure out something. I have to believe that the changes in Galatea present new vulnerabilities. She hates humans, but she is as ridiculous as Queen Magrit herself. Did you see her preening? And the hair. We always used their wares as costumes and as protections. This is not that. She almost seemed like she was enjoying herself."

I nodded in agreement. But I could not say what I was thinking: Hecate had changed too.

Perhaps if we had had room for vanity back then, we would not be here now. We had abstained from so many things for so long. Now that we have had them, we gorged on them like starving children.

That applied to everything, even love. I tried to dismiss what I felt for Mather in that light. I had been starved and then fed. It was only the first meal I had ever had. That did not make it the best or the last or the one that was meant for me. Still, even as I tried to logic it away, Mather's visage swam in my memory. Not just his face—his touch, and his words. Was it possible for the first love to indeed be the truest?

Hecate, reading my immediate Future, produced the mirror and showed me Mather and Cinderella again.

Inexplicably they were still having tea with the Rook.

"I don't understand. They're in exactly the same position as when we last looked at them. They are still having tea."

"The Rooks can slow time too. They're still figuring out what to do with their new guests."

"Should I be scared for them?"

"I sense no fear from them, only wariness, which is exactly the right temperament to meet a Rook King."

Again, I was not comforted. But Hecate knew that too.

Before she put the mirror away, I gazed into the glass and saw an abrupt shift, a sudden disturbance. Mather and Cinderella hadn't moved. But something did. The air spun, and Galatea stepped out of the swirl and into the room.

The Rook King stirred and cocked his head at her—he was surprised but not seemingly at all scared of her. "Galatea, we were just having tea. It has been too long, and yet I don't remember sending you an invitation."

"I can see that."

Mather and Cinderella were still frozen in place.

"Mother, we have to go there," I urged.

"Wait," she said.

"Your guests belong to the Queendoms," noted Galatea.

"They seek asylum here. You cannot have them," the Rook King asserted.

"For their sake, perhaps it is best if you keep them indefinitely. I am not here for them though. I am here for you."

"Whatever for?"

"I think it is time for us to renegotiate the covenant."

"And what do you have in mind?" asked the Rook King.

"Your freedom to roam the Queendoms could be returned to you," Galatea responded.

"After the last time your kind said that, my kind could not trust that they would be able to roam free."

"You wanted the matriarchy to become a patriarchy."

"I still do. Why would you allow it now?"

"I want something else entirely: a magi-archy."

"A what?" he asked, arching an eyebrow.

"Magical people will rule every Queendom."

"And where do I and my brothers come in? A war, no doubt."

"Just the opposite. We do not need to go to war. We just need to outnumber the humans, and they will never dare rise up against us." Galatea continued, her voice full of passion, "There are not enough Entente. There are not enough Rooks. That must change. There must be more of us. There must be legions."

The Rook took her in a beat, examining her face as if to confirm that she was serious.

"That is clever. You always were clever, Galatea," he said finally.

"That is not an answer. But you do not have to answer at this moment. Digest it with your tea."

"I do not regret wanting equality between the magical peoples. Or equality among the humans. But I have never wanted to rule over the humans. That is not our way," the Rook King declared.

"So you are rejecting my offer," Galatea said icily.

"Without reservation," the Rook responded.

"You would choose their freedom over your own? Look at the mess they have made of the Queendoms. This is our chance together to make it right."

A flicker of doubt crossed the Rook's face, but then he shook his head. "It was good to talk to you, Galatea. 'Til next season," he said, bowing.

Galatea sighed, raised her wand, and disappeared.

When the mirror went black, my eyes met Hecate's.

"She is serious about repopulating the Queendoms with magical people," Hectate concluded.

I almost laughed at the prospect. The Entente were, by our very magical nature, extremely rare. But Hecate wasn't laughing.

"That is a magical impossibility," I said.

Hecate shook her head. "She isn't wrong. With enough will and enough magic, anything is possible."

The room almost seemed to spin. Galatea's musings about a world filled with magic were not just idle chatter. They were part of her plan. "There are too many plots. How do we stop them all?"

"I told you we needed more magic. This is why."

"We can't possibly have enough. Even with your new power, even if I grant a million wishes—"

"Shhhhh. You are not alone anymore, Farrow. We can do this together. We will need the Rooks as well—and as many of your sisters as we can turn, and South and the humans as well."

"Mather and Cinderella are captive. The Resistance has gone quiet, and even if they hadn't, what could they do?"

It had been such a surprise when I first discovered that there were humans who were opposed to the Queen's cruelty. Who had banded together to try and undermine her. I was more surprised still that Cinderella was at the center of the Resistance. It made sense that they had not come forward after Galatea killed Queen Magrit. The Resistance had never trusted the Entente and had helped me, Cinderella, and South stop Bari from enchanting Mather at his ball.

"We will need every one of them to fight Galatea—and then it might not be nearly enough," Hecate observed.

"They helped me once, perhaps they would help me again."

There was a knock on the door. Hecate opened it with a wave of her wand, and seamstresses carrying armfuls of dresses entered.

It was time to get fitted for the first of many balls.

In the middle of the night, I woke again to find Hecate missing.

I reached out, hoping to hear her wishes. But I heard something else.

There were desperate wishes coming from the unlikeliest of places—the Couterie.

*Please help us . . .* The wish was from Holocene. I answered her call and arrived there the next moment.

The Couterie was on fire. Was my mother to blame? I had seen the rage rise in her when we talked about how the doctor changed my face. I had seen how impulsive she was since she returned from the ashes. I had heard her say she wished she could turn back time and undo the Couterie. Had she decided to do it in the Present instead?

The flames were building, and Hecate was nowhere to be found. I could see fire inching toward the window where Lavendra used to wait for me to return with her honeybread.

There were Couterie everywhere. They were in their nightclothes. They had formed a line with buckets of water. They were trying to douse the fire.

I spotted Jacoby and Holocene huddled on the lawn together. Despite the circumstances, I was grateful that each of them had finally found a friend.

She slipped out of her sweater and wrapped it around him. She looked up at him as the sweater came down around his shoulders. There was longing in the look and a slight smile, which he returned.

Perhaps they had found more than friendship. I hated breaking the moment. But I cleared my throat.

They looked up at me in wonder.

"Farrow," Jacoby whispered.

"What happened? Did everyone get out?" I asked over Holocene's shoulder.

Jacoby looked around. "All the Shadows and Couterie are accounted for."

I sighed in relief. "Why aren't you in the Third Queendom with the Queen?"

"She is on her honeymoon. We agreed that it would be a bit crowded for me to tag along."

I studied Jacoby for a moment. I knew how worried he was that he could not take Tork's place with the Queen. Was there more to his return to the Couterie than his story? Before I could press, the fire seemed to rise with intensity, and Holocene spoke, her voice urgent. "It's true then . . . You are Entente!"

Jacoby's face matched his brother's by natural means. They were twins. Holocene's, however, matched mine by unnatural means . . . the doctor. We had both been cut to match our Couterie. I had been Lavendra's Shadow, and once I had become Couterie, Holocene had been mine.

"Farrow, you really are magic. I had heard the rumor, but I don't think I truly believed. But when I saw the fire, I wished for you urgently and you came."

I felt a flood of emotion upon hearing her gratitude, when it was possible that I, or rather my mother, had brought the flames to their door.

Holocene got to her feet, and Jacoby followed. I noticed that he favored one leg when he stood. That was why Holocene was taking care of him while the others tried to put the fire out.

"Your leg?"

"It's nothing. Please don't," he began. They shared a look of trepidation. They did not want the doctor.

I bent down and looked at his leg—an angry red burn went up the side. It must have hurt like hell.

"Just wish for it to be better," I ordered.

He looked at me sheepishly.

"I wish for it to be better."

He began to bend his knee, and the skin began to heal.

Holocene hugged me fiercely.

One of the other Shadows approached us.

"Have you seen Linea?" the Shadow asked.

Holocene answered, "I saw her a few moments ago."

"She went back for her mirror," the Shadow said.

"Wish me to her, and I'll bring her back safely," I promised.

Holocene complied dutifully. "I wish you were where Linea is."

I realized my mistake too late. What if Linea was unconscious? I would not be able to save her. I would not be able to save myself. It would have been better to wish Linea to where we were, and then I never would have had to take a step inside. That was the thing about wishing. You had to be very specific. Be careful what you wish for . . . and be careful *how* you wished, indeed.

But what was wished was done. And I found myself in Linea's room, standing in the Couterie for the first time since the day I'd left it. Fortunately, Linea was alive. Her room had not yet been touched by the fire. But the smoke was beginning to drift under the door.

Linea was on her knees, looking beneath her dresser. I listened closely. I could hear her wish. It wouldn't help me to save her or the Couterie. She was wishing for her mirror.

"You told me yourself that it no longer worked. What use is it to you? You need to wish us out of here," I demanded.

She looked up at me sharply. "You take it for granted, don't you?"

"What?" I asked.

"Magic. You've lost it and found it again. But that mirror was the only magic that I have ever had."

I tried to put myself in her shoes, even though I was loath to. The mirror was an artifact from her only connection to the Entente, to magic. Linea was not ready to let it go.

"But it's just a piece of worthless glass now," I said forcefully.

"It's still mine. Can't you just wave your wand? Are you Entente, or aren't you?" she asked.

"I know it sounds rather ridiculous. But I am not like the other Entente. I can only fulfill people's deepest desires. How is it that yours is not to get the hells out of here?"

"Help me find it—hurry up!"

*It had to be Mother*, I thought again. The mirror had been given to Linea by Hecate. It showed Linea the faces of the future Couterie. That was how Linea had found us. She must've still thought she needed it to run the Couterie, even though it hadn't worked without Hecate.

I hated giving it back to her. The mirror was part of the Couterie's twisted history. But even though it pained me, I sensed that if I could produce the mirror, it would placate Linea and we could make it out of here alive.

"Wish for it then," I sighed.

She closed her eyes and wished for it. *I wish for the mirror of Gray Glass that shows me the faces of my Couterie.*

I waved my wand, and it appeared in her hands.

She smiled and looked at herself in the mirror. "Can you make it work again?"

"I can try," I said with difficulty. The idea of reactivating the mirror sickened me. So I added, "After you are safely outside."

From her studied countenance, I could see another idea forming. Was she going to insist on activating the mirror before we could leave this place? My stomach began to churn.

"Linea, we have to go. I need you to wish us out of here."

Linea, being Linea, surprised me. She was going to wish for something else. Something bigger than putting out the fire. She was going to try to blackmail me in this moment when both of our lives hung in the balance.

"I have spent all these years toiling and trying. It is thankless work at the hands of Queen and Entente alike."

"What is it that you want, Linea?"

"I want to be Queen."

# CHAPTER 20

## — Bari —

South and I disagreed, of course, about the flowers. I thought bringing them to the performance for Thiago would make me stand out.

As we approached the theater, I realized too late that South was right.

"You knew," I chided.

"I did warn you," he said with a smile.

"Thiago! Thiago! Thiago!" At the rear door of the theater, there were three dozen other girls in their best dresses, carrying flowers and shouting his name.

"They don't have seats; they're just hoping for a glimpse on the way in," South explained.

When we got inside, there were more ladies with more flowers.

"They will hear the play and throw their flowers down at particularly significant moments or just at will."

In fact, it seemed as if every woman, noble or common, in the theater had the same idea. The arrangements reflected their social standing. There were simple field flowers in the hands of girls of lesser means and elaborate bouquets of roses in the hands of the noble sort.

South was right. It would take more than flowers to win the actor's heart.

I tapped my wand to my flowers, and they withered and dried and became dust. I wiped my hands on my skirt.

"All right then, what is your plot?" I demanded in a whisper.

"Leave not so quietly in the middle of the first act. He'll think you're rude. You'll stand out—"

"But then he will find me rude."

"He likes drama . . . and you, Princess, are drama."

I looked up sharply at South, whose brown eyes glistened mischievously in the dark. Where was the obedient, enamored South of a few hours ago? Was that the sound of the spell slipping?

Before I could say anything, he continued to explain his plan. "Then we will return to the theater in the middle of the second act and interrupt him again."

"I'll be doubly rude."

"You'll be doubly noticed. He's used to being the center of attention. He'll need to know this girl who does not see him that way. Who has more earthly concerns."

"And what are my earthly concerns?"

"The baby, of course. He'll be humbled and intrigued. And smitten."

I frowned at the mention of the baby, but I nodded. It wasn't a bad plot, and it would have to do since I had no time to think of another.

"Besides, how could he not be smitten when he meets you?" he added, allaying my concern that the spell had eroded somehow.

We found our seats. The curtain finally began to rise.

I sat shoulder to shoulder with South in the back of the crowd that had filled the playhouse, which was open to the stars, and watched Thiago step onstage.

This was the prince. This was the man I was supposed to marry and control and ultimately kill. He was not at all what I had expected.

"That is he?" I whispered.

"You say it with such disdain," South assessed.

I cast a distraction spell so that we could speak freely and the other theatergoers would not pay attention to us. Our neighbors to the left and right looked everywhere but at us.

"I suppose I have never seen a prince with a profession before. If you can call it that," I quipped.

"She is disdainful of the arts. I am surprised."

I realized that by "she," he meant me.

"*She* rightly thinks that in a world as screwed up as ours, to have time for this kind of recreation is a luxury," I shot back.

"Actors bring light and joy and hope and sometimes even illuminate minds and reflect political moods."

"And when did you have time for the theater as a soldier?"

It occurred to me in this moment that, aside from what I had learned when we had restored his power, there was so much of South's life that I did not know. Nor had it occurred to me to ask.

"I spent most of the years after the Burning in the dungeon of the palace alongside the other Fallen. But Queen Magrit realized that she could use the Fallen to her advantage."

"How?"

"We were an example of the danger of the Entente. We were made part of her guard so we could make the Queendoms fear the Entente and see the Queen's benevolence."

"An insult upon an insult," I whispered bitterly.

South nodded.

"Once I was part of the guard, I was expected to enjoy the

pleasures the position allowed. There was a library of books we could read, and the theater was open to us. The first, I think, was to keep our minds busy so that we might not be idle, and the second—so that we might be seen as a warning to others about ever trusting the Entente."

"You confound me, South. We both have spent too long with the humans. You have taken on their affect. You sound like them. But then again I guess you always have. Where is your fury? Where is your desire to tear them limb from limb? It takes everything in me every day not to kill them one by one, slowly—"

"You think you insult me, but you don't," South said softly.

"They took Iolanta from us. They burned Hecate into a million pieces of ash—and from what Galatea says she didn't come back together the same way. How do you go on defending them?"

"Growing up as I did—a singular being among the Entente—I became very aware that every being, human or Entente, is entirely different. Iolanta was different from her sisters. And you, Bari, you are the only Bari in the whole world," he began.

I clutched my wand in my pocket. "Enough, South," I said, concentrating my magic into my wand and reinforcing the love spell.

His eyes glazed over, and he looked at me intently.

"Your hair is like ravens."

"We should pay attention. Perhaps there is something in Thiago's performance that will be of use to us."

We watched the play. It was a romance, in one of its final performances before the play Amantha had signed on for. Thiago was a common man in love with a Queen, and there was a witch who was in love with him. She had only appeared in the shadows wielding her wand.

There was another problem, which, given the resistance from Amantha, I was suddenly aware of. The troupe traveled. Meaning that my time with the man I had not yet met was already drawing short. I had days to make him love me and secure him for the Entente. Or I would have to chase after him like some stray puppy.

"Ticktock, Bari," South said. He wasn't supposed to be reading my Presents, but I'd let him in because I had been so very distracted.

"You really are insufferable. I should have left you at home with the baby, and Amantha should have accompanied me."

"Do you really think Amantha would have sat through an entire play without disappearing and reappearing?"

I bit my lip. It was one thing for me to complain about Amantha. South wasn't allowed to do the same.

"Don't say that. Amantha has been at my side for everything that matters."

"I know that, Bari. I meant no harm. But even I can see that she's not happy with taking second chair in this plan of Galatea's."

"Amantha will come around. She always does."

"It's not easy being in the shadow of Bari . . . ," he said.

I studied him a beat. Was what he said the result of the spell I had cast, or was that what he really thought?

I refocused on the task at hand. Thiago was an actor. Even though Amantha and Galatea and I had been pretending to be human for years, we had kept our circle small, and it had been easier to fool people than one would think. What Thiago did was something different. He was a bit of a savant and a bit of a clown. He wasn't changing faces like we could do with a flick of the wand. He was changing his own face with the acrobatics of expression and changing his voice with inflection.

"An actor who doesn't know he's a prince. Fate does have a way of making its own mirth, doesn't it?" I quipped.

South was not receptive. He didn't move toward me. He didn't even crack a smile.

"Why is an actor any worse a profession than any other? You're a snob, Bari. He brings joy to people. He's never done anyone any harm. The only reason he's ever held a sword is in jest."

I considered his words. There was some truth to them. But I would never let on. It seemed that too often I was finding that South's words challenged my long-held assumptions. I was not going to allow him the satisfaction of knowing that his opinions had gained any purchase with me.

The women from outside the theater were now seated at the edge of the stage. They weren't behaving like ladies were supposed to. Rather, they were in a frenzy. The blood had gone to their cheeks, their voices were high-pitched, and their hands were outstretched as if they needed to touch Thiago. For his part Thiago did not break character. He continued to make his case to the Queen. He loved her, but he was not noble. Would she return his love? The irony of the role was not lost on me.

"I take it by your silence that I am not wrong about the prince," South said.

"We do not yet know his character—you may glimpse his Present, but you do not know the whole of the man. He is human. I am sure there is some darkness there, whether it be in the Past or the Present."

"Or he could be harmless. Or, worse yet, he could be good," he countered.

I sighed.

"Right now I need him to be smitten. Besides, his very being is devoted to the one thing I loathe unless I am employing the tactic myself."

"What is that?"

"Distraction, while the people should be occupied with the political drama that is unfolding around them. The Entente are real, and we have taken one of their crowns. Instead, they are sitting in the dark watching someone play pretend. It's really unconscionable . . ."

"I don't know, Princess. There's something to be said for sitting in the dark and not thinking . . . just feeling."

South looked at me as if he was distracted himself. I noticed that his arm had inched toward mine until it rested against me. I left it there, not wanting to again see his damnable pout, which he had seemingly developed since the spell.

When the time came to test South's plan and cause a scene, South tapped my hand, and we made our exit.

I slipped my arm beneath my shawl and turned my arm into a sparkle of fireflies. They flew up in the air and surrounded me as we excused ourselves down the row.

I could see Thiago stop and look up, and his eyes met mine.

With my wand, I made the nightingales in the rafters begin their song.

I could see his face change from annoyance to curiosity to awe. But he tried to defy his wonder.

"Pardon me . . . Pardon me . . . ," I said loudly as we made our way to the aisle. I could feel the eyes of everyone else in the theater.

"How rude," muttered someone behind the curtain.

"How extraordinary," Thiago murmured.

When we had made it through the lobby and back out into the street, South and I were laughing.

"It worked. You were right," I exclaimed, the disbelief apparent in my voice.

"Say it again, Princess."

"You were right, South."

"I was, was I not?" he boasted.

He picked me up and swung me around, and suddenly we were somewhere else. We traveled to the same spot that he had taken me the day of the coronation.

"We can't," I said. I could see in his eyes what I had seen from the moment I cast the spell—him longing to kiss me.

He leaned down and concentrated his kisses along the nape of my neck. I found myself humming in response, and he echoed that hum.

"I think we should get back," I said. His lips strayed from my neck and reached my shoulder.

South extricated himself from me and reached out his hand for mine. I ignored him and stood up on my own two feet, straightening my posture and my dress, and only then did I take his hand to return to the street outside the theater.

There was clapping from inside. Thiago no doubt had just delivered another soliloquy. Just then, we stole the spotlight again, by noisily making our way through the theater and down our row before taking our seats again.

Thiago broke character and addressed us, seemingly unaccustomed to any interruption.

"Are you perfectly comfortable, madame?"

"It's mademoiselle. And I am quite comfortable," I projected, while trying to sound as dignified as possible.

"Then, with your permission, may the show go on?"

"You have it, but dare I say you do not need it. It is your stage, sir," I said with a rueful smile.

"Ah, indeed it is . . . ," he said with mock astonishment, as if it had not occurred to him.

The crowd laughed. Some of the women from the flower galley shot daggers of jealousy at me with their eyes.

Thiago bowed, and then he turned back to his costar and resumed the play without missing a beat. Despite his bravado, it was clear from the redness of his cheeks and the break in the play that I had rattled him. Drama, indeed.

South's arm continued to brush up against mine as we sat and continued to watch the play.

"What is it?" I exclaimed.

Behind us someone shushed. The audience was filled with Thiago-adoring fans. And I had not recast the distraction spell, because it was like being alone with South, and after our moments on the cliff, I felt like we needed the din of the crowd to create some distance between us. It was working, save for his arm against mine. If I removed it, he would be hurt. But every second we were still touching I was conscious of his skin against mine, of our closeness.

The rows of wooden benches shook with thunderous applause and the stomping of feet, which happened without fail every time Thiago stepped onto the stage.

"Look . . . ," South whispered a little too loudly, his voice laced with surprise. Had the spell really made him that jealous? He knew what the plan was.

"I am looking. He does have a way of courting the audience's attention, doesn't he?"

"Not at him. Look at her."

There was an actress playing a maid who was cleaning a hearth. There was nothing remarkable about her except that she did seem to have decent comic timing, something I had read was important for a romantic play. I wondered if we would have to put a pox on the actress to make sure she would not take the role in the next play, the one that Amantha had already cleared the way for.

"Really look at her. When the light hits her."

The stage was lit by candles, but it was open to the sky, and there was a large lantern that supplied moonlight for the play. When the lantern wasn't behind clouds, it created a natural spotlight. As surreptitiously as possible, I slipped my wand out of my pocket and created a gentle wind.

The clouds moved away from the lantern, and the light hit the stage. When it did, it went right through the comic actress. She was transparent. She was Amantha.

"Bari . . . ," South whispered, warning me.

I moved the cloud back. "Definitely Amantha," I said, sharing a look with South. I expected him to say that he had been right about me pushing her too far. But instead of gloating, he kept mum. I looked around. Had anyone else seen? No, everyone else's eyes were firmly planted on Thiago.

When we got back to the cottage, the baby was wailing at the top of its lungs.

Instinctively, I raced to it, picked it up, and cradled it in my arms.

"Shush," I whispered. I remembered what Queen Helene had said to do when the baby was upset. I began to sing an old Entente lullaby. South knew it too, and he joined in. Dora quieted, and I pulled the baby gently away from me and examined her. She seemed otherwise unaltered.

South said, "She's fine. I can feel it. But hungry."

The baby suddenly let out a guttural noise that I could only generously call a word.

"EEEEAT . . ."

"Damn, Amantha!" I exclaimed. "She really did it . . ."

"EEEEAT," the baby repeated.

South looked at me quizzically. When we first met the baby, Amantha had mused about doing a spell to make it tell us what it really wanted.

"Did what?"

"She spelled the baby so she could tell us what she wanted instead of crying."

"Clever," South assessed, then added, "but obviously wrong. Really, really wrong."

I waved my wand and produced a horn of milk. South reached for the baby, but I held on, waiting for her to drink.

Amantha appeared in the dress she had worn when we had left the cottage, not the one she wore onstage. She reached for the basinet.

I cleared my throat to make our presence known.

"I didn't see you come in. I was just getting some air," she lied.

"South, give us a moment," I said firmly.

South reached for the baby and said, "Allow me. I'll put her down."

It was still strange seeing South hold a baby. He was surprisingly adept at it. I wondered if that was a byproduct of being a Fate. He could see what the baby needed, how it wanted to be held.

My eyes followed him all the way to the door to the hallway.

Amantha cleared her throat, and I turned back to face her.

"Amantha, who was watching the baby?" I demanded.

"I don't know what you mean. I was, of course."

"We saw you on the stage at the theater. Don't bother denying it. So who was watching the child?"

Amantha pouted. "I was. I just came back and forth between scenes. I was only in a couple of them."

"Do you know what an enormous risk you took? We could have been exposed. Something could have happened to the child. Also, you did the talking spell even though I expressly forbade it," I said.

"You forbade it? You don't care about the child. You hate the child. You just hate that Thiago likes me more than he could ever like you. I have read every play he's ever been in. I actually like the theater. You think it is beneath the Entente. Do you think Thiago won't see through that?"

"You have to drop out of the play. And his life," I commanded.

Amantha's face twisted into a determined scowl. "Or what? We are supposed to get as close to Thiago as possible. Perhaps I will find out some information to help him fall in love with you. Or maybe, just maybe, he'll fall in love with me."

"If you don't drop out, I'll tell Galatea," I said.

Some part of me thought, *Good for you*, when Amantha challenged me. She had always followed me everywhere since we were small, and even more so after the day of the Burning. I was there to cover for her flickering. I was her anchor to this world—what she looked for when she slipped in and out of the Ever After. For her to challenge me—for her to choose another anchor, albeit an absolutely abysmal human one—felt like some sort of progress for her.

"Amantha, this is ridiculous. Enough. We never quarrel. You don't want me to tell her what you've done."

"Everything I have done is part of the plot. What you have done is an affront to the Fates . . . I'll tell her what you did to South," she mused.

She had me there.

"How's this? Whoever kisses first uses the love potion. The loser then plays a supporting role," I offered up.

Amantha smiled as if she was sure that she was going to win.

"I will not like beating you, sister," she said ruefully.

"That makes two of us," I countered. But I didn't mean it. I had to beat her to stop the chaos she was stirring up. That didn't mean I would like doing it.

We then went about the business of dividing up the remaining love potion. We performed the ritual twice. Once with a lock of her hair and once with a lock of mine. I didn't remember ever making a potion with Amantha before when we were not looking at each other or talking between spells. But now we were both serious and somber, and our eyes were on the ground or on the potion more than they were ever on each other.

When we were done, we shuffled off to bed.

In the middle of the night, I woke to the sound of wings outside my window. It was South, staying aloft by flapping his wings in place.

"What are you doing? Why didn't you just come to my door?"

"This felt more . . . dramatic."

"South."

"I know you and Amantha quarreled. I wanted to be sure it did not disturb your sleep—"

"You disturbed my sleep," I bit back, but I did not move from the window. And he did not move from his place in front of me, flapping his wings effortlessly.

"Perhaps I can occupy you until you get back to sleep," he offered with a smile.

There was no moon tonight, a fact I had not calculated in my spellwork. He would be under my power until the moon rose the next night.

"I am not the baby. I don't need someone to sing me a lullaby to get me to sleep . . ." I drifted off.

Perhaps it was because of my fight with Amantha. Perhaps it was because I could still feel his last kiss on my lips. Perhaps it was because I knew there was no way I could sleep after the night I had had. Whatever the reasons, I opened the window and let South fly in.

We kissed until our lips were raw. We kissed until I gently told him to stop but not to go. And I curled up against his chest and listened to the sound of his heart beating, knowing that it raced for me.

He lay beside me and he held my hand in his. South looked at my feathered fingers.

"How long?"

"Hmmm?" I murmured.

"How long have you not been able to control it?"

"What are you talking about?" I asked, bolting upright.

"Your feathers . . . They transformed while you were sleeping . . . dreaming maybe?"

"Maybe you were dreaming," I suggested feebly.

He shook his head.

"I was wide-awake. I was watching you sleep," he said without looking even remotely embarrassed.

"I can control it." I got up from the bed and gathered the blankets before me, stealing them from him. He sat up, his chest bare, completely unembarrassed. He leaned against the pillows. His eyes were still on me.

One of many problems with casting a love spell was that its object most likely had eyes on you whenever you were in the room. But South had been looking at me before the spell. Then, he'd been trying to keep an eye on me. Now his eyes had another purpose. They were looking after me. He cared about me—what happened to me, what I was feeling, what I was doing . . .

"I am not leaving until you tell me," he said defiantly.

"I could order you to leave," I said.

"But you won't. I think you need to tell someone. I can sense you haven't told anyone. Not even Amantha. When did the feathering start?" he repeated.

I sat down on the edge of the bed, out of his reach.

Since I cast the spell, he usually sought to have some part of me in contact with him. On the armrest in the theater, brushing the hair out of my face in the cottage . . . Now he refrained. Again, I reminded myself it was the spell; he cared about what I needed, but just for right now. And he could see that I needed space.

"It doesn't matter," I countered quietly.

"When, Bari?"

"I've been transforming since I was six."

"When did it change? When was the first time you transformed without willing it?"

It felt strange for him to put voice to it. I had never said it out loud myself. Saying it made it more real.

"After the Burning I could change at will. No wand required. I actually felt a little guilty about it. That day took so much from us. But I gained this gift."

"You have no reason to feel any guilt for that day," he said firmly, and then he paused, waiting for me to go on.

"Since Magrit's burning, something has shifted in me. Maybe it's from being around so many humans. Did you know that crows react defensively when trouble is near? Maybe that's all it is. Hells, maybe I'm reacting to you," I added.

South ignored my quip and remained serious. “It makes sense—the Burning was a period of extreme emotion and stress that elicited your stronger abilities. But why now?”

I looked at him unblinkingly as an errant thought crept in.

“Extreme emotion . . . like the abject hate that I feel for you? Would that be enough to transform me?”

“I am pretty sure you don’t hate me. There is another emotion that is just as strong as hate.”

His bizarre opinion was clearly the work of the spell. He thought he was in love. So he thought I was in love. And he thought that love was causing me to transform without me wanting to.

I shook my head, and I realized that I had let his musings go too far. Just as I had taken the spell too far.

“I can’t believe you just said that you thought I was so emotional that I can’t control my power. That is the most insulting thing I have ever heard.”

“That wasn’t what I said. I said that your power was linked to your emotions just like mine is. The day of the Burning, I flew my first—and I thought last—flight because I was inspired by the emotion of losing everyone I loved. I have noticed that I fly higher when I am happy. When I feel low, my ascension is lackluster. Is it the same for you?”

He’d shifted away from talk of love to talk of flying. He inched up on the bed and sat beside me.

“How long since you became a Fate? Not even a fortnight? You are new to your power. That explains your highs and lows, not emotion,” I countered.

“Really? Because right now I feel like I can barely keep my feet on the ground. Because I am near you.”

He finally reached over and touched me. He put his arms around me, and I did not stop him.

We floated toward the ceiling. It wasn't his wings that lifted us up; it was his will. He was a Fate, and he was getting stronger every day.

I kissed him then. I didn't want to be seen, but at the same time it felt good to be seen, to have someone know what plagued me—even if it was South, and even if it was just until the next moonrise.

I realized something then, something awful: South was a Fate. Hecate was back. Galatea was a Fate. There were only three, and I wasn't one of them. The only way for me to become a Fate was for another Fate to die.

# CHAPTER 21

## — FARROW —

"You want to take Galatea's throne?" I asked Madame Linea as the dark room began to fill with smoke.

"Any throne will do. That is my wish. If you don't grant it, we both burn."

"You always underestimated me, Linea. I think in some ways you underestimated all of us—"

"So that's a no then?" Linea said, sitting down in a cushioned armchair as if there were no fire at all.

"You never encouraged us to befriend one another. But before I came to you, I came from the Entente, and we relied upon one another," I rolled on.

"Where are your sisters now?" she said, looking around.

It was a very good question. Had Mother set the fire? If so, wouldn't she already know that I would end up here? And where was South? Why did he not answer my call? He was the only one who could, really. My wand was useless without a wish. But South could read my Present. He could come for me.

"South, I need your help this moment or I will fry!" I screamed, and I waved my wand out of habit.

I noticed there was some kind of movement in the dark outside the window.

*I am so sorry, Farrow. That I am not there. But I know that help is on the way.*

I could hear South's voice in my head.

Why would he not come himself? Had Bari and Amantha done something to stop him from coming to me?

The smoky air began to fill my lungs. I coughed. Linea began to cough too. But she still had not changed her wish. It was a challenge, and she was not giving up yet.

"I don't believe you will let us both die. I know that much about you."

# CHAPTER 22

## — BARI —

I woke when South bolted up in bed. His eyes were unfocused like he was in some kind of trance. I knew he was reading Presents. I hoped he was not reading mine.

"What is it, South?" I asked, putting a hand instinctively on his arm.

"Farrow's in trouble, I have to go," he said, his voice urgent.

I contemplated him for a second in the dark.

"Stay, I'll go. Tell me where she is," I insisted.

His eyes searched mine for a second. Perhaps his will was stronger than my magic. After all, he was a Fate.

"Tell me where she is," I repeated.

"She's at the Couterie."

"Go back to sleep," I ordered.

He blinked up at me for a moment and then closed his eyes and rolled over. Farrow was at the Couterie. Was that where she and Hecate had been since Hecate was returned?

I transformed and rushed there. I could see no sign of Hecate, but the building was on fire. I used my wand to put the fire out.

Farrow was coughing and struggling, but she still managed to ask me why I was helping her.

I had said I wanted to be the one who punished her. But it was more complicated than that. I did not want her to *not* be in the world. But what did I want her to be to me? Would we ever be what we had been as children? Or had all the human frailty that was the true sickness ruined her forever?

I was too tired and it was too late for answers. Sure that Farrow would indeed live, I transformed into a flock of black birds and flew back to the cottage and to South.

I slipped back into bed beside South. His breathing was rhythmic, and he did not stir when I snuggled against him. He truly must have been under my spell, because otherwise he would not have obeyed me; he would have been by her side. He must have been able to feel her Presents. She must have reached out for him. He loved her—or at the very least he was infatuated with her. Before the spell, he could not have denied her, and now, because of the spell but only because of the spell, he could not deny me.

"Is that smoke?" he said, nuzzling close to me.

"No, it's just a dream."

Tomorrow we would be strangers again, but right now, I nestled closer to him.

# CHAPTER 23

## — FARROW —

I could hear a buzzing like the beetles we'd heard in the Reverie. I knew that somehow Bari had answered my call instead of South. Beetles filled the space under the door, preventing more smoke from entering the room, giving us a few more moments of air.

A second later, the Couterie shook, and a tree branch broke through the window, reaching for me and Linea and pulling us out of the smoky room to safety.

It had to be Mother.

I'd seen her perform a similar feat when she made her wand. But where was she? Why didn't she stay?

Linea caught her breath and rose to her feet. She brushed off her gown and regained her composure. If I hadn't been with her, I never would have guessed she'd just tried to blackmail me, when our lives had been the potential cost.

I could see her calculating. Trying to think of another tactic.

"Forget about the crown. I wish for our home. I wish for you to restore the Couterie. I know that you do not want to do it for me, but for the Couterie, for all of them—" She gestured around the lawn where the Couterie were all gathered.

*There, you are safe.* South again, but he was not here.

*Why aren't you here?* I demanded in my head.

*I can't explain at the moment. I had to stay away, but I know that you are safe—*

*I could restore the Couterie with a single wish.*

South 's voice again. *But you don't want to.*

*I don't want to. I don't want to displace them. But I also do not want the practice to continue.*

*Is that up to you?*

"It could be . . ."

*South, I need to know, did my mother do this?*

*Hecate?*

*She expressed her guilt for my experience behind those walls. And now those walls have burned to the ground.*

Linea approached me—

"You could restore us with a single wave of your wand . . . couldn't you? Please, Farrow, I beg you . . ."

"You are asking me that after what you just—?"

"The smoke got to me. I was not myself."

"I think you were entirely yourself."

Just then, Galatea appeared, having apparently seen the immediate Past.

"Now, Linea, you do not beg *her.* You beg the Entente Queen."

"Pardon me, Your Highness." Linea curtsied deeply, and Galatea responded with a smile.

"Galatea, what are you doing here?" I asked.

"Farrow, I know that this situation is fraught for you—"

"If you don't rebuild this place, she will never do to another what she has done to me," I said plaintively.

"I know that this will be difficult for you, child. But right now, she and hers, they are of use to the Queendom of the Entente." Galatea waved her wand, and the Couterie began to restore itself—rebuilding itself brick by brick, room by room, as the crowd outside gasped, watching it all. Finally, even the wooden roof was reassembled.

Linea bowed in thanks. "I can never repay you," she said.

"I am sure I will find a way," Galatea returned.

# CHAPTER 24

## — BARI —

I woke, and it was still dark. South was gone. Had the spell worn off?

I could hear voices through the door. Had Amantha seen him exiting my room? Could she tell he was still spelled?

I crept up to the door and listened.

The cottage had gone quiet. Maybe she was considering telling him the truth about the spell?

"You kissed me. Why did you do that?" he asked, sounding curious.

My hand reached for the door, but I stopped myself. I needed to hear how Amantha responded. I opened the door just a slit and could see them.

"Was it so unpleasant?" she said cheekily.

"It was lovely, almost perfect, in fact," South said. But I couldn't see his face, so I couldn't gauge whether his answer was a kindness or if he'd actually liked kissing her.

Amantha, for her part, seemed unbothered. "And where was it lacking?"

"I believe a perfect kiss to be a convergence of not just lips but hearts and minds and wants. You do not want me, Amantha. So why did you kiss me?"

"You are surprisingly romantic, South."

"That is not an answer."

"I kissed you because Bari kissed you. I wanted to take something from her because she has so much. She has everything. I am but a shadow—"

"I know how close your bond is. She sees you as her equal—and the being closest to her in all the Queendoms."

"I thought so too until she supposed only she could use the potion and lead the plot. Clearly she thinks herself superior to me. Perhaps she always has, or perhaps since the day of the Burning . . ."

Standing on the other side of the door, I wanted to protest. The picture Amantha was painting did not match up to the relationship I thought I had with my sister. We were closer than close. We were partners in mischief and each other's confidants. Weren't we?

South's voice was full of empathy when he spoke again.

"We were all burned that day, Amantha. But I know that it affected you more than most."

Amantha countered, "I am the only one who lives between here and the Ever After."

South said, "There is Hecate."

Amantha rolled on. "We don't even really know that Hecate knows what's happened to her—if she feels the pain of her loss or if she's just remnants of consciousness."

South said, "I can feel her. She knows. She has always known. It has been excruciating for her."

Amantha digested this, swallowing hard.

"Then I feel for her."

South gently added, "I can feel your Presents too—your pain. Amantha, this is not the way to remedy it. I may disagree with what you and Bari have come here to do, but I can never argue with your kinship, your camaraderie, your bond. The last is perhaps the most precious. I do not want you to lose that; I do not want anything to come between you two. Especially not me," he said, sounding sincere.

"You are not between us. Bari's own ego, her hubris, is between us. I am no longer content in her shadow."

"Have you told her this, Amantha? I think she would want to know," South asked sincerely.

"You know her. She would laugh at my sensitivity, at my delicateness—she would not change."

"She has already changed, and so have you. I think you're just too close to see it."

Amantha was quiet. Perhaps she was considering his words and rethinking hers. After a moment, though, she answered with a new wave of defensiveness. "That's rich coming from you. You've had magic for only a very short time. And now you're an expert on us?"

"I have the benefit of distance. I am not judging, only observing."

Amantha sighed loudly. "And what do you see when you look at me?" she asked.

"Someone who has stepped out of the shadows and is trying to find her own light. I saw you onstage, Amantha. Even before I knew it was you, I could see your passion, your talent. Is that what you want to do? Amantha, it's not just about the actor, is it? It's about the art. Is that what you want to do? Act?"

Amantha straightened up and backed away from him as if she had touched something hot. After a long moment, she spoke, her voice sharp, her words clipped. "The Entente doesn't do things other than magic and saving the Queendoms."

South asked, "But I'm right, aren't I?"

Amantha spoke again, changing direction, gentling her tone. "I read a lot of plays. And we, the Entente, have spent so much time pretending. It is just a habit that I have allowed to become an indulgence. Please tell me you won't tell Galatea."

South said gently, "I won't betray your trust. But maybe it's time you talked to Bari. She may surprise you."

"Or she might crush me like she crushes her own bugs. Did you know that she did that when we were young? That she does it still?"

"No. Why would she . . . ," he began, his voice cracking a little when he spoke—like he was nervous about whatever Amantha was going to say next.

"She wants to get accustomed to the pain so that if and when she's injured in battle, she won't feel a thing. It has served her well. But it would not serve me in appealing to her sympathies. I will not find a comforting ear in my sister."

"She crushes herself . . . ," he mused, his voice filled with what sounded like wonder. He cocked his head. He didn't seem scared or put off—he seemed almost impressed. Then the rest of Amantha's speech seemed to hit him. And he refocused on her. "I think that Bari's heart has more capacity than even she knows. It is simply untested."

Amantha assessed: "Oh, poor South, you're in more trouble than I thought. You aren't scared by what I just said. You're intrigued—impressed even, maybe even a little more smitten with her than you already were."

South protested. "That's not . . ."

Amantha let him off the hook. "I am not judging you, I'm just being observant. You've changed too. You came here believing you could change us, and all the while she's changing you. The question is—are you a bug under her feet that she's going to crush or someone who she wants to fly at her side?"

Sounding curious, South asked, "And what do you think the answer is?"

Amantha said noncommittally, "I have an early rehearsal in the morning. Thiago's mother is a stickler for punctuality."

I assumed she was gone, because I could hear South calling after her: "Amantha—"

I entered the living room to find South alone.

"How much of that did you hear?" he asked sheepishly.

"All of it."

# CHAPTER 25

## — FARROW —

When I got home, Mother was there, in the drawing room, her needlepoint in her lap.

"You forgot your cloak," Hecate said. "You must promise me that you will wear it whenever you're granting wishes. It will be there for you when I am not."

"Mother . . . You're not planning on going anywhere, are you?" I asked, feeling fear rising in me.

"No, not at present," she reassured.

I pulled the cloak on and tightly around me. But what I really wanted was to pull my mother close. I never wanted to lose her again.

I decided to do just that, so I crossed the room and hugged her with a purpose. I inhaled deeply, which confirmed what I suspected. She smelled like smoke. When I parted from her, I stepped back and took the chaise beside her.

"I knew the tree had to be you. Why did you not show yourself?"

"I saw you in the mirror. I thought it was important for you to face Linea alone. But when I saw you needed me, I waved my wand and the tree saved you. I did not leave this spot."

"You never stepped foot in the Couterie today?" I demanded.

"On the Fates, I did not."

"Mother, did you do it? Did you start the fire? People could have been hurt. I could have been hurt."

"I saw all the Futures, and in all but one you were safe. I would never leave your life to chance."

She shifted in her seat and took a long sip of the drink next to her, as if the subject was closed.

Her face shifted, and she grabbed her wand. "Something's happening that you must see."

She produced the mirror. I could see on its surface Cinderella, Mather, and the Rook King still having their tea party.

*The Rook King suddenly put his teacup down and stood.*

*"Are you certain then? You refuse to take your birthright, the crown?"*

*"I will not be king under your terms."*

*"Very well," the Rook King said.*

*He clapped his hands, and Cinderella disappeared.*

*Mather demanded, "What did you do to her? Bring her back!"*

*"I am afraid that there is a cost for your stay, and if you will not pay it, she will. Nothing is free here, not even our hospitality."*

*"How? Bring her back here now."*

*"I cannot do that—you see, we have a sick Rook, and Cinderella is the only one who can help him."*

*"How?" Mather insisted, sounding confused.*

*"He needs stories. Human stories will keep him alive."*

*"That can't be possible," Mather protested.*

*"You know nothing of our ways."*

*"Then let me do it. I have stories," Mather volunteered.*

*"You will be otherwise occupied... You will be contemplating the throne."*

*"I have already given my answer," Mather said resolutely.*

*"We will show you that we can give you whatever you desire. We can give you untold rewards. You just have to tell us what you wish."*

*"I wish for Cinderella's return," Mather said firmly.*

*"You will see her at dinner. Until then . . . think on it. Have some tea."*

The Rook King disappeared. The mirror went blank.

I pleaded, "The Rook King separated them—wish me to them."

"You cannot interfere. We cannot step on their land. We have a covenant," my mother replied.

"*You* have a covenant."

Hecate's eyes glazed over. She was receiving a vision of the Future. When she refocused on me, she said, "Farrow, there has been a development. There has to be a wish from both sides—and Mather has finally given us the opening we need. He is wishing for you and I am wishing for you, and you can grant it. A mutual wish is the most powerful of all."

"Mother, what are you talking about?"

"Child, look over there."

I followed her wand. And the clock on the wall appeared to have stopped. On the ground beneath it, the cat that had been purring a moment ago was frozen in place.

"You stopped time," I said, marveling at the still animal.

"Slowed time," Hecate corrected.

She had done it before. South had done it before as well. It was something only the Fates could do—but not without an enormous outpouring of magic. Mother had done this for me at a cost to herself. She would be tired and vulnerable. I couldn't possibly leave her like this.

Hecate, having already known what I would say, was of course a step ahead of me.

"I am stronger than before. You can feel it. I can feel it too." She did indeed already look like she was recovering. The color had returned to her face, and her voice was already stronger.

"I am going to make a wish for you, and I want you to grant it. No thought of guilt. It will serve a dual purpose. Your heart's questions will be answered, and you can find out what is going on at the Rookery in Present time."

Before I could protest or ask another question, I could hear Hecate wishing.

"I will slow time a minute before midnight. While everyone else feels that minute, it will be an hour for you and Mather. I wish for you, daughter, and the prince that every second becomes a minute. Don't waste the time; make it yours. May you discover information that is of use only to the two of you and information that may save us all, Entente and human alike."

I studied my mother a beat and thought of the events of the last few days. She'd led me to Lavendra and Tork and to Hodder and now to Mather. This was not just a mother seeking comfort for her lovelorn daughter—this was a part of the plot.

"Mother, did you always know that he would wish for me—and that you would want me to ask him to spy for us?"

"I have no desire to keep anything from you, my child. Not anymore. I will only keep a fact in reserve if telling it to you would change an outcome."

"So that's a yes, then?" I said, not exactly mad at her. Since she'd returned, she'd become both sister and mother to me. It was hard sometimes to remember that she was still a Fate.

"Do not deny my wish, child. We do not waste magic already spent."

I sighed, uncertain. But, buoyed by her own certainty, I raised my wand and I granted the wish.

Then Hecate said, "May the hour before midnight belong to you and Mather. May you traverse space and time and be protected in the moonlight. And when that hour's up, may you return whence you came. And may the time feel longer than the twelve strikes of the clock."

It was a clever spell, and more than that, it was a gift from my mother. Was there some kind of cost to this wish? We were interfering with time itself. And for what—my happiness, our plot? In the scheme of what was happening all over the Queendoms, it seemed selfish to grant the wish that benefited me.

But my desire to see Mather won out. He had lost his mother, and I didn't even know if he knew yet. He was in untold danger no matter how civilized it looked in the mirror.

Suddenly, I was at the top of a staircase, and Mather was at the base of it. It was just like the night of his ball. I looked down. I was wearing the dress from that night, and he was wearing his suit. Had my mother sent us to another place and time or one we had inhabited before?

"Are you really, truly here?" he asked as I stepped down the stairs to meet him.

He pulled me to him, and we kissed deeply. When we parted, our arms stayed entangled, his fingers finding themselves still wrapped around me. He searched my face, his smile turning to utter sadness.

"Is she—?" he asked. I realized what he wanted, what he needed to know. I wished now that I had come sooner. His mother had been gone two whole days, and I was only now just telling him.

"She is. I am sorry, Mather."

"Why are you sorry? After what she did to you—"

I shook my head.

"When Queen Magrit was burned, Hecate returned to the flesh. It might be a miracle, but the cost was your mother's life."

"Do not feel sorrow for me. My mother earned this death."

"That does not mean that you do not miss her."

He grimaced. "I should not miss her."

"She was still your mother—and your heart longed for her to be the mother you deserved."

His eyes welled up.

"I kept thinking, hoping that she would change. But now she never will," he said quietly.

"I am so sorry," I said again, and hugged him again. He returned my embrace, and after a few seconds, I could feel him looking around.

"Where are we?"

I looked around too. It looked like the garden of the palace but without Galatea's recent improvements. There were no giant topiaries. Only the tasteful flower arrangements of old. But there was no Black Glass either.

"I don't know how to say it, but I think the wish created this space. You wished for me. And Hecate wished for us to be together. And this place was important to us."

"Hecate?"

"There is so much to explain, but she has returned to the flesh—and she hasn't aged a day."

"Returned to the flesh?"

I realized suddenly that in all our meetings I had told him about the day of the Burning. But not about her return as ashes. There had not been time, and before that, there had not been trust. But there were both now. Thanks to Hecate.

"Oh dear, there is so much to tell you about her. She gave us this time before midnight so that I could tell you about your mother and you could tell me what is really happening here."

"Well, thank her for me. I want to know everything about you, Farrow," he said, holding me closer.

"And I, you, but first I must know if you and Cinderella are in danger."

"I have never wanted to be king, except to right the wrongs that my mother had done. I know you sent me here, but is this the right path? And can we trust the Rooks?"

This was my opening. My chance to ask him to stay and find out more about the Rookery so we could sway them to our side.

"About that. Maybe you can't trust them . . . but you can use them."

"How so?"

"We need to know what their next move will be. And we need to find their treasures. Those hold the key to the Rooks' power. Each Rook is tied to an object. We may need them all."

"You want me to help you steal from the Rooks—like a heist?"

"I know it's a lot to ask."

He lit up. He was the same Mather who had secretly been blowing up his mother's Black Glass factories in an attempt to protect the Entente from her. He did not back down from a challenge or an adventure. And that made him irresistible. It also made me so very nervous. He and Cinderella were exceptionally brave, but they were human. Would all that bravery survive in the face of so much magic?

"Mather, a part of me wants you to wish you and Cinderella back to the Reverie. This could be so very dangerous."

"I want to stay. I want to help. I owe it to my people. I owe it to you."

"You have me and Hecate on your side. Hecate can stay ahead of them. And while we are together here, in this space, I can grant any wish you have."

"Any wish?"

His voice was flirtatious now. I felt my cheeks warm. How did he manage that at a time like this? And how did a few words from him affect me even across Queendoms?

"Until tomorrow then," he said wistfully.

"Until tomorrow," I repeated.

What a strange thing to have your own feelings tied to one outside your family. What a strange thing it was to choose to love, I thought as I found myself back in the sitting room.

Hecate was waiting for me. I rushed into her arms and hugged her and burst into tears. She ran her fingers through my hair, petting me until I was calm.

"I sent them there to make them safe."

"You sent them there to save the Queendoms. They want the same thing we do. Whatever the cost."

I knew she was right, and yet I felt so very responsible for both of them.

"Show me Cinderella," I commanded.

Hecate arched an eyebrow.

"I need to know that I am not asking too much of them. I need to know that they are both all right."

"Very well."

*Cinderella was led by the Rook King up the stairs of a circular tower and brought into an opulent room—*

*There was a figure lying on a bed in the darkness.*

*There was a chair across the room from the bed.*

*"What is it that you want me to do?" she asked fiercely.*

*"Tell him a story. That is what keeps him alive," said the Rook King.*

*The king disappeared. Cinderella got up and tried the door.*

*There was a moan from the bed.*

*Cinderella approached it and pulled back the covers.*

*Her face was filled with concern and recognition.*

*"It's you . . ."*

The mirror went blank.

"Hecate, who is it? Send me to her. Please."

"I cannot. You will know soon enough. I promise you that she is safe."

# CHAPTER 26

## — FARROW —

In the morning, Sadie entered our room carrying more dresses. We were supposed to spend the day in fittings. Galatea had sent Sadie to tell us that our dresses left much to be desired.

"What is she doing?" I asked Hecate.

"Galatea's drowning us in dresses, as if that would distract us from figuring out what her true plot was."

But even as she said it, I could see Hecate's eyes light on a particularly fetching pink frock.

I shot her a cautionary look.

"It *is* pretty," she said with a shrug.

"Mother, do you think you can keep the seamstresses busy? There's something I want to do. If I can't go to the Rookery, maybe I could go and tell Tork about Jacoby."

Mother agreed, so long as I wore my cloak.

Somehow, it seemed important for Tork to know that Jacoby had been in danger and now he was safe.

"Have you thought about asking him to join us?"

"I hate putting more people I care about in danger."

"It would be their choice. Just as it is our choice. The Queendoms do not just belong to us. They belong to the people too."

I asked Hecate to wish me to Tork and Lavendra's cottage, and she granted the wish promptly.

The two were curled up together on the small chaise in their living area. They were surprised but delighted to see me.

"There was a fire at the Couterie. Jacoby is all right. His leg was injured, but I healed it."

"Oh no," Tork said, touching his own leg as if he could feel the pain just by hearing about it.

"And you are sure he is all right? Can I see him?"

"If you wish it . . ."

"Something is troubling you, Farrow?" Lavendra asked.

"The Couterie burned to the ground, and I wanted it to remain so."

"That choice isn't just up to you—the Couterie themselves deserve a chance to decide their own Fates, just like we did."

I nodded, and Tork and I traveled to the Couterie.

Jacoby was by the pond reading a book. His eyes lit up when he saw his twin. Looking at the brothers together made my heart refill with magic.

I took my leave of them and went to find Holocene. I snuck into the Couterie through the back and found her in my old room.

She was happy to see me.

"How do you fare?" I asked.

"I am a Couterie without a prince; in some ways I am the luckiest of all. Linea cannot cast me aside because it's her prayer that the Couterie will forever be cared for."

"What does she have you do?"

"Errands. Sometimes she dictates and I write her letters."

"What does she write to the Queen?"

Linea provided the Entente Queen with gossip from around

the Queendoms. No doubt that was why Galatea had restored the Couterie.

I thought about this. Why hadn't my aunt relied on the Entente, who were in every Queendom? Did she not trust them? Or was this just Galatea being extra careful? Holocene searched my face, clearly wanting to know if the information pleased me.

"Was that helpful?" she asked eagerly.

"Can I ask you something, Holocene?"

"Anything."

"Do you think the world would be better off without the practice of the Couterie?"

"The Couterie saved me from the orphanage . . . and offered me an education, an occupation—"

"But what if there is another way?"

"I have yet to see it."

I changed the subject to her and Jacoby.

"Are my Couterie skills rusty or did I see a spark between you and Jacoby?"

Her eyes lit up. "Perhaps, but you know that it can never be."

"I have just come from seeing Lavendra and Tork, and I tell you they are the picture of love and happiness."

"But how do they live without the Couterie?"

"They found a way, and I am there to help. I could do the same for you and anyone who wants to."

Holocene's mouth made a thin line of indecision.

"All you'd have to do is make a wish," I told her.

"I will consider it," Holocene said finally. Lavendra was right; it would have to be every person's choice. It was not up to me.

Holocene walked me back to Jacoby and Tork, who hugged again, looking happier and closer for their time together.

They both thanked me before Tork returned to my side and wished for home and Lavendra. Before I complied, I addressed the three of them.

"I didn't bring you here just to reunite you with your brother."

"Why then?"

"I need your help. All of you."

They listened as I described our plan.

"I want the Couterie to warn the other Queens of Galatea's plot to take them down. And, Tork, I want you and Lavendra to renew the Resistance."

"Pardon—" Jacoby and Tork said at once.

"We are so very grateful for your gifts, Farrow. But we are not suited to this. We have just begun to fit in with the people in our new Queendom," said Tork.

"And yet you are doing so in record time. Your charm and your understanding of people will work in any setting, and you can convince them of our cause."

"I do not think we could ever leave the shop and the bees. It's good, honest work. We've made a place for ourselves."

"Just think about it, my friend. There isn't much time. There is so much mischief afoot."

"Wc just escaped all the madness. I don't really know if we can go back."

I could see the conflict in his face. What was I doing? I was pushing for too much.

"I understand, Tork. Forget I asked."

He hung his head. "I am sorry, Farrow."

To my surprise, Jacoby stepped forward.

"I would like to help."

Holocene stepped forward as well. "Me too."

# CHAPTER 27

## — BARI —

Has anyone ever told you that you have the most delicious ears?" South said, sitting across from me at breakfast. I dropped my spoon and glanced up, realizing that he was looking at me with the same intensity as he had last night.

I had every intention of honoring my deal with Amantha. I just hadn't accounted for the moonless night. Without raising my wand, I still had another day of South's adoration. Or at least so I thought.

But I had to be sure the love spell was working. And that South hadn't somehow figured out that I had spelled him. I studied him another beat, and an idea occurred to me. I needed to test his obedience.

"Show me Farrow."

"Pardon?"

"Her Present. Show me her Present. Wherever she is, whatever she is doing. I need to know."

He grabbed his wand and placed it at my temple.

I could see her. She was standing outside a cottage, wearing a cloak. She waved her wand. She was granting a wish—

"Show me inside the cottage."

The view changed. I could see inside. I didn't recognize the couple. They were cuddling on a small couch. They seemed happy and very much in love.

"Who are they to Farrow?"

"They were Couterie. Their names are Lavendra and Tork. Farrow has great affection for them, but it was not always so in the case of the girl. But Farrow granted their wishes anyway."

"Which wishes?"

From what I could see they were living very, very modestly.

"A library for the boy. An oven for the girl."

"I don't understand," I said honestly as he removed the wand, and I focused on him again and our Present.

"From what I can read of their Presents they desire very little except each other. Farrow offered them some of the comforts they were missing from the Couterie."

"But why would Farrow help them now? Shouldn't she be working on a plot of her own with Hecate to interfere with us?"

South shrugged.

"I can only show you what I can see," he said simply.

"But you can feel her Present too if she allows it. What is Farrow feeling? What is she doing, really?"

"She still believes steadfastly that there is another way than the one you and Amantha and Galatea and the others have taken."

Then his face shifted into a flirtatious smile.

"Was that what you wanted to know? Have I pleased you?"

"Very much and not at all," I murmured. But I rewarded him with another kiss.

And another. I told myself I was just reinforcing the spell.

# CHAPTER 28

## — FARROW —

The palace was full of Queens, and Galatea had made it clear that she thought it best that we steer clear of the royal houseguests except for appearances at the nightly balls. If Galatea had invited us to the palace to keep an eye on us, she was doing it surreptitiously. So Mother and I were thankfully left to our own devices. We were some days away from the ball that was indicated to be Queen Helene's downfall. But we had not yet decided how to stop Galatea from replacing the Queen with Bari's beau, Thiago.

Before this evening's ball, we ran into a familiar face in the hallway. Only it was much changed.

Freya had spent nearly ten years looking seventeen, but now she looked every bit of her age. She was still stunningly beautiful, if not more so. Her dewy dark-brown skin now stretched over a more angular face with cheekbones that made themselves known and lips that parted in a voluminous pout and eyes that shone a brownish gray, the color of a mourning dove.

Freya barely took me in. She was already hugging Hecate, who hugged her back.

"Freya?" Hecate said as they released each other.

“I am glad you are in the flesh,” Freya exclaimed.

“I am glad to be in the flesh,” Hecate returned, laughing.

“I wanted to come as soon as we found out you were here, but you know how impossible that is now. I miss us all being together.”

“Your face . . .”

“Isn’t it marvelous?” Freya said, touching it.

Hecate’s own face fell, but then she smiled again.

“Our spells are real. So it is real.” In her hand Freya held a small vial, which she pocketed.

I was familiar with the vial. I remembered that Bari had had the same kind when she made the spell that had given her my face so that Mather would see me when he looked upon her. It had nearly worked. But Mather recognized the real me at his ball.

“Freya, whatever does Galatea have you doing?” I asked.

“What must be done.”

With that, she pulled her wand out of her pocket and traveled away.

When she was gone, I locked eyes with Hecate.

“I promise you I am keeping an eye on every Queendom. Galatea is sticking to the chronology of her plan. We cannot intercede until the time is right. And besides, Bari has yet to win Thiago’s hand.”

Later that afternoon, we found Amantha and Bari in the study with Galatea.

They were supposed to be on some mysterious mission with South, but here they were. Amantha was on the piano, and Bari was dutifully working on her needlepoint.

Hecate looked at them skeptically. “Who are they? Because they certainly are not Entente,” she said.

"You are right. Sister, meet Ester and Annie. They have been kind enough to stand in for Bari and Amantha for the benefit of the Queens. I fear I have been the worst hostess. I haven't paid you any attention at all. Are you enjoying your stay?"

"We are quite comfortable," Hecate said.

"Thank you, Galatea," I forced myself to say with a smile before we ducked out of the room.

The afternoon dwindled into evening, and after donning our new gowns, Hecate and I entered the ballroom for the first of Galatea's fêtes. If I was honest with myself there was a jolt of electricity in seeing Galatea on the throne. She was Entente. And the Entente had always been behind the throne, never sitting in it, hosting a ball.

The Couterie were in attendance, and I took the opportunity to approach Jacoby, who was with Queen Papillion of Blenheim.

Jacoby grinned at me—and then at Holocene, who was across the room, but they only really had eyes for each other. Then he cast a knowing look toward me, accompanied by a wish he wanted me to hear.

*I wish Farrow to know that I have warned Queen Papillion. She was hesitant at first, but I believe that she believes me. We await further instruction.*

I raised my glass in acknowledgment. He smiled and returned his attention to his Queen.

Holocene was not anyone's Couterie. She, like me and Lavendra before me, was intended for Mather. Madame Linea, acting under the rules of the Couterie, had kept her promise to all Couterie that once one entered the Couterie, one was a Couterie for life unless one chose to leave. Holocene was to be cared for by the Couterie all the days of her life. So she attended the ball at Linea's side.

The other Queens of the Queen's Council were wary of Galatea. But from their wishes, I gathered that some of them still thought of the Entente quite fondly.

Galatea's plan to win over the Queendoms seemed to be working. I wanted to warn them all against her. But at the same time some part of me wondered if she felt respected enough that perhaps her thirst for revenge would be, if not quenched, at least tempered.

Between dances, Mother excused us suddenly, then took me to the balcony to show me the mirror.

"There is something that you must see," she whispered.

I followed her, my trepidation rising. Every glimpse in the mirror had brought a new complication.

A moment later, we were looking at Amantha in the mirror. She was inexplicably standing in front of a theater in the middle of the night.

"What is this place? What are you showing me? I don't understand."

"Change. I am showing you change. It's infectious."

Amantha took a small vial out of her pocket and slathered her finger with its contents.

It had to be a potion, another love spell . . .

"That man, that actor named Thiago, is the long-lost son of Queen Delphine. Now we know that means Galatea wants him to take the throne from Helene with Bari or Amantha at his side."

"We need to intercede," I pleaded.

My mother shook her head.

The playhouse was made of wood and open to the sky. The troupe was called the Royal Play Group, but they belonged to neither the royal class nor the common one. They were free of the social mores of the royals and not subject to the same domestic toil as the townspeople and farmers. They had their own toil, building sets, traveling, and performing. They lived a nomadic existence traveling from town to town, entertaining the masses and then leaving again. What kind of prince would a man from this background be, a free spirit or a rogue? Or would he even want the crown? I did not know, based on my experience with Mather. He had been raised by a monster. Somehow, he was decidedly the opposite.

*"We don't get a lot of ladies who want to be on the stage," Thiago said.*

*"Who says that I am a lady?" Amantha said with a flirtatious lilt in her voice.*

*"What are you doing here, Amantha? We don't rehearse for hours."*

*"I couldn't sleep. I was trying to memorize the pages, but I have a problem with them."*

*"And that couldn't wait till rehearsal?"*

*"There's a kiss on page seven."*

*"And you think I should remove it?"*

*"I think we should practice it."*

*"It is customary to save those moments for the stage. So that they are fresh."*

*"But that's the thing. I don't want my character to have her first kiss before I have mine."*

*"Ah . . ."*

*"I would like my first kiss to be something private and special, not in front of hundreds."*

*"And there is no one else you would want to give that honor?"*

*"In the interest of time, I'm afraid it has to be you," she said with a smile. Amantha ran her fingers over her gown, wiping away the potion, and she kissed him.*

The mirror went blank.

"She chose not to use the love potion. Why?"

"She is changing . . . Maybe we all are."

# CHAPTER 29

## — BARI —

South stopped kissing me suddenly and asked me about Amantha.

"What harm would it be to have Amantha perform the spell? Give her this."

If I didn't know better, I would have thought the spell had worn off, but it was still daylight outside. Another idea occurred to me.

"Are you saying that because you want to give her the chance or because you are jealous?"

"She has already taken your role. Why don't you support her? Why can't you let her take the lead for once?"

"Mistakes were made with Magrit . . . with Farrow, with you, the prince's ball, the Resistance. Nothing can go wrong this time."

"Do you have so little faith in Amantha?"

"I have plenty of faith in her. But she is so impetuous. She left the baby. She cannot fully control her power. She almost gave us all away on that stage."

"So she made a mistake. Bari, tell me that there's nothing you have ever done that you regret."

"This is salvageable. I just need to think—stop talking, South."

I grabbed my wand, and he complied.

An hour later, South was disagreeing with me again.

"It won't be that easy," South said roundly.

"Why not?"

"He doesn't believe himself capable of love, and he does not long for it."

"Then we make it undeniable. Make me undeniable. What does he want in his heart of hearts?" I asked.

"You know that's Farrow's territory, not mine. I can only tell you his truth right now."

"And what is that?" I demanded.

"He wants a love like his plays. High stakes, high drama. Heightened emotion."

"If he wants to play hero, we can do that. You made it sound like it was going to be hard."

South looked conflicted.

"I still do not like this," he said.

"Why is that?" I wondered.

"I am compelled to help you, and yet the prospect of seeing you in someone else's arms . . . I feel an urge to . . . do damage to him."

The spell was definitely working. That was the most un-South thing I had ever heard South say.

I looked at him a long beat, took in his determined, sincere countenance, and then I said, "As much as I'd like to see that, let's focus on creating the perfect moment."

It was too bad Amantha wasn't on board with the plot; she'd know exactly what to do. She'd read more plays than any Entente.

Even though South was in my thrall, and despite the flare of jealousy, in most ways he still seemed himself. He watched my every move before the potion touched his lips and after it. The only difference was, before he was trying to stop the plot for the sake of humankind, and now he was doing it for my sake, because he cared so deeply for me. Despite his qualms, we came up with a plan, one that did not include Amantha. It had to work.

Royalty was just a construct; it wasn't real. Still, the humans believed in it. And to them, just because of Thiago's lineage, his life would somehow be valued over others.

He didn't know yet. Right now, he was completely unaware of his Fate.

The Entente were architects of moments. The moments that could change one's Fate. Before the Burning, we'd only used our powers to keep humanity on course. Now we used them to bend humanity to our will.

Amantha and South were reluctant helpers for very different reasons. South, because he wanted to slow down my plan, and Amantha, because she wanted to be the one the prince fell in love with.

Using his gift, South could tell me all the things I needed to know about the future prince. What he was like. What he liked. Who he was. And Amantha, using her gift, could do the same—by appearing and disappearing at will to spy on him.

Farrow had spent too long with humans. She cared about human things too much. She was obsessed with her parentage. She had wanted an actual trial for Magrit. She had left us.

It wasn't her fault, really. It was all of the Entente's. We had not found Farrow after the Burning. She had been left alone except for Hecate's ashes, with only humans to influence her.

It wasn't that the question of my and Amantha's parentage hadn't ever occurred to me. It was that it didn't matter. All the Fates were our mothers. That was what we'd been taught; that was what we believed. Wasn't it?

Still, when I looked at Galatea's eyes and knew they were like my own, wasn't that the reason she had kept us so close?

South was in my head. We orchestrated the perfect Present, based on what South could gather about Thiago.

With South's instruction, I approached Thiago.

He was on his horse, nearing the road to the theater, and had stopped at a storefront. The proprietor had handed him an apple.

Thiago was examining it with the same intensity with which he examined a skull and gave a soliloquy onstage.

Every moment was theatrical for him. *He wants the real world to be like his plays: heightened action, heightened emotion.* South's voice rung in my head as he made the wind pick up around us. The sky opened up above us just as I made it past Thiago on my own horse. I rolled up my sleeves, revealing a tiny section of my arm, which I transformed into bees. I made them swarm around me. I dug my knees into the horse's sides, and I screamed my best damsel-in-distress scream.

My horse dove right by Thiago, who reacted, his mouth agape and his eyes wide, but to my surprise he did not move.

"Help!" I yelled. As my horse raced forward, I could hear the apple drop to the ground behind me.

After a moment or two, the thunder of his horse's hooves reached me.

"Madame!" Thiago shouted over the din of the hooves. "I am here to aid you! The bees are attracted to your bonnet. Cast it off," he demanded as he rode alongside me. "Leave it be and move to my horse."

"I can't. I'm scared!" I screamed. The last were words I thought I would never utter.

Thiago wrapped his arms around my waist and pulled me to his horse in front of him. The bees, of course, followed.

"There is a lake ahead. We must douse ourselves. It is the only way," he called out as he guided the horse to the water. We jumped out of the saddle and into the lake. The bees flew away.

Thiago and I stood looking at each other, soaking wet.

"You," he said suddenly. He did recognize me from the theater after all.

"Me?" I asked innocently.

"No matter. Let's get you to land."

He reached to lift me up, and with some difficulty he deposited me on the bank of the pond. He climbed up next to me. We were both breathless from our exertions, and we leaned back onto the grass. He turned his head to face me and asked, "Were you on your way to further insult my performance? Perhaps you intended to bring the horse onstage and let it relieve itself?"

"I did not mean to offend. There is an explanation."

"Let's hear it then. Saying you would like to apologize is not an actual apology," he said, turning over on his side to face me.

"A true gentleman would think the preamble was enough," I retorted.

"I have never claimed to be a gentleman. I am an actor."

"I am sorry that I insulted your work. Upon reflection, I see its merit," I quipped, my tone light as I remembered what South had said about Thiago's ego.

"And what's that? What makes it of value?"

"I liked the part when you were quiet."

He laughed. Then he aided me to my feet. He helped me find my horse, and we rode slowly back to the cottage. Along the way, I offered my explanation. It was closer to the truth than South and I had originally planned.

"I am a nanny. The baby I care for with another was suddenly left alone. I got word, and I had to make haste. But it turned out it was a false alarm. The baby was fine after all, and I returned. I so wanted to see the end of the play."

His face fell. "You must think me a monster. You had a completely noble reason for interrupting my play, and I behaved as a narcissistic beast."

"You saved my life. How could I ever think that?" I asked innocently.

"I demanded an apology, when all you were doing was caring for a sick babe."

I had never said that the baby was sick. Thiago had added that detail. The story was indeed getting more heroic by the moment.

"Can I let you in on a little secret? I have never saved anyone in real life. Onstage I have, but off the stage I have never experienced anything like that. It was exhilarating," he said suddenly.

We had arrived at the front door. He jumped from his horse and helped me down, clearly enjoying his new role as hero.

He gave me a quick bow. "I must take my leave."

I was half-certain he wanted to kiss my lips, but instead he kissed my hand and asked, "Wait, I did not ask your name . . ."

I thought about using an alias, but my lips moved faster than my mind. "It's Bari."

"What an arresting name for an arresting woman. Good day, Bari."

"You could come in . . . I could make you some tea," I offered.

"I could not imagine a more perfect second meeting. I will not mess with Fate. Till we meet again, fair Bari."

It seemed South was right. We'd turned the imperfect meeting to our advantage.

There was just one hiccup. Why hadn't he kissed me? Had South undermined the plot because he thought he was in love with me?

I asked him as much when we analyzed my adventure with Thiago.

"You might not know this, because maybe your heart is made of Black Glass, but humans sometimes wait to kiss someone because they really like them," South quipped.

"That is ridiculous."

Moonlight poured through the windows of the cottage. But I should have known that the spell had expired already by his behavior. South was no longer in my thrall. He was back to being his more-annoying self. All I had to do was slip my fingers into the potion and kiss him and renew the spell.

I remembered Amantha's warning, but I also remembered that she was off right now practicing lines with Thiago.

I touched my fingers to the potion and swiped them across my lips and reached for South again. He looked surprised, and then we both leaned in at once. We kissed, and we kept on kissing. When we broke apart, I repeated the spell.

South whispered, "I take back what I said. For the life of me I can't fathom why anyone would wait to kiss you, Princess."

# CHAPTER 30

## — FARROW —

After yet another ball, Hecate and I were ensconced in the drawing room doing our best impression of court ladies. Hecate had a quilt lying dormant in her lap. She'd grown tired of the needle and was using magic to weave the pieces of the fabric together. I sat in front of the pianoforte, and I played a melancholy tune that I remembered from the Couterie.

"There are so many things that you know how to do without magic. I could not play a tune with fingers to save my life," Hecate mused.

"I could teach you," I volunteered.

"I would like that, after . . ."

I knew what she meant by "after." After we defeated Galatea, or after we brought her back to her senses. After the peace was brought to the Queendoms.

Hecate looked around to be sure we weren't being observed, and she produced her mirror. There was no change. Cinderella was still animatedly sitting next to the shadowy Rook's bed telling him a fairy tale that sounded a little like her own life.

*"Once upon a time . . . there was a kind man, the kindest man in all the Queendoms, and somehow he found the kindest and most*

*beautiful woman. They were happy for a time, and happier still when they had their daughter . . .”*

The mirror went blank again.

“See, she’s fine.”

“But what happens when she runs out of stories?”

“The girl had no one to talk to but barn animals for years. She will not run out. We are going to find a way to get them out of there. Tell Mather not to wish for anything from a Rook. They use their wish magic to twist things to their own ends.”

I nodded. I was counting down to seeing Mather again. I would feel better when he could confirm what we saw in the mirror.

But when the clock struck eleven, Hecate suddenly put down her quilting.

“I’m sorry. I have to go—”

“What could be more important than whatever plot the sisters are up to?” I said, genuinely surprised as she got to her feet.

“I have an appointment, I am afraid. And I cannot be late.”

“How do you have appointments that I don’t know about? Are you meeting with one of the other sisters without me? Has Galatea saddled you with another dressmaker—?”

“After a decade without any privacy, my child, do you think that I have not earned a moment alone?” she mused.

“Of course. Take all the moments you want . . . ,” I said, her words stinging perhaps more than she intended them to.

Hecate took another glimpse in the glass and poufed up her hair. It was an uncharacteristic gesture. My mother did not care about how she looked unless she was perfecting a disguise.

She kissed my cheek. “I knew you would understand,” she said as she wafted out of the room, leaving behind the very distinct smell of a new perfume—grapefruit and flowers and a hint of death.

After the door closed behind her, I counted to ten and I followed.

I knew I had promised Hecate her privacy, and Fate knew she had more than earned it, but these were dangerous times. Mother was lying and I needed to know why. Had Galatea spelled her? Or was this just more of the strange behavior that she had exhibited since returning?

*Sorry, Hecate, you deserve some time alone, but I must know,* I thought to myself.

# CHAPTER 31

## — BARI —

After some discussion, it was agreed that South would take care of the child while Amantha and I would go to the theater. But when we parted, South looked at me mournfully.

"Promise me that you won't like him more than you like me," he whispered a little too loudly in my ear before Amantha and I left.

"You know I cannot. But he is human, so you have a chance . . ."

He smiled then and returned to the baby.

When we got outside, Amantha admonished me.

"You still are renewing the love spell with South."

"We are already acting at cross-purposes on this mission, Amantha. We do not need South in the way," I defended.

"Harrumph . . ."

We didn't speak again until we got to the theater and parted ways. She went through the door where the actors entered. A few of the girls who had waited for Thiago now waited for her. They were peppering her with questions about Thiago but also offering compliments on her performance. Amantha beamed.

Every night the play changed, and every night Amantha had a larger role than the last.

And I had to admit, she was good. She seemed completely in her element. And when Thiago acted opposite her, I could see the connection between them. I wondered how that would compare with the dramatic scene that South and I had successfully ensnared the thespian in.

After the play, I waited for Thiago at the stage door and he insisted on showing me around.

"You made it through the entire play . . . ," he commented ruefully. I looped my arm through his, and he led me through the theater. "It's all smoke and mirrors," he said as he gave me the tour.

"You paint the sets?" I asked.

"Who do you think did? The Entente? The only magic we have here, we make for ourselves," he explained.

"Do you object to the Entente?" I asked.

"I accept the idea of the Entente, and I am glad they have come out of the shadows. I only wish they would help the people as much as they have aided the nobles and the Queens."

I nodded, feeling a little caught off guard by his words. His critique of the Entente wasn't wrong. We had chosen to focus on the Queens and noble people because they held the strings of power in the human world. Perhaps if we had focused on the entirety of the human population instead of its leaders, the Entente could have had a different Fate. Maybe the Burning never would have happened at all.

He pressed on, showing me the back of one of the sets. There was a crack running through it. A worker was covering it with paint.

"With the right lighting and a little paint, you're in the Seventh Queendom. With a lot—we can take you to the stars."

"Well, you do a fine job. I almost feel the breeze from the Corsican Sea," I mused.

"The girl knows the name of the sea on the moon. Are you

Entente?" the worker asked, turning around. I was surprised she was a woman, with an arresting, expressive face surrounded by beatific curls.

"Pardon?" I asked.

Thiago laughed. "Bari, meet Dame Brianna Montagne, my mother. She is the heart of our theater. And she has her own particular sense of wit."

I reacted. This was the woman who raised him. The only mother he had ever known.

Another actor called Thiago away to talk about new pages. He took my hand and kissed it. "Would you mind terribly? It will only take a second. Don't let Dame Montagne break the spell while I'm gone."

I nodded my permission. I was left alone with his mother, who seemed to be in charge of everything.

"Let's have a look at you then, the girl who has bewitched my son. I was making light before, but I am serious now."

"Pardon?" I asked again.

She broke into a smile. "He doesn't usually bring his girls back here. The theater is sacred to him. It may not look like much. But it's his home."

"Don't you take any funding from Queen Helene? I hear she is a great patron of the arts."

"We have no quarrel with the Queen. She has proven herself quite kind and benevolent. But it was important to me—to us—that the theater . . . that it remain completely independent."

I knew her secret. If I had doubted it in the least before, I knew it for sure now. She loved her son, and she wanted to keep him as far away from his true family as possible.

Thinking of our own new status and Galatea's embrace of it, I said, "I think being independent of the crown is truly noble. You have a fine theater. And I have found it to be magical indeed."

"And what are your intentions with my son?"

"He is a hero on and off the stage. I have never met anyone like him," I mused, doing my best impression of a girl in love.

Thiago returned, and Brianna huffed. "I see what you see in her now . . ."

"What is that?" I asked.

"You got me to talk about myself, and I don't know a thing about you."

We all laughed, and Thiago offered to walk me home.

We stopped by the same lake where he had "saved" me, and we looked at the water.

Amantha would be home by now, taking South's place with the baby. I knew he was somewhere in the sky with his wand, touching our evening with bits of magic. South was in the gust of cold wind that made Thiago wrap his arm around me. Then South moved the clouds and even made the stars twinkle. Every action must have pained him, but he had no choice. He had to obey me and make this night the way it needed to be.

When Thiago walked me to the door, he pulled me close and kissed me. I had already put the potion on my lips. And under my breath I whispered, *"From this kiss forward, may your heart belong to me. May I invade your thoughts and compel your actions. May I be the center of all you hold dear, and may all you want is to keep me near . . ."*

"What was that?" he asked, confused.

But then he quieted, and he gazed at me as dreamily as South had.

"All I want is to keep you near," Thiago repeated, and kissed me again.

# CHAPTER 32

## — FARROW —

I walked through the halls of the palace looking for Hecate, wondering if perhaps she had gone to the Reverie.

It took me a moment to comprehend what I was seeing. They could have been any couple necking in the shadows. But they were not any couple. It was my mother and a guard.

Mother broke from him and raced down the hall.

The guard looked breathless, happy. He called after her.

"When can we meet again?" he asked.

She didn't answer.

Shaken by what I had seen, I reached for South in my mind. When he did not answer, I found myself in front of Galatea's room. She should have still been at her ball, but I could hear her voice through the door.

"Come on in then," she said, "or you are going to wear out my brand-new rug."

Beneath my feet there was indeed a new rug, but if I was honest, it was more of a living mat.

For all Galatea's talk about wanting to court the people and the court, the palace was looking more and more like the Reverie had after the forest had encroached on it. Perhaps, despite her attempts to seem in control, she was feeling the weight of her Pasts, specifically the one wherein she had killed Magrit.

"I only have a few minutes. I am changing my dress for the end of the ball. I was surprised that you and your mother left early—" Galatea took in my expression. "What's wrong? Let me get you some tea," she said.

"I just saw Mother with one of the guards."

"The palace is teeming with guards."

"She was kissing one."

Galatea paused thoughtfully before speaking. "When did you become so judgmental, Farrow? We didn't teach you that," she chided.

"I just want to know how she's different, who she really is now," I pleaded.

I hated having to ask Galatea. I wasn't sure if I could really trust her to be honest with me, or if by telling her I was giving her some new ammunition.

"We have deprived ourselves of so many things for so long. Don't you want to indulge a bit?"

"My sisters are out there trying to take down the Queendoms, and you want me to stop and indulge?" I asked, incredulous.

"I have encouraged all your sisters to do the same when the opportunity presents itself. As long as they are not discovered, their loves are their own."

I felt conflicted. She was right—we had all missed out on so much. Was this the moment to make up for lost time though? But perhaps while my sisters were distracted by their romantic pursuits—and by decorating and balls—there was an opportunity for me to get to them, to dismantle them. Something told me that maybe these new freedoms were not distracting them; they were fueling them.

I thought of Mather again, even though I knew I shouldn't.

A few minutes later, I met Hecate back in the drawing room. A satisfied smile danced upon her lips.

I wondered if I should ask her about it or if I shouldn't.

To my consternation, she volunteered. "His name's Craven. He tastes like strawberries."

I forced up a supportive smile.

"That's lovely?" I offered, my voice cracking under the pressure of embarrassment.

"You don't approve. I know all this must be very strange to you. But take heart, Farrow. I think that kissing is a part of life—like breathing. You should be doing it too."

"Mother . . . I know all about kissing from the Couterie. There was more to that kiss than just kissing . . ."

"You know how I kept objects from the Past to keep me from drifting off into all those Futures?" she began.

I knew that. There was no way to forget it. The same way I remembered the bones in the walls of Iolanta's room at the Reverie, there to keep Iolanta from the weight of all the Presents crushing in on her. And then there were the live flowers in Galatea's walls, and her dresses that kept her from staying too much in the Past. And Hecate had kept brushes that belonged to dead Fates on her dressing table in her room to keep her from drifting off too far into visions of the Future.

"Yes . . . and?"

"I find kissing is a much better anchor than brushes. It's like cake, don't you think?"

I felt the warmth rush to my cheeks again.

"Yes, it is like cake," I began with a smile. "Mother, I am sorry I followed you. You deserved your privacy."

"You can always ask me, Farrow. My door is always open. Don't go to Galatea's," Hecate said.

Shame washed over me. "I didn't intend . . . I was just so surprised. I— For a few moments I felt like Galatea was her old self again. Like she was still in there."

"I've felt it too. But other times, it's like she's a whole new person." Mother looked over to the clock, which was ticking closer to midnight. "It's almost time. See what you can find. But make time for cake."

"Are you sure we shouldn't have stayed at the ball?" I queried my mother as I prepared to leave.

"Sometimes absence is the best way to prove our trust."

"Pardon?"

Mother looked at me and explained, "If Galatea doesn't think we're watching her every second, she may begin to trust us. Sometimes our absence earns trust more than our presence."

# CHAPTER 33

## — FARROW —

Only mere minutes after my mother's revelation, it was time to see Mather. I hated parting with her when we still had so much to discuss, but I had to leave at the agreed-upon time.

We took a risk, based on my belief that my strange half magic would go unnoticed at the Rookery, and Hecate wished me there. I was dying to tell Mather about my mother's paramour, but when I broached the subject, he put a finger to his lips.

"What have you learned of the Rook King? How is Cinderella?" I whispered.

"I want to give you counsel, but I fear I have been compromised."

"Compromised how?"

"The longer we spend at the Rookery, the more I forget about my life before we landed here. I still remember you, though—but even Mother is fading away. Perhaps that is a blessing."

"You think the Rookery is altering your memories?"

"I don't think it's specific to me. I think there's something in the Rookery that makes everyone forget, so that we are all blissfully in the Present."

"How is Cinderella faring? Is it happening to her as well?"

"We see each other at breakfast and dinner. I am not privy to her hours in between. Perhaps because she is female, she seems unaffected by whatever spell is causing the memory fading."

"Hecate thinks that the Rooks need you and Cinderella for your wishes. They have been starved of wishes to grant since they are stuck here. I think I need to get you out. Bring you home—or at least to some other Queendom where you are safe."

"And which one is that? Galatea has her tentacles in every Queendom, as you said. And the Resistance has gone quiet."

"I can find them. I can get you to them," I protested.

"I think we stay. Cinderella can remind me of who I am and so can you whenever you visit at midnight. In fact, I think you could help me remember right now."

He leaned in for a kiss. And I gave in to it. This kiss was different from all the ones that had come before; this kiss had a particular fervor that promised indelibleness.

When we broke apart, we each took a second to catch our breath, to wait for our hearts to slow back down to their normal rhythms, to search each other's eyes and confirm that the kiss that had shook me to my core had also shook him. Satisfied, I finally spoke.

"You could wish to remember."

Mather shook his head. "The Rooks would sense that you had granted my wish. They might already sense that I have met you. You must have seen it in your visions: they are erratic and temperamental and mischievous."

"People could say the same about the Entente. Is there any chance that we have misjudged them, that they are playing into what we expect of them?"

"I have considered that—I have considered that I have brought my own prejudices to the table."

"What does Cinderella think?"

"She is reserving judgment—and charming everyone. You were right about her, Farrow. She is finely suited for diplomacy."

I felt a part of myself lurch. Was he saying that Cinderella would be a better match for him?

He read my face and touched my cheek.

"Cinderella has many gifts. But she is not you."

I accepted this, feeling slightly foolish for my jealousy. Cinderella was my friend. And she and Mather had never had any romantic interest in each other.

"I come with many complications," I said quietly.

"Have you taken a look at the Queendoms? No one is a stranger to complications anymore. I come with complications too," Mather responded without hesitation.

He put his arms around me and pulled me closer.

"Farrow, I know you're second-guessing the plan—maybe you're even second-guessing us."

I looked down guiltily. "We are supposed to steal the Rooks' objects if they do not agree to help us willingly. We are supposed to stop my sisters from overthrowing the other Queens, but there is not enough time and there are not enough of us. We are supposed to start reorganizing the Resistance, but I do not even know where to begin. It's all so hard and so complicated, and all I want to do is be here in this hour with you instead of everything that we should be doing."

"That's what I want too. Once we save the Queendoms, we will have all the hours in the world together."

"Do you really believe that or are you just saying that because I need to hear it?"

"Can it be both?"

I looked up then and smiled at him. The clock began to chime.

"Time to part," I insisted.

He leaned down and kissed my hand. It was such a princely, formal thing to do I was taken aback.

"Till tomorrow, then," he said, sounding ever the prince he no longer wanted to be.

The clock struck again, and I was back in my room at the palace. The kiss lingered on my hand. I hugged it to my chest.

I hoped Mather was right.

# CHAPTER 34

## — BARI —

When I got inside, I rushed to tell Amantha the news about my victory kissing Thiago. I assumed South knew, and I wasn't ready to face him yet.

She was sitting by the fire, curled up with her script pages. She looked at me with disdain.

"I have kissed him and I have used the potion. He is in my thrall."

"Of course you have." She looked back down at the pages, pretending not to care. But I saw a tear roll down her cheek onto a page, and then she flickered away.

South moved in from the kitchen, holding the baby and a bottle.

I asked him, "Where did she go?"

He closed his eyes and said, "To the palace of the Hinter."

"Stay with the baby," I ordered. I had to follow her. There was nothing stopping her from tattling to Galatea now.

"No, we will go together. We will leave the baby somewhere safe," he said.

He disappeared with the baby, then reappeared without her.

"Let's go."

"Where did you leave her?" I asked, sounding more concerned than I expected.

"With Tere."

Tere was the most nurturing of my sisters. I approved of South's choice. He and I traveled to the palace.

South read Amantha's Present. She was already talking to Galatea. "I'll wait here for you."

Amantha was already in the sitting room with Galatea. She smirked when she saw me.

"You should have seen her with the baby. She was a natural . . . disaster."

Amantha was pleased with her own joke. Galatea not so much.

"Hello, Bari. I was just telling your sister how much I trust you girls to take this seriously."

"Of course we are, Galatea. We have it all in hand," I vowed, joining them.

Galatea floated me over a teacup.

"What will the court think if they encounter two Baris and two Amanthas? You simply cannot stay."

Since when did we care what the court thought—what humans thought—beyond our own safety? I counted to ten and reminded myself that Galatea always had a plan.

"Tell me of your progress," she demanded.

"We have kissed, but he has yet to propose."

"You could force it with the spell. But we did agree that it is better if he thinks it is his own idea. Something is holding him back?" Galatea smiled. "Perhaps Amantha should stop kissing him," she said, surprising us both.

Amantha nearly spilled her tea. Galatea had cast an image of them kissing on the surface of it.

"Pardon. I have to kiss him in the play," she said defensively.

"Outside of the play, there was a kiss. I looked at your Pasts,

Amantha. This was before Bari's first kiss. Can you explain why you did not use the potion?"

Did Galatea see my Pasts too? Did she know about me and South? She didn't seem to be focused on me.

All her energy was on Amantha, who began to flicker.

I stayed on message. "Amantha wasn't certain that you wanted me to lead the mission. There was some confusion between us on that point. In the end she chose to let me lead."

Galatea seemed to accept this. But I knew I was just making up an excuse. Amantha had had the opportunity to win, and she chose not to. Why? Because she didn't believe she could? Or because she cared for Thiago that much?

"But that kiss lingers with the prince. Find a way to make him forget about it. Perhaps Amantha should drop out of the play," Galatea suggested.

Amantha flickered again, clearly distraught and trying to cover.

"I think that would only make him miss her more," I offered.

"I have a plan to reveal the truth in two days. I expect a proposal by then—whatever the means."

"You will have it," Amantha and I said in unison.

Galatea then rose and wafted off to check on her guests. Amantha and I were left to absorb her revelation.

"You didn't tell on me. You covered for me," Amantha said, surprised.

"And you covered for me."

It was as close to a truce as we had come in days. I missed her even though she was standing beside me. But a moment later, Amantha's face fell.

Amantha whispered, "She didn't even consider me. It's always you, Bari."

"We have to be practical, Amantha. What happens if you disappear in front of the prince?"

"And what if you start to sprout feathers? I've seen them, Bari. Galatea doesn't notice—but I do."

"I've got it under control," I said, keeping my tone hushed.

"And if you didn't, would you tell me?" Amantha retorted.

"Do you really think I want to do this either? I'd swap places with you in a minute." I let the words hang between us.

"Liar. Even if it means touching a human, currying Galatea's favor is everything to you, Bari. You can't lie to me. I know you better than anyone," Amantha countered.

We stood silent until Amantha spoke first, insisting that before returning to the cottage, she wanted to stop by our rooms and pick up a few things to make it more like home.

She also wanted more of her books, and I did wonder if we ran into our doppelgängers or the other staff or the Queens, if we might get a sense of what Galatea was up to. We walked through the palace toward the drawing room, where Amantha kept some of her books.

"I never would have told her about you and South. I only wanted you to think I had," Amantha ventured.

"Well played . . . ," I admitted, trailing off as I opened the drawing room door. What we saw stopped us in our tracks.

To my surprise, I found Farrow in the room, and another girl. I assumed she was another Entente based on the simple gray dress she wore, which was identical to those that my sisters and I wore every day at the Reverie.

She turned her head, and I could see her face. It was remarkable—like Hecate but younger.

"Hecate?" I marveled.

We did not drop our wands. Was this some kind of ambush?

"We spared you, and you judged us," I said, looking at Farrow. Then I turned to Hecate. "And you left . . . and now you're back. Why should we trust you?"

Galatea entered, and she waved her own wand, removing ours from our hands with a gust of strong wind.

She began to defend their presence. "Put down your wands. We are all sisters here. You do not understand. I asked them to stay, and in time they will agree to join the fight."

I could not believe what Galatea was saying. "Do you really think that? And how is Hecate so young?"

Galatea explained, "We believe the spell gave Hecate back the time she lost."

"We are rejoining our sisters—without condition, without judgment. It is good to see you again, Bari, Amantha. You are exactly as I pictured you," Hecate offered.

Had she also pictured my scar and Amantha's loss of her form?

Hecate straightened her spine. "I never wanted any of you to be hurt. I looked at all the possible Futures. I chose the one wherein the least number of you would suffer."

We had all known that she must have foreseen she would burn, and yet she had still resolved to meet Magrit that day. We had never known her reasoning.

"You chose to burn for us," Farrow whispered. She rushed to Hecate's side and hugged her.

Amantha surprised me by flickering away and showing up across the room next to them. She hugged Hecate too.

I stepped across the room and joined them.

Before we could travel away, Farrow approached me and grabbed my arm.

"You saved me at the Couterie. Why?" she demanded.

"I meant what I said. Stay away from our plot. I don't trust you to take part in it."

"That's not your decision to make. Galatea's invited us. We could not turn down her hospitality."

"I will not warn you again," I vowed. I took Amantha's hand, and we traveled away.

# CHAPTER 35

## — FARROW —

How could you not tell me that we were going to see them?" I challenged Hecate, who absolutely must have known this reunion was going to happen.

"It would have changed the way you reacted to them. And I think it is important for each of you to understand how deeply you still affect one another—how much, at heart, you are still sisters."

I sighed.

"Can we ever really be sisters again? Bari doesn't even feel any remorse for what she did to Cinderella's parents."

"Love doesn't stop because someone does something wrong, no matter how wrong. Speaking of which, perhaps I will ask Galatea to have some cake made . . ."

When she said the last, there was a sharp look in her eyes that said this time cake was not just cake.

"Do you want me to come?" I asked.

She shook her head. "Perhaps she will spill something if we are alone."

I nodded. I sank into one of the chairs, feeling spent.

Suddenly, South appeared in the center of the room. He was cradling a baby.

"You came," I said, relieved to see him. And I was completely perplexed about the infant he carried.

"Long story."

He waved his wand and produced a crib, which he deftly put the child into, and she fell fast asleep.

As we watched the sleeping babe, I wrapped my arms around him.

He hugged me back, and I remembered it was probably unfair of me to hug him. South had made no secret of his feelings for me. As I stepped away, I felt relief; he was smiling.

"I'm sorry, Farrow. I couldn't come before. Things are complicated with Amantha and Bari—"

"Complicated how? That's not your baby, is it?"

"It's Queen Helene's."

"A kidnapping?"

South arched his eyebrow as if the thought had never occurred to him.

"No. Or at least I don't think so. It's a cover. But I suppose it's also insurance for Galatea while the Queen's Council plays out. There's another plot afoot. Helene has a brother, and Amantha and Bari are vying for his hand."

"And they allowed you to accompany them? Why would Galatea take that risk? They all know that you do not agree with their aims."

"I think Galatea wanted them to keep me out of the fray at the palace. But I assure you I have it all in hand. I am the spoiler."

"How?"

"Bari won't go through with the plot if she thinks she's in love with someone else."

I did not think I could be any more surprised than when my mother came back from the ashes, but this nearly accomplished that feat.

"You think you can make Bari fall in love with you and abandon the plan?"

He looked hurt. "Aside from you, most women are not immune to my charms."

"South . . ."

He smiled.

"I did not mean it that way. I—you are quite charming, but Bari has eyes for revenge, not romance."

"I do not kiss and tell. But if I did my lips would tell another story."

"You can't be serious. Have you forgotten everything she has done?"

"She thinks I am on her side. She thinks that she can control me."

"She has killed people—the Grays. When she was just a child she turned men into the Fallen."

A dark look crossed his handsome face. No doubt he was thinking of the Fallen. He had been mistaken for one of them because of his wings. Bari had made one guard into a half man, half scorpion, and one man had become all scorpion. Our magic usually expired by moonrise, but in the case of South's wings and the Fallen and the spell that Hecate had used to bind me, the magic had somehow lasted for years.

"I haven't forgotten, but I have gotten glimpses of her Presents, and I can see there's still good in her."

The baby stirred in the crib. And South responded immediately.

"EAAAT . . ."

"Did the baby just talk?"

There had been babies in the orphanage where I had spent a few years before being taken in by the Couterie. And I knew for a fact that this baby was too young to talk.

“Amantha did a spell,” he said with a shrug, as if spelling a baby were commonplace.

I studied South for a beat. “Are you absolutely sure you have this under control?” I asked.

“I am a Fate, remember?” Gathering up the baby, he turned to me and spoke. “I have to get back now, Farrow.”

# CHAPTER 36

## — FARROW —

I had never been more happy to see the clock ticking toward midnight. I was spent, and seeing Mather was the only thing that lifted me up. This time when I met him, he seemed more himself. Clearer.

"I missed you," he said as soon as we met.

"I need to know what is happening to you and Cinderella. Are you safe?"

"The Rook King has been kind—but there is a lock on the door when we are not with him."

"You are prisoners."

"We are guests he does not trust," Mather explained and then continued, "he wants me to take the throne back."

"We want that too."

"He wants to do it with a wish."

"Perhaps he has enough power to accomplish a coup without hurting anyone," I mused, but shook my head as I said it.

"That's the thing—he wants the wish to be without conditions from me. He will choose the means, and I find that unacceptable."

"Then we need to find a way to get you and Cinderella out of there."

"I will continue to try to persuade him. If you break us out, you will start a war with the Rooks. The exact opposite of what we are here for."

I looked at him for a long beat. He was still very much a prince. He wanted to negotiate a peace. He wanted to protect his people.

"I did make one wish though."

"Oh, Mather. What was it?"

"To protect the people of the Queendoms and to protect you and Cinderella and Hecate and South."

"And King Waid, he granted it?"

"Don't worry, I was exceedingly careful."

"Did he tell you the means? How he planned to protect us? He could decide to rid the Queendoms of all the other Entente if he decided they were a danger to us."

"He wouldn't do that."

"How do you know?"

"I know we can't trust him, but you can trust me. I chose my words carefully, Farrow, don't worry."

But I was worried.

Our time was nearly up.

"Can you please send Cinderella my best?"

"I will. It's going to be all right, Farrow. I know it."

"But you don't know the means."

"I do not."

We kissed again, and we continued kissing until the clock struck twelve.

Suddenly, I was standing back in the room I shared with Hecate. Thankfully, she wasn't there waiting for me. She would have seen me kissing the air.

# CHAPTER 37

## — FARROW —

Something was very wrong. The clock's hand was at a moment past midnight, but there was no Hecate. Where was she? She always waited for me.

As impulsive as she was, she wouldn't slip off to see Craven until after she knew I was safely back from the Rookery.

I had another thought. Perhaps Galatea had called Hecate away to tonight's ball. She very well couldn't have explained that I was secretly, magically meeting Mather at the Rookery.

I rushed into the ballroom to look for Hecate when I noticed something strange instead. No, I noticed lots of strange things.

The Black Glass that Galatea had so painstakingly removed from the palace was now covering one of the walls. Stranger still, Hecate and the rest of the Entente, save South and Iolanta and me, were surrounding the throne like they were standing in for the Queen's court. And strangest of all, Magrit was very much alive and sitting on that throne.

I slipped into the empty seat next to my mother and whispered to her.

To my surprise, Mather entered with Cinderella on his arm. Cinderella was wearing the dress her mother had made for her, and

Mather was wearing the suit of a peasant. But he also wore a rucksack across his chest. I recognized the sack from the Past. He used it to carry explosives. He was here to blow something up.

I scanned the room. In this reality, he was not a prince. And the Entente was firmly on Magrit's side.

Mather was part of some kind of resistance—but to what? To Magrit herself?

I had to know. Also, I had to stop him. Didn't I?

"Mother, I think I'd like to dance," I volunteered. I needed to get close to him.

Magrit, somehow hearing us, said, "What a marvelous idea. Entente, I think you should all dance."

She clapped her hands with glee, and when she did, all the Entente rose at once in unison and headed for the dance floor and began to find partners. I spotted Bari wearing an expression of confusion as the music started, and I made a beeline to be her partner.

"Bari, do you know what is happening?"

"Magic, obviously," she said nonchalantly, but her eyes told another story. She was in the dark, as I was.

"Yours?" I asked.

She shook her head. "Yours?" she demanded. I shook mine.

'Then whose, South's?" I asked.

"I don't think so."

"Maybe we could . . . ," I began. Was I desperate enough to ask for Bari's help to get out of this, whatever this was?

Bari pressed. "Maybe what?"

"Never mind," I said.

She let out an annoyed exhale and released my hands ahead of the end of the song and began to walk off. The music changed, and I moved toward Cinderella and Mather.

I slipped on to the dance floor and cut in.

"No," Cinderella said firmly, glancing over at me.

Mather gave her a look that said he did not want to call attention to us, and he and I began to dance.

"Ladies of the court don't usually dance with peasants," he quipped.

"Well, you aren't just any peasant, are you?" I returned. Then, I lowered my voice. "I know what's in the sack, Mather."

"How could you know?"

I could hear his wishes even though he was trying hard not to think them.

*I want the Queen to die tonight.*

*Why do you want to kill the Queen?*

*She cares nothing for the people. She is using the Entente to kill the other Queens. We are trying to stop her, and you.*

"Me?" I gasped aloud.

"The Entente."

"Why do you think I am Entente?"

"The necklace you wear, all the Entente wear. There is a rumor that you cannot take them off. That you are just as much a prisoner to her whims as the people are . . ." He drifted off.

*Please don't let her notice the time*, he wished.

I realized then he was stalling.

And I could hear a faint ticking from his bag.

My lips involuntarily began to form around the word "traitor."

I looked at the necklace again. I was somehow bound to Margit.

I would have no choice but to tell on Mather—but even then, it would be too late. His bomb was ready to go off.

Instead, I made a choice, and I kissed him.

He responded for a moment, then gently pushed me away. There were fireworks along the edges of the ballroom, and the walls began to melt Black Glass.

Beside us a man wearing gold flickered into existence. I recognized him immediately from Hecate's mirror. It was the Rook King.

"Your Highness," Mather said.

"I would think you would recognize a wish, fair Farrow," King Waid said with a smile.

The clock struck again, and I found myself back in the garden with Mather. I didn't understand. I should have been returned to the study in the palace, but instead I was back here. Was I still stuck inside the wish?

"Mather?"

"Farrow . . . was that real?"

"It was a wish. Mather, did you wish for anything else—other than our safety? You can tell me."

His face crumpled with recognition.

"No—yes, maybe. I was trying to explain my relationship with my mother. I said I wished I'd known what she would have been like if she'd never had me. I wanted to know if she was the way she was because she was trying to make me king. I wanted to know that it wasn't all my fault—"

"What wasn't?"

"All of the death and all the hurt. Mother used to claim she did it all in my name to guarantee me the throne. Persecuting the Entente was supposedly for me. All those deaths, all that hurt, for me. I wanted to know—what if I had never been hers? What would life be?"

"And you now see that she would have been a monster no matter what. I am sorry, Mather."

I wondered if this made him feel better. His guilt had been

lifted, but in its place he had the knowledge that perhaps Magrit was irredeemable. I embraced him again.

"It's fine. It's better to know. Remind me if I forget, please." He tried to make his voice light, but I could feel the weight of his wish on him. I hugged him tighter.

"It's going to be all right, Mather. I promise. I will make it so."

The clock began chiming again, but I did not let go of him.

Just then, the clock struck midnight, and I traveled away back to Hecate. Even as I went, I could hear Mather asking, "You mentioned Cinderella. Are you she?" Mather was forgetting again.

The Entente aside, the plot against the Queendoms aside, I could not bear for Mather to forget me.

# CHAPTER 38

## — BARI —

One moment I had been in the cottage with South, and the next I was in the ballroom at the palace, my hands in Farrow's. What magic was this?

I looked down. I was wearing a plain lavender dress. I glanced around, and Farrow was inexplicably beside me.

"Bari, do you know what is happening?" she asked.

"Magic, obviously." I feigned nonchalance, but I could tell Farrow saw I was just as lost as she was.

"Yours?" she asked.

I shook my head. "Yours?" I shot back, and it was her turn to shake her head.

"Then whose, South's?" Farrow was clearly as disoriented as I was.

"I don't think so."

"Maybe we could . . ." She trailed off, but I could tell she was trying to piece something together in her head.

I pressed, "Maybe what?"

"Never mind," she muttered.

She had almost asked me for my help, but she couldn't bring herself to ask, and I couldn't bring myself to offer.

I stalked off, heading for the doors that led to the garden. I wanted to get as far away from Farrow as I could, but something stopped me—or rather someone. A hand found mine. I knew it was South even before I turned. When I did, he was bowing in front of me. "Care to dance?"

The way he grasped my hand confirmed we were something to each other in this strange landscape. There was a familiarity to his touch. He pulled me into the garden and began kissing my neck. I allowed it for a beat, then I said, "South, stop."

"Did you change your mind? Are you ready to tell the others about us? You know that's what I want."

"South, do you know what's happening here?"

"What if I stop kissing you? I could withhold my kisses until you shout it out for everyone to hear. Look at us, secretly in—!"

Was he going to say "love"?

"South," I said sternly, stopping him. "Do you know what is happening here? Not between us—in there?"

He took a peek at the ballroom, where Magrit was still sitting on her throne. He seemed to come to his senses.

"That's Magrit. If Magrit is here . . . then Iolanta is here."

I followed his logic. "Oh, South, we don't even know if it's real. It could be an illusion."

There was a loud bang, and when we ran back into the ballroom, Magrit was yelling for the guard.

The Black Glass was melting on all the walls.

Farrow was in the center of the ballroom with Mather, kissing him—and then they disappeared.

"South, we need to get out of here too. I don't know what it means if something happens to us while we are stuck in this magic."

"I have to find Iolonta. She could be locked in a cell upstairs like before."

I took his hand. When they were both alive, Magrit had kidnapped and kept Iolonta for years in a cage, torturing her with objects from the Present.

"South, we will find her."

He was already heading down the hall, no doubt to where she had been kept before by Magrit.

The air beside him flickered, and Iolanta suddenly appeared. She fell into step with us.

"South, I see you are looking for me," she said.

"Mother," he said, and he leaned down and hugged her. She looked healthy and happy.

But just as quickly as she'd appeared, she flickered away.

Just then, there was another standing beside us. He was a man dressed in gold. He had to be a Rook. I had never seen one in person, but I had seen them in Galatea's visions.

"Who are you?" I demanded.

"I think you know," the man said with a smile.

"What do you want? Did you orchestrate all this?" I demanded.

"Hardly. Let's just say I gave Fate a hand. And I can give your Fate a hand too."

He tapped South's shoulder, and within seconds, the back of South's shirt opened and, with an incredible cracking noise, wings of flesh and feathers burst out of his back, fully grown.

South screamed in pain, but then looked at them in wonder.

"South, you are living proof that wishes can be made permanent. Find me again and make all your wishes come true."

A second later, we were standing in the cottage again. South touched his own wings, then he touched my face.

We looked at each other. We knew it was some strange magic that had given us a taste of another time line, but the idea that we would still end up in each other's arms again—

"It wasn't real," I said.

"It felt real," he countered. "I had you, I had my mother, there had never been a Burning . . . It was better."

"It was an illusion. A wish—no, worse than that, a trick. Galatea told us about the Rooks."

"That doesn't mean that it can't be made true."

"We were still on the side of Magrit. She did not deserve us. And the Black Glass was back."

"But your hand was in mine. There had never been a Burning. The Rook King was right—Hecate was right, with enough will and enough magic, anything is possible."

He desperately wanted me to believe him. But I would not lie to him.

I put a hand on his wing.

"South, you are very tired. We are going to go back to sleep."

I could have taken away his memory of tonight, but I could not bear to do that to him. The Rook we had just encountered was most probably South's father.

# CHAPTER 39

## — FARROW —

Suddenly I was in the drawing room again and it was empty. Hecate always waited for me. Something was wrong.

When I found Hecate at the ball, she was dancing with her beau, their heads together, his arms around her waist. Spotting me, she left the dance floor. He trailed behind her dutifully as she moved toward me to make her introductions. "I don't believe you've met Craven."

He turned and spoke. "Charmed. You are as beautiful as your mother." He added, "You could be sisters." Another time this would have been a compliment. Since we now looked like we were truly the same age, it was just awkward as pairs whirled by on the dance floor.

"Craven, would you mind if I borrowed my mother for a moment?"

Hecate extricated herself from his embrace. She looped her arm through mine as she queried, "Tell me, did Mather's kisses measure up to what you remembered?"

I felt my cheeks warm. That was not the question I was expecting from my mother. I glanced over at the throne where Galatea was holding court. The ladies were fawning over her dress, covered in still-blooming white mums.

I led Hecate down the hall back to the drawing room, shutting the door firmly behind me. "Did you see the Rook King? Or was I the only one?"

Mother shook her head. "I've been dancing with Craven the whole time. Tell me what exactly happened." Before I could begin, Mother's eyes fell on the clock.

It was well past twelve. Surprised, I spoke. "Look at the time!" The Rook's magic had somehow touched me in true time, in the Queendom.

After I filled her in, Hecate was certain that the Rook's magic found not just me in the moment but also South and Bari and everyone I had seen in that vision.

"But how?" I asked my mother. "I thought the Rooks weren't allowed in the rest of the Queendoms."

"Think of Hark."

"He is magical. We know that from his disappearance the day of Magrit's burning." I paused and then queried my mother, "But is Hark definitely a Rook?"

"I cannot explain his presence that day. Perhaps the Rooks somehow managed to break the covenant so he could spy on Magrit. Or perhaps there is some other explanation." Worry settled on my mother's brow as she continued. "I am more concerned about the magic you just experienced, because we were all just touched by it."

"Still, how? I thought there were rules against Rooks using magic in our realm."

"For all these years, they have not had access to any wishes. They need humans to make wishes. Only then are they able to use their most powerful magic. So they can break out of the prison we've built for them," my mother explained.

"I think we absolutely miscalculated sending Cinderella and

Mather to the Rookery," I said as I continued to put the pieces together.

"How so?" Hecate pressed.

"They now have not one but two humans to grant wishes for," I observed. "Mather made a wish. He thought it was a perfectly harmless one. He wished for our safety and the safety of the humans. All over the Queendoms. He also accidentally wished to know what it would have been like if he had not been born a prince."

"Ah, there's the rub."

"Which part?"

"His wish was so broad. The part about the Queendoms. Mather's wish opened the door for Waid to reenter the other Queendoms."

"I thought that the Rooks couldn't come here without their objects."

"Waid's acting on a wish. It's what he's been waiting for. He is obligated by that wish to check on you and South."

"South? Oh no, he hasn't even met Waid yet. If the Rook just showed up in front of him, I don't know what it would do to South."

Hecate put her own wand to her temple. "South has safely returned to Bari and Amantha. I don't think he had any contact with his father."

I began to sigh with relief. "Wait, King Waid is his father. Does South know?"

"Not yet. But I believe we must tell him before the Rook King tries to visit again."

I absorbed this.

"There's something else, Mother. Mather said he's starting to forget, and I think they are taking his memories. Maybe as a punishment for not agreeing to retake the crown."

"That sounds like something the Rooks would do."

Hecate took me to our rooms and began to tell me more about the Rooks.

Aside from sharing magical origins, the Rookery operated in almost every way opposite to the Entente.

The Entente's decor mirrored that of the palace before Magrit had covered it in Black Glass.

The Rookery was dripping with opulence. Gold adorned the walls and floors and ceilings. Even the fabrics that covered the sofas and chairs seemed to be embroidered with gold.

There were no wands. Rooks didn't use them.

Their magic differed from ours too.

I had sent Cinderella and Mather to the Rookery without knowing anything real about them. Had I sent the two into more danger than I could have anticipated? "Tell me more," I pressed.

"The Rooks are not like us. Or at least they are not like we were before the Burning. Now I think perhaps they were just ahead of us. They became disenchanted with the humans long before we did."

I needed to know more details: why were the Rooks the way they were now? Why had they been confined to one Queendom? "Can you start from the beginning?"

"Once upon a time, the Entente and the Rooks were spread out all over the Queendoms."

"Then how did the Rooks end up just in the Thirteenth Queendom?"

"We put them there. The Entente."

"We?" I asked, incredulous.

"Our foremothers . . . The Rooks became out of control. They are known for their excess, and we the Entente were forced to do something to temper them."

"And how did you do that?"

"We decided it was better to put magic in the shadows, to shroud it in mystery. Otherwise there would be unrest among the people and wantonness among the magical. We bound the Rooks to the Rookery, and then bound them to objects. The Fates before us thought it was the right thing to do. But now—I wonder."

As it stood, even if the Rooks wanted to help us, they could not. Being tied to an object seemed almost as bad as being made into ash. I asked my mother, "And there is no way to undo the magic?"

"I do not see how without the force of all the Fates and all the Rooks in unison. I do not know how much of the story the present Rookery knows. But this is our history," Hecate said.

"Why would they not know?" I asked.

"The elders knew, but they did not pass down the story because they were afraid of retaliation. That secrecy has served us. This way we can continue to make new generations without recrimination and resentment."

"So what are we to do now?"

"If we take their objects, they will come back into the Queendoms, and they will serve us if we hold the objects. If we promise them their freedom, they may come willingly."

"Are you proposing we make them fight for us against Galatea, for their freedom?"

"I am proposing that they make a show of force for their freedom. If they stand with us, it may be enough to make Galatea and our sisters back down."

"And if she will not? Isn't it better to give them their freedom and then ask for their help?"

"It is, perhaps. If that is the gamble you wish to take. But I dare you to meet a Rook and trust him."

"I have. South . . . me—we are all half Rook."

"And the Entente half tempers us, but in your case I believe when I bound your Entente magic and Galatea attempted to unleash your Rook magic, your Rook magic became more dominant."

"I have heard the story, Hecate, and their resentment seems just. If we further push this injustice, are we no worse than Galatea?"

"Perhaps, but in every Future I see there is no positive outcome for any of us."

"Then let us make a new one. Hecate, I want to meet the Rook King. But first, I want to see Cinderella."

"And you shall, but first you must find South. He is going to need you more—"

"Why? What's happened?"

"I think he should learn from you who his father is."

# CHAPTER 40

## — BARI —

In the morning, South was in a strange mood.

After Amantha was gone, he returned from the nursery. He was holding the baby for no reason at all.

"South, why did you pick it up again? It did not express a need for any food or fresh linens."

"Humans need to be held. We were largely deprived of such comfort. But since I received my gift, I have seen so many Presents. They comfort one another. It's how they connect. I believe in some ways it's how they survive. Perhaps we could learn a thing or two from them."

"Forming an attachment is counter to our objectives. If you ask me, all the coddling may be what creates the worst of the human condition."

"How do I measure against Mather then? I was raised believing I was human," he said.

"Comparison and jealousy are so very human," I said archly, leveling him with a sharp look.

South smiled, acknowledging my petty insult. "How else am I to measure a man except with myself as a guide?" he retorted.

"Look at your human poets and dramatists that you favor so

much. They would compare him to the moon—to the forest and the stars."

He looked at me intently. "I have no interest in their opinions of him, only yours. What's he like, then?" South said, taking another tack.

"He's more interesting than you," I quipped.

"I doubt that. I am a Fate with wings, with a Rook father and an Entente mother. I spent a third of my life believing I was human, another third in a cell in Magrit's palace, and most of the rest as a part of the royal guard. I am a lot of things, Bari, but I am not boring."

I smiled despite myself. Had my spell somehow made him less inhibited? "Don't pretend you aren't loving this—me having to pretend to be a docile creature who would not hurt a fly," I countered.

"It's not the flies I'm worried about. You are quite fond of them. You would not hurt one of them. It's Thiago whose well-being is in danger," he said ruefully.

But then his face grew serious. "Bari, I am not loving this. Just the opposite. Whatever I think of you, the idea of your having to seduce someone you feel nothing for is untenable."

"This is my choice. Our plan," I said firmly.

"It's Galatea's plan."

"You don't understand anything. The Entente is all for one and one for all. Galatea's plan *is* our plan."

"Is it? Because the lips he kissed . . . the waist he wrapped his hands around . . . the hair that he moved out of those piercing eyes . . . those belong to you. No one should get to do that, unless you truly want them to."

I inhaled a shallow breath, and I felt my pulse betray me.

I looked down, expecting my hands to twitch into feathers. But my fingers were still very much flesh. I inhaled again. The only thing worse than not being able to control my feathers was realizing that there was no twitch because I was very much exactly where I wanted to be. My body wanted nothing more than to be here and to be touched by South.

"Who do you want to kiss you, Bari?"

After what he said, I expected him to kiss me like he had dozens of times before. But his lips did not seek mine.

I took his hands and placed them on my waist. He did not lean down to kiss me. Instead, he said, "Just say it once. Out loud."

Instead of saying what I couldn't, I said, "Thiago is an actor. And a rather good one at that. I am not sure if I have yet seen the real man or the real face behind his mannerisms and affects. Sometimes there is but a glimmer. Sometimes I wonder if there is anything there at all."

# CHAPTER 41

## — FARROW —

South, did you see any of that? Do you remember it?" I asked when I found him on one of his favorite cliffs in the Twelfth Queendom. He was looking off into the distance, his feathers rustling with the wind.

"Iolanta. She looked so happy. It was as if the Burning never happened. We had never been apart."

"But the problem of Magrit was still there—she was still tearing the Queendoms apart. She still would have begun rooting out magic after that explosion."

His sorrowful look brightened unexpectedly. "Or maybe if the wish had been better, we could have everything."

"South, you don't really mean that," I said gently.

"Says the girl who wished her mother back into existence."

I wanted to say it was different—Hecate had never left this plane. But I held my tongue.

"South?"

"No, you're right. I understand. I have to go," he said, standing up to launch himself into the sky.

"South, wait . . . There's more."

"What more?"

"The Rook who came—he's your father."

South laughed almost bitterly, and then a look of comprehension crossed his face. "Ah, of course he is. How is it that I am the Fate of the Present and I am supposed to know the truth of everything, and yet somehow I know less than I ever have before?"

I reached for South's hand to offer him support, but his hand slipped through mine. Before I could come up with a proper reply, Mother returned me to her with a wish. She had cake and tea waiting for me.

We ate in silence until she clapped her hands. "Farrow, be consoled that he has another who can comfort him now."

"You mean Bari. They aren't real."

"That has not yet been determined."

I took another bite of cake and tried not to think about South and Bari together. Mother and I spent the rest of the day checking in on the other Queendoms. My sisters were all remarkably quiet. Too quiet, we thought.

Later that night I visited Mather, who recognized me and kissed me but now seemed not to remember much of our encounter with the Rook King in the wish. He also told me that Cinderella had missed dinner and breakfast today.

When I returned to Hecate, I was full of concern for Cinderella. What if she had made a wish too, and I had not been there to help her? Hecate, ever a step ahead of me, surprised me with news of Cinderella.

"We are in luck, Farrow. Cinderella is wishing for you."

Mother made a wish, and I met Cinderella in what looked like the Gray manor.

She was sitting at the hearth.

"It's different than you think with the Rooks," she tried to explain.

"Good different or bad different?"

"Just different," she said simply.

But her tone and her face looked exactly as they had when she had been with my sisters. There was a hint of fear underneath her bravery.

"Tell me, Ella. Tell me so I can help."

"They want to be entertained."

"What does that mean?"

"I tell him stories about your world, and they allow me to keep my memories."

"They are extorting you."

Cinderella remained still and silent as if considering a protest. I studied her for a moment.

I shook my head, piecing the parts together. They were feeding off her stories. They needed them. But to what end? The Entente had chosen to help humans all the years before the Burning. We literally did need them.

"You are right. They should have asked me without condition. After I heard his tale, I am sure that I would have volunteered. He needs the stories to keep him alive. He, like you, is a product of magic."

What if this was another trick?

"What evidence have you of his claims?" I asked.

"He was beyond fatigued. He appeared near death, but after a few stories from me, he was revived. I watched the color come back into his skin. I watched his energy return. It was a thing to behold. Is that what it feels like for you to use your wand?"

I did not want to take this away from Cinderella. I did not know if she was being fooled—but she was being held captive; she was being manipulated.

"I am not explaining this well—you'll understand better when you meet him again. I will wish him here . . ."

Cinderella made her wish. And despite my mother's warnings about Rook magic, I granted it. A few seconds later a sleeping Hark was on the floor next to us.

This was not the outcome I was expecting. Cinderella was defending Hark, and here he was. I had not imagined our paths crossing again.

The first time I had seen Hark, we had been children, and he had been next to Magrit on the day of the Burning. When I had met Hark at the palace, he was sitting in Mather's throne. Then he had been Mather's best friend, and I discovered he was also the Queen's Right Hand. The second-to-last time I'd seen Hark, he had betrayed Mather, leading the Queen to Cinderella's door to expose the Entente and me. He had then disappeared into thin air when the Queen burned, revealing himself to be magical. He was now at the Rookery. He was a Rook, if an injured one.

"You do remember what Hark did to Mather and to us?"

"I have not forgotten. But I have also seen a bigger picture, gained an understanding that I did not have before. He was taken as a child. He was forced to be her Right Hand. Mather will come to understand that—"

"There is nothing in his covenant that precluded him from telling Mather, a royal heir to the throne, the truth."

"He wanted a friend. You know exactly what it is like to keep your magic secret and just want to have a friend."

"You will not make me forgive him."

"That is up to you. He is remorseful. Talk to him. Read him if you can."

Hark stirred and looked up at the both of us.

"Farrow?"

"Cinderella tells me that you are a Rook."

"I know you have no reason to believe me . . . ," he began.

Hark did look weak. His brown skin was dull instead of glowing. His eyes did not twinkle. But I knew that appearances could be deceiving.

"Magrit acquired me when I was a child. She took my object and I was beholden to her. When she died, the object went missing. I now belong nowhere. I am nothing . . ."

"That's not true," Cinderella piped in, holding his hand.

I sighed.

"All right, Hark. Tell me your story . . ."

# CHAPTER 42

## — BARI —

The house was empty. South was still gone with the baby. Probably taking it for a walk or a flight in another Queendom. Amantha had gone to the theater to practice with Thiago. All alone, I started making a potion. This one was not for South though; this one would be a sleeping potion.

Yesterday had been lost to me with South and the strange wish magic distracting me. Now I could finally do what Galatea had asked.

I sat in the dark and transformed. My entire body became bees and scorpions and wasps. I usually chose at least one flying thing. This was the only way to make the potion. I deposited the venoms in one repository, mixed them all together, and then I settled myself into the vat. It was my secret and Galatea and Amantha's. None of the other sisters knew.

South returned earlier than expected, and I could not transform myself quickly enough. After calling for me and receiving no answer, he entered the room and stopped, taking me in. "Bari, what is this? What are you doing?"

"I don't have to explain anything to you. You should turn around and . . ." I trailed off. His expression was so strange and dark and sad. I could not bring myself to make him obey me.

"I want to know you—the truth of you. Whatever this is, I will not judge. I want you to know the truth of me too," he said.

South did not seem repulsed, only curious—another product of the love spell, I was sure. But the intensity of his stare, the sincerity I read in his eyes, really did make me want to be known.

"Bari . . ."

I transformed back to my usual form and reached for a cloth to cover myself. Stepping out of the vat, I wrapped the cloth around me.

"It's a mixture of all the poisons of everything that I have transformed into. You won't remember this of course. You will keep my secrets even from yourself."

For the moment, I liked him knowing. I couldn't explain why, but it felt good to tell him the secret. He could do nothing with the information, and—Fates help me—for whatever reason, it seemed that he needed to know my essence, even fleetingly.

"I've tried other poisons and other spells, but I've found this one to be quite effective," I explained. "But I make more than one potion. Did you know that there is a queen bee, and all the other bees are in her thrall? They work for her. They exist for her. You are in my thrall now . . . that is the other potion, the one for love."

He nodded like that made sense and as if it had nothing at all to do with him.

"The potion in the vat is a sleeping potion. It's what spiders use to put their prey to sleep. They paralyze them. But their prey can still see everything and feel everything. The victim can't move."

"That's horrifying."

"A much more painful punishment than death."

"Do people ever wake from the spell?"

"In time perhaps they would, but by then they are already long buried."

"Who is it for?"

"No matter. I think it's time for bed," I replied, getting back to my feet and leading him to my room.

# CHAPTER 43

## — FARROW —

After Hark was done with his tale, I could hear Mother wishing me home. I knew she had seen it all in her magic mirror.

"Now the Rook King," I commanded.

Mother steeled herself and made the wish.

I was suddenly in a new place. I was in a golden room. Every surface was covered in gold, and in the center of the room stood a man also dressed in gold. The Rook King.

I curtsied, out of habit.

"I need to know what you have done to them," I demanded as I rose, knowing that the gesture had already undermined my power.

"The Entente of the Wish, it is a pleasure to have you in our home," he said with an overly deep bow.

"You know who I am?"

"We may not have a Past, Present, or Future, but we can see much farther than you imagine."

"And you saw me?"

"And your feats of wonder are only matched by your beauty."

"Your reputation precedes you as well."

"But your tone indicates that may not be a good thing."

"I make up my own mind."

"That is rare for an Entente."

"Not as rare as you think."

I had so many questions about wish magic, but I needed to help Mather and Cinderella.

"What have you done with Cinderella and Mather—?"

"Prince Mather refused my offer," he explained.

"Which was?"

"To restore him to the crown with a single wish. But he would not make it."

"So what did you do?"

"I granted another one."

"He asked you to keep the Queendoms safe. And so you twisted that wish. If Mather refuses to be king, it is 'safer' if he is nothing at all—not a distraction for me or the Queens or the humans. Just forgotten. Is that your logic?"

"Mather was right about one thing: you are incredibly bright. Can you see inside my head right now? Is that how you are bewitching me?"

"You know I cannot."

"There's the rub. I have encountered the Fates, I have encountered the Entente—but you are different from them all. I need to know if that difference is a danger or an aid to us."

"I seek no conflict with the Rookery. I—we want your help."

"You are asking us to venture into a world that we have not set foot in for centuries. That feels like danger to me."

"It's an invitation, which I hope that you will accept, to have a broader life. I know that you have wondered about the world outside these walls, and I know that some of you have tasted that world. You get to choose how much of a role you have out there."

"Once we are known out there, we may no longer have a choice. You're potentially drawing us into a war."

"Or a wider peace. Please consider my words. There is not much time. I do not know what will become of the Queendoms without your help."

"You have not yet fully explored your power, Bright One. What if you alone can remedy this?"

"Even if I could, if I have learned anything from the Entente and humans alike it's that going it alone never ends in the Ever After you want. Please consider our offer."

"We will."

"There is another matter I would like to discuss. Hark . . . I don't understand the cruelty. He is one of your own and you're punishing him for coming home without his object. He was a child when he was taken from you."

"But he was not a child when he returned. If I allowed him mercy, him most of all, then there would be dissent and chaos. You must know how much order matters, especially when you are dealing with those with magic."

I looked around. It seemed like there was not much order here.

"Ah, you judge. But my kind are not able to leave at will, so I give them all the freedom that I can. But that makes the few rules we have indelible."

"Why did you say Hark 'most of all'?"

"It wouldn't be proper for me to show favor to my own son."

"Hark is your child?"

I wrapped my head around this new wrinkle.

South was Hark's brother. I thought of their features. I could see no similarity between them—except that they were both beautiful.

South had spent so much time feeling left out of our Entente family—but now he had two. This new one might be more dangerous than the first.

"He can be yours if you like."

"Who? Hark?"

"In fact I would like that very much. It would seal our deal quite nicely."

"I don't know if you have figured it out yet, but I am not the most favored Entente."

"I don't want the most favored Entente. I want the most powerful one."

"Then you would want my mother, Hecate."

"Yes, she is powerful—but you have not even begun to reach your potential yet. Your wish magic is not bound by the Past, Present, or Future—it is bound only by the imagination of the wisher."

I sized the Rook up, realizing that there was something else he wanted—something only I could give him.

"I can bring you your son."

# PART III

# CHAPTER 44

## — BARI —

Everything was mostly going to plan. Amantha relented but with one concession: she would continue in the play. South and I had put the wish nonsense behind us, and it seemed like he had truly forgotten all about the potions. The obstacle was Thiago. He grew closer to a proposal, and yet it did not come. Mother was right. Something was holding him back. His heart was in conflict with the spell. He had feelings for Amantha.

"So what do we do?" I asked South. He stepped closer to me, and I let myself lean into him. *Once Thiago proposes, we can't continue like this*, I told myself. But until then. what was the harm?

Of course, Fate had other plans for us . . .

Farrow appeared in our living room. She took us in. I wondered if she could see what was between me and South. We were not touching at the exact moment she arrived. But we had been only a moment before and would probably be touching again at any moment after she left.

"We need to talk," she said, solely addressing South, as if I weren't there. "Cinderella and Mather are in trouble. They need your help. It's the Rooks," she continued.

South stood, ready to draw his wand and travel away with her to help.

"I'm coming with you," I insisted.

"So you can stop us?" Farrow dared to ask.

"We have all grown up knowing what a danger the Rooks are. I have no love lost for Cinderella. But I would not see this as her end or yours, Farrow."

"I appreciate the offer, Bari. Truly, I do. But I think you should stay," Farrow said gently but firmly.

"Because you don't trust me?" I bit back, betraying a little more emotion than I intended.

"Because it wouldn't just be you there, would it? Wherever you go, wherever you are . . . Galatea would know. Galatea would follow," South said gently.

"I am not ashamed to be part of the Entente."

South cleared his throat. "Bari, I'm sorry, but I really need to do this on my own."

# CHAPTER 45

## — FARROW —

South and his father met on neutral ground. I knew my friend wanted to see where the other half of him came from. But it was determined by Hecate that it would be too dangerous to meet at the Rook palace.

So we traveled by wish to the center of the sea. We stood on a tiny island that belonged to no one—not Rook or human or Entente.

South, Hecate, and I arrived early.

"The Rooks are never on time. Today will be no different," Hecate asserted knowingly.

"What is this place? I feel its magic," South said, closing his eyes.

"This is where every Entente and Rook were made—save one."

"I was not made here," South guessed.

Hecate nodded. "Iolanta and the Rook King snuck away. They made you in the flesh instead of by magic. There is a cove in the Twelfth Queendom. They were there for days before the Rooks and the Entente tracked them down."

"And separated them?" he asked, seemingly already certain of the answer.

"Yes. We thought we were doing the right thing then . . . Now I am not so sure."

Before South could respond, the air began to flicker around us. Three Rooks were there. They were all wearing silver.

The one in the center was the Rook King, Waid. He bowed to South.

"I never thought I would see you again, son."

South stood in front of his father. He straightened up, and then he relaxed. The first gesture was reflexive—he wanted his father to see him as taller. The second was reflective—he didn't want his father to know how much he cared.

I wondered if I would ever have a similar moment with my own father. I wondered how much I would care. Or not care. South and I were sometimes so different, and yet in some ways we were the same.

South bowed to the Rook King.

And the Rook King surprised him by bowing right back.

"That is not the way a son greets his father. When I imagined this moment in my head so many times, I had thought there would be an embrace. But perhaps it is too soon."

I looked from South to the Rook King and felt the immediate connection between the two, even if South was fighting it.

"We want you to come home, son, and take up your crown. You can rule by my side."

"I cannot. I have another life, another family . . . but I do want to know you. And to that end . . . I am told I have a brother. I would like to know him too."

I took heart that South's refusal meant there was some sense left in him. Still, in the same moment, the nagging feeling of worry clawed at me from the inside. Our fragile plan rested on his loyalty—and more than that, another, more selfish thought entered my mind. Even though I did not think of South romantically, South belonged to me somehow, and I did not want to lose him. Not to the Rook King and not to Galatea and not to Bari.

The Rook King Waid snapped his fingers, and Hark and Cinderella appeared, looking a little stunned.

"Hark, I am South," my friend said, locking eyes with his brother.

Hark nodded.

"As an act of faith, I would like his release as well that of my friends Cinderella and Mather."

The Rook King snapped again, and Mather appeared, looking a little lost.

"I would like his memories returned to him."

Another snap. "I see the Entente has taught you well," said Waid. "You must be very specific what you ask of a Rook."

"Cinderella, wish everyone home. I will find my own way," said South.

Cinderella complied.

I protested. I did not want to leave him.

"Farrow, grant the wish," he said sternly.

I raised my wand, and we were back at the palace. Hecate was waiting for us.

"What happens now?" I asked, needing to know what was going to transpire between South and his father.

"The Rook King offers him a wish he can't refuse."

# CHAPTER 46

## — FARROW —

I have decided to take the Rook up on his offer," South announced unceremoniously.

Hecate picked up her magic mirror with a sigh. She was clearly not an advocate of South's plan.

"No, South, you cannot. You know that what we saw in Mather's wish was just another ruse to get what they want," I protested.

"They've offered me something that I cannot turn down," he said resolutely.

"You know that they cannot be trusted. You know that there will be a cost," Hecate added.

"The cost is worth it. I saw Iolanta, Farrow. Not in the wish; I saw her right now. She was better, not haunted by the Presents. She was herself—"

"How did you see her?" Hecate pressed.

"In Rooks' Glass. And more than that, I can feel her. If I agree to take the crown, I will get her all the way back."

"South, I know how much you want this, and I can't ask you not to do this. But I can ask you one thing," I said plaintively.

"What's that?" he said as his eyes searched mine.

“That you be careful,” I said, willing him to not just say yes but to actually do what I asked.

“I’m always careful,” he said with a rueful smile.

I looked back at South. I loved my friend, but I did not believe him.

# CHAPTER 47

## — BARI —

Farrow reappeared without South.

"Tell me what happened to South," I demanded.

"First, I think we need to talk," Farrow said, looking squarely at me.

"Would you like some tea?" I offered.

She looked at me warily and shook her head.

"When we were young you thought there should be no rules, no limits to our magic," Farrow said.

I countered, "Look at the power you have now, look at South. If we had explored our magic to its limits back then, imagine how different everything would be. Perhaps the Burning would have never happened. Perhaps we never would have been separated."

"I think South should be the limit now. I hurt him once when we were young, when I gave him wings, and I hurt him again not so long ago," Farrow said, guilt washing over her face.

"I would argue that the wings were a gift. And perhaps a missed clue of the magic that lay within him," I concluded.

She shook her head. "South spent years trying to rid himself of those wings. You don't know or care about his pain. You don't care if he is hurt again."

“What makes you think I want to hurt him?” I countered.

She replied without hesitation. “When we were young, you weren’t above hurting yourself just to test your magic. What would you do to another who you have never loved or respected? You only care about the results, not the path you take to get there. You want more power; you want more magic, and you are using him to gain those things. You have no limits, Bari, and see what that makes you? There isn’t anyone or anything that you aren’t willing to hurt, even yourself. You know what the ironic thing is? The thing you think you’re fighting for, it’s a fairy tale—it’s not real. It’s not anything at all, not if all of us become monsters trying to get it back.”

Farrow’s words stung more than I anticipated. This was what she thought of me. This was how she saw me. Once upon a time she had been my favorite sister. Now we were further apart than when I thought she was in the Ever After.

“We were children, and I knew that he was not one of us. He is ours now. He is a Fate. Like him or not, he belongs to us,” I insisted.

*He belongs to me,* I almost added, but I stopped myself.

“I like him, a lot. He’s going to the Ever After with the Rook King to find Iolanta. I thought you would want to know,” Farrow finally said before disappearing.

We disagreed on so many things, but Farrow was right. I did want to know.

# CHAPTER 48

## — FARROW —

Hecate and I watched in the mirror, Hark and Cinderella beside us.

South took his father's hands, and the ground opened up. They began to descend, and the earth glowed white.

But as South and the Rook King traveled downward, Hark and Cinderella disappeared. Hecate looked at me. "I told you, never trust a Rook."

In the glowing white glass South and his father faced each other as they fell. Cinderella and Hark appeared in the mirror; they were falling too.

All four landed softly in a field. There was no one else there but Iolanta. She looked healthy, peaceful even.

"Iolanta . . . ," Hecate and I whispered simultaneously.

*Hark and Cinderella gathered themselves. Hark even put a protective arm around a fierce Cinderella.*

*South rushed to his mother. Iolanta recognized him and smiled and hugged him.*

*"Mother, it's me . . ."*

*"I am so glad to see you, but you should not have come. Your father is the love of my life, but he is not to be trusted. It is good to see you, Waid."*

*"My love . . ."*

*Waid moved to her and kissed her cheek. For a few moments, South's family was whole.*

*But the Rook King broke from them and turned to Hark.*

*"Son, you can have your mother. But your brother must stay behind."*

*Hark reacted. So did South.*

*"The ferryman requires payment. This is the cost. One soul for another. And so long as Hark is without his object there is no place for him among the Rooks. There is no place for him anywhere."*

*The thin, golden bracelet that Iolanta wore on her wrist faded away and appeared on Hark's wrist. He looked at it in bitter understanding. The bracelet would tie him to the Ever After.*

*"I should have known something was wrong when you were kind to me, Father."*

*Cinderella examined his wrist.*

*"Another trick—what kind of father are you?"*

*"I do not accept this," South said, looking horrified.*

*"Nor do I," said Hark.*

*"It is already arranged," the Rook King said resolutely. If he felt any emotion, I couldn't see it.*

*South took Hark's hand.*

*"Brother, you're missing an object. I believe you can have his." South waved his wand, and his father's crown appeared in his hands. The band around his brother's wrist began to fade away.*

*Hark looked at South and then took Cinderella's hand, and they flickered away.*

*"What are you doing?" Waid asked.*

*"I am sure the ferryman will let you go. Mother and I will find our own way back." South grabbed his mother's arm and began to walk away.*

*"You have broken the deal I made. There is no way back without me," the Rook King called after him.*

*But South kept walking.*

*Iolanta looked up at him. "Well, that was rather brave and rather foolish."*

*"I take after my mother."*

*They both looked down at the bracelet, which had appeared on his wrist.*

"Mother, we have to go to them," I told Hecate.

"Just wait. He already has help . . ."

# CHAPTER 49

## — BARI —

"Amantha, I need your help. I need to get to the Ever After. South is in trouble."

Without hesitating, Amantha took my hand and grabbed her wand.

The floor beneath us opened up, and we began to fall, down, down, down. We landed softy, looked up, and there was the bluest sky I'd even seen. I looked down, and there was the greenest grass.

"Welcome to the Ever After," Amantha announced with dramatic flourish.

Before I could say anything more, South appeared in the distance, carrying Iolanta and walking toward us.

"It's against the rules to take away someone the Ever After has claimed without leaving someone else behind," Amantha explained.

"We don't know if South has been claimed. But I have an idea." I whispered my plan to her.

"That could work, but Roo will not be happy," she responded.

"Who is Roo?"

"The Rook who runs the Ever After."

"Why have you never told me about Roo?"

"You never asked," she replied.

I had not asked her so many things.

"You are right, and I should have. And I will in the future," I vowed.

Amantha looked at me before South appeared before us, still carrying Iolanta in his arms.

"Bari, what are you doing here?" he said, sounding genuinely surprised at my presence.

"I knew the Rook's invitation to the Ever After was a trick," I said.

"And you came to save me," he said with that smile. The one that shot right through me.

"I came to tell you that I was right," I began, needing to be defiant.

"But since I am here . . . ," I added, looking around, realizing that this was not the time for a conversation.

Gently, South put Iolanta down.

My eyes met Iolanta's, and I said quietly, "Iolanta, it's me, Bari."

Amantha gave me a look. "And Amantha," she added.

Iolanta's gaze swept over us. "Bari, Amantha, is the whole Entente down here? You foolish girls making such a fuss over me," she said. Her eyes were clear and bright, her smile wide with recognition.

Amantha's eyes caught mine. "I am going to go distract Roo," she said. She kissed Iolanta on the cheek and flickered away.

"Iolanta, you are yourself again," I said.

"And you, child, I wouldn't recognize but for the bees," she said, studying me intently.

"Is that a good thing or a bad thing?" I said.

"It just is," she replied.

"I am so glad to see you, Iolanta."

"It is good to be seen," she said matter-of-factly.

"I am going to talk to South for a moment," I commented pointedly.

I spoke gently to South, wanting to give him the chance to say goodbye to his mother. "When you are ready, I can take you back. Amantha is distracting Roo. We have some time but not much."

"You don't understand. I want you to take Iolanta back in my stead," he said, holding up his wrist. There was a thin gold chain around it. I knew what the chain meant—it was a tie to the Ever After. Iolanta's wrists were decidedly bare.

I was surprised and yet not surprised at all. I thought of the moments we had staged to get Thiago close enough for me to spell, moments orchestrated to make the actor feel heroic. I thought of South now: a hero without any effort at all.

"You traded your freedom for your mother's?"

"For Hark actually—Father was going to free Mother and imprison Hark down here. I could not have that."

"You traded yourself for the brother you never knew—the rogue who helped Magrit?"

"I traded myself for the brother who had been imprisoned by Magrit and was about to be imprisoned by his father."

"I thought we had to slip you out of here in case your father tried to trick you. That maybe he didn't want you to come for his crown one day."

"Just the opposite. He wanted to reunite our family for a price—Hark's freedom—I thought that was a cost too high."

"I never imagined you volunteering to stay for Hark." I shook my head in disbelief, trying to make sense of this new wrinkle.

South's gaze moved from Iolanta to me. "My mother missed out on so much. Her life above was filled with so much pain. I want her to have a chance to live again, but better, happier. I understand if it's too much to ask. It's against the rules of the Entente. It's against the rules of the Ever After," he finished, his expression earnest.

I looked from him to Iolanta. Even though I did not know if the gods of the underworld would allow it, I was ready to try. But there was no way in the Ever After that I was going to leave him down here.

I had half a dozen arch responses in mind, but my answer was a simple one instead. "The only way Iolanta could live a happy life in the Queendoms is with you by her side. Let's take you and your mother home," I told him.

He held up his wrist again.

"The bracelet ties me to the Ever After. I will need to find another way. Maybe make a deal with the ferryman. Fates hold weight even down here. I imagine," he offered, sounding more certain than his eyes conveyed.

"I think you'll be in a better position to make a deal back in the Queendoms."

"The Rook King said that this bracelet will prevent anyone from crossing the river."

"There is another way out of the Ever After. We can bypass the river."

"How?"

"Let me take care of the how. You just have to carry your mother. What do you say, South?"

He paused and looked at Iolanta, who was touching her bare wrist where the bracelet had been.

We walked over to her.

"Iolanta, just hang on to me and South."

"It's very sweet, dear, that you want to save me, but your magic won't work the same down here, as uniquely powerful as you are.

I'm a bit afraid that you two will be stuck down here with me forever. Not that I would not love the company. But I want more for you, up there . . ."

When we were small and Farrow had accidentally given South feathers, Hecate had taken us to see Iolanta. It was meant as a punishment. But for me it had been a gift. Iolanta, like South now, had the power to see the truth of one's Present. When I was alone with Iolanta, she had told me about that ability.

Seeing Iolanta now and knowing the fullness of her story, I felt a rush of guilt. Amantha and I had not been kind to her when we were small. But as the years wore on, I felt a kinship with Iolanta even in her absence. Her only fault had been that she was not able to control her immense power. As I struggled with my own misbehaving feathers, I felt more sympathetic to her plight.

"Who needs magic, when you have flying things?" I said ruefully.

"Bari, I always knew your gifts would serve us. The girl made of bees and birds . . ."

"Iolanta, I—" I felt the apology rush to my lips.

"No need for that then or now. You think I couldn't see past the hard shells of your beetles? You chose them first because they could protect what's underneath."

South had looked away, but I could see a knowing smile on his lips as if he agreed. As if he thought he'd seen beneath my hard shells too.

Amantha hurried toward us, speaking quickly. "We need to leave, now."

I transformed partially, leaving my upper torso to wrap myself around Iolanta, who was beautifully lucid. And then I whistled for my friends. There were birds and other flying things, alive and dead, that went back and forth into the Ever After. I called on them to help us now.

*Winged friends, hear my call, large and small.*
*Help us take our dear Iolanta back to the surface where she belongs.*

My eyes met South's over Iolanta's head, and he smiled at me.

"You're not going to say that it's against the rules of the Ever After again, are you?" South said, surprised.

"The old rules are gone now," I replied, and when his eyes met mine, they twinkled with gratitude.

Birds of all shapes and sizes came and lifted us up. I whistled—a bird call that I'd learned in my time as different birds.

"That's the thing about animals. They are often overlooked and underestimated too. They slip into places unnoticed. And the one in control of this realm never bothered to make any rules for them," I assessed.

After we landed back at the Reverie, South wanted to know how I had done what I did.

"Whenever I transformed into flying things, they listened to me and I listened to them. I called for help, and they came as if I was one of them."

"That's incredible. Thank you, Bari."

"Don't thank me yet," I said, glancing down at his wrist. The bracelet was still there.

# CHAPTER 50

## — BARI —

Are we not going to talk about it?" Amantha asked as we watched Iolanta and South in the garden.

She was referring to the bracelet and whatever repercussions were coming from the Ever After.

"I was thinking not," I said.

"Roo is not happy. And when he is not happy, his grip on the Veil between realms could slip."

"What are you saying?" I asked. "We call his bluff. I don't think Roo is going to unleash all of the Ever After over one soul."

"And what if you are wrong?"

"We'll cross the river if we have to," I said with a smile.

Amantha shifted and smiled too. "They do look happy, don't they?"

I nodded.

"Should we gather our sisters? Surely, everyone will want to reunite with her?"

"Let them have the day. Then we will call our sisters," I replied.

Calling our sisters meant calling Galatea. "Amantha, how much trouble do you think we'll be in with Galatea?" I had to ask.

"Less than you would imagine," Amantha said, her smile becoming a little mysterious.

Before I could question her further, South waved me over.

"We were discussing when to call the others. We thought it might be nice if you had each other to yourselves for the day," I told him as I approached.

"Thank you, Bari," he mouthed.

Iolanta gently touched the bracelet on his wrist.

"You know that this belongs on my wrist, not yours," she said.

"I think you are owed years and years of freedom and clarity and joy. You were not given your due the first time around. And purely selfishly we are owed each other, Mother. We are owed time."

Iolanta's eyes watered, but she still smiled. "Yes, we are owed, my son. But the Keeper of the Ever After might not see it as time due."

"Let us worry about that, Iolanta," I gently commanded.

South shot me a grateful look. Then he picked a flower and offered it to Iolanta. She took the blossom and tucked it behind an ear. From the bloom a flower crown grew, framing her face.

"How do I look?" she asked.

"Beautiful," he responded.

The sadness faded from Iolanta's eyes. She was choosing to embrace the moment. However many or few they were meant to have.

As I moved to slip away, South grabbed my hand. "Mother and I would love it if you stayed for a little while."

I sat down, surprised, stopping myself from asking him why.

Iolanta locked eyes with me. "We are all too clever to pretend not to know why, child."

South and I shared a look.

The day was perfect. "Happy" was the only word to describe it—and I didn't remember using that word once in all my years.

I nearly cried as I watched South and his mother share their memories, their heads leaning against each other, their wands touching each other's temples.

We started at the Reverie, but also traveled to other places in the Queendoms that Iolanta wanted to show her son. She took us to the edges of Queendoms, the tops of mountains, the plains and beaches. All places where humans had not dared tread. "There is a quiet place in every Queendom. I've found them all. They will be of use to you when the Presents get too loud," Iolanta advised her son.

After a few hours, we returned to the Reverie, and Iolanta asked South to call her sisters. There was a distinct sadness that pierced the perfection of the day, although they each attempted to paper over it with smiles.

"What is it?" I asked.

"She has another day, maybe two, before the Presents begin to crush her again. She wants to go back before then."

"Oh, South, maybe there is a spell. When we gather them—"

He shook his head. "She is content there, and she thinks that the ferryman will allow me to visit. So long as I can find my own way out again."

I squeezed his hand. I did not understand how Fate could be so unfair. For a day South had had all he wanted, but it would expire almost as quick as a spell.

When Farrow and the others appeared, despite the circumstances, I could see South react to Farrow. He lit up when he saw her, and his eyes never left her as long as she was close by. My fingers on my free hand shuddered and turned into feathers and back again. I told myself that I did not care. He belonged with someone like her. They felt the same way about humans. Their moral compasses pointed in the same direction. Mine pointed in another.

# CHAPTER 51

## — FARROW —

We were reunited with Iolanta at the Reverie only to say goodbye to her again. But this time was different. This time Hecate and Iolanta and Galatea were able to join hands in the flesh, to talk and sing and be with all of us.

Iolanta explained how much she loved her life in the Ever After except for how she missed all of us, but that she followed our every move. "I can see the Presents there, but I cannot feel them—they do not crush me," she said.

It made sense. She was surrounded by the dead. She could still see the Presents, and now she was balanced by a world of Pasts.

"Thank you for saving me. Thank you for giving me your gift," South said, his voice full of emotion.

"It seems to be treating you better than me," Iolanta said, her voice filled with pride.

Looking at her, I found myself thinking about Rook King Waid and his offer to grant my wish. What I wouldn't give to be able to set things right for Iolanta. We had all this magic around us and not enough to keep her here.

As we made our goodbyes, there was a sudden rumbling in the ground. I looked to Hecate, thinking of the time she had caused the earth to shake when she grew a new tree from her wand.

My sisters held their wands at the ready. Shadows shaped like people began to appear all around us. Some were standing behind us while others seemed to be floating in the air, blotting out the sun.

The shadows parted, and a beautiful man dressed in silver stepped forward. He wore a crown, and his skin was silver as well. He had to be a Rook.

We stood, our wands poised. South stepped in front of his mother. Hecate stepped forward too.

Galatea called out to the Entente, ordering, "Cast a protective spell for both of them."

She began chanting the words of the spell. The other Entente repeated after her.

*It's not too late,*
*protect our Fates.*
*For them there is no cost,*
*We will not accept their loss,*
*It's not too late,*
*protect our Fates.*

"Roo, you know the covenant. Rooks are not allowed here," Hecate reminded him.

His eyes glimmered with recognition.

"It's been a long time, Hecate. You know the rules of the Ever After. I know you found a way to avoid your stay with me, but that does not mean that every Fate can. You have something that belongs to me." The silver Rook was undaunted.

He held up his arms, and South was pulled toward him.

Hecate raised her hand and pulled South back toward us. The Rook pulled him back again, leaving South suspended midair, obviously in pain.

"Ahhh . . . ," South gasped, moaning.

Bari transformed into a swarm of bees, and she headed toward the offending Rook, but she was stopped by a wall of shadows. South was frozen, helplessly waiting for someone to make a wish that I could grant to help him.

"South, you must try to wish yourself free!" I yelled.

But South still couldn't or wouldn't wish.

"Ahhhh," he moaned again, looking a bit faint.

Her face grimaced by pain, Iolanta spoke. "Unhand him, I come willingly."

"You did not break the deal, he did," the silver Rook pointed out. But as he spoke, his hold on South weakened and South fell to the ground.

Bari's bees swarmed toward him, reached for his arms, and asked him if he was hurt. I ran over and joined them, relieved to find that he seemed only a bit dazed but otherwise intact. He was already trying to get on his feet again to move toward Iolanta.

"Roo, we both know it was a trick. Do not make my son pay for the Rook King's actions," Iolanta vowed.

"I have to think," Roo said, clearly confused by the choices before him.

"I am better suited for life down there, and I do believe you have missed me."

"You left without saying goodbye," he said, his hurt showing and perhaps something else. He was looking more like a spurned lover than a scorned Keeper of the Ever After.

"That was wrong of me. I was already on my way back to you," Iolanta pleaded.

"Were you really or are you just saying this because I . . . ?" Roo countered.

Almost killed her son, I thought.

Hecate spoke up. "She was, until you so rudely interrupted our goodbyes."

Roo lifted his chin, seemingly comforted, but his pride still smarted.

"Let us dispense with this ugliness and make peace. Let us go home now," Iolanta commanded. "Perhaps you will allow my son to visit," she added.

"Perhaps, but I cannot promise. There may still yet be retribution." But even as Roo said this, the bracelet that had been on South's wrist appeared on Iolanta's. Roo had been swayed, and the shadows began to fade.

"Mother, are you sure?" South said, plaintively.

"Roo has a soft spot for me. There will be no retribution, not for us anyway. Though the Rook King should be wary." Iolanta was whispering, but I was close enough to hear.

After a minute or two, Iolanta kissed her son on the cheek and returned to Roo's side. They faded together, hand in hand.

The sisters took turns embracing South and giving condolences before they traveled away. Finally there was only me and Bari and South and Amantha.

Amantha kissed South on the cheek, remembering she had to get ready for the theater. Then there were three.

Before we parted ways, I hugged South. I noticed Bari reacting to our embrace, and I held him tighter.

Bari turned herself into an unkindness of ravens and flew off without saying a word.

I asked South, "Why didn't you make a wish? Maybe there was a way to keep Iolanta here and wish away the crush of the Presents."

"You said once I should not make that wish," he countered solemnly.

I realized now how unfair that was, especially when I had Hecate.

"You could maybe make the wish still," I offered. Though I was uncertain if a wish I granted would have any weight at all, now that Iolanta was back in the Ever After.

"Thank you for offering that," South replied. "I thought of making the wish. I am thinking of making it still, but with all that is going on up here, with how perilous everything is, I think Mother might be safer down there. For now at least," he concluded sadly.

"For now," I repeated, hoping that one day we could indeed revisit that wish.

# CHAPTER 52

## — BARI —

When we returned to the cottage, we tucked the baby in her crib. Done with her preparations, Amantha excused herself to return to the theater.

I found South outside, looking at the sky. I reached for his hand.

"I thought I would get to keep her."

"You can still see her, and she you. It is not what you deserve but it is something. And look at all the souls that came to save you from the Ever After. You are not alone, South."

"You, Cinderella, Hark, Hecate, Farrow . . ."

"You still look at her like she is the sun," I mused when he said the last name.

"And I look at you like you are the moon. If I didn't know better, I would think that you were jealous."

"When you see Farrow . . . when you see the contrast between us, does it remind you of all the reasons we should stop?"

"I don't want to think about Farrow right now. And I don't think you do either." He kissed me again.

I allowed myself to surrender to the kiss. But when our lips parted again for air and his lips moved in again to meet mine, I pulled back. "No, we haven't been thinking at all."

I pushed him away. Hurt registered on his handsome face. My first instinct was to kiss the hurt away. And I felt a flash of anger at him and another at myself for my first impulse.

"Deep down you think that you can fix me—that you can change me. You want me to be like her, like Farrow."

Even in the falling darkness, I could see South shake his head.

"I don't want to change you. Your intensity, your passion, the way that you are free—I love those things. I just don't think that you want to be a killer."

'Then you don't really know me," I bit back.

"You have put vengeance at your center. I think that there is more to life than that. I think that there is more to *you*."

"What was done to us cannot go unanswered."

"It was answered when Magrit burned."

"And what about everyone who cowered and stood by? What about those who cheered? That is who all of them are."

"You have not met all of them. You do not know all of them. You complain that they paint us all with the same brush—and yet you do the same."

"We are the injured party. We are the ones who burned and who will burn again—if we do not stop them, if we do not have them in hand."

South sighed. "Answering tyranny with tyranny is no answer at all. The way things were was wrong, the way things are is wrong—we have to make something new."

I took in his words. He painted a romantic picture. But I could not trust it.

The sun was almost fully gone, and the room was painted in shadows. I reached for the potion in my pocket. I hated spelling him now. But I could not stop.

South closed his eyes before I kissed him. Like he was waiting for it. Like he expected it. Like he knew what I was about to do. I pulled back from him. He opened his eyes.

"How long?"

"How long what?"

"How long have you known?"

A smile crept across his face.

"I'm a Fate—or half a Fate—your spell did not work on me."

"So you played along?"

"I'm sorry. I'm the wounded party here."

"How are you wounded? You got to kiss me. It must have been so horrible for you."

South stepped closer.

"It was horrible," he said with a smile that told me he meant the opposite.

"Then you don't have to worry. It will never, ever happen again."

"Do you promise?" he whispered as he leaned in and nuzzled my neck.

My skin betrayed me as his lips brushed against it. I wanted his lips to return again and again and to move up to my lips, which had reflexively parted. My body, my skin, my lips, they waited for him.

I closed my eyes and willed my feathers to take me away. I could still feel his lips even as I broke apart into thousands of feathers.

I didn't look back.

# CHAPTER 53

## — BARI —

I flew to the palace, and when I arrived, Amantha was already there, to my surprise. She was holding a gold watch.

"Aren't you supposed to be at the theater?"

"I needed to . . . um . . . get a prop for the play—no matter. What is wrong with you? Are you still crying over Iolanta or did something else happen?"

"It's nothing."

"Do you call South nothing now?"

"Where is Galatea?" I asked.

"Why do you have to have everything?" Amantha returned.

"That's not true."

"Thiago and South," she countered.

"What in the Queendoms are you going on about? I hate him," I replied, feeling testier by the moment. Why was Amantha being so tedious? Was it all her time in the theater with the humans?

"Harrumph. It's the most obvious thing in the world, even to me."

"What is?" I asked. "For the life of me I don't know what you are talking about."

"South's the only one who can understand."

"Understand what?"

"You spent your whole life wanting to be up there." Amantha directed her wand to the sky.

"What's your point?"

"So did he. You made wings for yourself. You made yourself into a gaggle or swarm or school of birds and beetles so you could be up there. And he's had wings all these years that were useless, but now he can fly. He understands the longing and power that you have felt your whole life. And realized. And now he's realized it too."

"That's ridiculous, Amantha. That's like comparing a raven to a . . ."

I tried to think of some kind of criticism, but Amantha wasn't having it.

"I'm comparing a girl who turns herself into a flock of birds to a boy who has wings. I can't think of anyone who would actually be closer to you in want and deed."

As was her custom, Amantha disappeared after making her point and left me to sit with it.

South had stronger magic than mine. I had to admit it. He was a Fate. I had been foolish to think a love spell could work on him. And more foolish still to think his feelings for me could sway him to my side. It was time for me to tell Galatea. She would know what to do.

Galatea was on the balcony of the ballroom when I appeared in front of her, but then I quickly disappeared to the dressing room. I had seen a flash of anger cross her face, because, of course, for a single moment there had been two Baris at the ball.

But then she appeared by my side, her face filled with concern for me. "What is it? What's happened?"

I spilled the whole terrible story of how I had thought I controlled South's heart but I hadn't—

"Is it salvageable, Galatea?"

She laughed and clapped her hands together.

"He is a Fate, child, how did you think you could outspell him?"

"He is a novice, and I should be a Fate, I know it . . . ," I replied, the words sounding feeble as I said them.

"But you are not—at least not yet. But just because he was immune to the spell, doesn't mean he's immune to you."

I showed her my visions.

"I can see it in your Pasts. Your spell did accomplish something: you let each other in. He was reading you every time he kissed you, but you were also inside his head and heart. You can use that. You do affect him. You can distract him. That may be enough."

"Enough for what?"

"For him not to stop the next step in our plan."

South was sitting in the drawing room of the cottage as if nothing had happened.

"Why are you here?" I demanded. I had assumed he would not be there when I returned. I assumed he would go to the palace and try to explain to Galatea how he had tricked me. Or perhaps he would have even found his way back to Farrow and Hecate. I did not expect him to be calmly sipping tea.

"I made a promise to Galatea. I will help you finish the plan. We are not done until Thiago proposes," he vowed simply.

I thought of what Galatea had told me: I affected him. I could use him. What better time than the Present to test that theory?

"You asked me once who I wanted to kiss me . . ." I trailed off suggestively.

He stood up, his face filled with expectation.

"Ask me again," I demanded.

"Bari, who do you want to kiss you?"

"You. I want it to be you. Always you."

The words tumbled out, and it felt good to say them.

There was movement then. His hands caressed my back and pulled me closer to him. His eyes met mine, and a smile just for me, for what I had said, lit up his eyes and face. And then, only then, did he lean down to meet me.

The kiss was not like any other we'd had. This time, I knew he was immune to my spells—and he knew that I knew. The spell hadn't been a spell; it had been a lie, and now it was no longer between us. It was the most honest kiss I'd ever had, and the one by which all others would be measured.

Just as Galatea had said, I let him in, and he let me in. I knew I wasn't supposed to. I didn't know what else he could see about me, feel about me, but at the same time, I knew he could feel everything I was feeling. It heightened his pleasure, intensified it and my own.

I knew I had made a mess of controlling South, but I was still on course with the plan. Or at least that was what I told myself.

# CHAPTER 54

## — BARI —

In the morning, the cottage was quiet except for the baby's occasional request for food or changing. South and I sat across from each another eating breakfast bread and drinking our lavender tea. We didn't talk about last night. We didn't talk about Iolanta. We didn't talk at all. A part of me wished I could cast the same spell on South that Amantha had on the baby so he could tell me what he really wanted. That wasn't possible of course, and after last night, I couldn't see myself even wanting to try.

Our hands touched accidentally when we both reached for the honey. He did not pull his away. Instead, he clasped my hand in his. Within seconds South had pushed the table away and I found myself sitting in his lap, kissing him again.

Just as suddenly, he drew away and then kissed my hand. "What does it feel like when you crush your beetles?" he asked.

I tried to pull my hand away. No one had ever asked me. They had asked why but never how it felt.

"When I was small it was a dare to myself to test my mettle and magic. To make myself invincible."

"And now?"

"It blots out everything for a second so there is nothing but the pain. It's so vivid I can almost see and taste it. There's a certainty to it in an uncertain world. It keeps me still. It keeps the feathering at bay," I whispered, almost in awe of my honesty.

"Bari, you can control how and when you are hurt only for a very short while. You know deep down no one can control that for good. No matter how much power or magic they possess."

I leaned into him. "I can control this," I said, kissing him.

We were lost in the kiss for a moment. Then he gently made some distance between us, and my lips sought to close it.

"Amantha's coming," he whispered.

I scrambled from his lap and back into my chair just as she appeared, in the same dress she had worn last night to the theater.

"Galatea wants to see us," she said, looking at South and then me, as if she could somehow tell what we had just been doing.

South rose to get the baby.

Amantha returned her gaze to South. "Just me and Bari."

He sat back down, seemingly unaffected.

Galatea surprised us all with an announcement. "First, I'd like to thank Bari and Amantha for going to the Ever After and back for the cause," she began.

I swallowed guilt. I hadn't gone to the Ever After for the Entente. I'd gone for South.

"And I must give special thanks to Amantha for removing all of the hoard of Rooks' objects while the Rooks were occupied with King Waid's travels to the Ever After."

Galatea lifted her wand, and the courtyard of the Reverie was illuminated, revealing a cache of golden objects, each with stones of varying colors and sizes.

I remembered seeing Amantha with a watch in the palace when I' d come to tell Galatea about South. Amantha had been helping Galatea steal from the Rooks. And she had not mentioned it once to me.

"Amantha was essential to this mission. Her stealth allowed us to take every single object from the Rooks' hoard. And now we will consolidate them."

I glanced at Amantha, who was beaming. Galatea had finally given Amantha her due—but to what end?

Galatea assessed the objects, her smile wide as we all realized what this meant. We'd taken the Rooks' magic.

"What will you do with it?" Amantha ventured.

"We will make all of these objects into one. Now raise your wands."

We all raised our wands obediently as Galatea began to chant.

*All the Rook magic from many become one.*
*Make this gem the strongest under the sun . . .*

As she incanted the spell, the objects lifted up into the air and began to swirl faster and faster around us, rising higher and higher. There was a flash of light and a bang, and the swirling mass became a bright blue gem as tall and wide as one of us.

The gem was suspended in the air, and Galatea moved it closer to her with her wand.

"Thank you, sisters."

"Where will you take it, Galatea?" Freya asked, her perpetually pretty face full of wonder.

"We cannot hide it here. It's better that you do not know. I have a plan. Trust in it; trust in me."

She disappeared with the gem. We looked at one another. A murmur went through us.

There was no dissent, but there were questions. It was my duty to quiet them.

"Galatea has led us to this point. We will follow her all the way to victory," I assured my sisters.

The murmurs stopped. I had taken control.

Still, when we went back to the palace, I wondered aloud to Amantha, "What do you think she's going to do with all that magic?"

I didn't know. But to my surprise, I did care.

# CHAPTER 55

## — FARROW —

Hecate sounded impressed. "She has used the Past as prologue."

"Pardon?"

"Galatea has bested us."

"How?" I asked, still trying to put the pieces together.

"She knew that South could not resist seeing his father, and she used that time to rob the Rook King blind. She has taken all their objects, and their magic will be subject to her will."

"What do we do?"

"We will find a way to get it back, but first there is another fire to put out. We have to stop Bari from killing a Queen."

# CHAPTER 56

## — BARI —

Before we could go home to the cottage, Freya stopped Amantha and me by appearing in the center of the road that wound its way from town to our little cottage. It was strange seeing Freya there in the middle of our made-up life in the Eleventh Queendom. Just as it had been strange seeing any of our sisters the few times they had visited us at the Grays'. Amantha put her arms around Freya, spinning her around and disappearing and reappearing in her excitement. The effect was Freya appearing to spin in the air all alone. As she turned, I noticed how Freya's face looked slightly older and more beautiful than just a couple of nights ago, and she looked even more stunning as she smiled in response to Amantha's enthusiasm.

Both the age and the beauty were the product of spells. One that had arrested her at seventeen, the age she'd been on the day of the Burning, and the other, one that I had cast with my sisters, making her look every bit her real age. She had already been beautiful, but we had also cast a spell to intensify that beauty and make her the most gorgeous in her Queendom, Lasse.

Both spells were important to appeal to the then newly widowed king regent of Lasse, whose daughter, Briar Rose, was now in line for the throne but too young to fill it. As regent, the king was merely holding the title until his daughter was ready. Freya, armed with her beauty, had made quick work of wedding the king and controlling him. But every day her charge grew older, and the regent was ill and slipping in and out of consciousness, drawing Freya perilously close to a time when her stepdaughter could gain and then use the crown against us.

"Amantha, not everyone wants to be thrown around like a rag doll!" I exclaimed. Was Amantha so tired of me that she preferred Freya? Or was every moment spent in the theater just making her more dramatic?

Freya was deposited somewhat gently back on her own two feet. Amantha reappeared beside her, shrugging sheepishly.

"I don't mind. It really is good to see you both again." Freya's smile faded quickly though.

"What is it, Freya?" I asked.

"Come home with me. You must see for yourself."

I sighed. I had bigger problems to allay, but the look on Freya's face could not be ignored. Amantha and I joined hands with her, and we were suddenly in Freya's drawing room.

There was a large mirror there, on which we had cast our spell just a few weeks ago.

"I do not know what happened, but something is amiss." Freya began pacing in front of the mirror.

"What do you mean, sister? You know that we are in the middle of Galatea's plot. I cannot stay long."

"But mine is ruined. Galatea will be so disappointed in me," Freya said, her eyes and voice brimming with tears.

"Just tell us what happened," Amantha interjected.

"I'll let the mirror tell you."

She stood in front of it and asked, "Who is the fairest of them all?"

"There is another . . . ," the mirror intoned.

"Maybe your spell stopped working, Bari."

"Impossible. Maybe you just renewed it wrong—"

"I didn't," Freya answered. "Maybe she was somehow in the room when we cast the spell."

"Why would you think that, and who?"

"Somehow Briar Rose ended up even more beautiful than me. That's who the mirror is referring to. Is this a twist of Fate? Did Hecate do this? Or South? Or Farrow? Now everyone in the whole Queendom will do anything to help protect Briar Rose. She ran away, and I can't find her. And there's more. I sent a huntsman to search for her. He could not resist her beauty, and now he's fallen in love with her!"

"Well, she's out there. Let's make haste."

"What are you going to do?"

"I'm going to finish what you could not."

Galatea appeared suddenly and showed us in the mirror, commenting, "All of your theories are good ones but none of them are correct."

"Some Queens did not think that the Entente alone could help them. They took all the magical help that they could get," I countered.

"Yes, but Briar Rose's mother had her own Rook, and this mirror was his object. She used it to make her wishes. And she wished for her daughter to be so beautiful that the whole Queendom would protect her from any harm," Galatea explained. "The Rook granted that wish. And the closer Briar Rose gets to the crown, the stronger the spell gets. It is so strong that it overshadows ours."

"So what do we do? Break the mirror?" I asked.

"No, a Rook spell cannot be undone by the Entente," Galatea replied.

"What then?" Freya asked.

"We break the girl," Galatea said. She looked squarely at me. "I told you that we would need more of your potions, Bari. We need one now."

I took on the face of an old woman. Hecate had taught us once that no one paid attention to the old, and when they did, they trusted them. I would need Briar Rose to trust me. I performed a locator spell, and then I followed Briar Rose to where she was wandering through the forest.

"Child, what are you doing out here?"

"The woodsman was so kind to me—almost too kind. So I needed a break. I took a walk, and I found myself lost. But now I've found you. Can you tell me the way back to the woodsman's cottage?"

"I am afraid I cannot, but I can offer you something to eat. You must be famished."

I pulled the spelled apple out of my pocket and began to hand it to her. I hesitated. And I never hesitated. I suddenly remembered the moment I had given Cinderella's mother a spelled pie.

She had been in bed. I had brought the pie on a tray. "What is this?" she had asked.

"My mother and sister, we are so grateful for your hospitality. I wanted to make you something," I said, turning my mouth up into a wide smile.

Her face lit up. "Is it made of magic?"

"It is." At the time I had not hesitated. Getting rid of Madame Gray was the only way we could be certain that Mr. Gray would take us in permanently. She was an obstacle in the plot. I was merely performing my duty.

Briar Rose was the same, and yet I gripped the apple, somehow not able to release it to the girl. Inexplicably, South's words from a couple of nights ago pushed themselves into my consciousness: *You have not met all of them. You do not know all of them. You complain that they paint us all with the same brush—and yet you do the same.*

What was wrong with me? Why was I thinking of him at this of all moments?

*We are the injured party. We are the ones who burned and who will burn again—if we do not stop them, if we do not have them in hand,* I'd said.

*The way things were was wrong, the way things are is wrong—we have to make something new.* His words again.

I looked down at the apple in my hand, my fingers pressed so tightly around the fruit that I might leave a mark.

Briar snatched the apple from my hands and took a bite.

"Mmm . . . This is the most delicious apple I have ever had. You are a strange one. You are the first person not to moon over me in ages. I rather like the feeling—"

Before she could finish, she was falling. I caught her and carefully laid her on the ground. Then I left. It was done. Why did I not feel victorious?

"It's too late for something new," I whispered to myself.

# CHAPTER 57

## — FARROW —

I looked at Hecate, whose eyes were closed, and she was frowning.

"Mother, what is it?"

She opened her eyes and produced her mirror. In it, Galatea explained to Freya, Amantha, and Bari what had gone wrong with Freya's stepdaughter and how they planned to deal with Briar Rose.

Hecate turned to me and explained, "Briar Rose's story began with a wish. That wish was not granted by one of the Entente. It was granted by a Rook. But the Rook twisted the wish. Briar Rose is not just beautiful. She is so beautiful that her face inspires people to do dangerous things. She is so beautiful that anyone she encounters will want to help her, want to shield her. It makes the men in the forest protect her. Her beauty is so powerful that it is a defense against the Queen. But it is no match for Galatea and the full Entente."

As my mother recounted Briar Rose's story, it occurred to me that my gift—the gift to grant wishes—was more aligned with the Rooks than with the Entente. Was my magic like theirs? Was it trickster magic as Galatea seemed to attest? Or was Hecate right, and magic was just magic?

"Briar Rose is safe for now, but not for long," Hecate told me.

"So what do we do?" South asked, suddenly appearing behind

us. I felt a wave of relief. Whatever Galatea had planned, we had two Fates on our side. That had to be enough.

"We find Briar Rose," I suggested.

"It's too late for that," Hecate said, reaching for her mirror.

Bari had indeed been quicker than us. We watched in horror as she spelled the girl, who fell. Bari began to chant.

*The fairest girl of all must fall,*
*So that an Entente may rise in her stead, once and for all.*

An idea occurred to me that I didn't like, but I could think of no other.

"Hecate, you always taught us how careful we have to be with spells and more careful still with wishes. I think we can use the spell that Bari just cast against them."

South repeated the spell, frowning in confusion.

"What do you have in mind?" he asked.

"We break the Rook's wish."

"We make her ugly?"

"We lift the Rook magic so that when people see her, she is an ordinary beauty, not a magical one."

"Then we need a Rook," South said thoughtfully.

"We're both part Rook." I asked Hecate hopefully, "Is that enough?"

"A pure Rook," Hecate said with assurance.

"You can't mean Hark," I said.

"Do you know any other Rook who owes us a favor?" South smiled. "I wish for a Rook—"

Hark appeared with Cinderella. "You wished?"

"Brother, I need a favor," South said.

"I owe you my life. I think I can manage a little favor," Hark affirmed. We quickly explained Briar Rose's misfortune to Hark and Cinderella.

"But there may be a wrinkle. Rooks' gifts are not meant to be returned. A wish granted by a Rook is by design not so easily counter-wished," Hark insisted.

"You have two Fates and a wish granter at your disposal. I am sure that our magic combined with yours must offer some remedy," South insisted.

"The best way to break a spell is to give a kiss," Hark suggested.

"A kiss?" South asked, clearly surprised.

"Not just any kiss, a kiss of pure love. And for a girl who is sleeping like the dead, that might prove a bit more complicated," Hark explained.

South frowned as he got his brother's meaning. "Not just complicated, damn near impossible when the whole world is in love with her physical beauty. They do not know her."

"Someone does," Hecate said.

South added, "Her father."

"But he isn't conscious," Hark countered.

"Even if Briar Rose's father isn't completely with us, the body holds a memory. I believe if he kisses her, then she will come back. And maybe he will as well," Hecate counseled.

I looked over at Hecate. I thought about all the years she had been with me in ash. My mother had found a way to be with me even after death. If Briar Rose's father loved her even half as much as Hecate loved me . . .

"Her father doesn't have to wake to save her. He just has to be there," I said, my idea crystallizing.

Understanding, Hecate put her hands together.

South and I shared a look, and I assumed he read my Present.

Hark shrugged, clearly feeling a touch left out.

"Have you ever known anyone who walked in their sleep, Hark?"

Hark's eyes widened in recognition, and the corner of his mouth turned up in a smile.

Hecate and South took out their wands, and using the power of the Present, South placed himself in the old king regent's dreams. Meanwhile, Hecate physically put the old man next to Briar Rose in the forest. The king, seeing her in his dream, knelt down and kissed her. And they both awakened at once. The Entente spell was broken.

We had saved Briar Rose, and I felt the magic surging through me again. Hecate had said that magic was neither good nor evil. I wondered if I granted a bad wish, would I get the same amount of power from the act?

"Can you remove the curse of beauty?" Briar Rose asked after she was safely in the palace again.

Hecate shook her head no. "I am afraid you will forever be the fairest of them all."

"Then what are we to do? Lock her away? How will she live? How will she love? How will she rule? She will have an unfair, undue influence on the Queendom," I exclaimed, feeling for the poor girl.

Briar looked at me dutifully. "Can you make me less fair?"

In all the wishes I had ever heard, Briar Rose was the first human to ever wish herself less pretty.

"She cannot rule. Even though she would be the best kind of queen, she would have too much influence." Hecate echoed my conclusions.

"Why can you not reverse the wish?" I asked

"You cannot give back a gift to a Rook," Hecate reminded us.

"What is done is not to be undone. A wish is from now to the Ever After—and back again," Hark said almost sadly.

"What if someone who had enough power could wish Briar Rose free?" I asked, looking at South and my mother. Together, maybe we could break this spell.

Hecate caught my look and spoke forcefully. "Countering a spell like that will take more than you and me and South, I'm afraid. Though I wish it weren't so. That magic would take us, plus the power of the other Les Soeurs and the rest of the Entente. And we full well know that more than one would never ever, ever agree to it."

"But there may be another way," South offered.

Hark glanced over at South, clearing his throat before speaking. "Even if I could do it, I do not think it would be in our best interest right now to make Briar Rose less beautiful. Every person in the Queendom is motivated to protect her. That will keep Galatea from making another attempt—that will keep her safe. As long as Briar is the fairest of them all, she will be safe from your sisters and safe from magic."

"What happens now?" South interjected.

"When the time is appropriate, Briar Rose will become Queen, but in the meantime, she needs a way to stay connected with her people and remain safe," my mother explained. "We must act very carefully."

"The mirror," I suggested. "It will allow her to communicate with her future subjects, but it will also reverse her image, so the public will not be subjected to the unadulterated view of her beauty. If she is to learn how to be a good Queen she will need access to the people, and she can do so safely through the mirror."

Briar Rose protested, "I want to be able to touch my people. I want to see them face-to-face."

"I'd rather you be alive to see them at all," Hecate cut in.

Briar hated the idea. But she finally agreed to it.

"One day we will right this wrong," I said to her with a confidence that I did not entirely feel. *One day we will right* all *the wrongs*, I said to myself—it was part assertion, part wish.

# CHAPTER 58

## — BARI —

I returned triumphant. "Try the question now," I demanded.

Freya asked the mirror, "Who is the fairest of them all?"

The mirror responded to her, "You are."

We all sighed in relief.

But a moment later, the mirror made a coughing sound, and then uttered, "I'm afraid I was mistaken . . . There is another."

"Show her to me!" Galatea exclaimed.

We could see Briar Rose in the glass, very much awake, her father by her side. They were hand in hand.

"What is the meaning of this? He has not stirred for years," Amantha said.

I could not speak. I was stunned. This wasn't supposed to happen.

The mirror revealed all to Galatea, who recounted what had occurred. "It appears that the king regent somehow walked in his sleep to his daughter, and he kissed her forehead. The kiss apparently woke them both from their slumber."

"This could not have happened without magic," Amantha assessed.

"This couldn't have happened without Farrow," Galatea corrected.

We had lost. The townspeople were already on their way, bringing Briar Rose back to the palace, with her now-lucid father.

Farrow and Hecate had placed a mirror in the square in front of the palace. In it, Briar Rose's image could be seen, and she could answer questions from the townspeople. They gathered around the polished glass. It was a novelty to them, and they looked at it full of worship. The people loved their princess, and they would love her more as Queen.

"We could break that mirror," I suggested.

"And cause an uprising that would draw the attention of the other Queens," Galatea countered, squashing the proposed remedy.

"We need to leave before they discover that you are Entente and that you are the cause." Galatea's voice was taut.

"So we retreat?" Amantha asked.

"For the last time, my loves, for the last time . . . ," Galatea said.

We traveled home. Back at the palace, we stood awkwardly, Amantha and I avoiding each other's gaze.

Galatea assessed the situation and finally broke the silence. "I must prepare for tonight's ball. Perhaps it would do you both good to attend yourselves this evening. I can give the maids the night off."

She had given me an out, and I tried to make my tone calm and respectful as I spoke. “And what should I do, Galatea, now that I have failed you?”

“I have the perfect room for you here. You can nurse your wounds and attend the balls, with a new face, of course.” Galatea paused and her features sharpened. “When you are ready, you can go back to the Queendom and observe Briar Rose and her father’s every move. We will find a new approach. However, I will need some time to devise a new plan.”

# CHAPTER 59

## — FARROW —

We had won, but Hecate looked south of happy.

She tried to force a smile, but I knew something else was coming.

Meanwhile, South and Hark were having a bit of a moment, and Hecate was determined not to interrupt it.

"I don't think I ever thanked you properly for saving me in the Ever After."

"You did not have to. What he was trying to do was wrong."

"But I am sure that everything that you have heard about me is awful."

South began to protest, but Hark rolled on.

"And all true."

"I make up my own mind about people. Especially family."

"Father has proven himself a bit of a disappointment. I wish I could say that won't always be the case."

"Well, Hark, so far *you* have not been. And I'd say that's a start."

They beamed at each other, and my heart swelled for South. After losing Iolanta all over again, having a brother had to be some consolation, even if that brother was Hark.

Just then, I could hear a distant, alarming wish. It was made by Lavendra.

# CHAPTER 60

## — BARI —

Perhaps it was the loss, but suddenly all I could think about was what South and Farrow had said, and how it had hurt me. They had both in their own ways suggested that I was monstrous.

South's assessment of me had been in my head when I spelled Briar Rose. Farrow had successfully interfered with the plot. South had lied to me and attempted to interfere with my heart.

I would show them both what a monster I could be.

I transformed into a gaggle of geese and traveled to the Thirteenth Queendom. When I got to the cottage, Lavendra was alone.

I transformed into Farrow's form.

"Oh, it's you," Lavendra said with a wide smile. "Farrow, what are you doing here?"

"I just had a craving for some honey."

The Couterie were known for being able to read body language—being able to read people. That was their nonmagical magic.

Her face fell suddenly, and she looked afraid. But in a blink she was smiling again. "Let me make us some tea with honey that I harvested this morning."

She turned toward the kitchen, and while she chatted evenly, she slipped a knife from the butcher block on the counter into her pocket.

I looked down at my hands. One of my fingers had transformed into feathers. It wasn't necessarily her acute sense of observation that had exposed me. It could have been my own body that had betrayed my real identity.

With a wave of my wand, I lifted the knife from the girl's pocket and brought it to my nonfeathered hand.

"I think I want some of that honey direct from the hive."

"Who are you? Because you aren't Farrow," Lavendra said bravely.

The girl tried to run, but then I pulled her back with my wand and made her face me.

# CHAPTER 61

## — FARROW —

Lavendra?" I called.

She was in the middle of the hive, but she wasn't wearing her beekeeper suit.

"Lavendra? What are you doing? Where is your suit?"

When she finally spoke, I could hear a buzzing that seemed to be modulating her voice. A single bee escaped her mouth and climbed out onto her lip.

"You're not Lavendra— What did you do to her, Bari? Where is she?"

"If you don't touch my things, I won't touch your things."

"You don't have to do this. I don't care about her!" I lied.

Bari laughed at me, and it hurt just as it had when we were young, but even more so because I knew she held Lavendra's Fate in her hands.

"But you do care. You're here trying to protect a human who spent years belittling you."

"Where is she?" Bari pointed, and I swallowed hard as I took in the beehive some distance behind us. How had I not noticed? The hive had tripled in size.

As I raced toward it as fast as my feet could carry me, I noticed there was movement within. But was the motion the bees, or Lavendra herself? I felt a pang in my chest that echoed what I felt when Bari told me it was she who had killed Cinderella's parents and not Galatea.

"They won't hurt her, unless I want them to. It's not the same as a wish exactly. It's more like I am their Queen. I can make them do exactly what I want, when I want, without someone else having to wish it for me." Bari's tone was taunting.

Panting, I listened hard, beneath the buzzing, for Lavendra's wishes.

*Please help me... I tried to not bring you here. I am sorry*, Lavendra wished.

"Just let her go. I don't care about her. She means nothing to me," I cried out to Bari.

"That's why you traveled across Queendoms? Just to check in on her and grant her petty wishes?" Bari asked, her tone mocking me.

"Are you threatening me?"

"Like I said, I just want you to take your hands off my things."

"And your things include South."

"I was actually thinking of the plot, and what you and Hecate did back there with Briar Rose. It's interesting that your mind went to South—"

"You don't want him. Why do you care what I do with him?"

Bari paused.

"Or maybe you do. Have you grown bored of your prince now that South is both Fate and Rook?"

"Just stay away from him."

"He doesn't deserve to be hurt again."

"Like you hurt him?"

She was not wrong. I had hurt South when I rejected him.

"This isn't you, Bari. Whatever you are doing here you can undo—"

"I haven't done anything yet. They tell me that you have taken very good care of the beekeeper and her love, but I also know that she never took very good care of you. Doesn't a part of you want her punished? I know that you miss being able to act without a wish. Why don't I just grant this one? It'll just be a little sting. Or rather a thousand of them. After a few seconds, she'll be completely numb." With the last, Bari's voice had shifted from bullying to teasing.

"Please don't, Bari. Please," I begged.

"I will never understand you. You defend them all, even the ones who have done you damage."

With that, she transformed into thousands of bees and flew away.

I approached gingerly and waved my wand, lifting the hive gently away from Lavendra, who collapsed to the ground.

She was pale as a ghost and looked lifeless. But as I got closer, I could see that she was still breathing.

I knelt down beside her.

"I didn't mean what I said, I do care about you."

Her eyes fluttered open.

"I know. My bees didn't sting me, not even once," she said as I helped her to her feet.

"Were you . . . playing dead?"

"I wish I was that clever. I think I must have fainted."

"That's understandable. You were very brave."

"All that practice staying completely still at the Couterie," she said with a bitter laugh.

I helped her back into the cottage. "I am so sorry I brought danger to your door," I told her.

"That wasn't you—that was her. Whoever she is she was pretty scary—but she was scared too."

"You think?"

"She cares about that boy she mentioned and you and the bees. In my experience, if you've ever lost anyone or anything, you are more scared to lose what you still have."

"Lavendra," I began, assuming she was talking about her brief separation from Tork, but she could just as well have been talking about the life she could have had as a Couterie.

Before I could press, she spoke again. "Go, go save the Queendoms. I wish . . . I wish Tork were here."

I granted it, and he appeared, still holding a hoe for hay.

Lavendra and I both began to laugh.

"This is what you do with your magic. Interrupt my work and poke fun at me . . ."

"Lavendra's been through quite a scare. I need to make sure that this never happens again. I'll be back, I promise."

I left and returned quickly with Mother, and we cast a protection spell around the cottage and its lands.

"That should keep you safe for the night. We'll be back to renew it again," I promised.

"Thank you, Farrow," they said in unison. Tork held Lavendra's hand tightly. Whatever they were missing, they had each other.

Hecate reached for my hand and her wand, and we were about to travel back to the palace, when Tork stopped us.

"Wait," he said, and then whispered something to Lavendra, who nodded.

"I should not have turned down your request. We see now that there is still a role for us in the Queendoms. We may not be Couterie, but perhaps we can aid the Resistance."

I thanked them both, and I shared a look with my mother. She blinked innocently, but I sensed that she had known this outcome all along.

# PART IV

# CHAPTER 62

## — BARI —

Today we take the next step with Thiago—we move the needle," South announced in the morning. If he'd known what I was up to last night, his face did not betray him.

"How?"

"He needs to feel what it is to almost lose you. The pressure of time is not enough for him. He must feel that your life is in the balance. Do you trust me, Bari—with your life?"

"With my life, yes. With the plot, no. But I think your plan is sound."

Later in the day we set about nearly killing me, and South was right; it had the desired effect.

"Make it look real. Don't hesitate," I instructed.

"Watch your feathers," he countered.

We had planned and choreographed the stunt perfectly, but South, who did not hesitate when we were alone together, paused now when it came to putting my life in danger.

"You could turn . . . ," he warned.

I smiled. "You're worried about me."

"Just listen to me for once. You may be magical, but you are not invincible. I will not lose you."

I kissed him on the cheek, then immediately regretted it because it was not a gesture of passion but rather of affection.

He smiled wider, as if he knew the distinction too. "I'll be just out of sight."

He was not going to be the hero here. I was supposed to "die" and be revived by Thiago's kiss. Further proof to Thiago that he and I were meant to be.

I had suggested that we take a walk by our lake. By chance the lake had frozen over in an early frost. I convinced Thiago it was safe to skate there, that I did it all the time. As proof, I ran ahead of him onto the ice and pirouetted. Thiago clapped. Then there was a terrible cracking sound, and I fell through the ice. I didn't like water the way I liked the sky, but we needed a plausible accident.

When the cold water greeted me, I realized too late that South had been right. My instinct was to turn to my feathers. If I transformed into birds I could fly out of the water before I sank, but then I would also reveal myself to Thiago, and all that I had done to prepare would have been in vain. So I surrendered myself to the water, and for the first time in my life I was waiting to be saved. I sank down, down, down, but I could still see the light and the circle of water dancing above me where I had broken through the ice.

I could hear Thiago calling my name, and then there was a giant branch protruding into the water.

"Bari, just take it and hold on. I'll pull you up."

I reached for the branch, but my hands were not flesh; they were feathers. I was in trouble.

"Take the branch, please . . . ," a voice said.

Then, "I'm coming in to get you—"

There was a splash, and a few seconds later a pair of arms lifted me out of the water. But it wasn't Thiago. I found myself in South's arms.

"It's me. I'm here. You're all right. You're all right. I've got you now," South whispered. He was drenched. His eyes were wide with relief as they met mine.

I felt a wave of exhaustion like I'd never felt before wash over me, and I closed my eyes.

When I opened them, South was gone, and Thiago was at my side.

"Thiago . . ."

"You fell through the ice. I was trying to save you. Before I could, another young man, he jumped in—no, he flew. That boy, he had wings!"

"Wings?"

Thiago looked around, confused. "Where did he go? I need to thank him."

South had saved me. South put my well-being before the plot.

"I know my timing is the worst. And I have no idea how this would work. I am an actor, and we make notoriously horrible spouses. And yet, I still dare ask if you would take a chance on me. Then, I will make every attempt to be a far better man than the others who have walked the boards."

"I do believe you mean every word . . . ," I said, studying him. "And you are a far better human than any I have encountered."

"Is that a yes?"

"Yes, that's a yes," I said, and then he kissed me. I had won. I had won his heart, but mine was elsewhere.

When I finally got home, Amantha was absent. But South was waiting for me, his hair still wet from the lake.

"You were not supposed to do that."

He shrugged. "Wasn't I? Would you have rather I allowed you to drown? Because my heart could not bear it."

I ignored the part about his heart and the look of longing in his eyes.

"In any case, the plan worked. I need to tell Galatea that it is done."

"It can wait till morning. You need to get out of those wet things," he said, already helping me out of my dress.

# CHAPTER 63

## — BARI —

When I arrived at the palace in the morning intending to update Galatea with my success, I came face-to-face with my own face. The spelled maid who had taken my place was rushing down the hall heading for the throne room when she spotted me.

She had been skeptical the day that Galatea had cast her to take my place, but now she looked positively comfortable in my visage.

"You . . . ," she said, sounding a bit confused. "What are you doing here? You're not supposed to be here for another two days," she continued.

"Oh, Galatea wanted to see me."

"But she's got the meeting of the Queen's Council, which I am late for by the way."

I had come to give Galatea my news, but it suddenly hit me that Galatea had not really been giving us all her news about her success with the council, particularly with Helene. Suddenly I wanted to know what was going on in the council.

Galatea had been making so many moves without me. She'd included Amantha in the heist of the Rook objects but not me. I wanted, needed to know where I stood. Galatea had said she'd forgiven me for my indiscretion with South, but did she still trust me?

"Are you sure you want to go like that?" I asked, my hand gesturing toward the skirt of her dress.

"Like what?" She looked down. I had released a cloud of moths while she spoke. They had made quick work of the fabric.

"Oh no, my dress! It's as if a hundred moths ate through it at once. How did I not notice?"

"You should go back and change. In fact, perhaps you need a new outfit altogether. I'll take your place at the meeting."

"You would do that for me?"

"It would be my pleasure, and I won't even mention this little indiscretion to the others."

When I slipped into the throne room, I found Amantha's doppelgänger and sat beside her. But when she turned to me, I realized she was the real Amantha.

"Why didn't you tell me you were coming?" I asked.

"Why didn't you tell me the same?"

Galatea cleared her throat and looked squarely at us, clearly realizing we both had made our way here. She smiled as if she was pleased to see us.

Amantha waved happily in return, happy to have passed this test of our mettle. I found it out of character for Galatea, who usually gave orders and expected us to follow them rather than presenting problems for us to solve. But perhaps this was Galatea trusting us, allowing us to act independently of her.

Some part of me was just relieved that despite her punishing schedule, Galatea apparently was not too busy with her daily dances to keep an eye on the plan. She'd stolen the Rooks' hoard, and now she was ready to serve up Helene to the council. So much had happened in such a short period of time, perhaps I had been too critical of Galatea: the balls, the crown, the pomp and circumstance were all a ruse. She was still very much our Galatea, and we were still on the cusp of another victory, another throne in our grasp. I couldn't wait to tell her my news about Thiago.

Galatea had ostensibly summoned the Queen's Council together to negotiate peace and to introduce herself, but there was of course another reason. It was here, at the end of the summit, that she planned on revealing the secret, one that would change the world.

The Queens and the few members of the court they had brought were gathered in the throne room, when Galatea brought in the doctor.

Queen Helene and the others recognized her. She was the one every Queen turned to when they had an illness or a birth.

"You all know the doctor. She is known for her secrecy, but just this once I am asking her to break her confidence for the betterment of the Queendoms."

The Queens gasped.

"We do not wish to hear her confidence. Our very system is based on privacy," Queen Osprey of the Eighth Queendom spoke first.

There were crowns nodding in agreement all around the throne room.

"And that is the problem. I promised when I took the throne to remove the Black Glass and let the light in. It is time for the truth and nothing but," Galatea declared, and the Queens gasped again.

"What truth have you for us?" one of the Queens ventured to ask. "And how can we be sure that it is the truth and not a spell?"

There were more gasps.

Galatea hushed them, then spoke. "That is a fair question."

She paused for a dramatic beat, then continued.

"To make things fair, I will cast a spell on all of us, and we will all be compelled to tell the truth for a few moments."

I could see from the looks on their faces, from shock to concern, that all the Queens would have objected to the spell. But Galatea did not hesitate; she was already waving her wand.

Queen Papillion of Blenheim exclaimed, "It is not working."

"Let's see then. Queen Papillion, tell Queen Charlotte what you think of her dress," Galatea suggested.

"It's positively awful—I did not mean that," Queen Papillion said, then covered her mouth.

"Queen Verna, tell Queen Nostra what you did with her crops last year."

"We set them on fire. We needed the water," Queen Verna deadpanned.

"You what?"

"I am sorry. I will make reparations."

'That's enough. We would like to hear from the doctor now," Galatea commanded.

"What is the question you intend to ask me?"

"I would like you to tell us about the son of the Eleventh Queendom, Nimolet."

Queen Helene exclaimed, "This is some kind of trick. I and my progeny are the only children of that Queendom!"

"There is another. Your mother, knowing what could become of him, had me hide him away and declare him stillborn," said the doctor.

"I don't believe you."

"I wish I could lie, but I am compelled to tell the truth."

The other Queens reacted.

"We all know that Prince Mather was an anomaly."

The doctor spoke again. "I am a woman of science. The fact that only two Queens have given birth to males in hundreds of years seems a scientific improbability. If there are two, there may be more."

"Queen Helene, what do you say?"

"If there is proof that I have a brother, then I will embrace him. If this is folly, we will rain hell on the Entente."

"That seems fair," Galatea said diplomatically.

"What else can you tell me of the boy's whereabouts? If there was a birth, where is the child now?" Queen Helene asked.

"There was a woman at court who was also a lover of the theater. She took the baby and took her troupe on the road, vowing only to spend one week every year in your Queendom," explained the doctor.

Helene's expression shifted, and she whispered, "Thiago . . ."

One of the other Queens asked, "Who is this Thiago?"

"Mother took us to the theater every year, without fail. She was enamored with this child performer. I liked him too. He grew up to be a bit of a star . . . I will need confirmation from his adoptive mother."

She stood up and bowed to the other Queens.

"I must take my leave. I need to know now." Her face a mess of emotion, Helene added, "It gladdens my heart to have more family when Mother has long been gone. As for the crown, it does not belong to me. I will give it to its rightful owner."

Queen Helene, for a human, seemed to be genuinely without fault, even under a truth spell.

Amantha and I slipped off to the balcony.

"We must go," I whispered to her. "There is much to do before we meet her again in the Eleventh Queendom."

# CHAPTER 64

## — BARI —

We waited in the wings for the truth to come out. I cast a distraction spell for privacy for me and South. Thiago was onstage finishing his performance. South and I were behind the curtain watching him.

South asked, "What happens if he doesn't want it? The throne?"

"Everyone wants it," I countered.

"I don't want it. And down deep I don't think that you want it either. The girl I remember led us places. I didn't always like where, but I don't think that this is what you dreamed of. You wanted magic with no limits. To see what you could do, what you could become. You weren't interested in humans; you were interested in you."

"That's true. But then one day they tore us apart, literally. They set Hecate on fire. They peeled you from the sky. Amantha barely came back from the Ever After . . ." I touched my face. "I never would have been interested in them, but they took from us and they must pay."

"That actor had nothing to do with my wings or your face or any of the injuries the Entente suffered that day and all the days since. He's lived an honorable life. He seems to be honorable still. Why put him on this course, to hurt or be hurt?"

"You're right. I like him as much as I like any human. But he does not get to be safe from us. We did not get to be safe from his kind," I said firmly.

"You know in your heart that that's not fair or just," South protested.

I laughed then. "How can you not understand that better than anyone? You have lived in both worlds and yet you remain so optimistic and naive. Is that your Rook blood? How do you not know that 'fair' and 'just' are just make-believe? They are foreign, imaginary lands that we will never ever reach."

"So what would you have us do, never even try? That doesn't begin to sound like the Bari I knew once upon a time."

"Just because you knew me as a child, South, doesn't mean that you know me now."

South blinked hard. Had I hurt his feelings?

"You dismiss my assessment of you. And yet, you are guilty of judging me on the same basis. Despite my efforts to the contrary, you still see the boy you derided for being human."

I paused, considering.

"I don't think you're that little boy anymore. That's not what I see."

"Then what do you see?"

"You know what's real? Power and magic and blood."

"And this . . . this is also real. Maybe even more so." He stepped closer, and he kissed my neck. And I allowed it, before pushing him away.

"There is no time for this. There is no room for this," I whispered to him.

Just then, Queen Helene swept onstage from the other side of the curtain and greeted Thiago.

"Queen Helene. What an honor . . ."

He bowed to her.

She surprised the audience and Thiago himself by bowing to him.

"I don't understand," he said, seemingly forgetting the audience. "You are my brother. You are the king."

Behind the curtain we could hear a scramble. Brianna was ordering the curtain dropped.

I used my wand and did it myself. After the curtain fell, Helene bowed to Thiago again.

"You can find me at the palace. We will talk more," she vowed.

And then she swept as quickly offstage as she had on.

# CHAPTER 65

## — BARI —

Watching his face, I realized that this was not how he should learn the truth. But it had to be done. For Galatea, for the Entente . . .

"Mother!"

I could see the struggle in the face of the woman Thiago knew as his mother.

"This is not the way I wanted you to find out," Brianna said quietly as she moved to stand in front of him.

I rushed to his side and took his hand.

"Did you ever want me to find out?"

"I swore I would never tell. It was my promise to the Queen, your mother. But I never would have told you. I was so very happy being your mother."

"How? Why?"

"I couldn't have children. I was a member of your mother's court. She did not want what happened in the First Queendom to happen here. The unrest of the people, and then all that Magrit did to protect Prince Mather . . . Her intentions were good, but she got carried away. It seemed a cautionary tale. Your mother loved you so very much. She thought that this was better for you, safer for you and for the Queendom. I am so sorry, my love," Brianna said as her eyes brimmed with tears.

Thiago stood rigid as he listened. Finally, he spoke. "So my life, our life in the theater, all the audiences that we had with her, all her encouragement had nothing to do with my talent? It was her guilt . . . ?"

His mother shook her head violently.

"Never guilt, always love. The Queen, she wanted you to have a life that was not of toil but of art. And she was so very proud of you."

"I thought I had won my spot in the lights with my talent, but it was pity and guilt and matriarchy—"

"Do not doubt your talent. You're the finest actor I have ever seen in any Queendom. And I say that not as your mother but as an artist . . . as a thespian."

"No, Mother, you are the greatest actress in all the Queendoms. You completely fooled me," he said, walking away.

His mother began to crumple. I was surprised as Amantha flickered into place and approached him, stopping him from leaving the stage.

His eyes widened in wonder.

"Not you too. You are Entente? Is everything a lie?"

"No, you are true, Thiago. Your mother is true. Look at her. You do not mean your harsh words. I know how much you love her. When we were alone, you gave her credit for all that you are. I have never seen a child prouder of his mother," Amantha said gently.

"But she is not my maker," he protested flatly.

"She is the one who taught you to act, who taught you to love . . . I should know. I have benefitted from that training—I mean onstage, of course."

I could see him melt and look at her. He crossed to his mother. He wrapped his arms around her.

# CHAPTER 66

## — BARI —

I led a shell-shocked Thiago backstage.

"There is something I must tell you, Thiago. After I am done, you decide if you still want me to keep this," I said, putting the ring he had given me in his hand.

"I thought I was the dramatic one. There is nothing you can say or do to tear us apart."

"I am not who I say I am. I came here and so did my sister in hopes of knowing you. Before the truth came out, I did not expect to fall in love with you. You have to believe me—"

"What are you talking about? You're not making any sense."

"I am Bari, princess of the First Queendom and a member of the Entente. And Amantha is also princess of the First Queendom and a member of the Entente. We are sisters."

"Amantha told me that she is Entente. I don't know why I didn't put the pieces together. Did you and Amantha come here to spy on me? Why? To you I was just an actor. Yes, a beloved and talented one. Still, how did you know I was of any significance to any Queendom?"

I had watched him with Amantha, and the fact that she was Entente seemed to pale in comparison to the revelation about his parentage. But now, upon reflection or upon knowing that I was also Entente, he seemed livid.

"That is where you are wrong. You are everything to this Queendom. You are the rightful heir. You are a prince, Thiago."

"There is only one prince in all the Queendoms, and he is in exile," Thiago countered, shaking his head.

"You have written about the state of the Queendoms. You know what peril a male child faces. Your mother knew it too, and she sought to save you from it—"

"Enough. I believe you."

He stopped and then he approached me.

"You do not have to decide right now. I know that I have just presented you with so much. I know that I have lied to you," I said as innocently as I could manage.

"I should have known you were magic. Thank you for telling me the truth." He took my hand and slipped the ring back onto my finger.

"What are you doing?" I had not expected him to accept the facts so easily, but he did.

Perhaps, with his ego, he had always believed he was meant for greater things.

But he seemed somehow unsurprised by all the developments—or perhaps he wanted to hold on to me because in an instant his whole world had changed.

I watched him in amazement. Thiago was doing the strangest thing. He was packing.

"What are you doing?"

"Packing. If I leave now maybe, just maybe, I can get out of the Queendom before the guard notices."

"You want to leave? You just found out that you are the prince. All of this belongs to you."

"There is just one thing that I want in this place."

He stopped packing and walked toward me purposefully, the expression in his eyes full of longing. I'd seen the same in South when he looked at me while I thought he was under the spell.

"Thiago, you are sweet but you're not thinking this through."

"How is that?"

He arched his eyebrow, which reminded me of the way he looked at me before he thought he'd gotten to know me. Before he trusted me.

"Your plays question everything. You have an opportunity to change things if you take the crown," I said, trying another tack: flattery.

Thiago shook his head again.

"Yes, I see opportunities for the Crown to improve. Hells, I see ways for all the Queendoms to improve," Thiago said, not completely immune to a compliment on his work.

"And now you can be that change."

"Art can change things. The people offer up their hearts and minds to me willingly."

"I do not disagree. However, art takes a lot longer than the Crown."

"I love what I do. It's who I am."

"Then you can be the king who stars in his own productions. You make the rules, my love . . . my lord."

"After all these years, I have family. I am not going to take the crown away from my sister. She is a fine Queen."

At every turn he had a new excuse to not take up the crown.

"She is a stranger. You would be superior to her."

"I've made up my mind. Now it's time for you to make up yours. Are you coming with me, my love, or do you only want me if I am a prince?"

I looked at him for a long beat. I made up my mind. I had tried it South's way, but it had not worked. I would have to use the spell again.

I kissed him then, knowing that my kiss was a weapon. And regretting it more than I imagined I would.

"I thought we could do this the easy way, not the hard way . . ."

"What are you talking about, Bari? What's that in your hand?"

"Haven't you ever seen a wand before?" I lifted mine and said firmly, "May my will be yours."

"This isn't funny, my love."

"I know. But this is what you get when you've fallen in love with an Entente . . ."

He took me in for a moment, his eyes widening, recognizing what I was about to do. "How can you bespell me and to what end? You know I sympathize with the Entente."

"I believe you would have, which is one of the reasons you will make an excellent king. That is the intent of the spell I will cast."

"I have already told you that I will not do it."

"You want to take the throne from your sister. You want to be the best king that you can be—with me by your side."

"I want to be an actor. I want to keep my life as it is. That includes you, I don't care what you call yourself. Or what sect you come from. I want you by my side."

"You will be an excellent king. You will be my king. And I will be your Queen. You will send your sister into exile. She will be safer there."

"Safe from you?"

"She has nothing to fear from me. My sisters and my mother may not be as kind."

I understood him completely then. He loved his craft of acting like I loved mine of magic. He thought it was his calling, and I was taking that away from him. And he feared for his new family, even though he barely knew them.

# CHAPTER 67

## — BARI —

K-EEEEE-SSSS," baby Dora wailed.

South kissed her on the forehead, and Dora cooed again. And I suppressed a smile.

"I don't see why we have to give her back," Amantha said.

"You know we can't keep her, Amantha," I replied.

"You called her 'her,' " South observed.

"What else would I call her?"

Amantha and South shared a smirk.

A short time later, Amantha and I unspelled the baby.

*Forget your voice*
*Until you are the right age,*
*But remember that once upon a time you had not one, not two,*
*but three mage.*

Suddenly Amantha surprised me by adding to the spell.

*And if you are ever in need,*
*Call on us as friends, indeed.*

I surprised myself by not objecting.

The baby gave my finger one final squeeze, and Amantha tickled her side.

"We will miss you, Dora," South said, speaking for all of us.

An hour later, we took a carriage to the palace to hand her over. Already reeling from learning she had a new brother, Helene was shocked to see that Galatea's daughters were her nannies.

"How did I not recognize you back at the palace?" she said, her face marred by anger and guilt.

"Don't blame yourself. We cast a face-altering spell so even when you met us, you did not wholly remember our faces. It was not your fault. Your motherhood is not in question."

She was not placated by my explanation. Instead, her eyebrows knitted closer together, her ire growing. "Give her to me. Get your hands off my Dora."

Helene glared at me as I placed the baby gently in her arms. She cradled Dora close and examined her, as if to see if she had been harmed by us in any way. I felt unreasonably affronted by the idea that we would cause Dora harm.

"You posed as my nanny while your mother planned to dethrone me. Were you to hold the child for ransom if I did not comply?"

"It wasn't like that," I protested, but even as I said it, I knew it *was* like that. Galatea, despite being seemingly distracted by the trappings of the Crown, had planned for every contingency.

"At first we thought she was a little monster, but we grew rather fond of her," Amantha added unhelpfully.

"I know that this is a lot for you to digest, but I am afraid that there is a little more," I muttered.

Helene's eyes widened as I told her that Thiago and I were engaged.

She cuddled the baby closer and ordered me out of her palace.

As I was preparing to leave, there was a commotion outside, and South and I rose and looked out the window, the velvet drapery concealing us. It was Thiago arguing with Amantha in the courtyard.

"You must be quiet. Bari will be back at any minute," she warned.

"You lied to me."

"So did Bari, your fiancée."

"Somehow it matters more to me that you did."

When I heard this, something clicked into place. It was the love spell that had kept him anchored to me, had made him slip the ring back onto my finger. His true heart was with Amantha, and since she had not spelled him to love her and he still did, that was where his anger was, where this hurt was, where the recriminations were.

Would Amantha tell Thiago about the spell? Would she break the Entente's confidence? I could see by the look upon her face that she was torn. But she held fast.

"We were sent to find out what kind of man you were, what kind of prince you might be. We were doing it for our Queendom and for all of them. I did not expect to fall in love with you."

"Are you saying you love me?" he asked softly.

His anger had subsided, and there was hope in its place.

Amantha paused and flickered away.

South and I stepped back from the window. He whispered, "You'd better make some more of that potion, Princess. I think it's definitely worn off for the lover out in the courtyard."

We traveled back to the cottage. I stormed into my room and he followed. Frustrated at him and at myself for the tangled web that we now found ourselves in, I pushed him onto the bed and kissed him hard.

I had promised myself that I would stop with South as soon as Thaigo proposed, but here we were again, my lips on his, his arms wrapped around me.

In between kisses, I found myself making up a new excuse. Galatea still wanted me to hold sway over South and learn what he and Hecate and Farrow were up to. It wasn't that I wanted to keep kissing South; it was that I had to.

# CHAPTER 68

## — FARROW —

All of the Entente were to be reunited for the final balls, some still in disguise, since their missions in other lands were not yet complete. This ball was to announce Bari's upcoming nuptials.

She had secured Prince Thiago's hand. Fate help us all.

"You didn't think there was any chance that he would have changed his mind about marrying you once he knew he was the prince and that you had tricked him the whole time?" I asked, still marveling at the audacity of their plan. They hadn't even bothered to cover their faces.

Bari shrugged at the impossibility.

"Because you've spelled him?"

"Because he thinks he loves me. And he is a man of his word," she said matter-of-factly.

"What about Amantha?"

"What about her?"

"South says she cares for Thiago. Why did you not let her have him from the start?"

"Precisely because she cares for him. She might get muddled."

"Like you think that I have with Mather?" I asked.

"You said it, not me."

"It's funny, maybe it's because we've been apart for so long, but I never really imagined Amantha actually being in love with anyone."

"She's very competitive. Perhaps it isn't love at all."

"Mother—Hecate—seems to think that by depriving ourselves of the joys of the flesh all these years we have become more susceptible."

"That has never been an issue for me."

I leaned in, curious. I had never really thought of Bari kissing anyone until I learned about her and South.

"Oh my. Are you saying you actually enjoy kissing the prince? Have there been others? I mean, other humans? You hate humans."

"What's not to enjoy? Thiago is very handsome—and very skilled, from all the women he's kissed in the theater. But my heart is not in the least bit of danger from him."

There was something in the emphasis on the last two words that struck me.

"Is it possible that your heart is in danger from someone else?" I asked, thinking of South.

"Now you're speaking nonsense. We should get ready. Galatea will have our heads."

"Bari, have you noticed a change in Galatea?"

"She's just settling in. We have all been waiting for these moments our whole lives, and now that they are here, I think perhaps we cannot be held to account for our every action."

"After so much deprivation, I suppose it does take time to get accustomed to getting everything you really wanted," I said, studying her.

"I think there's an adjustment to not having anything to want anymore. I think Galatea's trying to fill that space and time with something else, and nothing quite fills the hole where the vengeance used to be. Luckily for us there are more Queendoms to fell—beginning, of course, with tonight."

Bari changed her dress multiple times with the wave of her wand and a touch against the hem. Each time the wand met the fabric, the dress changed color from black to red to blue and back again.

"I can't decide. Do I wear his favorite color or my own?"

"Well, yours is midnight, more of a color for mourning than for romance."

"He likes me in anything," she said, clearly determined to do what she wanted.

She touched the hem again and went defiantly back to black.

"Which color is South's favorite?" I asked, wanting to see if I could get a reaction from her.

"What does South have to do with anything?"

"You tell me," I said defiantly.

Bari's cool demeanor broke, and her lavender-gray eyes flashed angrily. I could see the beetles moving beneath a cheek. The skirt of her dress began to flutter. The delicate gossamer had been replaced with shiny black feathers.

Bari jerked her arm back, and her wand clattered to the floor. Had she been prepared to use her wand against me because of the mere mention of South?

As I slipped my hand into my pocket for my wand, I realized how vulnerable I was against her magic. I would need a wish if she raised her wand against me.

Before I could find out Bari's intentions, the door swung open and Galatea stepped into the room.

Galatea took us in, and Bari stooped to pick up her wand and slip it into her pocket.

"You can't possibly think you're wearing that," Galatea said, eyeing Bari's dress.

"Why not?"

"It will make the masses think of their dead Queen. We are ushering in a new era, filled with pastels and light." There was more than a hint of sarcasm in Galatea's voice. But as she touched Bari's hem and made the dress the palest of pinks, she smiled what seemed to be a genuine smile. Bari, meanwhile, examined herself in the glass and frowned.

Galatea commanded, "Bari, after your wedding night, you'll be in mourning, and you can wear black every day again and no one will say boo about it."

Bari smoothed down her dress and stared into the glass.

I rocked back on my heels. They were truly just getting started.

# CHAPTER 69

## — FARROW —

My heart quickened when I was alone with Bari once more. So much had happened. We were still so far apart. Still, there was an odd comfort and familiarity of being in the same room with her, readying ourselves for this evening as we had once readied ourselves for the day when we were young.

"I never thought I'd see you in a crown."

"I was thinking of designing something myself, but Galatea thought I should wear some of Thiago's family's jewels," she said simply, as if wearing jewels and crowns were commonplace.

"What would you design?"

"Something more me," she said.

A crown of feathers mixed with red jewels popped onto my head.

The tiara she was wearing now was clearly nothing like those jewels. It was spare and elegant and sparkly. The gown Galatea had just conjured for her too was not like anything I'd seen her wear before, even at the manse. It wasn't a dress meant for a lady; it was a dress meant for a Queen. There were pearls all over it—it must have weighed more than Hodder.

Bari shifted uncomfortably, and there was a rustling of wings beneath her voluminous skirt. She floated a few steps, and I realized she wasn't really walking; her birds were carrying her.

"Someone might notice. They know about our magic, but they don't know every way it manifests," I warned instinctively.

"Thiago has seen my flying things. He knows what I am, and now everyone else will too. When Galatea announces our engagement, it will be the first union between Entente and humans—a first step for them toward unity. A first step for us to have domination."

"Does Thiago have any idea about your plan?"

"He is smitten."

"You're taking him away from his vocation. He loves acting, passionately. Eventually his true desire will bleed through or break the spell."

"That won't happen until after we tie the knot. I don't want to quarrel. Come meet my future husband, maybe stay and dance." Her tone became commanding and she added, "It's time that I present you to the future king."

As strange as it was to have Bari invite me to her engagement celebration, it was stranger still to wrap my head around the idea that there really was going to be a king for the first time in the history of the Queendoms. And that king was not going to be Mather.

This whole time I had believed that Mather was the first male heir born to any sovereign. But it simply was not true. And the only Fate who knew it, Galatea, had kept it secret for so long.

There had been male firstborns, and they had been shipped off to parts unknown, adopted by maids, even swapped with the children of the court—all to preserve the matriarchy.

The humans had their secrets too. In order to maintain the Queendoms, they had to eradicate their past. Magrit had been the first to stand her ground and make her son her heir. For all her faults, and we knew better than anyone what they were, she had done this one noble thing. Everything that she had done after was traitorous.

Galatea was nervous about the ball. To our surprise, she had invited the Couterie. "This is a very delicate situation. We have to be sure to have some reliable friends in attendance," she defended, as the Couterie filed into the ballroom, led by a proud Linea.

The Couterie's existence had always been dependent on the Crown. It had been a strategic institution, but not one that meshed with Mather's plans for the Queendom. He wanted to change the Couterie—make it a purely diplomatic resource.

Galatea had yet to express how she planned on using the Couterie. Would the practice continue as it had for years, or would it morph into something more like what Mather had planned? Galatea had already surprised us with the never-ending balls. What was next, a Couterie for every guest?

My thoughts were interrupted by Hecate gliding to my side. I hadn't noticed her enter the ballroom. I spoke in a soft voice to my mother. "Galatea spent so much energy redecorating the Queendom. Maybe now she is weak enough for us to—"

"She is still stronger than me, Farrow," Hecate interrupted. "I grow stronger every day, but the Entente is not what it was. And Galatea's power is buoyed by that of the rest of the Entente, save me and you and South. As long as she has their full support, we will not defeat her. And if we tip our hand right now, we will lose our chance forever."

I sighed. A part of me wanted to skip ahead, past whatever ugly confrontation was in our Future to the Ever After, where we might find some kind of peace. I didn't know what that looked like, and from Hecate's visions, it didn't seem possible yet. But I was nowhere near giving up.

I wanted to be with Mather, but could I be with Mather? Was that what was right for the Queendoms? For the Entente? Probably not, and even if it were, I never wanted to be a princess—or a Queen.

Watching Galatea act as a Queen was stomach turning. Was there a Future where the Entente could just walk among the people? Where magic wasn't our vocation, but rather just a trait we possessed? Did the magic constitute a duty, as we had always been taught? Or could we just live? Amantha wanted to just live. I had felt the stirrings of that too. I had always tamped them down. Was there perhaps something in between, where we honored the responsibility of our magic and still carved out lives for ourselves? These were my questions, but Hecate did not have the answers.

"Stop thinking. You're hurting my head. Let's go dance," Hecate announced suddenly.

"But no one has asked me."

"I am asking you," she said.

Without a pause, my mother was on her feet and pulling me toward the dance floor. She wrapped herself around me and led—and laughed. I laughed too and let my shoulders relax as I followed her in a box step.

"Hecate, we shouldn't . . . There is so much to do."

"And right now, what we must do is dance." My mother's voice was surprisingly light.

The thing we did best was creating a moment that changed a whole life. We steered humans together and broke them apart, and they were almost never aware of our wands tipping the scales of their lives. We were the wind beneath the leaf that the Queen slips on before she bumps into the man she will marry . . . And then for us, on to the next Fate.

I had never been more aware of how the tiniest moments changed everything. But that did not apply only to humans; it applied to the Entente too. If I had never been apart from my sisters? If I had never met Mather? Would I be the same Entente? I didn't think so, and as fraught as everything still was, I didn't want to be unchanged either.

Hecate twirled me around and spoke over the music. "There it is, the happy seated beside the sad."

"Mother, as long as I had some part of you, even when you were still in ash, I could feel some happiness. But, this is much better."

Smiling, Mother twirled me again.

In the middle of dancing, I looked up just as Mather was entering with Cinderella. How was he here?

His eyes met mine. And when I tore my glance away from him and looked back at my mother, her look of satisfaction was confirmation.

I whispered to her, "Mother, how are they here? They were safely in the Reverie."

"I told you that Galatea would know. She sent the guard and invited them to the palace."

"And you're just telling me this now?"

Mother shrugged.

The footman announced Mather's presence and Cinderella's: "Prince Mather and Lady Cinderella Gray . . ."

The room gasped as the pair descended the stairs. Galatea clapped her hands together and smiled as if she had been expecting them all along.

The swirling groups of dancers parted. Cinderella hung back briefly while Mather made his way to me and Mother. He bowed, kissing her hand and then mine.

"It's a pleasure to meet you. I am glad you are no longer ash," Mather said simply.

"As am I. And we did meet once before, when you were small." Hecate smiled.

"I remember. I was a little tyrant," he noted ruefully.

"Yes, but the best kind—an open-minded one."

"My apologies."

"Accepted. Now dance with my daughter. I would very much like to talk with Cinderella."

Hecate led Cinderella away, leaving Mather and me in each other's arms. I could hear the beginning of their conversation.

"My dear, it seems that the Entente owes you ten times over," Hecate remarked.

"About that . . . ," Cinderella answered. I assumed she was about to plead the case of Hark.

"I know you told me all about your mother. But it's a wonder to see her like this . . . ," Mather marveled.

"With enough will and enough magic, anything is possible. She taught me that."

"And love—maybe she didn't say 'love,' but it is so apparent. The way she looks at you."

I felt myself beaming. I did not doubt Hecate's love in the least, but having Mather note it out loud felt good.

"It's strange being so happy in one way. And yet . . . ," I paused.

Looking intently at me, Mather slowed his steps and spoke softly. "The whole world does not fall in line with your own happiness. I sympathize with the feeling." He was silent for a moment and then continued, "You see, I have lately come into some happiness, and yet the world around me remains in total chaos."

"And what brought your happiness?"

"You," he whispered. At that moment, I wanted everyone around us to fall far, far away, but I noticed other pairs observing our closeness, and it was time to resume our dance, though we were soon interrupted.

Signaling for the musicians to stop playing, Galatea called for attention. Mather and I rejoined my mother. She and Cinderella had found seats. All the others around us taken, I stood next to Hecate's seat and Mather edged a little closer to Cinderella.

Projecting her voice over the crowd, Galatea announced, "We are delighted to have not one but two blessings this evening."

Hecate's eyes widened and she gestured toward me. She knew what Galatea was about to do. "When Galatea says what she's about to say, stay calm," she whispered in my ear as I leaned down.

Mother's warnings were rare. I felt my body tense in anticipation for whatever Galatea had planned. It must have something to do with Mather. Otherwise, why would she have brought him here? Whatever the reason, it couldn't be good.

Galatea stood in front of her throne, readying herself to address the room again. As a murmur went through the crowd, I stepped toward Mather and spoke softly. "Mother says we should brace ourselves. Galatea is going to say or do something shocking—likely something terrible." The last detail was purely my own, but with Galatea involved, how could any other outcome but bad be possible?

"I know." His voice was barely audible.

"What do you know?"

"I wouldn't be here if she didn't have something positively awful planned. Either she needs me to cosign whatever evil thing it is. Or I am the awful thing—perhaps another public execution." Somehow, Mather's tone stayed calm as he voiced the worst of my fears.

"Mather, you should have wished yourself away the second she showed up at the Reverie! Why didn't you? Why don't you wish now?" I struggled to keep my voice low and calm.

"I had to see you," he whispered as his lips almost grazed my ear.

Galatea began, "Our Queendoms have been through so much. These are strange times indeed. And in times like these, when it feels like everything is shifting and changing so rapidly, it is so very important to celebrate where and when we are able to come together. Where we have found love. When we have found peace."

She stopped, seeming to take a breath, but really pausing to assess her audience. Satisfied she had their undivided attention, Galatea continued, "Just as the Queen's Council completed so much work to unify the Queendoms, we were oh so surprised to lose a Queen. Yet we are poised to welcome a new royal into the fold."

This unexpected news stilled the crowd into silence. Pleased with her revelation's effect, Galatea raised her voice to a dramatic pitch. "I have seen all our Pasts, and I am committed to change. I am committed to a Future that looks nothing like the Past. No doubt you are wondering, 'What does the Future hold?' I will show you. The Future does not belong to the Entente alone or to Queens alone or to kings alone or even to Rooks alone. It belongs to all of us. Imagine a Future where a king marries an Entente. Imagine a Future where a king-turned-commoner marries a commoner. But we don't have to imagine the last. It will happen in the very near Future."

That news caused the crowd to murmur again, surprise crossing almost every face in the room. I felt my sense of dread building.

Galatea gave her guests a moment to settle, and triumphant, she sprang her surprise. "Not one but two couples are heading down the aisle: Prince Thiago and our Bari and . . . Lady Cinderella and Prince Mather!"

Galatea had found a way to neutralize Prince Mather. She was making him part of her Queendom instead of a scorned heir. He would become a son-in-law through her adopted daughter. It was brilliant and horrible.

Galatea smiled widely, sweeping her arms toward Mather and Cinderella, and she finished with a flourish. "Cinderella is my daughter, and Prince Mather is like a son to me. I see a bright Future in theirs!"

The guests applauded. Mather and Cinderella forced up smiles. Publicly objecting to Galatea's claim could result in a scene or worse. Galatea could throw them in the dungeon or stop their breaths on the spot with a wave of her wand.

Galatea raised a glass, and everyone toasted. It was excruciating.

Hecate held my hand to keep me from using my wand.

"Must she take everything?" I whispered to my mother.

"Only the things she knows matter most. She wants our loyalty. She's destroying every obstacle she can find to gain that."

"Or does she want to punish us?" I interjected. "She punished the humans. Why not me? South and I disobeyed her, tried to stop her. There was no way that never crept back up on us. There's no way she ever forgot about what we did."

# CHAPTER 70

## — FARROW —

After more dancing there was a sumptuous dinner. Exuding maternal concern, Galatea encircled Cinderella and Mather in her arms, and announced, "My two darlings, you've had a long day and night. You need your rest." She instructed the guard to escort them to their respective rooms. The crowd voiced their approval of Galatea's wisdom and caring, and then happily returned to finishing their dessert course.

As the servants were clearing the tables, the Rook King appeared suddenly, filling Mather's empty chair next to Galatea. The king's voice was edged with anger. "You took something from us—our boy. And we are owed a debt." He was looking at Galatea, but then he turned to South.

"What are you doing here, King Waid?" South asked, his voice formal, but I could see the pain underneath, shown in his eyes.

"I never collected because I loved your mother so much and I thought maybe she was right, maybe you deserved a life outside of the Rookery," the Rook King continued, as if he were speaking only to South and there was not a ballroom full of people.

"But when I thought Iolanta had passed, I wanted you back, and Les Soeurs refused me."

He turned back, facing Galatea again. "It is ironic that you hemmed us in, and it was your kind that ended up taking over Queendoms—that ended up killing a Queen."

"I saw Hecate's visions of your Futures. Whatever our actions, they are nothing compared to the chaos that yours would have caused," Galatea defended.

"So after all these years, you offer no remorse, and you feel no empathy for our position. After all, we were right about the humans."

"That does not mean I wasn't also right about you. I understand you better now, and there is still a way that we can help each other."

"In exchange for our freedom?"

"Something like that . . . While you were busy with South, I took your things. You may live among us, but you will be subject to our will," Galatea said, not flinching.

The Rook King protested. "I don't understand. You don't need us for our magic. You have your own. You even have Farrow to grant your wishes."

"Oh, there is something that you can do that no one else can." She leaned in and whispered something to him. They conferred in hushed voices for a moment.

"I will think on it," the Rook King said, "but in the meantime I would like to invite my son home for his coronation."

"But of course, Father," South said, raising a glass. And then the Rook King disappeared.

Later, when I was alone with Hecate, she showed me what Galatea and the Rook King had whispered about.

*"I want to make more of us—enough to fill the Queendoms," Galatea explained.*

*"And what will become of the humans?" the Rook King asked.*

*"Once there are enough of us, there will be no need for them."*

*"What are you proposing?"*

*"We fill the Queendoms with magic," she said ruefully.*

"What does she mean by that?" I asked Hecate when she put down the mirror.

"You know now how magical babies are created. Galatea wants to create more. A lot more—enough to fill the Queendoms."

"And what will happen to the people who don't have magic?" I asked, a sick thought occurring to me.

"There will be more of us than there are of them. And then they will be of no use to us. Or at least that is how Galatea sees it."

I felt a chill.

"Do you think she will eliminate them?"

"I have seen versions of the Future where she does. At the same time, despite herself, she seems to be developing an affection for the humans. She enjoys their rituals almost as much as she enjoys our own."

"I think she enjoys controlling them. If the world is filled with magical people and no one else, who will she control?"

"That is a very sound point. One that I hope we will not need to reckon with."

I was not comforted. Even the Fate of the Future could not make me feel better.

# CHAPTER 71

## — FARROW —

At a moment before midnight, I met Mather in our wish garden.

"I will not do it," he said, pacing toward me.

"You have to play along until we find a way out," I said, even though the idea pained my heart.

"I thought you'd found a way out, and now it looks like they have aligned—into an even more formidable force."

"Looks can be deceiving," I reminded him.

"You think the Rook will double-cross Galatea?"

"The Rooks want freedom. I think Galatea wants to rule them too. She's just offering them a bigger cage to roam in."

"So what do we do? Do you have a plan?"

"Not yet, but we will figure this out." I tried to sound much more certain than I felt.

"I have faith in you, Farrow. But I can help. Give me something to do," he offered earnestly.

"Blow something up? It's too dangerous right now, Mather. Galatea's going to watch you every minute and Cinderella too. The best thing you can do is play the part."

"Pretending to be in love with anyone other than you is much harder than blowing up Black Glass factories."

I felt my cheeks warm, and he took my hand.

"We shouldn't. She could be watching."

"I don't care."

He kissed me then, and the world went away for a moment. But when we parted, it crashed in again, and Mather could read it on my face.

"You look so troubled."

"Mother says we need to find a very precise path out of our predicament."

Mather smiled. "For anyone else that would be a trial, but for you it's wishes and a wave of the wand."

"My magic doesn't work quite like that, and Bari and Amantha are working awfully hard to keep their wishes opaque to me."

But Mather's comment about wishes reminded me that Thiago had them too. Maybe his were the key to unraveling Galatea's plot.

I kissed Mather, remarking, "Did anyone ever tell you that you are brilliant?"

"For a puppet . . . ," he whispered back.

"No. You reminded me that another key player, Thiago, has his own desires, and maybe we can work with those."

Mather's face lit up, and we kissed a few more times. After we drew apart, I closed my eyes, settling myself, listening for what Thiago was hoping for. That he was under a love spell was problematic but not insurmountable.

Thiago's wishes surprised us both. "I don't know what to make of him. The only thing that he seems to be wishing for is to be back on the stage again," I told Mather after I opened my eyes. Then I clapped my hands together as an idea grew. "Maybe that's exactly what we need!"

"What are you thinking?" Mathew queried.

"An after-dinner performance on the wedding eve."

"Can you not say that again?" he said with a sad smile, before kissing me once more.

It was strange to be this happy and unhappy at once. Trepidation coursed through me, but every moment with him—even when everything was awful—was filled to the brim with joy.

He made me laugh, he made me think, and when he touched me, he made me not think, except to think about how much I wanted him to kiss me, about where I wanted his hands to go. It was maddening sometimes, the waiting—waiting for him to touch me, deciding whether or not I should touch him first. And then when we made contact skin to skin, there was this euphoria, a rush of senses and endorphins and comfort and longing all at once, every time. I could not tire of him. Nor did I want to.

He hummed beneath his breath, and I hummed back, as if we were making our own song.

When we were readying to part, I said, "We have to be more careful. Galatea could cast a spell and make you forget all about me."

"Not possible," he said intently.

We both knew better, unfortunately. He had never forgotten me, but we knew how close we had already come to losing each other. And we still might. No matter how much we wanted the outcome to be a happy one.

"I promise to be careful so long as you promise to let me help," he said resolutely.

I took a breath and agreed. I wanted to protect him, but I also trusted him to fight. He was resourceful and quick and even without magic would be an asset.

"I promise," I said, and I meant it.

We kissed one more time as the clock struck twelve.

When I returned to my room, Hecate was up waiting for me.

"Do you think we have to stop? Is Galatea catching on?" I asked my mother.

"I am confident in my spell," she assured me. "I stayed up to see if you're all right. I know how you feel about him."

"I'm fine. Only more determined than ever to stop Galatea. Mother, Mather wants to help. So does Cinderella. We keep thinking we are the ones to save them, but what if they make the difference? What if they are the missing ingredient? What if they need to play a role in saving themselves?"

# CHAPTER 72

## — BARI —

The wedding was drawing closer and closer. All of the Queendoms was invited.

Thiago's sister, Queen Helene, agreed to attend the wedding before leaving for exile. Everything was falling into place.

An outsider would think they were witnessing two beautiful romances. But of all the parties involved, there was only one of them who actually believed he was in love with his intended. And he was under a love spell.

"I was thinking it would be better if we do not kill him," I ventured, once more looking around at Galatea's handiwork. There were so many peonies growing out of the eastern side of the room, I could no longer see the wall.

"Whatever do you mean?" Galatea asked.

"I've gotten to know Thiago, and I think he would make a better patsy than a corpse."

"Corpses are much easier to control... Besides, the Queendoms are much more comfortable with a Queen than a king."

"But, Galatea—"

"I've made up my mind. You were supposed to have this crown, but Magrit's actions and Farrow's necessitated that I take it instead. This is your chance to have your birthright."

"This is my chance to be your pawn."

Galatea rolled her eyes and walked out the door. Suddenly, Amantha flickered into the room. She'd clearly been listening.

"I won't let you kill him."

"I have no intention of killing him," I told her.

Amantha's face opened with surprise.

"Then what's your plan?"

"I haven't figured it out yet, but I will. Or better yet, we can figure it out together."

"I don't know if I believe you. What if you're just buying time so that you can kill him and I can't stop you?"

There was a time not so long ago that all of us sisters trusted each other without hesitation, Amantha and I most of all. I didn't like the suspicious-shaped feeling that was lodged in my head and my heart. I wanted it gone. But it was stuck there. And I could see it reflected back in Amantha's cooler-than-usual eyes.

"I know that you don't approve of how I handled Thiago."

"That's an understatement. I should have been given a chance. You and Galatea . . . You two didn't trust me to be able to do it."

"I don't know if maybe that isn't a good thing. I know that we have all agreed that it's revenge at all costs. But I don't want that for you. You've already lost enough."

Amantha looked more hurt than I had ever seen her. "Galatea looks at me differently. Some of our sisters do too, even though almost all of them were affected by that day. You never pity me. I will not take pity from you. Not from you. From anyone else, but not from you, Bari."

"That is not what it was. I saw the way you looked at him. No one should have to kill what they love."

"I don't love him. I like him . . ."

I rolled my eyes at her, but she continued.

"How can I know if it's him or just the idea of him? Pretending to be someone else felt so good. It was different from when we were pretending to be Cinderella's stepsisters. For the first time I felt free."

"That's what we're doing all of this for. So that we can be free. Not for pretend, but for real."

"And what about Thiago? How do I know what's real when you've spelled him into loving you, and our mother wants to put a wand through his heart?"

"You don't. But maybe there's a way to find out. But first he has to be alive."

Amantha sat down on the couch next to me. For the first time in a long time, she wasn't going anywhere.

# CHAPTER 73

## — FARROW —

I had seen Linea since the Couterie had burned down and been rebuilt, at the ball for Bari. But I had not expected to see her in Galatea's private study.

"What are you doing here?" I demanded.

"I was invited, of course." She demurred without missing a beat.

"What for?"

"The new Queen has very few friends she can rely upon."

"And what is she giving you in return for your friendship?"

"Just a chance to continue the Couterie as it has always been. A complement to the royals in whatever form they take. In this case, the new royals."

"I don't understand. Are you saying . . . ?"

"I am here to start the Ana for Galatea and Bari and Amantha—and, if you so choose, Hecate and yourself. Whatever you think of me, I taught you well. You certainly have come up in the world, just as I intended."

I found myself speechless. I disagreed with what she was proposing—and what she had done to the Couterie.

When I returned to Hecate, my mother could read me. She said quietly, "You are disappointed in me for my role in the Couterie before you were brought there. You are disappointed in me because you know that I did not stop you from ending up there."

"How could you give Linea the mirror that helped her choose the Couterie, when you knew what she did to them—to us? The doctor . . . But the doctor was just the beginning of our mutilation. Linea made us construct our whole lives around the royals, learning their likes and dislikes and mimicking moods and manners not our own."

"I made the compromise I thought was for the greater good. It is possible to look at all the options and find that there are no moral choices, only immoral ones. But you have to pick one or the story stops entirely."

"I don't believe what you're saying. You taught me the opposite of that."

"I saw all the Futures, and this was the one where I could spare you. The Couterie was the only place I was able to hide you. Otherwise you would have ended up in Galatea's hands."

"And you think that would have been worse for me?"

"I could not let her have you, raise you in that vengeance . . ."

"But I had vengeance in my heart without her, and I spent all those years away from my sisters."

Hecate shook her head. "And I am sorry for that. I am. But I saw you with Galatea—and it was worse."

She held her wand up to my temple and showed me flashes of other Futures that could have been.

My sisters finding me in the woods instead of going to the orphanage.

Then me with Mather at the ball, dancing in the courtyard.

"I don't understand. That was exactly as it happened."

"In every Ever After you ended up here."

My face in the vision shifted into a small smirk that chilled me.

We were in Mather's bedroom, and I danced for him again as I had that night, but instead of stopping short of stabbing Mather, I buried my knife in him and said, "I am sorry, Prince, but this is for my mother, for my sisters, for the Entente. I avenge them, and I punish your mother by ending her line before I end her. You are the only thing in the Queendom she cares about other than her own power and her own self, and so I take you from her. Good night, sweet prince."

Tears sprang to my eyes, it felt so real.

Hecate had done this for me to stop me from becoming a killer.

"You did it for me."

"There is a reason we have the rule about not telling which children were born to us. This is the reason. I was never supposed to show you favor. But I did every time I visited Linea and when I gave her the mirror. I feel for all those children, but I fear that for you, I would do it again."

"Oh, Hecate."

I wrapped my arms around her and pulled her close. I could not wipe away her guilt, and now I felt some of my own. But knowing the truth of her association with Madame Linea answered a question that had gnawed at me for all the weeks since Linea told me about the mirror. This was not the answer I was looking for, but it was the truth, however ugly. And because of it, I felt like I now knew my mother better.

I went back to Galatea.

"I know that you have your own deal with Linea. But she should have no part in this wedding. I will teach Bari and Thiago and Mather and Cinderella the dance. I know it from my days in the Couterie."

Galatea looked at me surprised.

"Very well."

It was a small victory.

"I never expected to be in this position—leader of the Entente. The irony was not lost on me," Galatea added, after a pause.

"How so? You are just as much a Fate as Iolanta or Hecate."

"You would think so, but I was not to be the leader. I lived in my sisters' shadows. The shadow of Hecate's certainty. The shadow of Iolanta's passion and chaos . . ."

I accepted this, but I wondered something new. What if Galatea's plot was not singularly based on revenge? What if she was acting out of untold insecurities from her youth? We all carried things with us from when we were young. I certainly did. I carried Bari, South, Amantha, and our sisters with me every day. I wanted to impress them. I wanted us all to be better. I still felt a twinge of insecurity about my magic around Bari and Amantha. I still felt guilt about South's wings. What did Galatea carry with her, and was it affecting all the Queendoms now?

I went straight to Hecate, who listened carefully to what I told her.

"Maybe if you could just assure her that you have not come to take her place . . . ," I suggested.

Hecate leaned back on the pillows of the couch where she lounged.

"I will not lie to her. I have come to take the Entente and return it to its former glory. Her path is the wrong path. She knows this and is still going down it because of some hurt she perceives from our youth."

Hecate got to her feet.

"Where are you going? We aren't done talking about this."

"I'm meeting Craven."

Hecate stormed off.

I sighed. She was so stubborn and petulant. The Hecate of old would have stood her ground perhaps, but she would most likely have been much, much more polite about it.

I didn't chase after her. She was already gone.

# CHAPTER 74

## — FARROW —

I had not expected so many eyes on us," I whispered a few hours later, when I was leading the rehearsal dance.

The room was filled with the entire court, some Queens, and the Couterie, as well as select servants and the townspeople. But Mather looked only at me.

In the days since her nuptials announcement, Galatea had doubled the unions' value: political, as well as love, and everyone wanted to see the new couples. The townspeople were hoping for peace and romance. And the Couterie . . . They likely had already figured out how fake the two matches were through those preternaturally acute observation skills.

"Stop. I'm supposed to be your teacher," I warned.

"Stop what?"

"Looking at me that way. You're supposed to be looking at Cinderella like that."

"I have agreed to go along with this pretense only to be close to you," Mather whispered defiantly.

"How does it feel to be reunited with your own court?"

"It is not the same without Hark. But then again, I guess he was never my friend in the first place."

I wished I could hug him then, but I had to keep our bodies at arm's length. The only thing I could do was squeeze his hand.

He squeezed back. And his eyes met mine. And that same fluttering I felt in my chest every time he was near happened all over again. I wondered if it happened to him too. I knew I affected him, but was it the same for him? Did his heart pound for me in equal measure?

Bari and Thiago danced on the other side of the room. He never looked away from her face as they traversed the floor. His wishes were temporarily quieted, because having her in his arms was one thing that he was constantly wishing for.

She may have spelled him, but she could not spell herself. She kept stealing glances at South.

I longed to free Thiago and to somehow get through to Bari, but I knew at this moment all I could do was dance.

Playing the part of the dutiful sister, Amantha was lingering with the court. Her eyes betrayed her sadness as she flickered into and out of existence.

"I don't know if this place was ever really my home. It's prettier now, closer to the way I remember it being when Grandmother was Queen," Mather said, taking in the palace.

We had occupied his home. He would not or could not acknowledge the cost now that he was returned to it. Was it appealing at all to him, the chance to be prince to the First Queendom again—even though he knew that Galatea was using him, even though he would never be king? Or was every moment here just a reminder of all he had lost and all that could have been?

"I don't miss the Black Glass. At least we can thank Galatea for that," Mather commented.

Interrupting our quiet conversation so obviously her goal,

Galatea approached us, her smile frosty. I spoke first, offering a polite, "Good evening, Galatea."

"Farrow, in royal company, you must address me as Queen."

This was a moment I could never have anticipated. Galatea crowing herself as Queen was one thing. Her demanding we call her Queen was quite another. I fixed a smile on my face and spoke again. "Of course, Your Highness." This placated Galatea, and she stepped away to mingle with others in the court.

"We are the proof of the new Future Galatea has promised. Also, everyone loves a wedding," Mather mused.

He was acting as the royal courtier he was reared to be. I admired that, but I yearned to know, to feel all he truly wanted. I struggled, but I couldn't resist glimpsing his wishes.

*I wish I were dancing with Farrow anyplace else. I wish we were practicing for our own first wedding dance.*

I was overwhelmed by these wishes, ones that might never be granted.

I felt Mather's thoughts brush up against mine again, and I brought my focus back to him. *The crown was always tied to the idea of losing Mother. She is gone, but I do not have the crown. But I don't wish for the crown. I wish for Farrow.*

"What is truly in your heart?" I asked, as close to his ear as I dared. I wanted, needed to hear him tell me.

He answered me in words softly spoken. "With you in this moment, I have never been more free. The only thing my heart is tied to, the only thing I want to be tied to is you, only you."

"But that's not entirely true, is it?" I pressed, my words barely above a murmur.

Mather's face tightened, and his whispered response brimmed with urgency. "I love my Queendom. I want to help make it better.

Seeing it in Galatea's hands terrifies me. She has not hurt anyone yet, except Helene, and yes, she has taken down the glass. But I am waiting for the other shoe to drop. Perhaps it already has. She's moving people and Entente around like chess pieces for her own amusement and agenda, and I am petrified."

# CHAPTER 75

## — BARI —

I snuck into the room where Galatea was keeping Queen Helene and Dora. When I entered, Helene was sitting, holding the baby. At the sight of me, Dora cooed and her mother's face went taut.

Nestled tightly in Helene's arms, the baby cooed again. "Ma-Ma!" she exclaimed.

I felt my heart contract. Dora didn't need our spells to let the world know what she thought and what she wanted.

Helene stood, gently rocking Dora. "What do I call you? Princess Bari? Or future sister-in-law?" she demanded, her tone harsh.

"I know you have no reason to trust me, but this is your only chance. Wish yourself somewhere safe. Somewhere only you know."

I noticed something was very wrong about the interior of the room. The walls were made of Black Glass.

"Wish? And if I do, do I wish me and Dora out of existence?" she asked, her voice rising with anger and skepticism in equal measure. Dora's coos shifted to whimpers.

"There is no time to explain, but I have grown rather fond of Dora and I would like her to live. And since you are her best chance of survival, I suppose I want you to live too. You will not be in my hands; you will be in Farrow's. She is quite fond of your kind and she will make sure you are safe. Now please, when you make your wish, you must be very specific."

I could see Helene relent. She was ready.

"There is one more thing I want you to add to your wish. I want you to take—"

Before I could say I wanted her to bring Thiago along with her too, the door swung open, and Galatea stood before it. I could not finish my plea—not because I was afraid of Galatea, even though I most definitely was, but because my lips could not move.

"Why are you disturbing our guests? It's a big day tomorrow," Galatea said, holding her wand.

I kept my lips together and looked pointedly at Helene, who closed her eyes and presumably made her wish. She and her baby disappeared in an instant.

Farrow had done it. She had rescued them. From the look on Galatea's face, I was the one who needed rescuing now.

"I know you are disappointed in me, Galatea. But the baby . . . I grew attached to her on the mission, and I wanted her to be safe."

"Safe from me?"

"She has no part in this plot, and Queen Helene never betrayed the Entente. They have earned their freedom."

Galatea didn't say anything. Instead she put her wand on my temple. My head flooded with Pasts.

Some of the visions I remembered: the horror of Hecate's Burning and South's wings on fire took on new light now that I knew South in a new way. And seeing Hecate again . . . That day had been beyond horrifying when we were small but was even more visceral now.

Then I saw myself standing on that pyre. Being burned for who I was. In the Future, not the Pasts.

"How did you do that? You cannot see the Future," I said, surprised.

"I am not sure if it is a new gift or only my imagination. But the Past informs the Present. And this is what it is telling me. If you are not the danger now, you will be in danger . . . You must trust me—you must trust the plan."

The vision had shaken me. I could feel my fingers beginning to feather, and I slipped them into my pockets.

"You are right, Galatea. I was mistaken." I put my head down in shame, and she wrapped her arms around me.

# CHAPTER 76

## — BARI —

I walked back to my room, and South was waiting there.

"I am afraid I might miss the performance," he told me.

"Why is that?" I asked lightly.

"I have to be crowned."

"After what happened in the Ever After, you can't be going through with it—"

"I made a promise."

"But they tried to trick you."

"The Rook King thought he was doing what he had to when it came to my brother. It still sounds strange saying that. And his love for Mother clouded his actions."

"South—don't go."

"Why?"

*Because I am afraid for you*, I thought.

"Because we'll be down a player, and the play just will not work without you."

"That's all then . . . ," he said, drifting off, clearly wanting more of a reason. One I could not give.

"Yes."

"I'll see you when I return, Princess."

# CHAPTER 77

## — BARI —

Bari, what are you doing here? How are you even here—?" South asked when I appeared beside him at the Rookery a few moments later.

"Just like the Ever After, very little thought is taken in keeping flying things out," I boasted.

"Well, that was very brave of you. Stupid, but brave. The Rooks are not known for their hospitality," he said. The light in his eyes betrayed how happy he was to see me, but I saw fear too. South clearly wanted to protect me.

"And yet you've agreed to be their king."

He shrugged.

"Have you asked your father how this would even work? You belong to us. You are a Fate. A Present. You are not tied to a stone or an object. What are they going to do? Rip out a bit of your heart?"

"It's a rib actually," he said matter-of-factly.

I thought he was being facetious, but his face remained serious.

I reacted, nearly reaching for South's chest but stopping myself. "It's barbaric."

"It's tradition. They take the rib and place it inside a piece of stone and set that in a piece of jewelry or some other object," he said simply, as if that made it all right.

"It must be part of the covenant, a punishment for Rooks mostly long gone," I suggested.

"Are you saying the practice should be suspended?" he said, arching his eyebrow.

"I am saying the practice should not apply to you."

"Because I'm special? Or because you care what happens to me?"

For a moment I felt muddled. Was he calling me a hypocrite for wanting better for him? Or saying that I wanted better for him because I had grown too close to him?

"Relax, Bari. Because I am a Fate, I will not be giving up my bones—or a piece of my heart. But it would almost be worth doing so to see how much you're worried about it."

"I truly hate you."

"Only you truly don't."

There were footsteps coming down the hall.

"You have to go."

"I'll be in the rafters if you change your mind," I said, surprising myself.

"You're staying to rescue me? I do not need rescuing."

"Then I am staying to witness South getting his crown. Or should I say Prince South?" I transferred into a host of moths and camouflaged myself against the ceiling. The door opened to reveal South's father, the Rook King Waid.

"I thought I heard voices," he said.

"Just talking to myself . . . ," South covered.

"I never thought this monumental day would come."

A few moments later, South stood in the center of the Rooks' throne room, his father before him holding the crown. In many ways his investiture was the same as the coronation Amantha and I had had. And still, there were so many ways that this ceremony was uniquely Rook.

Galatea was trying to make us fit into the Queendoms, weaving her magic into every moment of her subjects' lives without them knowing it. The Rooks were unabashedly displaying theirs. The crown floated through the air and placed itself on South's head.

"Today we welcome our brother home. He will lead us to a new chapter, one where we walk free in the Queendoms," Waid told the gathered crowd.

"Welcome, brother," intoned the other Rooks.

"Do you have anything to say to the brotherhood?"

"I am one of you, but I am also one of the Entente, and for a long time I thought I was one of the people. I promise to represent you, but also to broker a peace between the humans and the Entente. There is a better way for all of us. We will find it together."

The Rooks responded with resounding cheers.

From the ceiling of the throne room, I watched South smile before I flew back toward home.

When I got back to the palace, Thiago was waiting for me.

"Where did you go? Where have you been?" He seemed restless and angry. It was time to cast the love spell again—but every time I did, I sensed his resistance. I couldn't help but think it was because of his growing feelings for Amantha.

I slid my fingers into the potion and wiped it over my lips, and I greeted him with a kiss. After a few seconds he began to calm down.

"I don't know what came over me. I just missed you, I guess . . . ," he said, looking slightly befuddled as he wrapped his arms around me. "I was thinking that perhaps we should cancel the play. It's undignified for a future prince."

Arranging my face into a pout, I retorted, "My mother has her heart set on it. And I would have thought you would love giving one last performance."

"Perhaps you could learn Amantha's part then."

"What is the trouble with Amantha? You told me she was a genius," I asked, feigning innocence.

"You're quite right. Ignore me—there is no reason it shouldn't be Amantha."

# CHAPTER 78

## — BARI —

All the Queens of all the Queendoms, save Helene, were in attendance, as were their respective courts, the Couterie, the servants, and a handful of commoners.

When the moment came for Amantha and Thiago to kiss onstage though, he kissed her passionately, and longer than the script called for. So long that the audience began to react, some shifting uncomfortably, some waving their fans in response. There was even a low whistle coming from the direction of the household staff.

Galatea cleared her throat, and I could see her wand flash out of her pocket. The curtain began to descend as she whispered under her breath and flicked her wrist.

It would have been quite mortifying if my heart were at all invested in Thiago's, but I pretended it was part of the play and I clapped louder and smiled wider than I thought possible.

Just before the curtain obscured them, I saw them come apart. Amantha and Thiago looked at each other as if quite surprised by the kiss itself. As far as I knew, the last time they had spoken had been their fight the night before we came here.

# CHAPTER 79

## — FARROW —

When Amantha and Thiago took the stage, I read him, and I wondered if the love spell had somehow slipped away.

"I wish Calliope would forget her station and choose me, choose love over all," he exclaimed with his hands over his heart and his eyes on Amantha, who stood, wearing a diaphanous gown, on a balcony above him.

*Would Amantha ever forget her station and choose me, choose love over all?* he wondered.

His wishes completely in sync with his character's every word and deed, Thiago seemed to literally become the hero. The second he ascended the stage, his wishes changed from a constant need to be with Bari to a pure love for Amantha.

As he walked the boards of the stage that had been erected that very day, it was as if he had shed Thiago and become his character, Archer, who was free to love Amantha's character, Calliope. Had his talent to transform actually given him a respite from the spell? He was the most curious subject I had ever heard wish. And then there was Amantha's wish . . .

*I wish I had used the love spell. But then again, I would never have felt this.*

My heart broke for her.

But at the close of the play, he climbed the balcony's ivy-entwined trellis and he kissed her. And my heart broke for him too. Because, for a moment at least, I was sure the spell was broken. I could hear him wish for her by her real name, Amantha, and her for him. And they kissed for what seemed like an eternity. Afterward, he returned to Bari's side and dutifully took her hand. And she clapped and laughed as if she were in on the joke. But she most definitely was not. I had not undone this marriage plot. But perhaps I had planted the seeds to weaken it.

I watched Bari watching Thiago. There was no love there.

# CHAPTER 80

## — FARROW —

After we watched the play, Hecate and I discussed my plan for what to do next.

"To answer your earlier question, I don't know if it's right to punish them forever, and at the same time I do not know what they will do when they are free—" I said.

"The same arguments could have been made by the humans against us," Hecate countered patiently.

I absorbed her words. She was not wrong. How was this any different?

Everything was more complicated than I wanted it to be. The more I learned, the worse it was. There had been Fates before Iolanta, Hecate, and Galatea, and others before that, and before that. Once upon a time our foremothers had contained the Rooks. And, Hecate had just told me, the humans had attempted to contain us. We did not take kindly to being persecuted then either.

"What was it that the Rookery did to deserve this?" I asked.

"They tried to secure the patriarchy."

"What's that?"

"The Queendoms ruled by men," Hecate replied. The very idea felt inconceivable to me. "They want it still."

"What do we do, Hecate? There are too many people wanting too many things . . ."

Hecate looked at me a long moment and then spoke. "There is a precise path of actions that, if followed, may allow us to find our way, Farrow," reminding me of what she had counseled before.

"And if we don't . . . ?"

"Chaos, destruction—death," she said matter-of-factly.

"Don't tell me, show me."

Hecate didn't ask me if I was sure. She put the wand to my temple, and I closed my eyes.

What I saw was worse than I imagined.

"Farrow?"

"I am still committed. I can see no other way."

# CHAPTER 81

## — FARROW —

When Mather saw Sadie, he pulled her into an embrace. She stepped back from him, surprised.

"It's me. Mather . . . ," he began, sounding hurt.

Was Sadie so afraid of Galatea that she could no longer hug her former charge?

"Oh yes, of course, good to see you," she said as if through a fog. "You're looking well, Your Highness." As she spoke, I could hear her wishes.

*I know he is the prince. But I wish I could place his face. Were we close? He seems to think we are. For the life of me I cannot remember. I wish I could.*

"Was it just me or was Sadie a little cold?" he asked.

I pushed him into one of the rooms. His hands went immediately to my waist, and he was already kissing me before the door was shut.

I pushed him gently back from me.

"Mather," I said, my voice a whisper of the longing that I had to tamp down. "I think I know what is happening here. I mean, not exactly—but I have an idea."

“We’re stealing this moment,” he said, closing the gap between us, kissing my neck.

“And this one,” he added, kissing the skin just below it.

“And this one,” he whispered as he planted another kiss even lower.

“Yes, and you are exceedingly good at that . . . ,” I whispered back, momentarily surrendering to the feel of his lips on my skin.

After they trailed still lower, I spoke again.

“Speaking of stolen, I think I know what Galatea is doing. She’s stealing memories. She’s making over the worlds so they forget about the Queendoms, so they forget there was ever any other royal than her.”

He lifted his lips, and his eyes met mine. I instantly missed his touch and resisted an urge to kiss him. I focused instead on what he was saying.

“I’m sorry, Farrow. It must hurt to see how much Galatea has changed from the Fate you looked up to when you were young to who she is now. All of what she’s doing, all of it sounds like what my mother would have done, if she had true magic. Thankfully, she never really did.”

Mather’s words reminded me that I had to accept Galatea as she was in the Present. I had to stay clear-eyed about who she was now. “It seems like she’s gotten worse since the crown was placed on her head. She is in love with this new power. She is in love with being able to exert her power not in the shadows but out in the open. And Fate help us, I think she’ll do absolutely anything to hold on to it.”

“But how is she administering the spell?” Mather asked.

“Normally it would have to be cast daily. There have been very few exceptions. But what if this is one? What if she used all that power to create permanent change?” I reasoned. The prospect was terrifying, but possible. "Either way, we have to do something, find out for certain."

"We have to find the magic," Mather said.

"Galatea spent her life up till now in the Reverie, the Grays' mansion, and the palace. Her world is small. Perhaps she would have hidden the magic she's using in one of those places," I observed.

"Is her world so small?" he countered. "From what my mother told me, Galatea and Iolanta and Hecate used to travel to the different Queendoms to resolve disputes. She could have hidden her magic in any of those realms."

"Perhaps," I said. "But I've found that the Entente always return to what we know. What we . . . I know all her places. That is the beauty of sisterhood. Let us begin our search."

"And what if she's no longer like the other Entente?" Mather questioned.

"Then we keep on searching."

And so we began; we searched the Reverie, the palace, the forest, and still nothing . . . Time was running out.

# CHAPTER 82

## — FARROW —

It was Bari's wedding day. Entente did not marry. That was how we were raised. But as Galatea said, the old ways were gone now.

I did not expect Bari to bow to the conventional white dress that most human brides wore on their day. But there she was in a white gown covered in pearls.

The result was beautiful and strange. Before the mirror, she tested out a smile.

Without a word, I crossed to her and began working on her hair. She allowed it. I had spent years braiding Lavendra's hair and my own to match.

"You could have used your wand."

"I've found that there are some things that are more satisfying without a hint of magic."

Bari looked up at me sharply, as if I had said something blasphemous. And then she caught herself in the mirror and tried to re-create the placid smile she'd been auditioning as I came in.

"All that time with the actor and you still cannot fake a smile."

"Do you think talent is contagious? The groom does not care. He loves me as I am."

"He loves you as you appear to be."

Bari waved her wand and revealed her scar, which was crawling with spiders. "Is this better?"

I didn't blink, and I took in her face as it was without the veil of magic she usually covered it with.

"I think that a groom should embrace you as you are. As you really are."

"I could walk down the aisle like this and he would not know the difference, the spell is so tightly bound," she said with pride. "But it would take too much magic to spell the entire audience. So alas . . ." She waved her wand again, and her flesh returned.

"But that's the thing, isn't it? Galatea is spelling everyone. How is that sustainable? She would need so much more magic. Eventually, they'll wake up, Bari."

"You have so much faith in humans and so little in the Entente."

"I think I see both of our kinds clearly."

"You are right. We do not have enough magic on our own. But there is another source of magic that is just as powerful as ours . . ."

"The Rooks."

"They were safe in the Rookery. And their power was beyond our reach. But you brought the Rook King out of his realm when you reunited him with South and allowed us to take all their magical objects. You made their power accessible to us. You have given us the tools to take over the Queendoms."

I felt everything in me sink. It had been a trick. Galatea had always known that South and I would turn to the Rookery to seek out their help. Amantha used that opportunity to steal the Rooks' power. Galatea was not the Fate of the Future, but somehow she had predicted our every move. We had delivered the Rookery up to her.

Why hadn't Mother foreseen this and warned me? I knew that her visions were not the same. But it had seemed that the most important Futures had managed to get through to her. How had she missed this?

I looked at Bari again, remembering something I had seen in her face when she helped save South and Iolanta from the Ever After. She had been sincere in her efforts, hadn't she?

I carefully considered my next words to Bari. "You weren't part of the plot to steal, Amantha was. Your mind and heart were elsewhere, with South, with Iolanta. I'm right, aren't I?"

After a moment, Bari responded, her voice cold. "There is nothing that the Entente does that I am not part of. And down deep you miss being part of it too."

The tiny bit of hope I had felt dimmed as I looked at her. How many times could Bari break my heart?

"Don't look so down, Farrow. We are not going to kill them—or at least not many of them. We are going to kill as few people as possible," she boasted.

"Somehow that is the opposite of comforting. Are we going to talk about it?"

"What?"

"The wish I granted so Helene and Dora could escape. You had to be the one who let Thiago's sister and niece out of that room. I granted their wish for safety because of you."

"I have no idea what you are talking about. Perhaps you have me confused with Amantha," she said. Then she added, "It's my wedding day, Farrow. I believe it is customary to cater to the bride's every happiness."

I tried a different tack.

"But you're not happy, are you, Bari?"

"We are on the cusp of having every single thing we ever wanted," she said, a little too firmly.

“That’s not an answer. I asked about you—not the Entente collectively,” I pressed, feeling like I had found a way to her truth.

She looked at me quizzically. As ambitious as she was about her own magic, about becoming a Fate, she still thought of the Entente first and her own needs second.

“There is no separation between my desires and the Entente’s.”

“But there is. That’s the thing about all this change from old ways to the new. There is light between us and the Entente. We are not just physically spread out through the Queendoms. We did not ask for any of this. We were all content as we were as children, as part of the Entente—but we have been forced to grow. It wasn’t our will, but it was the result all the same. Your heart and your will are no longer solely aligned with the heart and will of the Entente.”

“I truly don’t know what you mean.”

“I don’t have to read your wishes to see how you feel about South.”

“Marriage might as well be one of Thiago’s plays. Marriage doesn’t mean anything to the Entente. So we can use it as a stepping stone to bring us closer to what we want.”

“Then how will you feel when you stand in front of South and profess your love for Thiago?”

“South knows that it is not real. That I am acting for the Entente. Not that there is anything real between me and South. That’s pretend too.”

“And exactly what are you pretending for? You could have subjected South to your magical will without using a love spell.”

“The love spell didn’t work, it turns out. Because he’s a Fate. So making him fall a little in love with me is perhaps the most control I can exert over him.” Bari’s mouth twisted as she admitted this. It was further proof that she was indeed affected by South.

“Does Thiago know that you have magic?”

"I am honestly not sure what he would have done if I had let him keep that knowledge. I think he would have been sympathetic to our cause. But in the interest of time, I had to be sure of his absolute compliance."

"You spelled him with a memory spell in addition to the love spell?" I asked, a little overwhelmed by the thought of Bari's double spelling.

"I did—" And Bari quickly shifted the topic. "You are right, as far as humans go. He is not the worst of his kind. His devotion to a sister he never really knew is rather sweet. He did not want to take the crown from her. There are other humans like Queen Magrit, who had no issue sinking those who stood in the way of the crown to the bottom of the sea."

"There was a time when you wouldn't even recognize the distinction between Magrit and other humans."

"Thiago had a lifetime without power. Give him time," she said with a smirk.

"I don't think you really believe that anymore," I said, cocking my head, examining her, waiting for a response.

Bari set her lips in a firm line, then she answered. "We have waited our whole lives to get to this point. Why do you insist on ruining it? Nothing will stop me from walking down that aisle. Not you. Not Thiago. Not Amantha, and definitely not South."

If I could have heard her wish to be with South, I could have granted it, but Bari was keeping her wishes away from me. Galatea had taught her well.

# CHAPTER 83

## — BARI —

Do you ever think that maybe we are stuck?" South asked after showing up in my room wearing his wedding suit.

"Stuck how?"

"Maybe we are stuck being sad?"

"You're kidding, right? You keep acting like it's over, but it isn't. Everyone seems to be doing that, and I am perfectly happy."

"The one thing this gift has shown me is that no one can stay in the same place forever—even if they want to."

"You think I'm stuck? I think you are all completely delusional. Just because Magrit's gone doesn't mean it all goes away."

"You're right. It never goes away, but she's still here. She's still victorious if we continue building our lives around her. You're keeping her alive with this vengeance."

"Or I'm making it so that another Magrit doesn't rise to power. So that all of this doesn't happen all over again."

"I do not disagree with your feelings, Bari. I just do not agree with your methods. I do not want you to miss out on the good. I do not want you to miss out on who you could be. Or what we could be . . ."

"You cannot seriously be making yourself a factor in my decision. We are not anything. We were a spell."

"It wasn't a spell."

"A pretense then, no more real than one of Amantha and Thiago's plays."

"You think you can just push me away. That you can hurt me. Do your worst. I will not be moved."

Was that a declaration of love from South—Farrow's South? Once-human South? Infuriating South . . . ?

"I can't do this now. This is my wedding day. Thiago is waiting at the end of that aisle. Galatea, all of our sisters . . . What do you think is going to happen between us? Entente do not marry one another. They don't marry half Rooks either. What is the outcome you seek? What do you want from me?"

He paused and then smiled a wry smile.

"Happily ever after," South said, without an ounce of sarcasm.

I scoffed at his audacity.

"That doesn't exist for the Entente. And the more I see of the human world, the more I wonder if it exists even for them. Or the Rooks."

"I beg to differ."

He produced his wand and placed it at my temple.

"Do your worst," I dared him.

He showed happy scenes of humans I did not know, and then he showed me. Me smiling with my sisters the night I had been reunited with him and Farrow. Me and Amantha when we were children. And a moment that I had forgotten when he was nice to me when we were small.

"How did you do that? That is not your gift. You deal in the Present."

"I am sharing my Present."

"I don't understand."

"I can show you my memories of you as I recall them."

This was how he saw me. Not with judgment, but with fondness and affection. Maybe even love.

"That is how you see me? That is how you remember me?" I said, not even bothering to hide my surprise. Then, I caught myself. "You are painting me with the brush of delusion. All those Presents, they drove Iolanta mad. Maybe they drove you to this—to me," I said defensively.

I wanted, needed, to push him away. He could see and feel my resistance.

"Walk down the aisle if you must. I will not be moved," he repeated.

# CHAPTER 84

## — FARROW —

It was almost time for the wedding, and Mother and I were putting the finishing touches on our outfits. She wore a dress of pale blue, and mine was yellow.

"What do you see when you look into Galatea's Future? I know you are looking for the moments when her guard is down," I said.

"She is at war with herself. Perhaps victory does not feel as she expected it to," Hecate mused.

Her face lit up suddenly.

"What is it, Mother?" I asked.

"With everyone so busy with the wedding, perhaps now is the perfect time to look again for the Rooks' magic."

"Perhaps you are right."

Hecate cast a locator spell and got nothing, so we decided to split up and go room to room.

In the southern wing of the palace, I spotted a door I had never seen before. It was grown over with a shock of peonies. Anything with that many flowers had to have more magic than usual, I reasoned.

Hecate, sensing my find, showed up beside me.

I opened the door to the room, and behind it was the

unimaginable. There were babies as far as the eye could see, in rows and rows of cribs. They were quiet, as if under a spell. The servants who wore Bari's and Amantha's faces were there, tending to them. Hecate put up a hand and slowed time. The servants were frozen in place.

"What the hells?" I whispered.

Hecate whispered back, "It's worse than I thought. The sickness . . . Remember Iolanta," she continued in a hushed tone, as if the words themselves were infectious. Iolanta had gone to great lengths to keep the Presents, which haunted her, at bay.

Galatea had been growing more and more things in the palace. The walls and ceilings were covered by plants. But I'd thought she was just trying to wipe out all memories of Magrit. I never attributed the abundant greenery to any kind of sickness. I just thought it was her conscience or her vanity at work.

"That doesn't make any sense. Galatea's dealt with the Pasts all her life. What changed?" I wondered out loud.

"Perhaps killing Magrit and then having to live in her home, where everything is a trigger to a Past, has been too much for her. Or perhaps the act of killing Magrit had changed Galatea. We are not by nature killers, and imagine if you had Galatea's gift. I believe she cannot put the moment of burning someone alive behind her, especially not while living here in the place where the former Queen had lived almost every moment of her life. Galatea is reliving that killing over and over again. It must be excruciating."

"I would think she'd rather enjoy it. She really wanted desperately to avenge you."

"As did you. But when the moment came, you could not do it. She could, and now she has to live with it. So the babies . . ."

"Keep her from reliving it." I finished her thought.

“Where did they come from?” Hecate asked as she reached into a crib and touched the baby’s hands.

I suddenly remembered the passing comment Linea had made about a baby being missing in Queensland, one of the towns. “Wait, Linea had mentioned something about a missing baby. I didn’t think anything of it at the time . . .”

“There are babies missing all over the Queendoms. She’s taking them and keeping them,” Hecate surmised.

“The closer following birth, the better she feels because the infants barely have any Pasts,” I added.

“Newborns, she needs newborns,” my mother concluded.

“Why doesn’t she just use her own forgetting spell on herself?” I interjected.

“I don’t think this Galatea knows who she is without Magrit’s death. Avenging me was all that she lived for—it defined her for all those years.”

“You are back, Mother. You are almost fully reunited. Can’t she redefine herself?”

“You will find that an object in motion continues in the same direction until something or someone changes it. It is not often of its own volition.”

I sighed. I had had many obstacles that changed my direction—Hecate herself, South, Mather, even witnessing my sister’s bloodlust. It all saved me from Galatea’s Fate. For the briefest of seconds I felt pity for her.

Galatea was stranger by the day, and now we’d found a secret room filled with babies.

“Farrow, I have my magic in hand, I believe. But I do not want to take any risks with infants . . . ,” Hecate began. I nodded, knowing instantly what she wanted. I waited for her to whisper the wish aloud.

*"I wish for the babies in our midst to be returned to the families from whence they were wrenched."*

Using my power of the wish, I matched the babies with all the desperate wishes of their parents.

It didn't take long to orchestrate each reunion. With each one I felt my power grow.

When I returned from my last delivery, Hecate was waiting for me. "Do you think the Rooks have spelled Galatea? There's something hugely amiss."

"Perhaps she has spent too much power in too short a time."

"But speaking of power, returning the babies must have increased yours tenfold," my mother said pointedly.

Hecate was different too. She had used Galatea's folly to my advantage. She knew the wishes of those parents were the most pure, and the power I attained from granting them was substantial.

"Hecate," I admonished.

"We must not miss any opportunity. Galatea is tired, but she will not misstep."

I nodded. I hated that this was our new reality. But at the same time, I knew we had to be ready for whatever was to come, including the wedding soon to start.

"Hecate, shouldn't we just find a way to stop the ceremony? Too many people are at risk from its outcome."

"Galatea may not be herself in ways we couldn't have imagined before. But from what I can see of the Future, the events of this day may be our only chance to save the Future," she said firmly.

# CHAPTER 85

## — BARI —

An hour later, I asked a member of my court to bring South a note.

*Meet me in the place where we kissed*
*on the palace grounds.*

There was a small shed that the gardener used, but South had used his wand and turned it into an exact replica of my room in the cottage.

We stood outside for a moment, and he took me in.

"I don't see why you would want to meet here," he began, but then he stopped and he just stared at me. "Bari, you look beautiful. Not that you don't always look beautiful . . ."

"South . . ."

"Tell me you'll go with me, and we can fly anywhere right now."

"You don't understand. I have to go through with this. I just wanted a little more time with you before . . . I have to do this."

He shook his head. "What if I don't want only a few moments?"

My response was to take his hand.

The lights were out.

"I know there isn't time, but then I remembered you can make time." I kissed him and he kissed back. When we broke apart, I whispered, "Please, South. Just give us a little more time."

I could feel him reaching for his wand in the dark.

"It isn't working," he said, frustrated.

"I know," I replied. "I'm sorry, South. I couldn't let you ruin it. If you were there, you would not be moved. So I had to move you."

"What did you do?" he asked, lighting the tip of his wand.

He looked down. The room was filled with objects belonging to other people. So many Presents that he would remain trapped.

"This is what Magrit did to Iolanta. How could you do it to me?" he asked, his handsome face wrapped in the sadness I had caused.

"I'm sorry, South. It's only for a couple of hours. Amantha will let you out after," I reasoned, barely able to look at him and barely able to look away. "You know I am right. You know I cannot let you ruin this."

But I did look, and the more I did, the more tempted I was to empty the room of the objects and take his hand again. Just then though, my fingers flickered into feathers.

"At least admit why. It's because if I'm in the throne room, you won't be able to go through with it. What does that say about what you are about to do?" he pleaded as I willed my feathers back to fingers and closed the door behind me.

# CHAPTER 86

## — FARROW —

Amantha walked down the aisle first, appearing and disappearing as she went. Thiago watched her with longing as if she were his real bride. Galatea, of course, insisted that all of the Entente except for South, Hecate, and me be part of the wedding procession. Mather and Thiago stood at the end of the aisle, awaiting their brides.

Walking toward Mather and knowing that he was to wed Cinderella was excruciating. Hecate was right behind me. I slid into the pew beside her, and she reached for my hand.

I looked back, and I watched Cinderella, looking resplendent in a white gown and veil. She joined Mather.

My stomach sank.

Suddenly, a voice rang out in the hushed church. "The palace is surrounded, Galatea. My wedding gift to you."

Hecate took my arm, and we floated up to the stained glass windows. Sure enough, there was a full force of Rooks forming a block of metallic uniforms in the square behind the townspeople.

We floated back down, and Hecate reported to Galatea. "It is true, sister."

Seemingly out of thin air, Rook King Waid appeared beside us.

"Have you decided to join me or fight me?" Galatea asked him without missing a beat.

"I suppose that depends on whether or not you return my objects," he said with a smile.

The already treacherous situation was getting more so.

Next, was Bari. She had indeed worn the dress of her own making. The crowd gasped as it took in her black gown made of feathers. There was beading that I knew was not beading. It was beetles.

She smiled.

But the closer she got to Thiago, the more her smile faltered. I could see she wasn't truly walking. Bari's gown was carried by her wings flapping beneath as she moved down the aisle.

I looked around for South. He wasn't there, but I could hear him in my head.

*Farrow, she's locked me in the shed. I wish you would release me.*

I granted the wish, and South appeared in the back of the church.

Bari turned and locked eyes with him.

Then she turned back to where Thiago stood.

"Bari . . . ," South pleaded.

# CHAPTER 87

## — BARI —

I began to transform.

I didn't want to.

But it was all too much.

"Bari . . ." South had appeared. I smelled the work of Farrow.

"I told you not to come," I said.

Thiago looked from me to South.

"You love him, not me," my fiancé assessed.

"That's not . . . I'm not . . ."

Galatea looked at me. "Bari, this is your wedding day. This is our day. Everyone is watching. Everyone is here. You can't do this to me . . ."

I looked at Galatea's face. My anger grew.

"I cannot do this *for* you. This is not what you promised us, Mother. We do not have to perform for them, marry for them. Maybe we'd be better off without them . . . all of them."

My feathers made their way up my arm, and I felt myself getting bigger. My head hit the ceiling, and my wings grew.

# CHAPTER 88

## — FARROW —

Bari had turned into a giant feathered dragon, and she could not be contained, despite South's cries, despite Galatea's demands.

She broke through the ceiling and into the air. South began flapping his wings, and he took off after her.

I turned back to the pews. Galatea was working to calm the masses. Unbelievably, the wedding guests had remained in their seats, even after Bari tore a hole in the roof.

Galatea stepped before the crowd, wand in hand, reminding them that they were having a wonderful time.

It was as Hecate and I thought: she was spelling them all.

Hecate took my hand.

"Something is wrong here. Something else . . ."

"Mother, wish me to Bari, please."

Hecate's eyes searched mine, and I could see her weighing my safety against my utility. She had allowed herself to be burned to protect me once; her instinct was to protect me again.

"Mother, I am capable."

"I know, but so is she."

"Mother . . ."

She nodded, letting go. "Very well. I can handle whatever is happening here."

# CHAPTER 89

## — BARI —

All I had to do was breathe, and the whole Queendom would be gone. I could take out humanity, and then it would be only us. Wouldn't it be better? Weren't they the root of our problems?

I just wanted it all to stop. I just wanted it to be the Entente again. And South. I wanted South.

"I am sorry about this, Bari," he said.

He came at me, knocking me from the tower I had flown to. I fell but righted myself. I was poised to take out the Hinter.

South was approaching again. I had to make all the pain go away. Maybe even make him go away.

I inhaled.

In the instant I had closed my eyes and opened them again, Farrow had appeared on the top of the tower where I had just stood. She spoke in a firm voice. "I know you blame the humans, but it isn't their fault. There are still ways we can make this right."

I growled.

"Please, Bari. I know you know better. I know you do. All you have to do is come back to us . . ."

We had missed years and years together, and in so many ways

we were strangers. We were on opposing sides, but somehow Farrow's words got through.

I hesitated for a second. In that moment, South appeared and came toward me again, wrapping his arms around me.

I could hear Farrow in the background, begging him to wish her back to the church.

Suddenly, South and I were on the cliff again. My feathers were turning back into flesh.

His voice soft, he implored, "We were raised to be agents of Fate, to know that life turns on moments and to create them. This is one of those moments, Bari. This is your chance to make your Fate. You can be the agent of revenge you were forced to be, or you can be something new, one you choose to be."

# CHAPTER 90

## — FARROW —

As I returned to Hecate's side, I took in the glassy-eyed faces in the pews. All had continued to stay seated and seemed unaware of the gaping hole in the ceiling and the bride who had transformed into a dragon and flown away. I shared a knowing look with my mother. Galatea had spelled her cherished guests into uncomprehending stillness.

Suddenly, Hark appeared, taking Cinderella's hand.

"You came back!" Cinderella's voice peaked in surprise.

"I was content to live in the darkness until I died of starvation, but you, Cinderella, you made me want to live again. I deserved to be punished forever for what I did to humanity," Hark declared.

"You had no choice. But you have a choice now. Tell them what Magrit's last wish was. Tell them," Cinderella urged.

Galatea brandished her wand. "I think that this wedding has had enough disruptions. Will no one allow me to have my celebration?"

Hecate raised her hand and steeled her own wand. The other sisters clamored for theirs.

"What are you waiting for, children? Our own Fate has raised her wand against us."

I stepped in front of them.

“That is not Galatea.”

“What are you talking about?” asked Galatea.

Looking at Galatea and then to Hecate, I began to put the pieces together. Why hadn’t we seen it before? It was right in front of us. *She* was right in front of us.

“Galatea never would have wanted this. She wanted the Queen dead. She did not want to be Queen—at least not like this.”

“Then who is she?”

Hark whispered, “She is Queen Magrit. Long live the Queen.”

# CHAPTER 91

## — FARROW —

Galatea-who-was-not-Galatea began to laugh.

"You really have missed a step, Hecate. I thought you were the Fate of the Future. How could you have not foreseen this—foreseen me?" Magrit exclaimed.

"Who says I did not? I was searching for a way to save my sister. I cannot eradicate you without eradicating her, it seems," Hecate retorted.

Mother had kept the truth from me, and that fact hurt me, but I also understood at once.

"It is a strange thing, sharing a soul with the kind that I so long hated. The kind that tried to kill me," Magrit continued.

"I imagine it must be more excruciating for Galatea," Hecate countered with utter disdain.

"Hark, I just need you to finish the job, complete my wish." Magrit addressed her former Right Hand.

"All my life I spent hiding from your prophecy. This is as free as I have ever been—and the magic is wondrous," she said, turning around.

"She never really hated us. She coveted us, our power," I gasped.

"Mother," Mather whispered, stepping forward.

"Hello, son," Magrit said. She was still wearing Galatea's face, but it was Magrit's voice we could hear now. And the expression, haughty and entitled and certain, was purely Magrit's.

"Mother . . . How is this possible?" Mather asked, his face a twist of pain and wonder at once.

"Hark granted my last wish," Magrit explained.

Mather looked at Magrit with disbelief. But we could see what she was saying was true. Galatea's actions since the day of the coronation, which we had thought so very odd, now made so much sense. The balls, the clothes—it was all her second chance.

Magrit produced a magic mirror, and a scene from the Past played out for everyone to see.

It was the day of her burning.

"When I died, I wished for myself, and Hark granted my final wish—and as with every Rook wish, there was a twist and a cost. I had wished for no pain too. And then I found myself inside the very object that had bound us together."

In the mirror, there was a servant delivering a necklace to Galatea in her drawing room.

*"What is this?"*

*"She was wearing it. It would not burn," the servant said.*

*Galatea picked up the necklace and examined it, then slipped it around her neck. Then she began screaming in pain as the necklace buried itself inside her chest. The servant ran from the room.*

Galatea smiled. But seeing that smile now, I recognized it as Magrit's.

She continued her tale. "The necklace was inside Galatea's chest. I was inside the necklace. I could feel her battling me—but I was too strong. I emerged, and Galatea began to fade away. I hope she gets to watch though." With great difficulty, Magrit clawed at her chest and pulled out the necklace for all to see.

In the largest gem was a tiny, screaming Galatea. It would have been comical if it weren't terrifyingly real.

Holding up the necklace, Magrit spoke again. "My mother, Queen Meena, made her children go into the army. She made us learn how to do many things, even though most royals don't even know how to change their own shoes. Meena stressed that it was important for us to learn what it was like to be one of the people. I learned something more important: how to adapt."

She continued. "With my transformation, after hating your magic all these years, I suddenly was stuck inside of it—all these Pasts. The visions were the worst. I kept returning over and over to the day of Hecate's Burning and so many other days I bore responsibility for. I believed it was somehow Galatea's doing. She was summoning those images to torture me, but I began to learn that all of that was just her existence. But instead of giving up and letting her win out—I can hear her trying to claw out even now—I found a way to quiet her . . ."

"The babies," I whispered.

"Yes, Farrow, the babies. I just borrowed them. I never devoured them or anything else. The Pasts, they were overwhelming, but babies, they barely had Pasts. I could finally rest." She closed her eyes. "I see you have already taken them home."

Hark stepped forward. "I did not want you to die. In some ways you were the only mother I had ever known. But I cannot let you keep my magic. It belongs to me."

Hark put his palm out, facing her.

There was a loud scream from Magrit as the gem glowed green in response to his power.

"Mother!" Mather yelled. He reached for her, but Hark held him back with his other palm.

"You cannot take the necklace away without killing them both," Hecate explained. "They are still bound." She put up her own hand, pushing back Hark.

"It belongs to me," Hark protested. He tried to come at Hecate, but it was like he was facing a strong wind, and he was pushed back again.

"Son, we have a covenant," the Rook King reminded him, adding his own power and pushing Hark to the ground.

But Hark wasn't done. "A covenant that would have allowed you to leave me in the underworld, for example," Hark countered, pain written on his attractive face.

"I could not be seen as showing favor. I regretted it as soon as I did that. Why else would I have come for you into the underworld?" the Rook King said gently, leaning down to Hark and offering a hand to help his son to his feet.

"You came for Iolanta—you loved her still. And you decided to make a trade," Hark said, not buying it.

"And I came for you and your brother. You have to believe me," King Waid said plaintively.

"Why should I?"

Cinderella spoke finally, and Hark's face shifted from anger to curiosity.

"Hark, let us see if there is another way," she said.

"Ella, not you too. You cannot owe her anything. You told me yourself how abhorrent she as Galatea was to you," Hark said, shaking his head.

"Galatea was horrible to me, but I will not follow her example and you do not have to follow your father's."

Hark put his hand down, and the gem stopped glowing.

"And what was your plan for me, Mother?" Mather asked. "I have no magic. Was I to die with the other humans?"

"Oh, my love, do not think that I would have forsaken you as you forsook me," Magrit said, her voice full of surprise. "I would have found a way to give you magic like it was given to me," she added with a creepy certainty.

"I don't understand," Mather said, a mix of confusion and continued disappointment on his handsome face.

"I have all the magic in the world. Or at least all the Rook magic and a bit of Galatea's too," Magrit exclaimed, triumphant.

Just then the Rook King flickered into place beside Magrit and spoke. "Not anymore."

Mather stepped forward. Reading his wishes, I knew what he was doing. He wished to say goodbye.

Hecate nodded, as if she realized it too.

"Mother, I want you to know that I never wanted the crown. I just wanted a mother. I wish that it could have been different."

Magrit's eyes seemed to soften as she took him in. "I did love you, in my way . . ."

She lifted her chin and added, "You are going to have to be so much stronger when you are king. Otherwise, the magical ones . . . they will eat you alive."

The words must have stung, but Mather looked unsurprised. He leaned in and kissed her on the cheek. I instinctively reached for my wand to protect him. Mather was sure that Magrit would not hurt him or use him. I did not share his faith in her.

"Goodbye, Mother," he said, stepping back.

My heart ached for him.

"What of Galatea? Is she gone? Could she be brought back?" one of my sisters asked quietly.

"I know you're still in there, sister. I have seen glimmers of you since we were first reunited," Hecate said, looking closer at Magrit.

I thought I had seen glimmers of her too. When we were in the drawing room and she had hugged me close. But every other action she'd taken had all been the actions of a Queen, and an evil one at that.

Magrit raised her wand and directed it at Hecate.

Hecate strained against the force of her, my mother's very body seeming to tear apart and regroup as ashes for a moment before returning to the flesh.

"Nooooo!" I screamed, raising my own wand. I needed a wish. And not unsurprisingly, I found no one was wishing to help Magrit.

Hecate turned to my sisters. "I need your help to restrain her."

They looked at one another, unsure.

"You will be helping Galatea, I promise."

My sisters raised their wands.

"I need the Rooks too, King Waid. I know our kind has done you a disservice, but I promise you that from this day forward it will be different. If you deign to trust me."

They all added their power to Hecate's, but Magrit was not subdued.

She was stronger than all of us together.

She laughed and addressed the wedding guests. "If my family has no love for me, perhaps you can show your love for your Queen."

And with that, the people began to march on the Entente and

the Rooks. It would have been comical if there were not so many of them.

Suddenly, South and Bari reappeared, hand in hand. His coat was wrapped around her. And she was wearing a new dress. She took in what was happening. I could see the shock and horror of what she was realizing, what we had all realized a moment before. "Magrit," she whispered. "How could I not see . . . ?" Then something clicked in my sister's expression, and she volunteered, "I know where she hid the Rooks' gem. I know what she is doing to everyone."

"The clock tower," I said.

Hecate looked at me and spoke. "We'll hold her. Go."

Bari, South, and I held hands, and we traveled to the top of the tower.

# CHAPTER 92

## — FARROW —

It was genius. The spell was in the clock's chime, which sounded on the hour, and Magrit had been using it to control the people.

We found the Rooks' gem hidden in the bell's clapper, which swung and hit the sides of the bell, making the magical tone. Every time the bell rang and the clock pointed to the hour, her spell was renewed.

"What do we do?" Bari asked.

"We give it back to the Rooks. They can break the gem apart and have their power back. It belongs to them."

Bari's eyes locked with mine.

"You can feel the power, can't you?" she whispered, sounding tempted by it.

"I can," I whispered back.

"Call the Rooks, South," I said.

He nodded.

Suddenly the Rooks filled the area beneath the tower. And just then, behind them, on foot and on horses, there were scores of humans. Judging from their clothes, they came from every Queendom. I could spot Tork and Lavendra and Jacoby and Holocene among them.

"We need our sisters," I told Bari.

"There isn't time. It's just us."

Just then, Amantha flickered into place, and then Freya.

"Let's do this," I whispered.

Suddenly I felt a tap on my shoulder. It was the Rook King. I looked around, and everyone else was still. He had stopped time, just as I had seen Hecate do.

"What are you up to?" I demanded.

"I thought we could have a moment."

"A moment for what?" My voice was wary. The Rooks were tricksters still, and perhaps they had one last trick left.

"We are at the tipping point, where the Queendoms could fall into the abyss, where the Entente could lose it all, where Bari could still eat you alive . . . Do you really want to let that all play out?"

"You just agreed to help us. You brought all the Rooks."

"Now is the perfect opportunity to negotiate. The first time was just an introductory taste of the magic. Now that you know what you are capable of, what is possible—"

"And now you are going to tell me that I am special, when I know my magic is broken."

"Is that what you think? You are exactly the way you should be. You are made for this moment. You can only give, never take. You can serve us. You can serve the magic. I believe you are Fate's best design. If you kept that jewel for yourself, if we used it to combine our power with yours, whatever you wish for we could make permanent."

"Why would you go along with that?" I asked, genuinely curious.

"You do not seek to keep us on this land. You seek equality. We could live well under those conditions."

"Or you would be free to do whatever you wanted, since my wishes had nothing to do with you. Is that it?"

"Why would you care? You would have the life you want—your sisters back, your love by your side, your human friends happy . . ."

I shook my head. Somehow the rest of the Queendoms had become important to me; humans had become important to me.

"Why ask me this?"

"Because I believe we are overdue for a little rebalancing. Fate takes and takes: years of our lives lost to the Queendoms for the Rooks, lost years of time with your sisters and time with your mother in the flesh. Why can it not be your turn?"

"And yours, right?" I said. "That wish of mine that you propose. There is no part in it for you and the Rooks, so you would be free to do whatever you want."

"Exactly. We would be free."

"But that is what we are promising you already."

"No, Farrow. You are offering us another chance to join another fight with no end. I am too tired to fight again."

"I don't think we ever get to stop, King Waid. I think even when there is peace, we always have to stay vigilant."

"I can make it so you control what happens after this moment. So that you will never ever lose anyone you love again. Including yourself . . ." The king's voice trailed off.

I countered quickly. "We are about to bring the closest thing to peace that this land has known in many, many years."

The Rook King pressed his case. "And, yes, we will bask in peace for a moment. But what always happens next? War. Death—maybe of someone you care about, someone close. Or even your own death. You can stop all that with a wish."

I shook my head. I knew what he was offering, and I was so very tempted. But I still believed that there had to be another way. And if there wasn't, I believed that, whatever the sacrifice, what we were fighting for was worth it.

Of course I wanted to undo the events of today. I wanted it to be easier. But then I remembered the look I shared in the tower with Bari only moments earlier. That was hard-fought and hard-won. That was worth it.

"I do not want it to be easy. I do not want to solve it with a single wish. You deserve your freedom, Fate knows you do, and I will not stand in the way of that. But I will not look the other way if some are somehow more free than everyone else."

"Very well, but I am just a wish away if you ever change your mind."

"Will you back out of your promise to help us?"

"This was an attempt at a renegotiation. Just because I failed does not mean I am going anywhere."

"Thank you for sticking by us."

"Thank you for being a worthy ally. I do hope we are never enemies. I just wish you were a little less worthy."

He chuckled and blinked, and within seconds I was exactly where I had been standing before he had tapped me on the shoulder. And so was he. He smiled a knowing smile at me.

"Farrow?" Bari said, calling me to attention. "Are you okay? You seemed distant."

"I am here. I am ready," I said firmly.

A part of me could not wait to tell Hecate what had transpired between me and King Waid. I thought she would be proud of me.

*May what we have done, be undone.*
*For human and Rook alike, may what was lost be found.*

*May the human minds again be sound.*
*May the Rooks have back what we stole and may this tale be forever told.*

With that, the giant gem shattered into a million pieces, projecting into the air and shooting across the sky and down, down, down in green streaks toward the Rooks who waited below.

# CHAPTER 93

## — FARROW —

When we returned, Hecate and my sisters were still battling with Magrit.

*Expel Magrit to the Ever After.*
*Welcome her never again in this body or this soul.*
*Take her back where she belongs . . .*

Hecate began the chant, and we added our voices.

Magrit appeared inside the gem again . . .

And then seemed to fade away.

We looked at Galatea, who had begun falling to the ground. Amantha appeared beside her and caught her. Bari rushed to her side. Despite all that had happened, they both cared for her still.

Hecate looked upon them. "Hurry, sisters, we must make haste. We must complete the spell."

We joined hands, and in a blink we were all at the Reverie.

We said the words. Hecate put her wand to the sky, and a bolt of lightning met it. The lightning coursed through her, and she touched Galatea's hand.

"She is gone, but we can bring her back," Hecate proclaimed.

She made us grab our wands, and we began to chant.

*Bring our sister to the surface.*
*Send the possession into the shadows.*
*We are with you now and forever.*
*Find the light—no one can hurt us.*
*There are wands to wave and spells to cast.*
*Put this possession in the Past.*
*Send Magrit to the shadow of your heart and mind; she has no power.*
*Rejoin your sisters. We wait for you.*

I could feel the energy of my sisters coursing through me. I felt whole—and once Galatea was back, I would feel more so.

I knew it was a risk, bringing her back. Which Galatea would return? The vengeful one, who was organizing the sisters to conquer the Queendoms? Or the gentle Fate I grew up with, who was always the most encouraging?

After a few excruciating seconds, Galatea's eyes fluttered open.

She asked, "Why did you save me? You could have let me go to the Ever After with Magrit."

Hecate answered simply. "You are my sister—now and always. Yes, you have made the worst of all mistakes, but our bond is still here. I will fight for you till the end of time, as you would for me."

Galatea reached for her wand. Did she intend to fight, or flee? We would not know, because her wand was not in her pocket; it was already in Hecate's hand. In fact, there were two of them there.

I could see Bari reach into her own pocket and find it empty.

"Galatea, Bari, I love you. Trust is indeed another matter," Hecate said with a smile.

# CHAPTER 94

## — FARROW —

What do we do with you, Galatea?" Hecate asked, cocking her head and looking sadly at her sister.

Galatea had not been responsible for any of the events of the days since Magrit's burning. She hadn't forced anyone to marry or stolen from the Rooks or tried to enslave the humans, but before all that she had killed Magrit. And there was no reason to believe that she was done with her need for vengeance.

Hecate tucked away Galatea's wand and Bari's.

"I will hang on to these while we figure it out."

"What does that mean?"

"You said once that you would persuade me to your side. I am going to see if I cannot do the same."

"You cannot watch me every second. Are you going to cage me like Magrit caged Iolanta?" Galatea asked without ire.

"No. But I can see every second of your Future. And until it changes, we will spend nearly every moment together. It will be good for us. I have missed you."

Galatea smiled then. "And I you. You do forget there is a chance that I will convince you instead."

“There is always a chance with Fate,” Hecate conceded, a truce made.

Mather took his place as king but with a caveat. He wanted to attempt my plan. The Queendoms would be ruled not just by Queens, and now a king. There would be a place for humans to be represented by themselves, and for the Entente and the Rooks. And even the Couterie.

As for my idea to give everyone a little bit of magic, I found resistance in the most surprising of places: Cinderella.

“I am not sure that every person should have magic,” she said, raising her hand as she spoke.

Given her words, I changed my mind.

“We will offer the humans who want to learn magic a chance to practice it. They can come to the Reverie.”

What Cinderella said crystallized my head.

I thought about a memory that Hecate had shown me once upon a time, of her and Iolanta and Galatea advising the Queendoms and forming a temporary peace.

Why could we not do the same now? Why could the people not represent themselves?

The solution was simple, but getting there seemed impossible. I gathered all the key players—South, Mather, Cinderella, Hecate . . .

“I am not proposing ending the Queendoms or the Crowns. I am proposing changing the way that the Queendoms are governed. There should be no one authority by accident of birth. There will be representatives from the people, who will have a say in what happens to them. The Queens will do what they have always done: hear their people’s grievances and ideas. They will not rule alone; they will rule alongside the people.”

“You would need the agreement of every Queen and king—including Galatea,” Mather said thoughtfully. “Meaning, the impossible . . .”

“Someone once told me that with enough will and enough magic anything was possible. I may not have magic, but I have plenty of will,” I pledged.

“So do I. And I know plenty of people who would support this plan,” Cinderella seconded.

“The Resistance. I thought it was all but quashed by Galatea,” Mather said.

Cinderella countered, her voice hopeful. “The household staff at the manor were not affected by Galatea’s spell, I think because you, Farrow, granted their wishes to be themselves. They have kept resisting alive in those who will listen.”

I felt a swell of pride to know that something I had done had made a difference. And more importantly, a sense of relief that the former animals were thriving.

“I can consult with the other Crowns,” said Mather.

“And we can handle Galatea,” Hecate added.

Cinderella chimed in. “I will go find Hodder and the others.”

It was strange seeing Hecate interact with Cinderella and Mather. I looked at Hecate’s face, wanting her to like him. It mattered to me that she liked him. I wanted her approval.

# CHAPTER 95

## — FARROW —

To our surprise, Cinderella had decided she wanted to go back to the Rooks' Queendom with Hark.

"Are you sure, Ella?"

"I think I can help make a new peace. And I want to know if this thing between me and Hark was just the pressure of the situation or something real. Besides, after being cooped up all my life, I want to travel. I want to help."

While Cinderella packed, Hark asked for an audience with me and South.

He showed us his Rook object, which he now wore on a chain around his neck. It turned out it worked like the Fates' mirrors.

"When we were in the Ever After, Cinderella asked me for something—a wish. She wanted to see her parents. She wanted to say goodbye."

*Cinderella looked to Hark. "I have never asked you for anything. I ask for this now. I want to see my parents. I want to say goodbye."*

*"I do not have the power to grant this without my Rook's magic, but I still know the Rook who guards the Ever After: Roo."*

*As he said the name, he and Cinderella were suddenly transported to a different part of the Ever After. They were standing in front of another Rook, I judged from the being's costume.*

*"I know it's been a long time, and I am out of favor. But this girl saved my life, and she has but one wish: to see her parents again," Hark said.*

*Roo looked at her and nodded his head and closed his eyes. But when he opened them, he said, "I have tried, but they are not here."*

*"How is that possible? From what we know of them, they were the best of people and they died by unjust means. They should be in the most exalted part of the Ever After."*

*Roo shook his head.*

*"They were never here. They are not in the Ever After."*

The Rook object went blank.

"What does that mean?" I queried.

"It can only mean one thing: Cinderella's parents are still alive," Hark said.

South closed his eyes, and he was gone. No doubt he was traveling to see Bari so he could ask her about this development.

I faced Hark. He had indeed changed. He didn't have to tell us this.

"What does Cinderella believe?"

"She thinks that they are somehow lost in magic. I did not correct her of this, because if I am wrong, she will endure their deaths all over again."

"And if you are right?"

"There is a chance to make her the happiest she has been since she lost them."

"Why put this in my hands?"

"You and South are Entente. Only you can find the truth. Cinderella and I will leave tomorrow. She has been through enough. I hope you find happy news to share with us."

"Thank you, Hark."

# CHAPTER 96

## — BARI —

I was in my room at the palace. I was not confined there. But I was still without my wand, and while I knew I could transform without it, there was a part of me that was afraid to. So I sat and stared at the wall, contemplating the events of the last few days, which had turned out to be so completely different from what I had imagined for an outcome.

How had I not seen Magrit for what she was? *So I stand here with one crown—but there are two of us beneath it.* She had said that during her coronation. I had thought it was an awkward attempt at a Queen's speech, but instead it was the truth. Magrit was clever and cruel, and she was flaunting it even then.

South appeared next to me. I turned to him, asking, "How did I not see the truth about Magrit? I should have seen it."

"I think we all missed things that were right in front of us, Bari. Come with me."

"Where are we going?"

Was I to be punished? Confined? What did Farrow and Hecate have planned for me?

South took me to our cliff.

"What are we doing here?" Why would he bring us back to a

place where we had talked about so many things when the Future had looked very, very different? I was completely confused.

"Why weren't Cinderella's parents in the Ever After?" he demanded.

"Perhaps they are in the other realm? The deeper one?" I offered.

"From what we know of Madame and Mr. Gray, they were the best of the humans. They took you in, and they were punished with their deaths by your hand—unfair deaths. They should be in the part of the Ever After where the best of all beings are rewarded, and yet they are not there." South paused, then spoke again, his voice unyielding. "Why aren't they?"

I put him off. "You are the Fate of the Present. You know why."

"I want to hear it from you."

"Why does it matter if it comes from me?"

"You know why." He repeated my words back at me.

I took his wand to my temple and showed him my memories from not long after we'd arrived at the Grays' manor. Mr. Gray was lying on a chaise where I had left him, his eyes closed, his body beyond still. A cup of tea emptied of my spelled potion sat on the floor by his side.

*"Is he really, truly dead?" Amantha asked.*

*Galatea looked at him.*

*They were examining my handiwork.*

*"He is dead enough for our purposes. He will sleep unless the spell is undone by someone who loves him. And since we will keep him far away from the one who does, he may as well be. Just like his wife before him."*

I pulled my wand away.

Buoyed by the vision showing that Mr. Gray still lived, South questioned me again. "Where are they?" Then he looked straight into my eyes, adding softly, "You can make this right. There is still a path for us."

I shook my head. "You claim to accept me as I am, but you want some better version of me, some fairy-tale version that does not exist."

"I don't want you to be a killer, and it turns out that you are not one. There is nothing that stands between us now."

"You do. You and your judgment. I had every right to kill every human in every Queendom for what they have done to us."

"But you did not, because when no one is looking, you do not want to kill them. Is admitting that you are not wicked that hard?"

"Is admitting that you really do not care if I am wicked, that you could still love me if I was wicked, that hard? Is admitting that there is no judgment between us, that there is no obstacle except of your own making that hard? You love me, the killer me, just as much as the one who would spare a human. Your stomach never turned. You were just conditioned by humans to think it did."

We stood at an impasse, shouting at each other, unable to cross the line of our principles. In my head, I could already imagine myself in his arms, his lips on my lips, making the rest of the Queendoms and all our conflicts slip away. Instead, we stood like that, staring at each other until a lightning strike in the distance and a downpour of rain sent us back to the Reverie. It was no doubt Hecate, trying either to push us together or to call us back home.

The rain clung to us, pouring down our skin and clothes. I was conscious of South's sculpted chest showing through his wet shirt, and I could not take my eyes off him.

"Take me back," I commanded, still afraid to transform on my own without my wand.

"Not yet. Not until you are honest with me."

I felt frustration tear through me. I would not admit that South was right. I could not. If I did, it would mean that everything I had believed, everything I had done was wrong. That I was wrong. I felt myself begin to feather all over again. It was like being back in the church—only my wand wasn't in my pocket. It was only my will and my magic. I broke apart into dozens of ravens, and I flew away from South without looking back.

# CHAPTER 97

## — FARROW —

South returned to me, his face a mess of emotions. He had clearly come from seeing Bari.

"What did she say?"

"Do you know where Cinderella's parents are supposed to be buried?"

"Sure, on the edge of the manor's property near a beautiful tree. I passed the spot on my walks. Why?"

"I think Hark is right. I think they are still alive."

"Did Bari confirm that? I know that she has your feelings wrapped around her wand. But you can't just bring Cinderella's parents back to life to make it okay for you to like her."

"It's not that. It's something she told me, not just now but while she thought I was under the spell. When we were staying in the cottage, I saw her making the sleeping potion. It isn't just magic; it's a venom. Bari's spelled the venom. I think it's what she gave Briar Rose. And I think that's what she gave Cinderella's parents."

"Is there an antidote?"

"Time, but you need something else to break the spell. You did it in the magic shop with a mother's wish. And it's like what the king regent did with Briar coupled with Hark's granting their wish.

What if we could do it again with a wish from Cinderella? I would think a daughter's wish would be just as effective."

"We get to give Cinderella her parents back. Let's pray we are right and this is not a trick," I said, wanting to believe but still unaccustomed to happy endings for those I was closest to or for myself.

"You know what this means also about Bari . . . ?" I whispered.

"She's not a killer," he finished.

# CHAPTER 98

## — FARROW —

South went to bring Cinderella and Hark back from the manor, and they were all at the palace now. We recounted our theory about Cinderella's parents.

"It isn't so," Cinderella said, her blue eyes wide.

"But it is. Bari's spell is one of sleep, not death, and it can be broken by love. Or at least that's what we think," I said.

She looked to Hark, and he nodded as he spoke. "I think so too. I didn't want to tell you until we had more proof. I did not want to disappoint you."

She took his hand, clearly a little overwhelmed and also more than a little smitten.

South led the way as together we traveled back to the manor.

We went straight to the small chapel where her parents had been entombed.

Cinderella gasped at the idea of disinterring them. "Are you certain?" she asked.

I swallowed hard. I believed South, but I also believed that he wanted to believe. If we were at all wrong, Cinderella would face her parents' deaths all over again, just as Hark had said.

I nodded. South waved his wand, and their caskets slid out of the tomb.

South opened them one by one, and the Grays were as Bari had described: they had not decayed at all. They were, I presumed, as alive looking as they'd been the day they were laid to rest.

Cinderella approached gingerly and kissed each upon the cheek. As she did so, she made a wish. She wished for them to return to her.

We waited one agonizing second after another, then finally her mother began to stir, and then her father.

"Mother! Father!"

"Ella, how is it you?" Madame Gray marveled.

"There is much to explain, but first let us hold one another," Cinderella said.

As they embraced, South and I took our leave.

Hark smiled at me and mouthed, "Thank you," before he also darted away.

As South and I stood at a distance, I couldn't help but break the silence between us.

"You are going to go to her, aren't you? You think that this absolves her?" I said to South.

He didn't answer.

"Bari may not have robbed them of their lives, but she did rob them of time with their child," I reminded him.

"We have all done things of which we are not proud."

"But she does not regret them. Do you love her that much, South?"

He looked at me a long beat and then said finally, "Don't you?"

With those words, he began to flap his wings, and he ascended. I looked around, and I noticed that the trees surrounding the chapel were full of ravens. Bari was there, and she was watching.

# CHAPTER 99

## — BARI —

I watched Cinderella reunite with her family, and despite myself I felt a flutter inside me akin to what I'd felt when baby Dora held my finger.

"You couldn't stay away, could you?" Farrow said.

I transformed out of my feathers and back into my flesh.

"It turns out I don't need my wand."

"Which means you are free, so why come here? I have been where you are, Bari. I wanted revenge just as much as you did. Now I want something else. And I think you do as well. You're too scared to admit it."

"That's not . . . ," I began, ready to protest.

"You don't have to admit it. And you don't have to go. You could help us remake the world." Farrow's voice was welcoming.

"Into what kind of world?" I asked.

"One that is filled with magic and peace and lots and lots of feathers," she said, smiling.

"I don't know if I can do that."

"Then we'll be here when you do know," Farrow offered.

I believed her.

# CHAPTER 100

## — BARI —

I found myself on the cliff again. South was there, looking forlorn. He saw me and offered a careful smile. "I knew you would come back."

"No, you didn't," I said, meaning for my voice to be light but in control. Instead, it came out soft and small.

I stepped closer to him and tried to explain. "You want to know why I did what I did? I wanted the power. I wanted to be a Fate. I wanted to please Galatea. I didn't care that I was stealing years from the Grays, the people who hadn't hurt us. The people who had saved us. I only cared about the Entente."

His smile grew. "Was that so hard?"

"Yes," I said honestly.

"And what do you care about now?"

"That's even harder to say . . ."

It would be easier to kiss him.

"South, I care about the Queendoms and even some humans. I care about Farrow. And Hecate. And Amantha. And our sisters. And I still care about Galatea—"

He broke in. "Anyone else?"

"You. I care about you. I love you."

He was silent for an excoriating moment. I felt myself threatening to feather. But I stayed still.

Finally he spoke. "When we were here before, I was going to give you this. So that whatever happened, the choice was yours. It turns out that you don't need it. So my grand gesture is a little less grand."

I looked down. To my surprise, he was holding my wand.

I felt the flutter again.

"No, it is still pretty grand. What happens now?"

"Happily ever after. Just like in the stories," he said with certainty.

"They don't write stories with beings like me at the center of them," I countered.

"Oh, but they will . . . I love you, Bari," he said, and then I kissed him.

# CHAPTER 101

## — Farrow —

Mother and I were sitting in her room in the palace. I could see Galatea's wand on her dresser. She had spelled it to herself. But we both knew that it was possible to use magic without a wand. Galatea must have known that too.

When your mother is the Fate of the Future, there is no way you cannot ask the question:

"What's going to happen to us, Mother?"

"We are going to live more happily ever than not."

"Can you be a touch more specific?"

"Where would be the fun in that?"

Suddenly, Amantha appeared and grabbed the wand before disappearing again.

"Wish me to follow her," I demanded.

"Let's give them both a head start," Hecate advised.

"Mother . . ."

"You asked me about the Future. The prince will propose to you many times. You will always think you have better things to do—more wishes to grant, more Queendoms to save. Until one day you will think, *Why did I wait so long?*" She continued, "Cinderella and Hark will have many adventures, and he will always be a bit of a rogue. Bari and South will spend more time in the air than on land and more time with each other than with anyone else. I will grow old but stay young, and I will have many years with my daughter."

"What about Amantha and Thiago?"

"He will give up the crown and return to acting, and he'll ask Amantha to come with him. She will refuse. But she will see him secretly until she disappears from the Entente one day and reappears onstage the next."

"And the rest of my sisters?"

"Some will choose our side. Some will choose Galatea's, and we will spend our lives trying to convince them otherwise. So, you see? More happily ever than not."

I reached for my wand and took my mother's hand, and I waited for the wish to take me.

# ACKNOWLEDGMENTS

To Chris Albers. My love, I will be crossing rooms to meet you for the rest of our lives.

When I wrote *Wish of the Wicked*, as when I write most of my books, I fell in love with my villains alongside my heroine. So I made room in this book for Bari's perspective alongside Farrow's. Because I believe firmly that there is good in almost all of us and I am rooting for Happily Ever Afters for all of us, even those who have made some detours along the way. This book is about the act of wishing—of putting voice to your deepest desires and making them come true. I think we don't always wish big enough.

Daddy, like every book I write, it would not have been possible if not for you and Mommy. You worked so hard to nurture me as a person and a writer. And your example as a brilliant, generous, and funny teacher and artist gave me all the tools I needed to make my wildest wishes come true. I love you so much. For my sister, Andrea, you are our family's heart and strength. You hold us up and take care of us. You are beautiful and loving and you are still the sun I wanted to follow around when I was little. To my brother-in-law, Josh, thank you for always reading and rooting me on. For Sienna, you are magic; being your aunt means so much to me. And watching you dance, grow, and become is just magic.

For Fiona, goddaughter, being your fairy godmother is such an honor. I love you to infinity and back again and I am so proud of the beautiful, brilliant, funny, and empathetic young woman you are becoming!!

For Lauren Goodman Dell, my forever friend, NY misses you and I do too.

To Annie Kojima, you told me to write a book ten years before I wrote one. You remind me of who I am when I forget. And you are always in my corner. And I am in yours. I love you, and I cannot wait to see your design firm become a big deal.

To Bonnie Datt, who I share so much more than dresses with. We have always been kindred spirits. Some friendships are tinged with fate.

To Carin Greenberg, who means so much to me, and I will do better and see more of!

And to Daryn Strauss, who is a literal fairy godmother and just the loveliest . . . And for so many other fairy godmothers both personal and professional.

Tina Sloan and Steve McPherson, I love you and you have brought me so much love, advice, glamour, and encouragement! Jill Lorie Hurst, my first writing mentor and forever family. To Nancy Williams Watt and all my *Guiding Light* fam.

To my beloved second families: Annie, Chris, Fiona and Jackson Rolland; Lauren Dell and Sandy and Don Goodman; Stephen Mcpherson and Tina Sloan; Jill Lorie and Tony Hurst.

To Josh Sabarra, Michele Wells, Kami Garcia, Frank Lesser, Sasha Alsberg, Stephanie Garber, Leslie Rider, Paloma Ramirez, Jeanne Marie Hudson, Megan Steintrager, Lexi Dwyer, Lisa Tollin, Sarah Kagan, Kristin Nelthorpe, Leslie Kendall Dye, Crystal Chappell, Melissa Salmons, Laura Wright, Jordan Vilasuso, Valeria

Tejada, Sasha Mote, Chris Lowe, Meg Cabot, Melissa de la Cruz . . . and so many more . . .

And to my dear Emily Williams! Thank you for all your light, help, and love! You know what you do!

To my brilliant editors, Mary Kate Castellani and Camille Kellog. Thank you for more fairy dust that pulled together my ambitious vision for this one.

And to Cindy Loh, the first fairy godmother of the series.

To Erica Barmash, and Kei and the rest of the team at Bloomsbury and off to bookstores with such inventiveness and enthusiasm.

To Charlie Bowater for the stunning cover.

And finally to all my readers. Thanks to everyone who picked up our book, who gave it a shout or drew some art. Munchkins, keep on wishing! I wish I had the power to grant every one! Here's to all your Happily Ever Afters.

**Danielle Paige** is the *New York Times* bestselling author of *Stealing Snow* and its prequel novellas *Before the Snow* and *Queen Rising*. Before turning to young adult literature, she worked in the television industry, where she received a Writers Guild of America Award and was nominated for several Daytime Emmys. She is a graduate of Columbia University and currently lives in New York City.

Twitter and Instagram: @daniellempaige